MW01639925

Treasure Island

by

ROBERT LOUIS STEVENSON

Illustrated Edition

4-5 North Parade Buildings, Bath

First published 1998.

Printed in China

TREASURE
ISLAND.

To

S. L. O.,

AN AMERICAN GENTLEMAN,

IN ACCORDANCE WITH WHOSE CLASSIC TASTE

THE FOLLOWING NARRATIVE HAS BEEN DESIGNED,

IT IS NOW, IN RETURN FOR NUMEROUS DELIGHTFUL HOURS,

AND WITH THE KINDEST WISHES

Dedicated

BY HIS AFFECTIONATE FRIEND,

THE AUTHOR.

TO THE HESITATING PURCHASER

If sailor tales to sailor tunes;
Storm and adventure, heat and cold;
If schooners, islands, and maroons
And Buccaneers and buried Gold,
And all the old romance, retold
Exactly in the ancient way,
Can please, as me they pleased of old,
The wiser youngsters of to-day:

—So be it, and fall on! If not,
If studious youth no longer crave,
His ancient appetites forgot,
Kingston, or Ballantyne the brave,
Or Cooper of the wood and wave:
So be it, also! And may I
And all my pirates share the grave
Where these and their creations lie!

CONTENTS

PART I – THE OLD BUCCANEER

PART II – THE SEA-COOK

PART III – MY SHORE ADVENTURE

CONTENTS

PART IV – THE STOCKADE

PART V – MY SEA ADVENTURE

PART VI – CAPTAIN SILVER

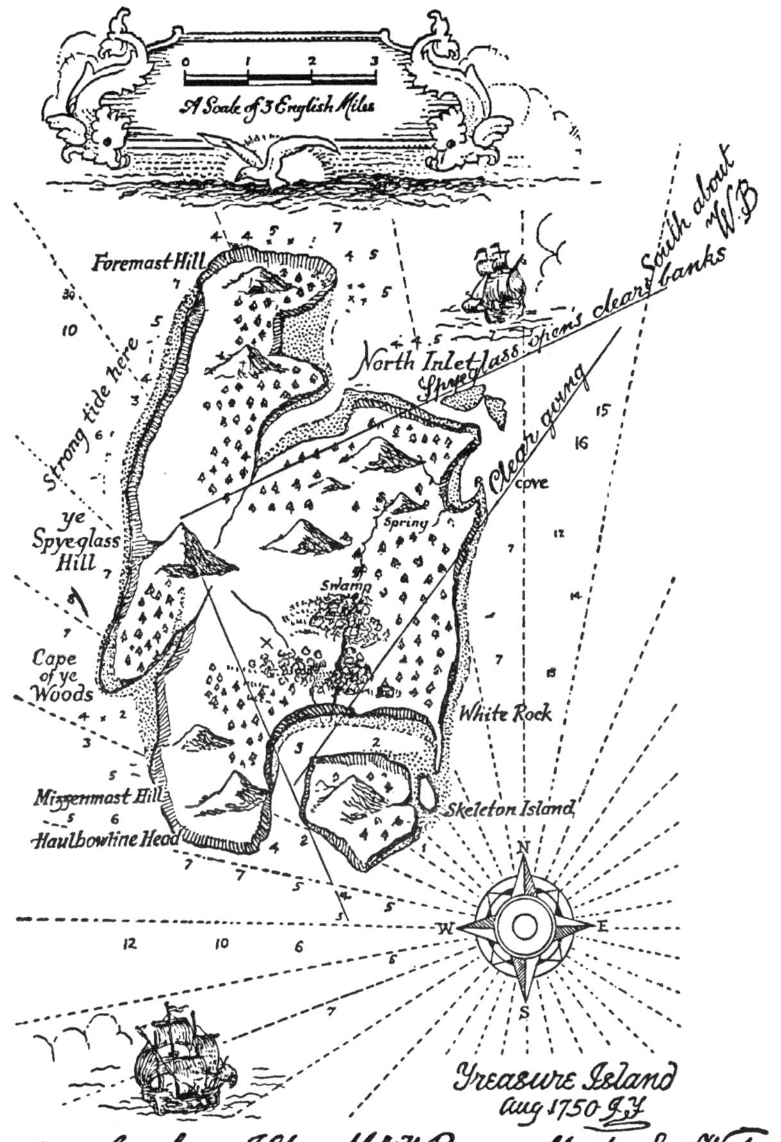

Given by above J.F. & Mr. W Bones Maite of ye Walrus Savannah this twenty July 1754 W.B.

Facsimile of Chart latitude and longitude struck out by J Hawkins

PART I THE OLD BUCCANEER

CHAPTER I

THE OLD SEA DOG AT THE "ADMIRAL BENBOW"

SQUIRE Trelawney, Dr. Livesey, and the rest of these gentlemen having asked me to write down the whole particulars about Treasure Island, from the beginning to the end, keeping nothing back but the bearings of the island, and that only because there is still treasure not yet lifted, I take up my pen in the year of grace 17—, and go back to the time when my father kept the Admiral Benbow inn, and the brown old seaman, with the sabre cut, first took up his lodging under our roof.

I remember him as if it were yesterday, as he came plodding to the inn door, his sea-chest following behind him in a hand-barrow; a tall, strong, heavy, nut-brown man; his tarry pigtail falling over the shoulders of his soiled blue coat; his hands ragged and scarred, with black, broken nails; and the sabre cut across one cheek, a dirty, livid white. I remember him looking round the cove and whistling to himself as he did so, and then breaking out in that old sea-song that he sang so often afterwards:

"Fifteen men on The Dead Man's Chest—
Yo-ho-ho, and a bottle of rum!"

in the high, old tottering voice that seemed to have been tuned and broken at the capstan bars. Then he rapped on the door with a bit of stick like a handspike that he carried, and when my father appeared, called roughly for a glass of rum. This, when it was brought to him, he drank slowly, like a connoisseur, lingering on the taste, and still looking about him at the cliffs and up at our signboard.

"This is a handy cove," says he at length; "and a pleasant sittyated grog-shop. Much company, mate?"

My father told him no, very little company, the more was the pity.

"Well, then," said he, "this is the berth for me. Here you, matey," he cried to the man who trundled the barrow; "bring up alongside and help up my chest. I'll stay here a bit," he continued. "I'm a plain man; rum and bacon and eggs is what I want, and that head up there for to watch ships off. What you mought call me? You mought call me captain. Oh, I see what you're at – there" and he threw down three or four gold pieces on the threshold. "You can tell me when I've worked through that," says he, looking as fierce as a commander.

And, indeed, bad as his clothes were, and coarsely as he spoke, he had none of the appearance of a man who sailed before the mast; but seemed like a mate or skipper, accustomed to be obeyed or to strike. The man who came with the barrow told us the mail had set him down the morning before at the Royal George; that he had inquired what inns there were along the coast, and hearing ours well spoken of, I suppose, and described as lonely, had chosen it from the others for his place of residence. And that was all we could learn of our guest.

He was a very silent man by custom. All day he hung round the cove, or upon the cliffs, with a brass telescope; all evening he sat in a corner of the parlour next the fire, and drank rum and water very strong. Mostly he would not speak when spoken to; only look up sudden and fierce, and blow through his nose like a fog-horn; and we and the people who came about our house soon learned to let him be. Every day, when he came back from his stroll, he would ask if any seafaring men had gone by along the road? At first we thought it was the want of company of his own kind that made him ask this question; but at last we began to see he was desirous to avoid them. When a seaman put up at the Admiral Benbow (as now and then some did, making by the coast road for Bristol), he would look in at him through the curtained door before he entered the parlour; and he was always sure to be as silent as a mouse when any such was present. For me, at least, there was no secret about the matter; for I was, in a way, a sharer in his alarms. He had taken me aside one day, and promised me a silver fourpenny on the first of every month if I would only keep my weather-eye open for a seafaring man with one leg," and let him

know the moment he appeared. Often enough, when the first of the month came round, and I applied to him for my wage, he would only blow through his nose at me, and stare me down; but before the week was out he was sure to think better of it, bring me my fourpenny piece, and repeat his orders to look out for "the seafaring man with one leg."

How that personage haunted my dreams, I need scarcely tell you. On stormy nights, when the wind shook the four corners of the house, and the surf roared along the cove and up the cliffs, I would see him in a thousand forms, and with a thousand diabolical expressions. Now the leg would be cut off at the knee, now at the hip; now he was a monstrous kind of a creature who had never had but the one leg, and that in the middle of his body. To see him leap and run and pursue me over hedge and ditch was the worst of nightmares. And altogether I paid pretty dear for my monthly fourpenny piece, in the shape of these abominable fancies. But though I was so terrified by the idea of the seafaring man with one leg, I was far less afraid of the captain himself than anybody else who knew him. There were nights when he took a deal more rum and water than his head would carry; and then he would sometimes sit and sing his wicked, old, wild sea-songs, minding nobody; but sometimes he would call for glasses round, and force all the trembling company to listen to his stories or bear a chorus to his singing. Often I have heard the house shaking with "Yo-ho-ho, and a bottle of rum"; all the neighbours joining in for dear life, with the fear of death upon them, and each singing louder than the other, to avoid remark. For in these fits he was the most overriding companion ever known; he would slap his hand on the table for silence all round; he would fly up in a passion of anger at a question, or sometimes because none was put, and so he judged the company was not following his story. Nor would he allow any one to leave the inn till he had drunk himself sleepy and reeled off to bed.

His stories were what frightened people worst of all. Dreadful stories they were; about hanging, and walking the plank, and storms at sea, and the Dry Tortugas, and wild deeds and places on the Spanish Main. By his own account he must have lived his life among some of the wickedest men that God ever allowed upon the sea; and the language in which he told these stories shocked our plain country people almost as much as the crimes that he described. My father was always saying the inn would be ruined, for people would soon cease coming there to be tyrannised over and put down, and sent shivering to their beds; but I really believe his presence did us good.

People were frightened at the time, but on looking back they rather liked it; it was a fine excitement in a quiet country life; and there was even a party of the younger men who pretended to admire him, calling him a "true sea-dog," and a "real old salt," and such like names, and saying there was the sort of man that made England terrible at sea.

In one way, indeed, he bade fair to ruin us; for he kept on staying week after week, and at last month after month, so that all the money had been long exhausted, and still my father never plucked up the heart to insist on having more. If ever he mentioned it, the captain blew through his nose so loudly that you might say he roared, and stared my poor father out of the room. I have seen him wringing his hands after such a rebuff, and I am sure the annoyance and the terror he lived in must have greatly hastened his early and unhappy death.

All the time he lived with us the captain made no change whatever in his dress but to buy some stockings from a hawker. One of the cocks of his hat having fallen down, he let it hang from that day forth, though it was a great annoyance when it blew. I remember the appearance of his coat, which he patched himself upstairs in his room, and which, before the end, was nothing but patches. He never wrote or received a letter, and he never spoke with any but the neighbours, and with these, for the most part, only when drunk on rum. The great sea-chest none of us had ever seen open.

He was only once crossed, and that was towards the end, when my poor father was far gone in a decline that took him off. Dr. Livesey came late one afternoon to see the patient, took a bit of dinner from my mother, and went into the parlour to smoke a pipe until his horse should come down from the hamlet, for we had no stabling at the old Benbow. I followed him in, and I remember observing the contrast the neat, bright doctor, with his powder as white as snow, and his bright, black eyes and pleasant manners, made with the coltish country folk, and above all, with that filthy, heavy, bleared scarecrow of a pirate of ours, sitting far gone in rum, with his arms on the table. Suddenly he – the captain, that is – began to pipe up his eternal song:

"Fifteen men on The Dead Man's Chest—
Yo-ho-ho, and a bottle of rum!
Drink and the devil had done for the rest—
Yo-ho-ho, and a bottle of rum!"

At first I had supposed "the dead man's chest" to be that identical big box

‘ “If you do not put that knife this instant in your pocket, I promise . . . you shall hang at the next assizes.” ’ (p. 6)

of his upstairs in the front room, and the thought had been mingled in my nightmares with that of the one-legged seafaring man. But by this time we had all long ceased to pay any particular notice to the song; it was new, that night, to nobody but Dr. Livesey, and on him I observed it did not produce an agreeable effect, for he looked up for a moment quite angrily before he went on with his talk to old Taylor, the gardener, on a new cure for the rheumatics. In the meantime, the captain gradually brightened up at his own music, and at last flapped his hand upon the table before him in a way we all knew to mean – silence. The voices stopped at once, all but Dr. Livesey's; he went on as before, speaking clear and kind, and drawing briskly at his pipe between every word or two. The captain glared at him for a while, flapped his hand again, glared still harder, and at last broke out with a villainous low oath: "Silence, there, between decks!"

"Were you addressing me, sir?" says the doctor; and when the ruffian had told him, with another oath, that this was so, "I have only one thing to say to you, sir," replies the doctor, "that if you keep on drinking rum, the world will soon be quit of a very dirty scoundrel!"

The old fellow's fury was awful. He sprang to his feet, drew and opened a sailor's claspknife, and, balancing it open on the palm of his hand, threatened to pin the doctor to the wall.

The doctor never so much as moved. He spoke to him, as before, over his shoulder, and in the same tone of voice; rather high, so that all the room might hear, but perfectly calm and steady.

"If you do not put that knife this instant in your pocket, I promise, upon my honour, you shall hang at next assizes."

Then followed a battle of looks between them; but the captain soon knuckled under, put up his weapon, and resumed his seat, grumbling like a beaten dog.

"And now, sir," continued the doctor, "since I now know there's such a fellow in my district, you may count I'll have an eye upon you day and night. I'm not a doctor only; I'm a magistrate; and if I catch a breath of complaint against you, if it's only for a piece of incivility like to-night's, I'll take effectual means to have you hunted down and routed out of this. Let that suffice."

Soon after Dr. Livesey's horse came to the door, and he rode away; but the captain held his peace that evening, and for many evenings to come.

CHAPTER II

BLACK DOG APPEARS AND DISAPPEARS

IT was not very long after this that there occurred the first of the mysterious events that rid us at last of the captain, though not, as you will see, of his affairs. It was a bitter cold winter, with long, hard frosts and heavy gales; and it was plain from the first that my poor father was little likely to see the spring. He sank daily, and my mother and I had all the inn upon our hands; and were kept busy enough, without paying much regard to our unpleasant guest.

It was one January morning, very early – a pinching, frosty morning – the cove all gray with hoar frost, the ripple lapping softly on the stones, the sun still low and only touching the hilltops and shining far to seaward. The captain had risen earlier than usual, and set out down the beach, his cutlass swinging under the broad skirts of the old blue coat, his brass telescope under his arm, his hat tilted back upon his head. I remember his breath hanging like smoke in his wake as he strode off, and the last sound I heard of him, as he turned the big rock, was a loud snort of indignation, as though his mind was still running upon Dr. Livesey.

Well, mother was upstairs with father; and I was laying the breakfast table against the captain's return, when the parlour door opened, and a man stepped in on whom I had never set my eyes before. He was a pale, tallowy creature, wanting two fingers of the left hand; and, though he wore a cutlass, he did not look much like a fighter. I had always my eye open for seafaring men, with one leg or two, and I remember this one puzzled me. He was not sailorly, and yet he had a smack of the sea about him too. I asked him what was for his service, and he said he would take rum; but as I was going out of the room to fetch it he sat down upon a table and motioned me to draw near. I paused where I was with my napkin in my hand.

"Come here, sonny," says he. "Come nearer here."

I took a step nearer.

"Is this here table for my mate Bill?" he asked, with a kind of leer.

I told him I did not know his mate Bill; and this was for a person who stayed in our house, whom we called the captain.

"Well," said he, "my mate Bill would be called the captain, as like as not. He has a cut on one cheek, and a mighty pleasant way with him, particularly in drink, has my mate Bill. We'll put it, for argument like, that your captain has a cut on one cheek – and we'll put it, if you like, that that cheek's the right one. Ah, well! I told you. Now, is my mate Bill in this here house?"

I told him he was out walking.

"Which way, sonny? Which way is he gone?"

And when I had pointed out the rock and told him how the captain was likely to return, and how soon, and answered a few other questions, "Ah," said he, "this'll be as good as drink to my mate Bill."

The expression on his face as he said these words was not at all pleasant, and I had my own reasons for thinking that the stranger was mistaken, even supposing he meant what he said. But it was no affair of mine, I thought; and, besides, it was difficult to know what to do. The stranger kept hanging about just inside the inn door, peering round the corner like a cat waiting for a mouse. Once I stepped out myself into the road, but he immediately called me back, and, as I did not obey quick enough for his fancy, a most horrible change came over his tallowy face, and he ordered me in, with an oath that made me jump. As soon as I was back again he returned to his former manner, half fawning, half sneering, patted me on the shoulder, told me I was a good boy, and he had taken quite a fancy to me. "I have a son of my own," said he, "as like you as two blocks, and he's all the pride of my 'art. But the great thing for boys is discipline, sonny – discipline. Now, if you had sailed along of Bill, you wouldn't have stood there to be spoke to twice – not you.

That was never Bill's way, nor the way of sich as sailed with him. And here, sure enough, is my mate Bill, with a spy glass under his arm, bless his old 'art to be sure. You and me'll just go back into the parlour, sonny, and get behind the door, and we'll give Bill a little surprise – bless his 'art, I say again."

So saying, the stranger backed along with me into the parlour, and put me behind him in the corner, so that we were both hidden by the open door. I was very uneasy and alarmed, as you may fancy, and it rather added to my fears to observe that the stranger was certainly frightened himself. He cleared the hilt of his cutlass and loosened the blade in the sheath; and all the time we were waiting there he kept swallowing as if he felt what we used to call a lump in the throat.

At last in strode the captain, slammed the door behind him, without looking to the right or left, and marched straight across the room to where his breakfast awaited him.

"Bill," said the stranger in a voice that I thought he had tried to make bold and big.

The captain spun round on his heel and fronted us; all the brown had gone out of his face, and even his nose was blue; he had the look of a man who sees a ghost, or the evil one, or something worse, if anything can be; and, upon my word, I felt sorry to see him, all in a moment, turn so old and sick.

"Come, Bill, you know me; you know an old shipmate, Bill, surely," said the stranger.

The captain made a sort of gasp.

"Black Dog!" said he.

"And who else?" returned the other, getting more at his ease. "Black Dog as ever was, come for to see his old shipmate Billy, at the Admiral Benbow inn. Ah, Bill, Bill, we have seen a sight of times, us two, since I lost them two talons," holding up his mutilated hand.

"Now, look here," said the captain; "you've run me down; here I am; well, then, speak up: what is it?"

"That's you, Bill," returned Black Dog, "you're in the right of it, Billy. I'll have a glass of rum from this dear child here, as I've took such a liking to; and we'll sit down, if you please, and talk square like old shipmates."

When I returned with the rum, they were already seated on either side of the captain's breakfast table – Black Dog next to the door, and sitting sideways, so as to have one eye on his old shipmate, and one, as I thought, on his retreat.

He bade me go, and leave the door wide open. "None of your keyholes for me, sonny," he said; and I left them together, and retired into the bar.

For a long time, though I certainly did my best to listen, I could hear nothing but a low gabbling; but at last the voices began to grow higher, and I could pick up a word or two, mostly oaths, from the captain.

"No, no, no, no; and an end of it!" he cried once. And again, "If it comes to swinging, swing all, say I."

Then all of a sudden there was a tremendous explosion of oaths and other noises – the chair and table went over in a lump, a clash of steel followed, and then a cry of pain, and the next instant I saw Black Dog in full flight, and the captain hotly pursuing, both with drawn cutlasses, and the former streaming blood from the left shoulder. Just at the door, the captain aimed at the fugitive one last tremendous cut, which would certainly have slit him to the chine had it not been intercepted by our big signboard of Admiral Benbow. You may see the notch on the lower side of the frame to this day.

The blow was the last of the battle. Once out upon the road, Black Dog, in spite of his wound, showed a wonderful clean pair of heels, and disappeared over the edge of the hill in half a minute. The captain, for his part, stood staring at the signboard like a bewildered man. Then he passed his hand over his eyes several times, and at last turned back into the house.

"Jim," says he, "rum"; and as he spoke, he reeled a little, and caught himself with one hand against the wall.

"Are you hurt?" cried I.

"Rum," he repeated. "I must get away from here. Rum! rum!"

I ran to fetch it; but I was quite unsteadied by all that had fallen out, and I broke one glass and fouled the tap, and while I was still getting in my own way, I heard a loud fall in the parlour, and, running in, beheld the captain lying full length upon the floor. At the same instant, my mother, alarmed by

the cries and fighting, came running downstairs to help me. Between us we raised his head. He was breathing very loud and hard; but his eyes were closed, and his face a horrible colour.

"Dear, deary me," cried my mother, "what a disgrace upon the house! And your poor father sick!"

In the meantime, we had no idea what to do to help the captain, nor any other thought but that he had got his death-hurt in the scuffle with the stranger. I got the rum, to be sure, and tried to put it down his throat; but his teeth were tightly shut, and his jaws as strong as iron. It was a happy relief for us when the door opened and Doctor Livesey came in, on his visit to my father.

"Oh, doctor," we cried, "what shall we do? Where is he wounded?"

"Wounded? A fiddle-stick's end!" said the doctor. "No more wounded than you or I. The man has had a stroke, as I warned him. Now, Mrs. Hawkins, just you run upstairs to your husband, and tell him, if possible, nothing about it. For my part I must do my best to save this fellow's trebly worthless life; and Jim here will get me a basin."

When I got back with the basin, the doctor had already ripped up the captain's sleeve, and exposed his great sinewy arm. It was tattooed in several places. "Here's luck," "A fair wind," and "Bill Bones his fancy," were very neatly and clearly executed on the forearm; and up near the shoulder there was a sketch of a gallows and a man hanging from it – done, as I thought, with great spirit.

"Prophetic," said the doctor, touching this picture with his finger. "And, now, Master Billy Bones, if that be your name, we'll have a look at the colour of your blood. Jim," he said, "are you afraid of blood?"

"No, sir," said I.

"Well, then," said he, "you hold the basin," and with that he took his lancet and opened a vein.

A great deal of blood was taken before the captain opened his eyes and looked mistily about him. First he recognised the doctor with an unmistakable frown; then his glance fell upon me, and he looked relieved. But suddenly his colour changed, and he tried to raise himself, crying:—

"Where's Black Dog?"

"There is no Black Dog here," said the doctor, "except what you have on your own back. You have been drinking rum; you have had a stroke, precisely as I told you; and I have just, very much against my own will, dragged you head-foremost out of the grave. Now, Mr. Bones—"

"That's not my name," he interrupted.

"Much I care," returned the doctor. "It's the name of a buccaneer of my acquaintance; and I call you by it for the sake of shortness, and what I have to say to you is this: one glass of rum won't kill you, but if you take one you'll take another and another, and I stake my wig if you don't break off short, you'll die – do you understand that? – die, and go to your own place like the man in the Bible. Come, now, make an effort. I'll help you to your bed for once."

Between us, with much trouble, we managed to hoist him upstairs, and laid him on his bed, where his head fell back on the pillow, as if he were almost fainting.

"Now, mind you," said the doctor, "I clear my conscience – the name of rum for you is death."

And with that he went off to see my father, taking me with him by the arm.

"This is nothing," he said, as soon as he had closed the door. "I have drawn blood enough to keep him quiet a while; he should lie for a week where he is – that is the best thing for him and you; but another stroke would settle him."

CHAPTER III

THE BLACK SPOT

ABOUT noon I stopped at the captain's door with some cooling drinks and medicines. He was lying very much as we had left him, only a little higher, and he seemed both weak and excited.

"Jim," he said, "you're the only one here that's worth anything; and you know I've been always good to you. Never a month but I've given you a silver fourpenny for yourself. And now you see, mate, I'm pretty low, and deserted by all; and Jim, you'll bring me one noggin of rum, now, won't you, matey?"

"The doctor—" I began.

But he broke in cursing the doctor, in a feeble voice, but heartily. "Doctors is all swabs," he said; "and that doctor there, why, what do he know about seafaring men? I been in places hot as pitch, and mates dropping round with Yellow Jack, and the blessed land a-heaving like the sea with earthquakes – what do the doctor know of lands like that? – and I lived on rum, I tell you. It's been meat and drink, and man and wife, to me; and if I'm not to have my rum now I'm a poor old hulk on a lee shore, my blood'll be on you, Jim, and that doctor swab;" and he ran on again for a while with curses. "Look, Jim, how my fingers fidges," he continued, in the pleading tone. "I can't keep 'em still, not I. I haven't had a drop this blessed day. That doctor's a fool, I tell you. If I don't have a drain o' rum, Jim, I'll have the horrors; I seen some on 'em already. I seen old Flint there in the corner, behind you; as plain as print, I seen him; and if I get the horrors, I'm a man that has lived rough, and I'll raise Cain. Your doctor hisself said one glass wouldn't hurt me. I'll give you a golden guinea for a noggin, Jim."

He was growing more and more excited, and this alarmed me for my father, who was very low that day, and needed quiet; besides, I was reassured by the doctor's words, now quoted to me, and rather offended by the offer of a bribe.

"I want none of your money," said I, "but what you owe my father. I'll get you one glass, and no more."

When I brought it to him, he seized it greedily, and drank it out.

"Ay, ay," said he, "that's some better, sure enough. And now, matey, did that doctor say how long I was to lie here in this old berth?"

"A week at least," said I.

"Thunder!" he cried. "A week! I can't do that; they'd have the black spot on me by then. The lubbers is going about to get the wind of me this blessed moment; lubbers as couldn't keep what they got, and want to nail what is another's. Is that seamanly behaviour, now, I want to know? But I'm a saving soul. I never wasted good money of mine, nor lost it neither; and I'll trick 'em again. I'm not afraid on 'em. I'll shake out another reef, matey, and daddle 'em again."

As he was thus speaking, he had risen from bed with great difficulty, holding to my shoulder with a grip that almost made me cry out, and moving his legs like so much dead weight. His words, spirited as they were in meaning, contrasted sadly with the weakness of the voice in which they were uttered. He paused when he had got into a sitting position on the edge.

"That doctor's done me," he murmured. "My ears is singing. Lay me back."

Before I could do much to help him he had fallen back again to his former place, where he lay for a while silent.

"Jim," he said at length, "you saw that seafaring man to-day?"

"Black Dog?" I asked.

"Ah! Black Dog," says he. *"He's* a bad 'un; but there's worse that put him on. Now, if I can't get away nohow, and they tip me the black spot, mind you, it's my old sea-chest they're after; you get on a horse – you can, can't you? Well, then, you get on a horse, and go to – well, yes, I will! – to that eternal doctor swab, and tell him to pipe all hands – magistrates and sich – and he'll lay 'em aboard at the Admiral Benbow – all old Flint's crew, man and boy, all on 'em that's left. I was first mate, I was, old Flint's first mate, and I'm the on'y one as knows the place. He gave it me to Savannah, when he lay a-dying, like as if I was to now, you see. But you won't peach unless they get the black spot on me, or unless you see that Black Dog again, or a seafaring man with one leg, Jim – him above all."

"But what is the black spot, captain?" I asked.

"That's a summons, mate. I'll tell you if they get that. But you keep your weather-eye open, Jim, and I'll share with you equals upon my honour."

He wandered a little longer, his voice growing weaker; but soon after I had given him his medicine, which he took like a child with the remark, "If ever a seaman wanted drugs, it's me," he fell at last into a heavy, swoon-like sleep, in which I left him. What I should have done had all gone well I do not know. Probably I should have told the whole story to the doctor; for I was in mortal fear lest the captain should repent of his confessions and make an end of me. But as things fell out, my poor father died quite suddenly that evening; which put all other matters on one side. Our natural distress, the visits of the neighbours, the arranging of the funeral, and all the work of the inn to be carried on in the meanwhile, kept me so busy that I had scarcely time to think of the captain, far less to be afraid of him.

He got downstairs next morning, to be sure, and had his meals as usual, though he ate little, and had more, I am afraid, than his usual supply of rum, for he helped himself out of the bar, scowling and blowing through his nose, and no one dared to cross him. On the night before the funeral he was as drunk as ever; and it was shocking, in that house of mourning, to hear him singing away at his ugly old sea-song; but, weak as he was, we were all in the fear of death for him, and the doctor was suddenly taken up with a case many miles away, and was never near the house after my father's death. I have said the captain was weak; and indeed he seemed rather to grow weaker than regain his strength. He clambered up and down stairs, and went from the parlour to the bar and back again, and sometimes put his nose out of doors to smell the sea, holding on to the walls as he went for support, and breathing hard and fast like a man on a steep mountain. He never particularly addressed me, and it is my belief he had as good as forgotten his confidences; but his temper was more flighty, and, allowing for his bodily weakness, more violent than ever. He had an alarming way now when he was drunk of drawing his cutlass and laying it bare before him on the table. But with all that, he minded people less, and seemed shut up in his own thoughts and rather wandering. Once, for instance, to our extreme wonder, he piped up to a different air, a kind of country love-song, that he must have learned in his youth before he had begun to follow the sea.

So things passed until, the day after the funeral, and about three o'clock of a bitter, foggy, frosty afternoon, I was standing at the door for a moment, full of sad thoughts about my father, when I saw some one drawing slowly near along the road. He was plainly blind, for he tapped before him with a stick, and wore a great green shade over his eyes and nose; and he was hunched, as if with age or weakness, and wore a huge old tattered sea-cloak with a hood, that made him appear positively deformed. I never saw in my life a more dreadful looking figure. He stopped a little from the inn, and, raising his voice in an odd sing-song, addressed the air in front of him.

"Will any kind friend inform a poor blind man, who has lost the precious sight of his eyes in the gracious defence of his native country, England, and God bless King George! – where or in what part of this country he may now be?"

"You are at the Admiral Benbow, Black Hill Cove, my good man," said I.

"I hear a voice," said he; "a young voice. Will you give me your hand, my kind young friend, and lead me in?"

I held out my hand, and the horrible, soft-spoken, eyeless creature gripped it in a moment like a vice. I was so much startled that I struggled to withdraw; but the blind man pulled me close up to him with a single action of his arm.

"Now, boy," he said, "take me in to the captain."

"Sir," said I, "upon my word I dare not."

"Oh," he sneered, "that's it! Take me in straight, or I'll break your arm."

And he gave it, as he spoke, a wrench that made me cry out.

"Sir," I said, "it is for yourself I mean. The captain is not what he used to be. He sits with a drawn cutlass. Another gentleman—"

"Come, now, march," interrupted he; and I never heard a voice so cruel, and cold, and ugly as that blind man's. It cowed me more than the pain; and

I began to obey him at once, walking straight in at the door and towards the parlour, where our sick old buccaneer was sitting, dazed with rum. The blind man clung close to me, holding me in one iron fist, and leaning almost more of his weight on me than I could carry. "Lead me straight up to him, and when I'm in view, cry out, 'Here's a friend for you, Bill.' If you don't, I'll do this" – and with that he gave me a twitch that I thought would have made me faint. Between this and that, I was so utterly terrified of the blind beggar that I forgot my terror of the captain, and as I opened the parlour door, cried out the words he had ordered in a trembling voice.

The poor captain raised his eyes, and at one look the rum went out of him, and left him staring sober. The expression of his face was not so much of terror as of mortal sickness. He made a movement to rise, but I do not believe he had enough force left in his body.

"Now, Bill, sit where you are," said the beggar. "If I can't see, I can hear a finger stirring. Business is business. Hold out your right hand. Boy, take his right hand by the wrist and bring it near to my right."

We both obeyed him to the letter, and I saw him pass something from the hollow of the hand that held his stick into the palm of the captain's, which closed upon it instantly.

"And now that's done," said the blind man; and at the words he suddenly left hold of me, and, with incredible accuracy and nimbleness, skipped out of the parlour and into the road, where, as I still stood motionless, I could hear his stick go tap-tap-tapping into the distance.

It was some time before either I or the captain seemed to gather our senses; but at length, and about at the same moment, I released his wrist, which I was still holding, and he drew in his hand and looked sharply into the palm.

"Ten o'clock!" he cried. "Six hours. We'll do them yet;" and he sprang to his feet.

Even as he did so, he reeled, put his hand to his throat, stood swaying for a moment, and then, with a peculiar sound, fell from his whole height face foremost to the floor.

I ran to him at once, calling to my mother. But haste was all in vain. The captain had been struck dead by thundering apoplexy. It is a curious thing to understand, for I had certainly never liked the man, though of late I had begun to pity him, but as soon as I saw that he was dead, I burst into a flood of tears. It was the second death I had known, and the sorrow of the first was still fresh in my heart.

'I saw him pass something from the hollow of his hand . . .' (p. 17)

CHAPTER IV

THE SEA CHEST

I LOST no time, of course, in telling my mother all that I knew, and perhaps should have told her long before, and we saw ourselves at once in a difficult and dangerous position. Some of the man's money – if he had any – was certainly due to us; but it was not likely that our captain's shipmates, above all the two specimens seen by me, Black Dog and the blind beggar, would be inclined to give up their booty in payment of the dead man's debts. The captain's order to mount at once and ride for Doctor Livesey would have left my mother alone and unprotected, which was not to be thought of. Indeed, it seemed impossible for either of us to remain much longer in the house: the fall of coals in the kitchen grate, the very ticking of the clock, filled us with alarms. The neighbourhood, to our ears, seemed haunted by approaching footsteps; and what between the dead body of the captain on the parlour floor, and the thought of that detestable blind beggar hovering near at hand, and ready to return, there were moments when, as the saying goes, I jumped in my skin for terror. Something must speedily be resolved upon; and it occurred to us at last to go forth together and seek help in the neighbouring hamlet. No sooner said than done. Bare-headed as we were, we ran out at once in the gathering evening and the frosty fog.

The hamlet lay not many hundred yards away though out of view, on the other side of the next cove; and what greatly encouraged me, it was in an opposite direction from that whence the blind man had made his appearance, and whither he had presumably returned. We were not many minutes on the road, though we sometimes stopped to lay hold of each other and hearken. But there was no unusual sound – nothing but the low wash of the ripple and the croaking of the crows in the wood.

It was already candle-light when we reached the hamlet, and I shall never forget how much I was cheered to see the yellow shine in doors and windows; but that, as it proved, was the best of the help we were likely to get in that quarter. For – you would have thought men would have been ashamed of themselves – no soul would consent to return with us to the Admiral Benbow. The more we told of our troubles, the more – man, woman, and child – they clung to the shelter of their houses. The name of Captain Flint, though it was strange to me, was well enough known to some there, and carried a great weight of terror. Some of the men who had been to field-work on the far side of the Admiral Benbow remembered, besides, to have seen several strangers on the road, and, taking them to be smugglers, to have bolted away; and one at least had seen a little lugger in what we called Kitt's Hole. For that matter, any one who was a comrade of the captain's was enough to frighten them to death. And the short and the long of the matter was, that while we could get several who were willing enough to ride to Dr. Livesey's, which lay in another direction, not one would help us to defend the inn.

They say cowardice is infectious; but then argument is, on the other hand, a great emboldener; and so when each had said his say, my mother made them a speech. She would not, she declared, lose money that belonged to her fatherless boy; "if none of the rest of you dare," she said, "Jim and I dare. Back we will go, the way we came, and small thanks to you big, hulking, chicken-hearted men. We'll have that chest open, if we die for it. And I'll thank you for that bag, Mrs. Crossley, to bring back our lawful money in."

Of course, I said I would go with my mother; and of course they all cried out at our foolhardiness; but even then not a man would go along with us. All they would do was to give me a loaded pistol, lest we were attacked; and to promise to have horses ready saddled, in case we were pursued on our return; while one lad was to ride forward to the doctor's in search of armed assistance.

My heart was beating finely when we two set forth in the cold night upon this dangerous venture. A full moon was beginning to rise and peered redly through the upper edges of the fog, and this increased our haste, for it was plain, before we came forth again, that all would be as bright as day, and our departure exposed to the eyes of any watchers. We slipped along the hedges, noiseless and swift, nor did we see or hear anything to increase our terrors, till, to our huge relief, the door of the Admiral Benbow had closed behind us.

I slipped the bolt at once, and we stood and panted for a moment in the dark, alone in the house with the dead captain's body. Then my mother got

' "He had till ten, mother," said I; and just as I said it, our old clock began striking.' (p. 22)

a candle in the bar, and, holding each other's hands, we advanced into the parlour. He lay as we had left him, on his back, with his eyes open, and one arm stretched out.

"Draw down the blind, Jim," whispered my mother; "they might come and watch outside. And now," said she, when I had done so, "we have to get the key off *that;* and who's to touch it, I should like to know!" and she gave a kind of sob as she said the words.

I went down on my knees at once. On the floor close to his hand there was a little round of paper, blackened on the one side. I could not doubt that this was the *black spot;* and taking it up, I found written on the other side, in a very good, clear hand, this short message: "You have till ten to-night."

"He had till ten, mother," said I; and just as I said it, our old clock began striking. This sudden noise startled us shockingly; but the news was good, for it was only six.

"Now, Jim," she said, "that key."

I felt in his pockets, one after another. A few small coins, a thimble, and some thread and big needles, a piece of pigtail tobacco bitten away at the end, his gully with a crooked handle, a pocket compass, and a tinder-box, were all that they contained, and I began to despair.

"Perhaps it's round his neck," suggested my mother.

Overcoming a strong repugnance, I tore open his shirt at the neck, and there, sure enough, hanging to a bit of tarry string, which I cut with his own gully, we found the key. At this triumph we were filled with hope, and hurried upstairs, without delay, to the little room where he had slept so long, and where his box had stood since the day of his arrival.

It was like any other seaman's chest on the outside, the initial "B" burned on the top of it with a hot iron, and the corners somewhat smashed and broken as by long, rough usage.

"Give me the key," said my mother; and though the lock was very stiff, she had turned it and thrown back the lid in a twinkling.

A strong smell of tobacco and tar rose from the interior, but nothing was to be seen on the top except a suit of very good clothes, carefully brushed and folded. They had never been worn, my mother said. Under that, the miscellany began – a quadrant, a tin canikin, several sticks of tobacco, two brace of very handsome pistols, a piece of bar silver, an old Spanish watch and some other trinkets of little value and mostly of foreign make, a pair of compasses mounted with brass, and five or six curious West Indian shells. It

has often set me thinking since that he should have carried about these shells with him in his wandering, guilty and hunted life.

In the meantime, we had found nothing of any value but the silver and the trinkets, and neither of these were in our way. Underneath there was an old boat-cloak, whitened with sea-salt on many a harbour-bar. My mother pulled it up with impatience, and there lay before us, the last things in the chest, a bundle tied up in oilcloth, and looking like papers, and a canvas bag, that gave forth, at a touch, the jingle of gold.

"I'll show these rogues that I'm an honest woman," said my mother. "I'll have my dues, and not a farthing over. Hold Mrs. Crossley's bag." And she began to count over the amount of the captain's score from the sailor's bag into the one that I was holding.

It was a long, difficult business, for the coins were of all countries and sizes – doubloons, and louis-d'ors, and guineas, and pieces of eight, and I know not what besides, all shaken together at random. The guineas, too, were about the scarcest, and it was with these only that my mother knew how to make her count.

When we were about half-way through, I suddenly put my hand upon her arm; for I had heard in the silent, frosty air, a sound that brought my heart into my mouth – the tap tapping of the blind man's stick upon the frozen road. It drew nearer and nearer, while we sat holding our breath. Then it struck sharp on the inn door, and then we could hear the handle being turned, and the bolt rattling as the wretched being tried to enter; and then there was a long time of silence both within and without. At last the tapping recommenced, and, to our indescribable joy and gratitude, died slowly away again until it ceased to be heard.

"Mother," said I, "take the whole and let's be going," for I was sure the bolted door must have seemed suspicious, and would bring the whole hornet's nest about our ears; though how thankful I was that I had bolted it, none could tell who had never met that terrible blind man.

But my mother, frightened as she was, would not consent to take a fraction more than was due to her, and was obstinately unwilling to be content with less. It was not yet seven, she said, by a long way; she knew her rights and she would have them; and she was still arguing with me, when a little low whistle sounded a good way off upon the hill. That was enough, and more than enough for both of us.

"I'll take what I have," she said, jumping to her feet.

"And I'll take this to square the count," said I, picking up the oilskin packet.

Next moment we were both groping downstairs, leaving the candle by the empty chest; and the next we had opened the door and were in full retreat. We had not started a moment too soon. The fog was rapidly dispersing; already the moon shone quite clear on the high ground on either side; and it was only in the exact bottom of the dell and round the tavern door that a thin veil still hung unbroken to conceal the first steps of our escape. Far less than half-way to the hamlet, very little beyond the bottom of the hill, we must come forth into the moonlight. Nor was this all; for the sound of several footsteps running came already to our ears, and as we looked back in their direction, a light tossing to and fro and still rapidly advancing, showed that one of the new-comers carried a lantern.

"My dear," said my mother suddenly, "take the money and run on. I am going to faint."

This was certainly the end for both of us, I thought. How I cursed the cowardice of the neighbours; how I blamed my poor mother for her honesty and her greed, for her past foolhardiness and present weakness! We were just at the little bridge, by good fortune; and I helped her, tottering as she was, to the edge of the bank, where, sure enough, she gave a sigh and fell on my shoulder. I do not know how I found the strength to do it at all, and I am afraid it was roughly done, but I managed to drag her down the bank and a little way under the arch. Farther I could not move her, for the bridge was too low to let me do more than crawl below it. So there we had to stay – my mother almost entirely exposed, and both of us within earshot of the inn.

CHAPTER V

THE LAST OF THE BLIND MAN

MY curiosity, in a sense, was stronger than my fear; for I could not remain where I was, but crept back to the bank again, whence, sheltering my head behind a bush of broom, I might command the road before our door. I was scarcely in position ere my enemies began to arrive, seven or eight of them, running hard, their feet beating out of time along the road, and the man with the lantern some paces in front. Three men ran together, hand in hand; and I made out, even through the mist, that the middle man of this trio was the blind beggar. The next moment his voice showed me that I was right.

"Down with the door!" he cried.

"Ay, ay, sir!" answered two or three; and a rush was made upon the Admiral Benbow, the lantern-bearer following; and then I could see them pause, and hear speeches passed in a lower key, as if they were surprised to find the door open. But the pause was brief, for the blind man again issued his commands. His voice sounded louder and higher, as if he were afire with eagerness and rage.

"In, in, in!" he shouted, and cursed them for their delay.

Four or five of them obeyed at once, two remaining on the road with the formidable beggar. There was a pause, then a cry of surprise, and then a voice shouting from the house:— "Bill's dead!"

But the blind man swore at them again for their delay.

"Search him, some of you shirking lubbers, and the rest of you aloft and get the chest," he cried. I could hear their feet rattling up our old stairs, so that the house must have shook with it. Promptly afterwards, fresh sounds of astonishment arose; the window of the captain's room was thrown open with a slam and a jingle of broken glass; and a man leaned out into the moonlight, head and shoulders, and addressed the blind beggar on the road below him.

"Pew," he cried, "they've been before us. Some one's turned the chest out alow and aloft."

"Is it there?" roared Pew.

"The money's there."

The blind man cursed the money.

"Flint's fist, I mean," he cried.

"We don't see it here nohow," returned the man.

"Here, you below there, is it on Bill?" cried the blind man again.

At that, another fellow, probably him who had remained below to search the captain's body, came to the door of the inn. "Bill's been overhauled a'ready," said he, "nothin' left."

"It's these people of the inn – it's that boy. I wish I had put his eyes out!" cried the blind man Pew. "They were here no time ago – they had the door bolted when I tried it. Scatter lads, and find 'em."

"Sure enough, they left their glim here," said the fellow from the window.

"Scatter and find 'em! Rout the house out!" reiterated Pew, striking with his stick upon the road.

Then there followed a great to-do through all our old inn, heavy feet pounding to and fro, furniture thrown over, doors kicked in, until the very rocks re-echoed, and the men came out again, one after another, on the road, and declared that we were nowhere to be found. And just then the same whistle that had alarmed my mother and myself over the dead captain's money was once more clearly audible through the night, but this time twice repeated. I had thought it to be the blind man's trumpet, so to speak, summoning his crew to the assault; but I now found that it was a signal from the hillside towards the hamlet, and, from its effect upon the buccaneers, a signal to warn them of approaching danger.

"There's Dirk again," said one. "Twice. We'll have to budge, mates."

"Budge, you skulk!" cried Pew. "Dirk was a fool and a coward from the first – you wouldn't mind him. They must be close by; they can't be far; you have your hands on it. Scatter and look for them, dogs! Oh, shiver my soul," he cried, "if I had eyes!"

This appeal seemed to produce some effect, for two of the fellows began to look here and there among the lumber, but half-heartedly, I thought, and with half an eye to their own danger all the time, while the rest stood irresolute on the road.

"You have your hands on thousands, you fools, and you hang a leg!

You'd be as rich as kings if you could find it, and you know it's here, and you stand there malingering. There wasn't one of you dared face Bill, and I did it – a blind man! And I'm to lose my chance through you! I'm to be a poor, crawling beggar, sponging for rum, when I might be rolling in a coach! If you had the pluck of a weevil in a biscuit you would catch them still."

"Hang it, Pew, we've got the doubloons!" grumbled one.

"They might have hid the blessed thing," said another. "Take the Georges, Pew, and don't stand here squalling."

Squalling was the word for it, Pew's anger rose so high at these objections; till at last, his passion completely taking the upper hand, he struck at them right and left in his blindness, and his stick sounded heavily on more than one.

These, in their turn, cursed back at the blind miscreant, threatened him in horrid terms, and tried in vain to catch the stick and wrest it from his grasp.

This quarrel was the saving of us; for while it was still raging another sound came from the top of the hill on the side of the hamlet – the tramp of horses galloping. Almost at the same time a pistol-shot, flash and report, came from the hedge-side. And that was plainly the last signal of danger; for the buccaneers turned at once and ran, separating in every direction, one seaward along the cove, one slant across the hill, and so on, so that in half a minute not a sign of them remained but Pew. Him they had deserted, whether in sheer panic or out of revenge for his ill words and blows, I know not; but there he remained behind, tapping up and down the road in a frenzy, and groping and calling for his comrades. Finally he took the wrong turn, and ran a few steps past me, towards the hamlet, crying:—

"Johnny, Black Dog, Dirk," and other names, "you won't leave old Pew, mates – not old Pew!"

Just then the noise of horses topped the rise, and four or five riders came in sight in the moonlight, and swept at full gallop down the slope.

At this Pew saw his error, turned with a scream, and ran straight for the ditch, into which he rolled. But he was on his feet again in a second, and made another dash, now utterly bewildered, right under the nearest of the coming horses.

The rider tried to save him, but in vain. Down went Pew with a cry that rang high into the night; and the four hoofs trampled and spurned him and passed by. He fell on his side, then gently collapsed upon his face, and moved no more.

'Down went Pew with a cry that rang high into the night; and the four hoofs trampled and spurned him and passed by.' (p. 27)

I leapt to my feet and hailed the riders. They were pulling up, at any rate, horrified at the accident; and I soon saw what they were. One, tailing out behind the rest, was a lad that had gone from the hamlet to Dr. Livesey's; the rest were revenue officers, whom he had met by the way, and with whom he had had the intelligence to return at once. Some news of the lugger in Kitt's Hole had found its way to Supervisor Dance, and set him forth that night in our direction, and to that circumstance my mother and I owed our preservation from death.

Pew was dead, stone dead. As for my mother, when we had carried her up to the hamlet, a little cold water and salts and that soon brought her back again, and she was none the worse for her terror, though she still continued to deplore the balance of the money. In the meantime the supervisor rode on, as fast as he could, to Kitt's Hole; but his men had to dismount and grope down the dingle, holding, and sometimes supporting, their horses, and in continual fear of ambushes; so it was no great matter for surprise that when they got down to the Hole the lugger was already under way, though still close in. He hailed her. A voice replied, telling him to keep out of the moonlight, or he would get some lead in him, and at the same time a bullet whistled close by his arm. Soon after, the lugger doubled the point and disappeared. Mr. Dance stood there as he said, "like a fish out of water," and all he could do was to despatch a man to B— to warn the cutter. "And that," said he, "is just about as good as nothing. They've got off clean, and there's an end. Only," he added, "I'm glad I trod on Master Pew's corns;" for by this time he had heard my story.

I went back with him to the Admiral Benbow, and you cannot imagine a house in such a state of smash; the very clock had been thrown down by these fellows in their furious hunt after my mother and myself; and though nothing had actually been taken away except the captain's money-bag and a little silver from the till. I could see at once that we were ruined. Mr. Dance could make nothing of the scene.

"They got the money, you say? Well, then, Hawkins, what in fortune were they after? More money, I suppose?"

"No, sir; not money, I think," replied I. "In fact, sir, I believe I have the thing in my breast-pocket; and, to tell you the truth. I should like to get it put in safety."

"To be sure, boy; quite right," said he. "I'll take it, if you like."

"I thought, perhaps, Dr. Livesey—" I began.

A Map of Treasure Island
(M. S. Orr)

I remember him as if it were yesterday as he came plodding to the inn door.
(M. Winter)

"BOY TAKE HIS RIGHT HAND BY THE WRIST."
(F. GILLET)

" 'Pew,' he cried, 'they've been before us.' "
(M. Winter)

"Perfectly right," he interrupted, very cheerily, "perfectly right – a gentleman and a magistrate. And, now I come to think of it, I might as well ride round there myself and report to him or squire. Master Pew's dead, when all's done; not that I regret it, but he's dead, you see, and people will make it out against an officer of his Majesty's revenue, if make it out they can. Now, I tell you, Hawkins; if you like, I'll take you along."

I thanked him heartily for the offer, and we walked back to the hamlet where the horses were. By the time I had told mother of my purpose they were all in the saddle.

"Dogger," said Mr. Dance, "you have a good horse; take up this lad behind you."

As soon as I was mounted, holding on to Dogger's belt, the supervisor gave the word, and the party struck out at a bouncing trot on to the road to Dr. Livesey's house.

CHAPTER VI

THE CAPTAIN'S PAPERS

WE rode all the way, till we drew up before Dr. Livesey's door. The house was all dark to the front. Mr. Dance told me to jump down and knock, and Dogger gave me a stirrup to descend by. The door was opened almost at once by the maid.

"Is Dr. Livesey in?" I asked.

No, she said; he had come home in the afternoon, but had gone up to the Hall to dine and pass the evening with the squire.

"So there we go, boys," said Mr. Dance.

This time, as the distance was short, I did not mount, but ran with Dogger's stirrup-leather to the lodge gates, and up the long, leafless, moonlit avenue to where the white line of the Hall buildings looked on either hand on great old gardens. Here Mr. Dance dismounted, and, taking me along with him, was admitted at a word into the house.

The servant led us down a matted passage, and showed us at the end into a great library, all lined with book-cases and busts upon the top of them, where the squire and Dr. Livesey sat, pipe in hand, on either side of a bright fire.

I had never seen the squire so near at hand. He was a tall man, over six feet high, and broad in proportion, and he had a bluff, rough-and-ready face, all roughened and reddened and lined in his long travels. His eyebrows were very black, and moved readily, and this gave him a look of some temper, not bad, you would say, but quick and high.

"Come in, Mr. Dance," says he, very stately and condescending.

"Good-evening, Dance," says the doctor, with a nod. "And good-evening to you, friend Jim. What good wind brings you here?"

The supervisor stood up straight and stiff, and told his story like a lesson; and you should have seen how the two gentlemen leaned forward and looked at each other, and forgot to smoke in their surprise and interest.

When they heard how my mother went back to the inn, Dr. Livesey fairly slapped his thigh, and the squire cried, "Bravo!" and broke his long pipe against the grate. Long before it was done, Mr. Trelawney (that, you will remember, was the squire's name), had got up from his seat, and was striding about the room, and the doctor, as if to hear the better, had taken off his powdered wig, and sat there, looking very strange indeed with his own close-cropped, black poll.

At last Mr. Dance finished the story.

"Mr. Dance," said the squire, "you are a very noble fellow. And as for riding down that black, atrocious miscreant, I regard it as an act of virtue, sir, like stamping on a cockroach. This lad Hawkins is a trump, I perceive. Hawkins, will you ring that bell? Mr. Dance must have some ale."

"And so, Jim," said the doctor, "you have the thing that they were after, have you?"

"Here it is, sir," said I, and gave him the oilskin packet.

The doctor looked it all over, as if his fingers were itching to open it; but, instead of doing that, he put it quietly in the pocket of his coat.

"Squire," said he, "when Dance has had his ale, he must, of course, be off on his Majesty's service; but I mean to keep Jim Hawkins here to sleep at my house, and, with your permission, I propose we should have up the cold pie, and let him sup."

"As you will, Livesey," said the squire; "Hawkins has earned better than cold pie."

So a big pigeon pie was brought in and put on a side-table, and I made a hearty supper, for I was as hungry as a hawk, while Mr. Dance was further complimented, and at last dismissed.

"And now, squire," said the doctor.

"And, now, Livesey," said the squire in the same breath.

"One at a time, one at a time," laughed Dr. Livesey. "You have heard of this Flint, I suppose?"

"Heard of him!" cried the squire. "Heard of him, you say! He was the bloodthirstiest buccaneer that sailed. Blackbeard was a child to Flint. The Spaniards were so prodigiously afraid of him, that, I tell you, sir, I was sometimes proud he was an Englishman. I've seen his top-sails with these eyes, off Trinidad, and the cowardly son of a rum-puncheon that I sailed with put back – put back, sir, into Port of Spain."

"Well, I've heard of him myself, in England," said the doctor. "But the

point is, had he money?"

"Money!" cried the squire. "Have you heard the story? What were these villains after but money? What do they care for but money? For what would they risk their rascal carcasses but money?"

"That we shall soon know," replied the doctor. "But you are so confoundedly hot-headed and exclamatory that I cannot get a word in. What I want to know is this: Supposing that I have here in my pocket some clue to where Flint buried his treasure, will that treasure amount to much?"

"Amount, sir!" cried the squire. "It will amount to this; if we have the clue you talk about, I fit out a ship in Bristol dock, and take you and Hawkins here along, and I'll have that treasure if I search a year."

"Very well," said the doctor. "Now, then, if Jim is agreeable, we'll open the packet;" and he laid it before him on the table.

The bundle was sewn together, and the doctor had to get out his instrument-case, and cut the stitches with his medical scissors. It contained two things – a book and a sealed paper.

"First of all we'll try the book," observed the doctor.

The squire and I were both peering over his shoulder as he opened it, for Dr. Livesey had kindly motioned me to come round from the side-table, where I had been eating, to enjoy the sport of the search. On the first page there were only some scraps of writing, such as a man with a pen in his hand might make for idleness or practice. One was the same as the tattoo mark, *"Billy Bones his fancy"*; then there was *"Mr. W. Bones, mate." "No more rum." "Off Palm Key he got itt"*; and some other snatches, mostly single words and unintelligible. I could not help wondering who it was that had *"got itt,"* and what *"itt"* was that he got. A knife in his back as like as not.

"Not much instruction there," said Dr. Livesey, as he passed on.

The next ten or twelve pages were filled with a curious series of entries. There was a date at one end of the line and at the other a sum of money, as in common account-books; but instead of explanatory writing, only a varying number of crosses between the two. On the 12th of June, 1745, for instance, a sum of seventy pounds had plainly become due to some one, and there was nothing but six crosses to explain the cause. In a few cases, to be sure, the name of a place would be added, as *"Offe Caraccas"*; or a mere entry of latitude and longitude, as *"62° 17′ 20″, 19° 2′ 40″."*

The record lasted over nearly twenty years, the amount of the separate entries growing larger as time went on, and at the end a grand total had been made out after five or six wrong additions, and these words appended, *"Bones, his pile."*

"I can't make head or tail of this," said Dr. Livesey.

"The thing is as clear as noonday," cried the squire. "This is the black-hearted hound's account-book. These crosses stand for the names of ships or towns that they sank or plundered. The sums are the scoundrel's share, and where he feared an ambiguity, you see he added something clearer. *'Offe Caraccas,'* now; you see, here was some unhappy vessel boarded off that coast. God help the poor souls that manned her – coral long ago."

"Right!" said the doctor. "See what it is to be a traveller. Right! And the amounts increase, you see, as he rose in rank."

There was little else in the volume but a few bearings of places noted in the blank leaves towards the end, and a table for reducing French, English, and Spanish moneys to a common value.

"Thrifty man!" cried the doctor. "He wasn't the one to be cheated."

"And now," said the squire, "for the other."

The paper had been sealed in several places with a thimble by way of seal; the very thimble, perhaps, that I had found in the captain's pocket. The doctor opened the seals with great care, and there fell out the map of an island, with latitude and longitude, soundings, names of hills, and bays, and inlets, and every particular that would be needed to bring a ship to a safe anchorage upon its shores. It was about nine miles long and five across, shaped, you might say, like a fat dragon standing up, and had two fine land-locked harbours, and a hill in the centre part marked *"The Spy-glass."* There were several additions of a later date; but, above all, three crosses of red ink – two on the north part of the island, one in the south-west, and, besides this

last, in the same red ink, and in a small, neat hand, very different from the captain's tottery characters, these words: *"Bulk of treasure here."*

Over on the back the same hand had written this further information:—

> *"Tall tree, Spy-glass shoulder, bearing a point to the N. of N.N.E.*
> *"Skeleton Island E.S.E. and by E.*
> *"Ten feet.*
> *"The bar silver is in the north cache; you can find it by the trend of the east hummock, ten fathoms south of the black crag with the face on it. "The arms are easy found, in the sand hill, N. point of north inlet cape, bearing E. and a quarter N.*
>
> *"J. F."*

That was all; but brief as it was, and, to me, incomprehensible, it filled the squire and Dr. Livesey with delight.

"Livesey," said the squire, "you will give up this wretched practice at once. To-morrow I start for Bristol. In three weeks' time – three weeks! – two weeks – ten days – we'll have the best ship, sir, and the choicest crew in England. Hawkins shall come as cabin-boy. You'll make a famous cabin-boy, Hawkins. You Livesey, are ship's doctor; I am admiral. We'll take Redruth, Joyce, and Hunter. We'll have favourable winds, a quick passage and not the least difficulty in finding the spot, and money to eat – to roll in – to play duck and drake with ever after."

"Trelawney," said the doctor, "I'll go with you; and, I'll go bail for it, so will Jim, and be a credit to the undertaking. There's only one man I'm afraid of."

"And who's that?" cried the squire. "Name the dog, sir!"

"You," replied the doctor; "for you cannot hold your tongue We are not the only men who knew of this paper. These fellows who attacked the inn to-night – bold, desperate blades, for sure – and the rest who stayed aboard that lugger, and more, I dare say, not far off, are, one and all, through thick and thin, bound that they'll get that money. We must none of us go alone till we get to sea. Jim and I shall stick together in the meanwhile; you'll take Joyce and Hunter when you ride to Bristol, and, from first to last, not one of us must breathe a word of what we've found."

"Livesey," returned the squire, "you are always in the right of it. I'll be as silent as the grave."

PART II THE SEA-COOK

CHAPTER VII

I GO TO BRISTOL

IT was longer than the squire imagined ere we were ready for the sea, and none of our first plans – not even Dr. Livesey's, of keeping me beside him – could be carried out as we intended. The doctor had to go to London for a physician to take charge of his practice; the squire was hard at work at Bristol; and I lived on at the Hall under the charge of old Redruth, the gamekeeper, almost a prisoner, but full of sea-dreams and the most charming anticipations of strange islands and adventures. I brooded by the hour together over the map, all the details of which I well remembered. Sitting by the fire in the housekeeper's room, I approached that island in my fancy, from every possible direction; I explored every acre of its surface; I climbed a thousand times to that tall hill they call the Spy-glass, and from the top enjoyed the most wonderful and changing prospects. Sometimes the isle was thick with savages, with whom we fought; sometimes full of dangerous animals that hunted us; but in all my fancies nothing occurred to me so strange and tragic as our actual adventures.

So the weeks passed on, till one fine day there came a letter addressed to Dr. Livesey, with this addition, "To be opened, in the case of his absence, by Tom Redruth, or young Hawkins." Obeying this order, we found, or rather I found – for the game-keeper was a poor hand at reading anything but print – the following important news:—

"OLD ANCHOR INN, BRISTOL,
"March 1, 17—.

"DEAR LIVESEY, – As I do not know whether you are at the Hall or still in London, I send this in double to both places.

"The ship is bought and fitted. She lies at anchor, ready for sea. You never imagined a sweeter schooner – a child might sail her – two hundred tons; name Hispaniola.

"I got her through my old friend, Blandly, who has proved himself throughout the most surprising trump. The admirable fellow literally slaved in my interest, and so, I may say, did every one in Bristol, as soon as they got wind of what port we sailed for – treasure, I mean."

"Redruth," said I, interrupting the letter, "Doctor Livesey will not like that. The squire has been talking, after all."

"Well, who's a better right?" growled the gamekeeper. "A pretty rum go if squire ain't to talk for Doctor Livesey, I should think."

At that I gave up all attempt at commentary, and read straight on:—

"Blandly himself found the Hispaniola, and by the most admirable management got her for the merest trifle. There is a class of men in Bristol monstrously prejudiced against Blandly. They go the length of declaring that this honest creature would do anything for money, that the Hispaniola belonged to him, and that he sold it me absurdly high – the most transparent calumnies. None of them dare, however, to deny the merits of the ship.

"So far there was not a hitch. The workpeople, to be sure – riggers and what not – were most annoyingly slow; but time cured that. It was the crew that troubled me.

"I wished a round score of men – in case of natives, buccaneers, or the odious French – and I had the worry of the deuce itself to find so much as half a dozen, till the most remarkable stroke of fortune brought me the very man that I required.

"I was standing on the dock, when, by the merest accident, I fell in talk with him. I found he was an old sailor, kept a public-house, knew all the seafaring men in Bristol, had lost his health ashore, and wanted a good berth as cook to get to sea again. He had hobbled down there that morning, he said, to get a smell of the salt.

"I was monstrously touched – so would you have been – and, out of pure pity, I engaged him on the spot to be ship's cook. Long John Silver, he is called, and has lost a leg; but that I regarded as a recommendation, since he lost it in his country's service under the immortal Hawke. He has no pension, Livesey. Imagine the abominable age we live in!

"Well, sir, I thought I had only found a cook, but it was a crew I had discovered. Between Silver and myself we got together in a few days a company of the toughest old salts imaginable – not pretty to look at, but fellows

by their faces, of the most indomitable spirit. I declare we could fight a frigate.

"Long John even got rid of two out of the six or seven I had already engaged. He showed me in a moment that they were just the sort of fresh-water swabs we had to fear in an adventure of importance.

"I am in the most magnificent health and spirits, eating like a bull, sleeping like a tree, yet I shall not enjoy a moment till I hear my old tarpaulins tramping round the capstan. Seaward ho! Hang the treasure! It's the glory of the sea that has turned my head. So now, Livesey, come post; do not lose an hour, if you respect me.

"Let young Hawkins go at once to see his mother, with Redruth for a guard; and then both come full speed to Bristol.

"JOHN TRELAWNEY."

"Postscript. – *I did not tell you that Blandly, who, by the way is to send a consort after us if we don't turn up by the end of August had found an admirable fellow for sailing master – a stiff man, which I regret, but, in all other respects, a treasure. Long John Silver unearthed a very competent man for a mate, a man named Arrow. I have a boatswain who pipes, Livesey; so things shall go man-o'-war fashion on board the good ship Hispaniola.*

"I forgot to tell you that Silver is a man of substance; I know of my own knowledge that he has a banker's account, which has never been overdrawn. He leaves his wife to manage the inn; and as she is a woman of colour, a pair of old bachelors like you and I may be excused for guessing that it is the wife, quite as much as the health, that send him back to roving.

"J.T."

"P.P.S. – Hawkins may stay one night with his mother.

"J.T."

You can fancy the excitement into which that letter put me. I was half beside myself with glee; and if ever I despised a man, it was old Tom Redruth, who could do nothing but grumble and lament. Any of the under gamekeepers would gladly have changed places with him; but such was not the squire's pleasure, and the squire's pleasure was like law among them all. Nobody but old Redruth would have dared so much as even to grumble.

The next morning he and I set out on foot for the Admiral Benbow, and there I found my mother in good health and spirits. The captain, who had so long been a cause of so much discomfort, was gone where the wicked

'I said good-bye to mother and the cove where I had lived since I was born, and the dear old Admiral Benbow . . .' *(p. 40)*

cease from troubling. The squire had had everything repaired, and the public rooms and the sign repainted, and had added some furniture – above all, a beautiful arm-chair for mother in the bar. He had found her a boy as an apprentice also, so that she should not want help while I was gone.

It was on seeing that boy that I understood, for the first time, my situation. I had thought up to that moment of the adventures before me, not at all of the home I was leaving; and now at the sight of this clumsy stranger, who was to stay here in my place beside my mother, I had my first attack of tears. I am afraid I led that boy a dog's life; for as he was new to the work, I had a hundred opportunities of setting him right and putting him down, and I was not slow to profit by them.

The night passed, and the next day, after dinner, Redruth and I were afoot again, and on the road. I said good-bye to mother and the cove where I had lived since I was born, and the dear old Admiral Benbow – since he was repainted, no longer quite so dear. One of my last thoughts was of the captain, who had so often strode along the beach with his cocked hat, his sabre-cut cheek, and his old brass telescope. Next moment we had turned the corner, and my home was out of sight.

The mail picked us up about dusk at the Royal George on the heath. I was wedged in between Redruth and a stout old gentleman, and in spite of the swift motion and the cold night air, I must have dozed a great deal from the very first, and then slept like a log up hill and down dale through stage after stage; for when I was awakened at last, it was by a punch in the ribs, and I opened my eyes to find that we were standing still before a large building in a city street, and that the day had already broken a long time.

"Where are we?" I asked.

"Bristol," said Tom. "Get down."

Mr. Trelawney had taken up his residence at an inn far down the docks,

to superintend the work upon the schooner. Thither we had now to walk, and our way, to my great delight, lay along the quays and beside the great multitude of ships of all sizes and rigs and nations. In one, sailors were singing at their work; in another there were men aloft, high over my head, hanging to threads that seemed no thicker than a spider's. Though I had lived by the shore all my life, I seemed never to have been near the sea till then. The smell of tar and salt was something new. I saw the most wonderful figureheads, that had all been far over the ocean. I saw, besides, many old sailors, with rings in their ears, and whiskers curled in ringlets, and tarry pigtails, and their swaggering, clumsy sea-walk; and if I had seen as many kings or archbishops I could not have been more delighted.

And I was going to sea myself; to sea in a schooner, with a piping boatswain, and pigtailed singing seamen; to sea, bound for an unknown island, and to seek for buried treasures! While I was still in this delightful dream, we came suddenly in front of a large inn, and met Squire Trelawney, all dressed out like a sea-officer, in stout blue cloth, coming out of the door with a smile on his face, and a capital imitation of a sailor's walk.

"Here you are," he cried, "and the doctor came last night from London. Bravo! the ship's company complete!"

"Oh, sir," cried I, "when do we sail?"

"Sail!" says he. "We sail to-morrow!"

CHAPTER VIII

AT THE SIGN OF THE "SPY-GLASS"

WHEN I had done breakfasting the squire gave me a note addressed to John Silver, at the sign of the Spy-glass, and told me I should easily find the place by following the line of the docks, and keeping a bright look-out for a little tavern with a large brass telescope for sign. I set off, overjoyed at this opportunity to see some more of the ships and seamen, and picked my way among a great crowd of people and carts and bales, for the dock was now at its busiest, until I found the tavern in question.

It was a bright enough little place of entertainment. The sign was newly painted; the windows had neat red curtains; the floor was cleanly sanded. There was a street on either side, and an open door on both, which made the large, low room pretty clear to see in, in spite of clouds of tobacco smoke.

The customers were mostly seafaring men; and they talked so loudly that I hung at the door, almost afraid to enter.

As I was waiting, a man came out of a side room, and, at a glance, I was sure he must be Long John. His left leg was cut off close by the hip, and under the left shoulder he carried a crutch, which he managed with wonderful dexterity, hopping about upon it like a bird. He was very tall and strong, with a face as big as a ham – plain and pale, but intelligent and smiling. Indeed, he seemed in the most cheerful spirits, whistling as he moved about among the tables, with a merry word or a slap on the shoulder for the more favoured of his guests.

Now, to tell you the truth, from the very first mention of Long John in Squire Trelawney's letter, I had taken a fear in my mind that he might prove to be the very one-legged sailor whom I had watched for so long at the old Benbow. But one look at the man before me was enough. I had seen the captain, and Black Dog, and the blind man Pew, and I thought I knew what a buccaneer was like – a very different creature, according to me, from this

clean and pleasant-tempered landlord.

I plucked up courage at once, crossed the threshold, and walked right up to the man where he stood, propped on his crutch, talking to a customer.

"Mr. Silver, sir?" I asked, holding out the note.

"Yes, my lad," said he; "such is my name, to be sure. And who may you be?" And then as he saw the squire's letter, he seemed to me to give something almost like a start.

"Oh!" said he, quite loud, and offering his hand. "I see. You are our new cabin-boy; pleased I am to see you."

And he took my hand in his large, firm grasp.

Just then one of the customers at the far side rose suddenly and made for the door. It was close by him, and he was out in the street in a moment. But his hurry had attracted my notice, and I recognised him at a glance. It was the tallow-faced man, wanting two fingers, who had come first to the Admiral Benbow.

"Oh," I cried, "stop him! it's Black Dog!"

"I don't care two coppers who he is," cried Silver. "But he hasn't paid his score. Harry, run and catch him."

One of the others who was nearest the door leaped up and started in pursuit.

"If he were Admiral Hawke he shall pay his score," cried Silver; and then, relinquishing my hand – "Who did you say he was?" he asked. "Black what?"

"Dog, sir," said I. "Has Mr. Trelawney not told you of the buccaneers? He was one of them."

"So?" cried Silver. "In my house! Ben, run and help Harry. One of those swabs, was he? Was that you drinking with him, Morgan? Step up here."

The man whom he called Morgan – an old, gray-haired, mahogany-faced sailor – came forward pretty sheepishly, rolling his quid.

"Now, Morgan," said Long John, very sternly, "you never clapped your eyes on that Black – Black Dog before, did you, now?"

"Not I, sir," said Morgan, with a salute.

"You didn't know his name, did you?"

"No, sir."

"By the powers, Tom Morgan, it's as good for you!" exclaimed the landlord. "If you had been mixed up with the like of that, you would never have put another foot in my house, you may lay to that. And what was he saying to you?"

‘ “Oh,” I cried, “Stop him! it’s Black Dog!” ’ (p. 43)

"I don't rightly know, sir," answered Morgan.

"Do you call that a head on your shoulders, or a blessed dead eye?" cried Long John. "Don't rightly know, don't you! Perhaps you don't happen to rightly know who you was speaking to, perhaps? Come, now, what was he jawing – v'yages, cap'ns, ships? Pipe up! What was it?"

"We was a-talkin' of keel-hauling," answered Morgan.

"Keel-hauling, was you? and a mighty suitable thing, too, and you may lay to that. Get back to your place for a lubber, Tom."

And then, as Morgan rolled back to his seat, Silver added to me, in a confidential whisper, that was very flattering, as I thought:—

"He's quite an honest man, Tom Morgan; on'y stupid. And now," he ran on again aloud, "let's see – Black Dog? No, I don't know the name, not I. Yet I kind of think I've – yes, I've seen the swab. He used to come here with a blind beggar, he used."

"That he did, you may be sure," said I. "I knew that blind man, too. His name was Pew."

"It was!" cried Silver, now quite excited. "Pew! That were his name for certain. Ah, he looked a shark, he did. If we run down this Black Dog, now, there'll be news for Cap'n Trelawney! Ben's a good runner; few seamen run better than Ben. He should run him down, hand over hand, by the powers! He talked o' keel-hauling, did he? *I'll* keel-haul him!"

All the time he was jerking out these phrases he was stumping up and down the tavern on his crutch, slapping tables with his hand, and giving such a show of excitement as would have convinced an Old Bailey judge or a Bow Street runner. My suspicions had been thoroughly reawakened on finding Black Dog at the Spy-glass, and I watched the cook narrowly. But he was too deep, and too ready, and too clever for me, and by the time the two men had come back out of breath, and confessed that they had lost the track in a crowd, and been scolded like thieves, I would have gone bail for the innocence of Long John Silver.

"See here, now, Hawkins," said he, "here's a blessed hard thing on a man like me, now, ain't it? There's Cap'n Trelawney – what's he to think? Here I have this confounded son of a Dutchman sitting in my own house, drinking of my own rum! Here you comes and tells me of it plain; and here I let him give us all the slip before my blessed deadlights! Now, Hawkins, you do me justice with the cap'n. You're a lad, you are, but you're as smart as paint. I see that when you first came in. Now, here it is: What could I do, with this old timber I hobble on? When I was an A.B. master mariner I'd have come up alongside of him, hand over hand, and broached him to in a brace of old shakes, I would; but now—"

And then, all of a sudden, he stopped, and his jaw dropped as though he had remembered something.

"The score!" he burst out. "Three goes o' rum! Why, shiver my timbers, if I hadn't forgotten my score!"

And, falling on a bench, he laughed until the tears ran down his cheeks. I could not help joining; and we laughed together, peal after peal, until the tavern rang again.

"Why, what a precious old sea-calf I am!" he said at last wiping his cheeks. "You and me should get on well, Hawkins, for I'll take my davy I should be rated ship's boy. But, come now stand by to go about. This won't do. Dooty is dooty, messmates I'll put on my old cocked hat, and step along of you to Cap'n Trelawney, and report this here affair. For mind you, it's serious young Hawkins; and neither you nor me's come out of it with what I should make so bold as to call credit. Nor you neither, says you; not smart – none of the pair of us smart. But dash my buttons! that was a good 'un about my score."

And he began to laugh again, and that so heartily, that, though I did not see the joke as he did, I was again obliged to join him in his mirth.

On our little walk along the quays, he made himself the most interesting companion, telling me about the different ships that we passed by, their rig, tonnage, and nationality, explaining the work that was going forward – how one was discharging, another taking in cargo, and a third making ready for sea; and every now and then telling me some little anecdote of ships or seamen, or repeating a nautical phrase till I had learned it perfectly. I began to see that here was one of the best of possible shipmates.

When we got to the inn, the squire and Dr. Livesey were seated together, finishing a quart of ale with a toast in it, before they should go aboard the schooner on a visit of inspection.

Long John told the story from first to last with a great deal of spirit and the most perfect truth. "That was how it were, now, weren't it, Hawkins?" he would say, now and again, and I could always bear him entirely out.

The two gentlemen regretted that Black Dog had got away; but we all agreed there was nothing to be done, and after he had been complimented, Long John took up his crutch and departed.

'. . . our little walk along the quays . . .' (p. 46)

"All hands aboard by four this afternoon," shouted the squire after him.

"Ay, ay, sir," cried the cook, in the passage.

"Well, squire," said Dr. Livesey, "I don't put much faith in your discoveries, as a general thing; but I will say this, John Silver suits me."

"The man's a perfect trump," declared the squire.

"And now," added the doctor, "Jim may come on board with us, may he not?"

"To be sure he may," says squire. "Take your hat, Hawkins, and we'll see the ship."

CHAPTER IX

POWDER AND ARMS

THE *Hispaniola* lay some way out, and we went under the figureheads and round the sterns of many other ships, and their cables sometimes grated underneath our keel, and sometimes swung above us. At last, however, we got alongside, and were met and saluted as we stepped aboard by the mate, Mr. Arrow, a brown old sailor, with earrings in his ears and a squint. He and the squire were very thick and friendly, but I soon observed that things were not the same between Mr. Trelawney and the captain.

This last was a sharp-looking man, who seemed angry with everything on board, and was soon to tell us why, for we had hardly got down into the cabin when a sailor followed us.

"Captain Smollett, sir, axing to speak with you," said he.

"I am always at the captain's order. Show him in," said the squire.

The captain, who was close behind his messenger, entered at once and shut the door behind him.

"Well, Captain Smollett, what have you to say? All well, I hope; all shipshape and seaworthy."

"Well, sir," said the captain, "better speak plain, I believe, even at the risk of offence. I don't like this cruise; I don't like the men; and I don't like my officer. That's short and sweet."

"Perhaps, sir, you don't like the ship?" inquired the squire, very angry, as I could see.

"I can't speak as to that, sir, not having seen her tried," said the captain. "She seems a clever craft; more I can't say."

"Possibly, sir, you may not like your employer either?" says the squire.

But here Dr. Livesey cut in.

"Stay a bit," said he, "stay a bit. No use of such questions as that but to produce ill-feeling. The captain has said too much, or he has said too little, and I'm bound to say that I require an explanation of his words. You don't, you say, like this cruise. Now, why?"

"I was engaged, sir, on what we call sealed orders, to sail this ship for that gentleman where he should bid me," said the captain. "So far so good. But now I find that every man before the mast knows more than I do. I don't call that fair, now, do you?"

"No," said Dr. Livesey, "I don't."

"Next," said the captain, "I learn we are going after treasure – hear it from my own hands, mind you. Now, treasure is ticklish work; I don't like treasure voyages on any account; and I don't like them, above all, when they are secret, and when (begging your pardon, Mr. Trelawney) the secret has been told to the parrot."

"Silver's parrot?" asked the squire.

"It's a way of speaking," said the captain. "Blabbed, I mean. It's my belief neither of you gentlemen know what you are about, but I'll tell you my way of it – life or death, and a close run."

"That is all clear, and, I dare say, true enough," replied Dr. Livesey. "We take the risk; but we are not so ignorant as you believe us. Next, you say you don't like the crew. Are they not good seamen?"

"I don't like them, sir," returned Captain Smollett. "And I think I should have had the choosing of my own hands, if you go to that."

"Perhaps you should," replied the doctor. "My friend should perhaps, have taken you along with him; but the slight, if there be one, was unintentional. And you don't like Mr. Arrow?"

"I don't, sir. I believe he's a good seaman; but he's too free with the crew to be a good officer. A mate should keep himself to himself – shouldn't drink with the men before the mast!"

"Do you mean he drinks?" cried the squire.

"No, sir," replied the captain; "only that he's too familiar."

"Well, now, and the short and long of it, captain?" asked the doctor. "Tell us what you want."

"Well, gentlemen, are you determined to go on this cruise?"

"Like iron," answered the squire.

"Very good," said the captain. "Then, as you've heard me very patiently, saying things that I could not prove, hear me a few words more. They are putting the powder and the arms in the fore hold. Now, you have a good place under the cabin; why not put them there? – first point. Then you are bringing four of your own people with you, and they tell me some of them are to be berthed forward. Why not give them the berths here beside the cabin? – second point."

"Any more?" asked Mr. Trelawney.

"One more," said the captain. "There's been too much blabbing already."

"Far too much," agreed the doctor.

"I'll tell you what I've heard myself," continued Captain Smollett: "that you have a map of an island; that there's crosses on the map to show where treasure is; and that the island lies—" And then he named the latitude and longitude exactly.

"I never told that," cried the squire, "to a soul!"

"The hands know it, sir," returned the captain.

"Livesey, that must have been you or Hawkins," cried the squire.

"It doesn't much matter who it was," replied the doctor. And I could see that neither he nor the captain paid much regard to Mr. Trelawney's protestations. Neither did I, to be sure, he was so loose a talker; yet in this case I believe he was really right, and that nobody had told the situation of the island.

"Well, gentlemen," continued the captain, "I don't know who has this map; but I make it a point, it shall be kept secret even from me and Mr. Arrow. Otherwise I would ask you to let me resign."

"I see," said the doctor. "You wish us to keep this matter dark, and to make a garrison of the stern part of the ship, manned with my friend's own people, and provided with all the arms and powder on board. In other words, you fear a mutiny."

"Sir," said Captain Smollett, "with no intention to take offence, I deny your right to put words into my mouth. No captain, sir, would be justified in going to sea at all if he had ground enough to say that. As for Mr. Arrow, I believe him thoroughly honest; some of the men are the same; all may be, for what I know. But I am responsible for the ship's safety and the life of every man Jack aboard of her. I see things going, as I think, not quite right. And I ask you to take certain precautions, or let me resign my berth. And that's all."

"Captain Smollett," began the doctor, with a smile, "did ever you hear the fable of the mountain and the mouse? You'll excuse me, I dare say, but you remind me of that fable. When you came in here I'll stake my wig you meant more than this."

"Doctor," said the captain, "you are smart. When I came in here I meant to get discharged. I had no thought that Mr. Trelawney would hear a word."

"No more I would," cried the squire. "Had Livesey not been here I should have seen you to the deuce. As it is, I have heard you. I will do as you desire; but I think the worse of you."

"That's as you please, sir," said the captain. "You'll find I do my duty."

And with that he took his leave.

"Trelawney," said the doctor, "contrary to all my notions, I believe you have managed to get two honest men on board with you – that man and John Silver."

"Silver, if you like," cried the squire; "but as for that intolerable humbug, I declare I think his conduct unmanly, unsailorly, and downright un-English."

"Well," says the doctor, "we shall see."

When we came on deck, the men had begun already to take out the arms and powder, yo-ho-ing at their work, while the captain and Mr. Arrow stood by superintending.

The new arrangement was quite to my liking. The whole schooner had been overhauled; six berths had been made astern, out of what had been the after-part of the main hold; and this set of cabins was only joined to the galley and forecastle by a sparred passage on the port side. It had been originally meant that the captain, Mr. Arrow, Hunter, Joyce, the doctor, and the squire, were to occupy these six berths. Now, Redruth and I were to get two of them, and Mr. Arrow and the captain were to sleep on deck in the companion, which had been enlarged on each side till you might almost have called it a round-house. Very low it was still, of course; but there was room to swing two hammocks, and even the mate seemed pleased with the arrangement. Even he, perhaps, had been doubtful as to the crew, but that is only guess; for, as you shall hear, we had not long the benefit of his opinion.

We were all hard at work, changing the powder and the berths, when the last man or two, and Long John along with them, came off in a shore-boat.

The cook came up the side like a monkey for cleverness, and, as soon as he saw what was doing, "So ho, mates!" says he, "what's this?"

' "Here, you, ship's boy," he cried, "out o' that! Off with you to the cook anbd get some work." ' (p. 54)

"We're a-changing of the powder, Jack," answers one.

"Why, by the powers," cried Long John, "if we do, we'll miss the morning tide!"

"My orders!" said the captain shortly. "You may go below, my man. Hands will want supper."

"Ay, ay, sir," answered the cook; and, touching his forelock, he disappeared at once in the direction of his galley.

"That's a good man, captain," said the doctor.

"Very likely, sir," replied Captain Smollett. "Easy with that, men – easy," he ran on, to the fellows who were shifting the powder; and then suddenly observing me examining the swivel we carried amidships, a long brass nine—"Here, you ship's boy," he cried, "out o' that! Off with you to the cook and get some work."

And then, as I was hurrying off, I heard him say, quite loudly, to the doctor:—

"I'll have no favourites on my ship."

I assure you I was quite of the squire's way of thinking, and hated the captain deeply.

CHAPTER X

THE VOYAGE

ALL that night we were in a great bustle getting things stowed in their place, and boatfuls of the squire's friends, Mr. Blandly and the like, coming off to wish him a good voyage and a safe return. We never had a night at the Admiral Benbow when I had half the work; and I was dog-tired when, a little before dawn, the boatswain sounded his pipe, and the crew began to man the capstan-bars. I might have been twice as weary, yet I would not have left the deck; all was so new and interesting to me – the brief commands, the shrill note of the whistle, the men bustling to their places in the glimmer of the ship's lanterns.

"Now, Barbecue, tip us a stave," cried one voice.

"The old one," cried another.

"Ay, ay, mates," said Long John, who was standing by, with his crutch under his arm, and at once broke out in the air and words I knew so well:—

"Fifteen men on The Dead Man's Chest—"

And then the whole crew bore chorus:—

"Yo-ho-ho, and a bottle of rum!"

And at the third "ho!" drove the bars before them with a will. Even at that exciting moment it carried me back to the old Admiral Benbow in a second; and I seemed to hear the voice of the captain piping in the chorus. But soon the anchor was short up; soon it was hanging dripping at the bows; soon the sails began to draw, and the land and shipping to flit by on either side; and before I could lie down to snatch an hour of slumber the *Hispaniola* had begun her voyage to the Isle of Treasure.

I am not going to relate that voyage in detail. It was fairly prosperous. The ship proved to be a good ship, the crew were capable seamen, and the captain thoroughly understood his business. But before we came the length of

Treasure Island, two or three things had happened which require to be known.

Mr. Arrow, first of all, turned out even worse than the captain had feared. He had no command among the men, and people did what they pleased with him. But that was by no means the worst of it; for after a day or two at sea he began to appear on deck with hazy eye, red cheeks, stuttering tongue, and other marks of drunkenness. Time after time he was ordered below in disgrace. Sometimes he fell and cut himself; sometimes he lay all day long in his little bunk at one side of the companion; sometimes for a day or two he would be almost sober and attend to his work at least passably.

In the meantime, we could never make out where he got the drink. That was the ship's mystery. Watch him as we pleased, we could do nothing to solve it; and when we asked him to his face, he would only laugh, if he were drunk, and if he were sober, deny solemnly that he ever tasted anything but water.

He was not only useless as an officer, and a bad influence amongst the men, but it was plain that at this rate he must soon kill himself outright; so nobody was much surprised, nor very sorry when one dark night, with a head sea, he disappeared entirely and was seen no more.

"Overboard!" said the captain. "Well, gentlemen, that saves the trouble of putting him in irons."

But there we were, without a mate; and it was necessary, of course, to advance one of the men. The boatswain, Job Anderson, was the likeliest man aboard, and, though he kept his old title, he served in a way as mate. Mr. Trelawney had followed the sea, and his knowledge made him very useful, for he often took a watch himself in easy weather. And the coxswain, Israel Hands, was a careful, wily, old, experienced seaman, who could be trusted at a pinch with almost anything.

He was a great confidant of Long John Silver, and so the mention of his name leads me on to speak of our ship's cook, Barbecue, as the men called him.

Aboard ship he carried his crutch by a lanyard round his neck, to have both hands as free as possible. It was something to see him wedge the foot of the crutch against a bulkhead, and, propped against it, yielding to every movement of the ship, get on with his cooking like some one safe ashore. Still more strange was it to see him in the heaviest of weather cross the deck. He had a line or two rigged up to help him across the widest spaces – Long John's earrings, they were called; and he would hand himself from one place

to another, now using the crutch, now trailing it alongside by the lanyard, as quickly as another man could walk. Yet some of the men who had sailed with him before expressed their pity to see him so reduced.

"He's no common man, Barbecue," said the coxswain to me. "He had good schooling in his young days, and can speak like a book when so minded; and brave – a lion's nothing alongside of Long John! I seen him grapple four, and knock their heads together – him unarmed."

All the crew respected and even obeyed him. He had a way of talking to each, and doing everybody some particular service. To me he was unweariedly kind; and always glad to see me in the galley, which he kept as clean as a new pin; the dishes hanging up burnished, and his parrot in a cage in one corner.

"Come away, Hawkins," he would say; "come and have a yarn with John. Nobody more welcome than yourself, my son. Sit you down and hear the news. Here's Cap'n Flint – I calls my parrot Cap'n Flint, after the famous buccaneer – here's Cap'n Flint predicting success to our v'yage. Wasn't you, cap'n?"

And the parrot would say, with great rapidity, "Pieces of eight! pieces of eight! pieces of eight!" till you wondered that it was not out of breath, or till John threw his handkerchief over the cage.

"Now, that bird," he would say, "is, may be, two hundred years old, Hawkins – they lives for ever mostly; and if anybody's seen more wickedness, it must be the devil himself. She's sailed with England, the great Cap'n England, the pirate. She's been at Madagascar, and at Malabar, and Surinam, and Providence, and Portobello. She was at the fishing up of the wrecked plate ships. It's there she learned 'Pieces of eight,' and little wonder; three hundred and fifty thousand of 'em, Hawkins! She was at the boarding

of the Viceroy of the Indies out of Goa, she was; and to look at her you would think she was a babby. But you smelt powder – didn't you, cap'n?"

"Stand by to go about," the parrot would scream.

"Ah, she's a handsome craft, she is," the cook would say, and give her sugar from his pocket, and then the bird would peck at the bars and swear straight on, passing belief for wickedness. "There," John would add, "you can't touch pitch and not be mucked, lad. Here's this poor old innocent bird o' mine swearing blue fire, and none the wiser, you may lay to that. She would swear the same, in a manner of speaking, before chaplain." And John would touch his forelock with a solemn way he had, that made me think he was the best of men.

In the meantime, squire and Captain Smollett were still on pretty distant terms with one another. The squire made no bones about the matter; he despised the captain. The captain, on his part, never spoke but when he was spoken to, and then sharp and short and dry, and not a word wasted. He owned, when driven into a corner, that he seemed to have been wrong about the crew, that some of them were as brisk as he wanted to see, and all had behaved fairly well. As for the ship, he had taken a downright fancy to her. "She'll lie a point nearer the wind than a man has a right to expect of his own married wife, sir. But," he would add, "all I say is we're not home again, and I don't like the cruise."

The squire, at this, would turn away and march up and down the deck, chin in air.

"A trifle more of that man," he would say, "and I should explode."

We had some heavy weather, which only proved the qualities of the *Hispaniola*. Every man on board seemed well content, and they must have been hard to please if they had been otherwise; for it is my belief there was never a ship's company so spoiled since Noah put to sea. Double grog was going on the least excuse; there was duff on odd days, as, for instance, if the squire heard it was any man's birthday; and always a barrel of apples standing broached in the waist, for any one to help himself that had a fancy.

"Never knew good come of it yet," the captain said to Dr. Livesey. "Spoil foc's'le hands, make devils. That's my belief."

But good did come of the apple barrel, as you shall hear; for if it had not been for that, we should have had no note of warning, and might all have perished by the hand of treachery.

This was how it came about.

We had run up the trades to get the wind of the island we were after – I am not allowed to be more plain – and now we were running down for it with a bright look-out day and night. It was about the last day of our outward voyage, by the largest computation; some time that night, or, at least, before noon on the morrow, we should sight the Treasure Island. We were heading S.S.W., and had a steady breeze abeam and a quiet sea. The *Hispaniola* rolled steadily, dipping her bowsprit now and then with a whiff of spray. All was drawing alow and aloft; every one was in the bravest spirits, because we were now so near an end of the first part of our adventure.

Now, just after sundown, when all my work was over, and I was on my way to my berth, it occurred to me that I should like an apple. I ran on deck. The watch was all forward looking out for the island. The man at the helm was watching the luff of the sail, and whistling away gently to himself; and that was the only sound excepting the swish of the sea against the bows and around the sides of the ship.

In I got bodily into the apple barrel, and found there was scarce an apple left; but, sitting down there in the dark, what with the sound of the waters and the rocking movement of the ship, I had either fallen asleep, or was on the point of doing so, when a heavy man sat down with rather a clash close by. The barrel shook as he leaned his shoulders against it, and I was just about to jump up when the man began to speak. It was Silver's voice, and, before I had heard a dozen words, I would not have shown myself for all the world, but lay there, trembling and listening, in the extreme of fear and curiosity; for from these dozen words I understood that the lives of all the honest men aboard depended upon me alone.

CHAPTER XI

WHAT I HEARD IN THE APPLE BARREL

"NO, not I," said Silver. "Flint was cap'n; I was quartermaster, along of my timber leg. The same broadside I lost my leg, old Pew lost his deadlights. It was a master surgeon, him that ampytated me – out of college and all – Latin by the bucket, and what not; but he was hanged like a dog, and sun-dried like the rest, at Corso Castle. That was Roberts's men, that was, and comed of changing names to their ships – *Royal Fortune,* and so on. Now, what a ship was christened, so let her stay, I says. So it was with the *Cassandra,* as brought us all safe home from Malabar, after England took the Viceroy of the Indies; so it was with the old Walrus, Flint's old ship, as I've seen a-muck with the red blood and fit to sink with gold."

"Ah!" cried another voice, that of the youngest hand on board, and evidently full of admiration, "he was the flower of the flock, was Flint!"

"Davis was a man, too, by all accounts," said Silver. "I never sailed along of him; first with England, then with Flint, that's my story; and now here on my account, in a manner of speaking. I laid by nine hundred safe, from England, and two thousand after Flint. That ain't bad for a man before the mast – all safe in bank. 'Tain't earning now, it's saving does it, you may lay to that. Where's all England's men now? I dunno. Where's Flint's? Why, most of 'em aboard here, and glad to get the duff – been begging before that, some on 'em. Old Pew, as had lost his sight, and might have thought shame, spends twelve hundred pound in a year, like a lord in Parliament. Where is he now? Well, he's dead now and under hatches; but for two year before that, shiver my timbers! the man was starving. He begged, and he stole, and he cut throats, and starved at that, by the powers!"

"Well, it ain't much use, after all," said the young seaman.

"'Tain't much use for fools, you may lay to it – that, nor nothing," cried Silver. "But now, you look here: you're young, you are, but you're as smart as paint. I see that when I set my eyes on you, and I'll talk to you like a man."

'. . . I lay there, trembling and listening, in the extreme of fear and curiosity.' (p. 59)

You may imagine how I felt when I heard this abominable old rogue addressing another in the very same words of flattery as he had used to myself. I think, if I had been able, that I would have killed him through the barrel. Meantime, he ran on, little supposing he was overheard.

"Here it is about gentlemen of fortune. They lives rough, and they risk swinging, but they eat and drink like fighting-cocks, and when a cruise is done, why it's hundreds of pounds instead of hundreds of farthings in their pockets. Now, the most goes for rum and a good fling, and to sea again in their shirts. But that's not the course I lay. I puts it all away, some here, some there, and none too much anywheres, by reason of suspicion. I'm fifty, mark you; once back from this cruise, I set up gentleman in earnest. Time enough, too, says you. Ah, but I've lived easy in the meantime; never denied myself o' nothing heart desires, and slep' soft and ate dainty all my days, but when at sea. And how did I begin? Before the mast, like you!"

"Well," said the other, "but all the other money's gone now, ain't it? You daren't show face in Bristol after this."

"Why, where might you suppose it was?" asked Silver, derisively.

"At Bristol, in banks and places," answered his companion.

"It were," said the cook; "it were when we weighed anchor. But my old missis has it all by now. And the Spy-glass is sold, lease and good-will and rigging; and the old girl's off to meet me. I would tell you where, for I trust you; but it 'ud make jealousy among the mates."

"And can you trust your missis?" asked the other.

"Gentlemen of fortune," returned the cook, "usually trusts little among themselves, and right they are, you may lay to it. But I have a way with me, I have. When a mate brings a slip on his cable – one as knows me, I mean – it won't be in the same world with old John. There was some that was feared of Pew, and some that was feared of Flint; but Flint his own self was feared of me. Feared he was, and proud. They was the roughest crew afloat, was Flint's; the devil himself would have been feared to go to sea with them. Well, now, I tell you, I'm not a boasting man, and you seen yourself how easy I keep company; but when I was quartermaster, lambs wasn't the word for Flint's old buccaneers. Ah, you may be sure of yourself in old John's ship."

"Well, I tell you now," replied the lad, "I didn't half a quarter like the job till I had this talk with you, John; but there's my hand on it now."

"And a brave lad you were, and smart, too," answered Silver, shaking hands so heartily that all the barrel shook, "and a finer figurehead for a

gentleman of fortune I never clapped my eyes on."

By this time I had begun to understand the meaning of their terms. By a "gentleman of fortune" they plainly meant neither more nor less than a common pirate, and the little scene that I had overheard was the last act in the corruption of one of the honest hands – perhaps of the last one left aboard. But on this point I was soon to be relieved, for Silver giving a little whistle, a third man strolled up and sat down by the party.

"Dick's square," said Silver.

"Oh, I know'd Dick was square," returned the voice of the coxswain, Israel Hands. "He's no fool, is Dick." And he turned his quid and spat. "But, look here," he went on, "here's what I want to know, Barbecue: how long are we a-going to stand off and on like a blessed bumboat? I've had a'most enough o' Cap'n Smollett; he's hazed me long enough, by thunder! I want to go into that cabin, I do. I want their pickles and wines, and that."

"Israel," said Silver, "your head ain't much account, nor ever was. But you're able to hear, I reckon; leastways, your ears is big enough. Now, here's what I say: you'll berth forward, and you'll live hard, and you'll speak soft, and you'll keep sober, till I give the word; and you may lay to that, my son."

"Well, I don't say no, do I?" growled the coxswain. "What I say is, when? That's what I say."

"When! by the powers!" cried Silver. "Well, now, if you want to know I'll tell you when. The last moment I can manage; and that's when. Here's a first-rate seaman, Cap'n Smollett, sails the blessed ship for us. Here's this squire and doctor with a map and such – I don't know where it is, do I? No more do you, says you. Well, then, I mean this squire and doctor shall find the stuff and help us to get it aboard, by the powers. Then we'll see. If I was sure of you all, sons of double Dutchmen, I'd have Cap'n Smollett navigate us half-way back again before I struck."

"Why, we're all seamen aboard here, I should think," said the lad Dick.

"We're all foc's'le hands, you mean," snapped Silver. "We can steer a course, but who's to set one? That's what all you gentlemen split on, first and last. If I had my way, I'd have Cap'n Smollett work us back into the trades at least; then we'd have no blessed miscalculations and a spoonful of water a day. But I know the sort you are. I'll finish with 'em at the island, as soon's the blunt's on board, and a pity it is. But you're never happy till you're drunk. Split my sides, I've a sick heart to sail with the likes of you!"

"Easy all, Long John," cried Israel. "Who's a-crossin' of you?"

"Why, how many tall ships, think ye, now, have I seen laid aboard? and how many brisk lads drying in the sun at Execution Dock?" cried Silver, "and all for this same hurry and hurry and hurry. You hear me? I seen a thing or two at sea, I have. If you would on'y lay your course, and a p'int to windward, you would ride in carriages, you would. But not you! I know you. You'll have your mouthful of rum to-morrow, and go hang."

"Everybody know'd you was a kind of a chapling, John; but there's others as could hand and steer as well as you," said Israel. "They liked a bit o' fun, they did. They wasn't so high and dry, nohow, but took their fling, like jolly companions every one."

"So?" says Silver. "Well, and where are they now? Pew was that sort, and he died a beggar-man. Flint was, and he died of rum at Savannah. Ah, they was a sweet crew, they was! on'y, where are they?"

"But," asked Dick, "when we do lay 'em athwart, what are we to do with 'em, anyhow?"

"There's the man for me!" cried the cook admiringly. "That's what I call business. Well, what would you think? Put 'em ashore like maroons? That would have been England's way. Or cut 'em down like that much pork? That would have been Flint's or Billy Bones's."

"Billy was the man for that," said Israel. "'Dead men don't bite,' says he. Well, he's dead now hisself; he knows the long and short on it now; and if ever a rough hand come to port, it was Billy."

"Right you are," said Silver, "rough and ready. But mark you here; I'm an easy man – I'm quite the gentleman, says you; but this time it's serious. Dooty is dooty, mates. I give my vote – death. When I'm in Parlyment, and riding in my coach, I don't want none of these sea-lawyers in the cabin a-coming home, unlooked for, like the devil at prayers. Wait is what I say; but when the time comes, why, let her rip!"

"John," cried the coxswain, "you're a man!"

"You'll say so, Israel, when you see," said Silver. "Only one thing I claim – I claim Trelawney. I'll wring his calf's head off his body with these hands. Dick!" he added, breaking off, "you just jump up, like a sweet lad, and get me an apple, to wet my pipe like."

You may fancy the terror I was in! I should have leaped out and run for it, if I had found the strength; but my limbs and heart alike misgave me. I heard Dick begin to rise, and then some one seemingly stopped him, and the voice of Hands exclaimed:—

"Oh, stow that! Don't you get sucking of that bilge, John. Let's have a go of the rum."

"Dick," said Silver, "I trust you. I've a gauge on the keg, mind. There's the key; you fill a pannikin and bring it up."

Terrified as I was, I could not help thinking to myself that this must have been how Mr. Arrow got the strong waters that destroyed him.

Dick was gone but a little while, and during his absence Israel spoke straight on in the cook's ear. It was but a word or two that I could catch, and yet I gathered some important news; for, besides other scraps that tended to the same purpose, this whole clause was audible: "Not another man of them 'll jine." Hence there were still faithful men on board.

When Dick returned, one after another of the trio took the pannikin and drank – one "To luck"; another with a "Here's to old Flint"; and Silver himself saying, in a kind of song, "Here's to ourselves, and hold your luff, plenty of prizes and plenty of duff."

Just then a sort of brightness fell upon me in the barrel, and, looking up, I found the moon had risen, and was silvering the mizzen-top and shining white on the luff of the fore-sail; and almost at the same time the voice of the look-out shouted "Land-ho!"

CHAPTER XII

COUNCIL OF WAR

THERE was a great rush of feet across the deck. I could hear people tumbling up from the cabin and the foc's'le; and, slipping in an instant outside my barrel, I dived behind the fore-sail, made a double towards the stern, and came out upon the open deck in time to join Hunter and Dr. Livesey in the rush for the weather bow.

There all hands were already congregated. A belt of fog had lifted almost simultaneously with the appearance of the moon. Away to the south-west of us we saw two low hills, about a couple of miles apart, and rising behind one of them a third and higher hill, whose peak was still buried in the fog. All three seemed sharp and conical in figure.

So much I saw, almost in a dream, for I had not yet recovered from my horrid fear of a minute or two before. And then I heard the voice of Captain Smollett issuing orders. The *Hispaniola* was laid a couple of points nearer the wind, and now sailed a course that would just clear the island on the east.

"And now, men," said the captain, when all was sheeted home, "has any one of you ever seen that land ahead?"

"I have, sir," said Silver. "I've watered there with a trader I was cook in."

"The anchorage is on the south, behind an islet, I fancy?" asked the captain.

"Yes, sir; Skeleton Island they calls it. It were a main place for pirates once, and a hand we had on board knowed all their names for it. That hill to the nor'ard they calls the Fore-mast Hill; there are three hills in a row running south'ard – fore, main, and mizzen, sir. But the main – that's the big 'un with the cloud on it – they usually calls the Spy-glass, by reason of a look-out they kept when they was in the anchorage cleaning; for it's there they cleaned their ships, sir, asking your pardon."

"I have a chart here," says Captain Smollett. "See if that's the place."

Long John's eyes burned in his head as he took the chart; but, by the fresh

look of the paper, I knew he was doomed to disappointment. This was not the map we found in Billy Bones's chest, but an accurate copy, complete in all things – names and heights and soundings – with the single exception of the red crosses and the written notes. Sharp as must have been this annoyance, Silver had the strength of mind to hide it.

"Yes, sir," said he, "this is the spot to be sure; and very prettily drawed out. Who might have done that, I wonder? The pirates were too ignorant, I reckon. Ay, here it is: 'Capt. Kidd's Anchorage' – just the name my shipmate called it. There's a strong current runs along the south, and then away nor'ard up the west coast. Right you was, sir," says he, "to haul your wind and keep the weather of the island. Leastways, if such was your intention as to enter and careen, and there ain't no better place for that in these waters."

"Thank you, my man," says Captain Smollett. "I'll ask you, later on, to give us a help. You may go."

I was surprised at the coolness with which John avowed his knowledge of the island; and I own I was half-frightened when I saw him drawing nearer to myself. He did not know, to be sure, that I had overheard his council from the apple barrel, and yet I had, by this time, taken such a horror of his cruelty, duplicity, and power, that I could scarce conceal a shudder when he laid his hand upon my arm.

"Ah," says he, "this here is a sweet spot, this island – a sweet spot for a lad to get ashore on. You'll bathe, and you'll climb trees, and you'll hunt goats, you will – and you'll get aloft on them hills like a goat yourself. Why, it makes me young again. I was going to forget my timber leg, I was. It's a pleasant thing to be young, and have ten toes, and you may lay to that. When you want to go a bit of exploring, you just ask old John, and he'll put up a snack for you to take along."

And clapping me in the friendliest way upon the shoulder, he hobbled off forward and went below.

Captain Smollett, the squire, and Dr. Livesey were talking together on the quarter-deck, and, anxious as I was to tell them my story, I durst not interrupt them openly. While I was still casting about in my thoughts to find some probable excuse, Dr. Livesey called me to his side. He had left his pipe below, and being a slave to tobacco, had meant that I should fetch it; but as soon as I was near enough to speak and not to be overheard, I broke out immediately: "Doctor, let me speak. Get the captain and squire down to the cabin, and then make some pretence to send for me. I have terrible news."

' "Yes, Sir," said he, "this is the spot to be sure; and very prettily drawed out." ' (p. 67)

The doctor changed countenance a little, but next moment he was master of himself.

"Thank you, Jim," said he, quite loudly, "that was all I wanted to know," as if he had asked me a question.

And with that he turned on his heel and rejoined the other two. They spoke together for a little, and though none of them started, or raised his voice, or so much as whistled, it was plain enough that Dr. Livesey had communicated my request; for the next thing that I heard was the captain giving an order to Job Anderson, and all hands were piped on deck.

"My lads," said Captain Smollett, "I've a word to say to you. This land that we have sighted is the place we have been sailing to. Mr. Trelawney, being a very open-handed gentleman, as we all know, has just asked me a word or two, and as I was able to tell him that every man on board had done his duty, alow and aloft, as I never ask to see it done better, why, he and I and the doctor are going below to the cabin to drink your health and luck, and you'll have grog served out for you to drink our health and luck. I'll tell you what I think of this: I think it handsome. And if you think as I do, you'll give a good sea cheer for the gentleman that does it."

The cheer followed – that was a matter of course; but it rang out so full and hearty, that I confess I could hardly believe these same men were plotting for our blood.

"One more cheer for Cap'n Smollett," cried Long John, when the first had subsided.

And this also was given with a will.

On the top of that the three gentlemen went below, and not long after, word was sent forward that Jim Hawkins was wanted in the cabin.

I found them all three seated round the table, a bottle of Spanish wine and some raisins before them, and the doctor smoking away, with his wig on his lap, and that, I knew, was a sign that he was agitated. The stern window was open, for it was a warm night, and you could see the moon shining behind on the ship's wake.

"Now, Hawkins," said the squire, "you have something to say. Speak up."

I did as I was bid, and, as short as I could make it, told the whole details of Silver's conversation. Nobody interrupted me till I was done, nor did any one of the three of them make so much as a movement, but they kept their eyes upon my face from first to last.

"Jim," said Dr. Livesey, "take a seat."

And they made me sit down at table beside them, poured me out a glass of wine, filled my hands with raisins, and all three, one after the other, and each with a bow, drank my good health, and their service to me, for my luck and courage.

"Now, captain," said the squire, "you were right, and I was wrong. I own myself an ass, and I await your orders."

"No more an ass than I, sir," returned the captain. "I never heard of a crew that meant to mutiny but what showed signs before, for any man that had an eye in his head to see the mischief and take steps according. But this crew," he added, "beats me."

"Captain," said the doctor, "with your permission, that's Silver. A very remarkable man."

"He'd look remarkably well from a yard-arm, sir," returned the captain. "But this is talk; this don't lead to anything. I see three or four points, and with Mr. Trelawney's permission, I'll name them."

"You, sir, are the captain. It is for you to speak," says Mr. Trelawney grandly.

"First point," began Mr. Smollett. "We must go on, because we can't turn back. If I gave the word to go about, they would rise at once. Second point, we have time before us – at least, until this treasure's found. Third point, there are faithful hands. Now, sir, it's got to come to blows sooner or later; and what I propose is, to take time by the forelock, as the saying is, and come to blows some fine day when they least expect it. We can count, I take it, on your own home servants, Mr. Trelawney?"

"As upon myself," declared the squire.

"Three," reckoned the captain, "ourselves make seven, counting Hawkins here. Now, about the honest hands?"

"Most likely Trelawney's own men," said the doctor; "those he had picked up for himself, before he lit on Silver."

"Nay," replied the squire, "Hands was one of mine."

"I did think I could have trusted Hands," added the captain.

"And to think that they're all Englishmen!" broke out the squire. "Sir, I could find it in my heart to blow the ship up."

"Well, gentlemen," said the captain, "the best that I can say is not much. We must lay to, if you please, and keep a bright look-out. It's trying on a man, I know. It would be pleasanter to come to blows. But there's no help for it till we know our men. Lay to, and whistle for a wind, that's my view."

"Jim here," said the doctor, "can help us more than any one. The men are not shy with him, and Jim is a noticing lad."

"Hawkins, I put prodigious faith in you," added the squire.

I began to feel pretty desperate at this, for I felt altogether helpless; and yet, by an odd train of circumstances, it was indeed through me that safety came. In the meantime, talk as we pleased, there were only seven out of the twenty-six on whom we knew we could rely; and out of these seven one was a boy, so that the grown men on our side were six to their nineteen.

PART III MY SHORE ADVENTURE

CHAPTER XIII

HOW I BEGAN MY SHORE ADVENTURE

THE appearance of the island when I came on deck next morning was altogether changed. Although the breeze had now utterly failed, we had made a great deal of way during the night, and were now lying becalmed about half a mile to the south-east of the low eastern coast. Gray-coloured woods covered a large part of the surface. This even tint was indeed broken up by streaks of yellow sandbreak in the lower lands, and by many tall trees of the pine family, out-topping the others – some singly, some in clumps; but the general colouring was uniform and sad. The hills ran up clear above the vegetation in spires of naked rock. All were strangely shaped, and the Spy-glass, which was by three or four hundred feet the tallest on the island, was likewise the strangest in configuration, running up sheer from almost every side, and then suddenly cut off at the top like a pedestal to put a statue on.

The *Hispaniola* was rolling scuppers under in the ocean swell. The booms were tearing at the blocks, the rudder was banging to and fro, and the whole ship creaking, groaning, and jumping like a manufactory. I had to cling tight to the backstay, and the world turned giddily before my eyes; for though I was a good enough sailor when there was way on, this standing still and being rolled about like a bottle was a thing I never learned to stand without a qualm or so, above all in the morning, on an empty stomach.

Perhaps it was this – perhaps it was the look of the island, with its gray, melancholy woods, and wild stone spires, and the surf that we could both see and hear foaming and thundering on the steep beach – at least, although the sun shone bright and hot, and the shore birds were fishing and crying all around us, and you would have thought any one would have been glad to get to land after being so long at sea, my heart sank, as the saying is, into my boots; and from that first look onward, I hated the very thought of Treasure Island.

We had a dreary morning's work before us, for there was no sign of any wind, and the boats had to be got out and manned, and the ship warped three or four miles round the corner of the island, and up the narrow passage to the haven behind Skeleton Island. I volunteered for one of the boats, where I had, of course, no business. The heat was sweltering, and the men grumbled fiercely over their work. Anderson was in command of my boat, and instead of keeping the crew in order, he grumbled as loud as the worst.

"Well," he said, with an oath, "it's not for ever."

I thought this was a very bad sign; for, up to that day, the men had gone briskly and willingly about their business; but the very sight of the island had relaxed the cords of discipline.

All the way in, Long John stood by the steersman and conned the ship. He knew the passage like the palm of his hand; and though the man in the chains got everywhere more water than was down in the chart, John never hesitated once.

"There's a strong scour with the ebb," he said, "and this here passage has been dug out, in a manner of speaking, with a spade."

We brought up just where the anchor was in the chart, about a third of a mile from either shore, the mainland on one side, and Skeleton Island on the other. The bottom was clean sand. The plunge of our anchor sent up clouds of birds wheeling and crying over the woods; but in less than a minute they were down again, and all was once more silent.

The place was entirely land-locked, buried in woods, the trees coming right down to high-water mark, the shores mostly flat, and the hill-tops standing round at a distance in a sort of amphitheatre, one here, one there. Two little rivers, or, rather, two swamps, emptied out into this pond, as you might call it; and the foliage round that part of the shore had a kind of poisonous brightness. From the ship, we could see nothing of the house or stockade, for they were quite buried among trees; and if it had not been for the chart on the companion, we might have been the first that had ever anchored there since the island arose out of the seas.

There was not a breath of air moving, nor a sound but that of the surf booming half a mile away along the beaches and against the rocks outside. A peculiar stagnant smell hung over the anchorage – a smell of sodden leaves and rotted tree trunks. I observed the doctor sniffing and sniffing, like some one tasting a bad egg.

"I don't know about treasure," he said, "but I'll stake my wig there's fever here."

If the conduct of the men had been alarming in the boat, it became truly threatening when they had come aboard. They lay about the deck growling together in talk. The slightest order was received with a black look, and grudgingly and carelessly obeyed. Even the honest hands must have caught the infection, for there was not one man aboard to mend another. Mutiny, it was plain, hung over us like a thunder-cloud.

And it was not only we of the cabin party who perceived the danger. Long John was hard at work going from group to group, spending himself in good advice, and as for example no man could have shown a better. He fairly outstripped himself in willingness and civility; he was all smiles to every one. If an order were given, John would be on his crutch in an instant, with the cheeriest "Ay, ay, sir!" in the world; and when there was nothing else to do, he kept up one song after another, as if to conceal the discontent of the rest.

Of all the gloomy features of that gloomy afternoon, this obvious anxiety on the part of Long John appeared the worst.

We held a council in the cabin.

"Sir," said the captain, "If I risk another order, the whole ship'll come about our ears by the run. You see, sir, here it is. I get a rough answer, do I not? Well, if I speak back, pikes will be going in two shakes; if I don't, Silver will see there's something under that, and the game's up. Now, we've only one man to rely on."

"And who is that?" asked the squire.

"Silver, sir," returned the captain; "he's as anxious as you and I to smother things up. This is a tiff; he'd soon talk 'em out of it if he had the chance, and what I propose to do is to give him the chance. Let's allow the men an

afternoon ashore. If they all go, why, we'll fight the ship. If they none of them go, well, then, we hold the cabin, and God defend the right. If some go, you mark my words, sir. Silver'll bring 'em aboard again as mild as lambs."

It was so decided; loaded pistols were served out to all the sure men; Hunter, Joyce, and Redruth were taken into our confidence, and received the news with less surprise and a better spirit than we had looked for, and then the captain went on deck and addressed the crew.

"My lads," said he, "we've had a hot day, and are all tired and out of sorts. A turn ashore'll hurt nobody – the boats are still in the water; you can take the gigs, and as many as please can go ashore for the afternoon. I'll fire a gun half an hour before sundown."

I believe the silly fellows must have thought they would break their shins over treasure as soon as they were landed; for they all came out of their sulks in a moment, and gave a cheer that started the echo in a far-away hill, and set the birds once more flying and squalling round the anchorage.

The captain was too bright to be in the way. He whipped out of sight in a moment, leaving Silver to arrange the party; and I fancy it was as well he did so. Had he been on deck he could no longer so much as have pretended not to understand the situation. It was as plain as day. Silver was the captain and a mighty rebellious crew he had of it. The honest hands – and I was soon to see it proved that there were such on board – must have been very stupid fellows. Or, rather, I suppose the truth was this, that all hands were disaffected by the example of the ringleaders – only some more, some less; and a few, being good fellows in the main, could neither be led nor driven any further. It is one thing to be idle and skulk, and quite another to take a ship and murder a number of innocent men.

At last, however, the party was made up. Six fellows were to stay on board, and the remaining thirteen, including Silver, began to embark.

Then it was that there came into my head the first of the mad notions that contributed so much to save our lives. If six men were left by Silver, it was plain our party could not take and fight the ship; and since only six were left, it was equally plain that the cabin party had no present need of my assistance. It occurred to me at once to go ashore. In a jiffy I had slipped over the side, and curled up in the fore-sheets of the nearest boat, and almost at the same moment she shoved off. No one took notice of me, only the bow oar saying, "Is that you, Jim? Keep your head down." But Silver, from the other boat, looked sharply over and called out to know if that were me; and from that moment I began to regret what I had done.

The crews raced for the beach; but the boat I was in, having some start, and being at once the lighter and the better manned, shot far ahead of her consort, and the bow had struck among the shoreside trees, and I had caught a branch and swung myself out, and plunged into the nearest thicket, while Silver and the rest were still a hundred yards behind.

"Jim, Jim!" I heard him shouting.

But you may suppose I paid no heed; jumping, ducking, and breaking through, I ran straight before my nose, till I could run no longer.

CHAPTER XIV

THE FIRST BLOW

I WAS so pleased at having given the slip to Long John, that I began to enjoy myself and look around me with some interest on the strange land that I was in.

I had crossed a marshy tract full of willows, bulrushes, and odd, outlandish, swampy trees; and I had now come out upon the skirts of an open piece of undulating, sandy country, about a mile long, dotted with a few pines, and a great number of contorted trees, not unlike the oak in growth, but pale in the foliage, like willows. On the far side of the open stood one of the hills, with two quaint, craggy peaks, shining vividly in the sun.

I now felt for the first time the joy of exploration. The isle was uninhabited; my shipmates I had left behind, and nothing lived in front of me but dumb brutes and fowls. I turned hither and thither among the trees. Here and there were flowering plants unknown to me; here and there I saw snakes, and one raised his head from a ledge of rock and hissed at me with a noise not unlike the spinning of a top. Little did I suppose that he was a deadly enemy, and that the noise was the famous rattle.

Then I came to a long thicket of these oak-like trees – live, or evergreen, oaks, I heard afterwards, they should be called – which grew low along the sand like brambles, the boughs curiously twisted, the foliage compact, like thatch. The thicket stretched down from the top of one of the sandy knolls, spreading and growing taller as it went, until it reached the margin of the broad, reedy fen, through which the nearest of the little rivers soaked its way into the anchorage. The marsh was steaming in the strong sun, and the outline of the Spy-glass trembled through the haze.

All at once there began to go a sort of bustle among the bulrushes; a wild duck flew up with a quack, another followed, and soon over the whole surface of the marsh a great cloud of birds hung screaming and circling in the air. I judged at once that some of my shipmates must be drawing near

Black Dog - At the sign of the "spy-glass"
(M. S. Orr)

IT WAS SOMETHING TO SEE HIM GET ON WITH HIS COOKING LIKE SOMEONE SAFE ASHORE.
(M. WINTER)

"Of all the beggar-men that I had seen or fancied, he was the chief for raggedness."
(M. S. Orr)

"THEY HAD THE GUN, BY THIS TIME, SLEWED AROUND UPON THE SWIVEL..."
(M. WINTER)

'Here and there I saw snakes, and one raised his head from a ledge of rock and hissed at me with a noise not unlike the spinning of a top.' *(p. 77)*

along the borders of the fen. Nor was I deceived; for soon I heard the very distant and low tones of a human voice, which, as I continued to give ear, grew steadily louder and nearer.

This put me in a great fear, and I crawled under cover of the nearest live-oak, and squatted there, hearkening, as silent as a mouse.

Another voice answered; and then the first voice, which I now recognised to be Silver's, once more took up the story, and ran on for a long while in a stream, only now and again interrupted by the other. By the sound they must have been talking earnestly, and almost fiercely; but no distinct word came to my hearing.

At last the speakers seemed to have paused, and perhaps to have sat down; for not only did they cease to draw any nearer, but the birds themselves began to grow more quiet, and to settle again to their places in the swamp.

And now I began to feel that I was neglecting my business; that since I had been so foolhardy as to come ashore with these desperadoes, the least I could do was to overhear them at their councils; and that my plain and obvious duty was to draw as close as I could manage, under the favourable ambush of the crouching trees.

I could tell the direction of the speakers pretty exactly, not only by the sound of their voices, but by the behaviour of the few birds that still hung in alarm above the heads of the intruders.

Crawling on all-fours, I made steadily but slowly towards them; till at last, raising my head to an aperture among the leaves, I could see clear down into a little green dell beside the marsh, and closely set about with trees, where Long John Silver and another of the crew stood face to face in conversation.

The sun beat full upon them. Silver had thrown his hat beside him on the ground, and his great, smooth, blond face, all shining with heat, was lifted to the other man's in a kind of appeal.

"Mate," he was saying, "it's because I thinks gold dust of you – gold dust, and you may lay to that! If I hadn't took to you like pitch, do you think I'd have been a-warning of you? All's up – you can't make nor mend; it's to save your neck that I'm a-speaking, and if one of the wild 'uns knew it, where 'ud I be, Tom – now, tell me, where 'ud I be?"

"Silver," said the other man – and I observed he was not only red in the face, but spoke as hoarse as a crow, and his voice shook, too, like a taut rope – "Silver," says he, "you're old, and you're honest, or has the name for it; and you've money, too, which lots of poor sailors hasn't; and you're brave, or I'm mistook. And will you tell me you'll let yourself be led away with that kind of a mess of swabs? not you! As sure as God sees me, I'd sooner lose my hand. If I turn agin my dooty—"

And then all of a sudden he was interrupted by a noise. I had found one of the honest hands – well, here, at that same moment, came news of another. Far away out in the marsh there arose, all of a sudden, a sound like the cry of anger, then another on the back of it; and then one horrid, long-drawn scream. The rocks of the Spy-glass re-echoed it a score of times; the whole troop of marsh-birds rose again, darkening heaven, with a simultaneous whirr; and long after that death yell was still ringing in my brain, silence had re-established its empire, and only the rustle of the redescending birds and the boom of the distant surges disturbed the languor of the afternoon.

Tom had leaped at the sound, like a horse at the spur; but Silver had not winked an eye. He stood where he was, resting lightly on his crutch, watching his companion like a snake about to spring.

"John!" said the sailor, stretching out his hand.

"Hands off!" cried Silver, leaping back a yard, as it seemed to me, with the speed and security of a trained gymnast.

"Hands off, if you like, John Silver," said the other. "It's a black conscience that can make you feared of me. But, in heaven's name, tell me what was that?"

"That?" returned Silver, smiling away, but warier than ever, his eye a mere pin-point in his big face, but gleaming like a crumb of glass. "That? Oh, I reckon that'll be Alan."

At this poor Tom flashed out like a hero.

"Alan!" he cried. "Then rest his soul for a true seaman! And as for you, John Silver, long you've been a mate of mine, but you're mate of mine no more. If I die like a dog, I'll die in my dooty. You've killed Alan, have you? Kill me, too, if you can. But I defies you."

And with that, this brave fellow turned his back directly on the cook, and set off walking for the beach. But he was not destined to go far. With a cry, John seized the branch of a tree, whipped the crutch out of his armpit, and sent that uncouth missile hurtling through the air. It struck poor Tom, point foremost, and with stunning violence, right between the shoulders in the middle of his back. His hands flew up, he gave a sort of gasp, and fell.

'. . . cleansing his blood-stained knife the while upon a wisp of grass.' *(p. 82)*

Whether he were injured much or little, none could ever tell. Like enough, to judge from the sound, his back was broken on the spot. But he had no time given him to recover. Silver, agile as a monkey, even without leg or crutch, was on the top of him next moment, and had twice buried his knife up to the hilt in that defenceless body. From my place of ambush, I could hear him pant aloud as he struck the blows.

I do not know what it rightly is to faint, but I do know that for the next little while the whole world swam away from before me in a whirling mist; Silver and the birds, and the tall Spy-glass hill-top, going round and round and topsy-turvy before my eyes, and all manner of bells ringing and distant voices shouting in my ear.

When I came again to myself, the monster had pulled himself together, his crutch under his arm, his hat upon his head. Just before him Tom lay motionless upon the sward; but the murderer minded him not a whit, cleansing his blood-stained knife the while upon a wisp of grass. Everything else was unchanged, the sun still shining mercilessly on the steaming marsh and the tall pinnacle of the mountain, and I could scarce persuade myself that murder had been actually done, and a human life cruelly cut short a moment since, before my eyes.

But now John put his hand into his pocket, brought out a whistle, and blew upon it several modulated blasts, that rang far across the heated air. I could not tell, of course, the meaning of the signal; but it instantly awoke my fears. More men would be coming. I might be discovered. They had already slain two of the honest people; after Tom and Alan, might not I come next?

Instantly I began to extricate myself and crawl back again, with what speed and silence I could manage, to the more open portion of the wood. As I did so, I could hear hails coming and going between the old buccaneer and his comrades, and this sound of danger lent me wings. As soon as I was clear of the thicket, I ran as I never ran before, scarce minding the direction of my flight, so long as it led me from the murderers; and as I ran, fear grew and grew upon me, until it turned into a kind of frenzy.

Indeed, could any one be more entirely lost than I? When the gun fired, how should I dare to go down to the boats amongst those fiends, still smoking from their crime? Would not the first of them who saw me wring my neck like a snipe's? Would not my absence itself be an evidence to them of my alarm, and therefore of my fatal knowledge? It was all over, I thought. Good-bye to the *Hispaniola;* good-bye to the squire, the doctor, the captain!

There was nothing left for me but death by starvation, or death by the hands of the mutineers.

All this while, as I say, I was still running, and, without taking any notice, I had drawn near to the foot of the little hill with the two peaks, and had got into a part of the island where the live-oaks grew more widely apart, and seemed more like forest trees in their bearing and dimensions. Mingled with these were a few scattered pines, some fifty, some nearer seventy, feet high. The air, too, smelt more freshly than down beside the marsh.

And here a fresh alarm brought me to a standstill with a thumping heart.

CHAPTER XV

THE MAN OF THE ISLAND

FROM the side of the hill, which was here steep and stony, a spout of gravel was dislodged, and fell rattling and bounding through the trees. My eyes turned instinctively in that direction, and I saw a figure leap with great rapidity behind the trunk of a pine. What it was, whether bear or man or monkey, I could in no wise tell. It seemed dark and shaggy; more I knew not. But the terror of this new apparition brought me to a stand.

I was now, it seemed, cut off upon both sides; behind me the murderers, before me this lurking nondescript. And immediately I began to prefer the dangers that I knew to those I knew not. Silver himself appeared less terrible in contrast with this creature of the woods, and I turned on my heel, and, looking sharply behind me over my shoulder, began to retrace my steps in the direction of the boats.

Instantly the figure reappeared, and, making a wide circuit, began to head me off. I was tired, at any rate; but had I been as fresh as when I rose, I could see it was in vain for me to contend in speed with such an adversary. From trunk to trunk the creature flitted like a deer, running manlike on two legs, but unlike any man that I had ever seen, stooping almost double as it ran. Yet a man it was, I could no longer be in doubt about that.

I began to recall what I had heard of cannibals. I was within an ace of calling for help. But the mere fact that he was a man, however wild, had somewhat reassured me, and my fear of Silver began to revive in proportion. I stood still, therefore, and cast about for some method of escape; and as I was so thinking, the recollection of my pistol flashed into my mind. As soon as I remembered I was not defenceless, courage glowed again in my heart; and I set my face resolutely for this man of the island, and walked briskly towards him.

He was concealed by this time behind another tree trunk; but he must have been watching me closely, for as soon as I began to move in his

direction he reappeared and took a step to meet me. Then he hesitated, drew back, came forward again, and at last, to my wonder and confusion, threw himself on his knees and held out his clasped hands in supplication.

At that I once more stopped.

"Who are you?" I asked.

"Ben Gunn," he answered, and his voice sounded hoarse and awkward, like a rusty lock. "I'm poor Ben Gunn, I am; and I haven't spoke with a Christian these three years."

I could now see that he was a white man like myself, and that his features were even pleasing. His skin, wherever it was exposed, was burnt by the sun; even his lips were black; and his fair eyes looked quite startling in so dark a face. Of all the beggar-men that I had seen or fancied, he was the chief for raggedness. He was clothed with tatters of old ship's canvas and old sea cloth; and this extraordinary patchwork was all held together by a system of the most various and incongruous fastenings, brass buttons, bits of stick, and loops of tarry gaskin. About his waist he wore an old brass-buckled leather belt, which was the one thing solid in his whole accoutrement.

"Three years!" I cried. "Were you shipwrecked?"

"Nay, mate," said he— "marooned."

I had heard the word, and I knew it stood for a horrible kind of punishment common enough among the buccaneers, in which the offender is put ashore with a little powder and shot, and left behind on some desolate and distant island.

"Marooned three years agone," he continued, "and lived on goats since then, and berries, and oysters. Wherever a man is, says I, a man can do for himself. But, mate, my heart is sore for Christian diet. You mightn't happen to have a piece of cheese about you, now? No? Well, many's the long night I've dreamed of cheese – toasted, mostly – and woke up again, and here I were."

"If ever I can get on board again," said I, "you shall have cheese by the stone."

All this time he had been feeling the stuff of my jacket, smoothing my hands, looking at my boots, and generally, in the intervals of his speech, showing a childish pleasure in the presence of a fellow-creature. But at my last words he perked up into a kind of startled slyness.

"If ever you can get aboard again, says you?" he repeated. "Why, now, who's to hinder you?"

"Not you, I know," was my reply.

"And right you was," he cried. "Now you – what do you call yourself, mate?"

"Jim," I told him.

"Jim, Jim," says he, quite pleased apparently. "Well, now, Jim, I've lived that rough as you'd be ashamed to hear of. Now, for instance, you wouldn't think I had a pious mother – to look at me?" he asked.

"Why, no, not in particular," I answered.

"Ah, well," said he, "but I had – remarkable pious. And I was a civil, pious boy, and could rattle off my catechism that fast, as you couldn't tell one word from another. And here's what it come to, Jim, and it begun with chuck-farthen on the blessed grave-stones! That's what it begun with, but it went further'n that; and so my mother told me, and predicked the whole, she did, the pious woman! But it were Providence that put me here. I've thought it all out in this here lonely island, and I'm back on piety. You don't catch me tasting rum so much; but just a thimbleful for luck, of course, the first chance I have. I'm bound I'll be good, and I see the way to. And, Jim" – looking all round him, and lowering his voice to a whisper – "I'm rich."

I now felt sure that the poor fellow had gone crazy in his solitude, and I suppose I must have shown the feeling in my face, for he repeated the statement hotly:—

"Rich! rich! I says. And I'll tell you what: I'll make a man of you, Jim. Ah, Jim, you'll bless your stars, you will, you was the first that found me!"

And at this there came suddenly a lowering shadow over his face, and he tightened his grasp upon my hand, and raised a forefinger threateningly before my eyes.

"Now, Jim, you tell me true: that ain't Flint's ship?" he asked.

At this I had a happy inspiration. I began to believe that I had found an ally, and I answered him at once.

"It's not Flint's ship, and Flint is dead; but I'll tell you true, as you ask me there are some of Flint's hands aboard; worse luck for the rest of us."

"Not a man – with one – leg?" he gasped.

"Silver?" I asked.

"Ah, Silver!" says he; "that were his name."

"He's the cook; and the ringleader, too."

He was still holding me by the wrist, and at that he gave it quite a wring.

"If you was sent by Long John," he said, "I'm as good as pork, and I know it. But where was you, do you suppose?"

I had made my mind up in a moment, and by way of answer told him the whole story of our voyage, and the predicament in which we found ourselves. He heard me with the keenest interest, and when I had done he patted me on the head.

"You're a good lad, Jim," he said; "and you're all in a clove hitch, ain't you? Well, you just put your trust in Ben Gunn – Ben Gunn's the man to do it. Would you think it likely, now, that your squire would prove a liberal-minded one in case of help – him being in a clove hitch, as you remark?"

I told him the squire was the most liberal of men.

"Ay, but you see," returned Ben Gunn, "I didn't mean giving me a gate to keep, and a shuit of livery clothes, and such; that's not my mark, Jim. What I mean is, would he be likely to come down to the toon of, say, one thousand pounds out of money that's as good as a man's own already?"

"I am sure he would," said I. "As it was, all hands were to share."

"And a passage home?" he added, with a look of great shrewdness.

"Why," I cried, "the squire's a gentleman. And besides, if we got rid of the others, we should want you to help work the vessel home."

"Ah," said he, "so you would." And he seemed very much relieved.

"Now, I'll tell you what," he went on. "So much I'll tell you and no more. I were in Flint's ship when he buried the treasure; he and six along – six strong seamen. They were ashore nigh on a week, and us standing off and on in the old *Walrus*. One fine day up went the signal, and here come Flint by himself in a little boat, and his head done up in a blue scarf. The sun was getting up, and mortal white he looked about the cut-water. But, there he was, you mind, and the six all dead – dead and buried. How he done it, not a man aboard us could make out. It was battle, murder, and sudden death, leastways – him against six. Billy Bones was the mate; Long John he was quartermaster; and they asked him where the treasure was. 'Ah,' says he, 'you can go ashore, if you like, and stay,' he says; 'but as for the ship, she'll beat up for more, by thunder!' That's what he said."

"Well, I was in another ship three years back, and we sighted this island. 'Boys,' said I, 'here's Flint's treasure; let's land and find it.' That cap'n was displeased at that; but my messmates were all of a mind, and landed. Twelve days they looked for it, and every day they had the worse word for me, until one fine morning all hands went aboard. 'As for you, Benjamin Gunn,' says they, 'here's a musket,' they says, 'and a spade, and pick-axe. You can stay here, and find Flint's money for yourself,' they says.

"Well, Jim, three years have I been here, and not a bite of Christian diet from that day to this. But now, you look here; look at me. Do I look like a man before the mast? No, says you. Nor I weren't, neither, I says."

With that he winked and pinched me hard.

"Just you mention them words to your squire, Jim" – he went on: "Nor he weren't, neither – that's the words. Three years he were the man of this island, light and dark, fair and rain; and sometimes he would, maybe, think upon a prayer (says you), and sometimes he would, maybe, think of his old mother, so be as she's alive (you'll say); but the most part of Gunn's time (this is what you'll say) – the most part of his time was took up with another matter. And then you'll give him a nip, like I do."

And he pinched me again in the most confidential manner.

"Then," he continued – "then you'll up, and you'll say this: Gunn is a good man (you'll say), and he puts a precious sight more confidence – a precious sight, mind that – in a gen'leman born than in these gen'lemen of fortune, having been one hisself."

"Well," I said, "I don't understand one word that you've been saying. But that's neither here nor there; for how am I to get on board?"

"Ah," said he, "that's the hitch, for sure. Well, there's my boat, that I made with my two hands. I keep her under the white rock. If the worst comes to the worst, we might try that after dark. Hi!" he broke out, "what's that?"

For just then, although the sun had still an hour or two to run, all the echoes of the island awoke and bellowed to the thunder of a cannon.

"They have begun to fight!" I cried. "Follow me."

And I began to run towards the anchorage, my terrors all forgotten; while,

close at my side, the marooned man in his goatskins trotted easily and lightly.

"Left, left," says he; "keep to your left hand, mate Jim! Under the trees with you! Theer's where I killed my first goat. They don't come down here now; they're all mast-headed on them mountings for the fear of Benjamin Gunn. Ah! and there's the cetemery" – cemetery, he must have meant. "You see the mounds? I come here and prayed, nows and thens, when I thought maybe a Sunday would be about doo. It weren't quite a chapel, but it seemed more solemn like; and then, says you, Ben Gunn was short-handed – no chapling, nor so much as a Bible and a flag, you says."

So he kept talking as I ran, neither expecting nor receiving any answer.

The cannon-shot was followed, after a considerable interval, by a volley of small arms.

Another pause, and then, not a quarter of a mile in front of me I beheld the Union Jack flutter in the air above a wood.

PART IV THE STOCKADE

CHAPTER XVI

NARRATIVE CONTINUED BY THE DOCTOR: HOW THE SHIP WAS ABANDONED

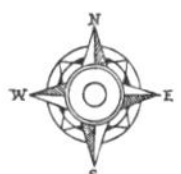

IT was about half-past one – three bells in the sea phrase – that the two boats went ashore from the *Hispaniola*. The captain, the squire, and I were talking matters over in the cabin. Had there been a breath of wind we should have fallen on the six mutineers who were left aboard with us, slipped our cable, and away to sea. But the wind was wanting; and, to complete our helplessness, down came Hunter with the news that Jim Hawkins had slipped into a boat and was gone ashore with the rest.

It never occurred to us to doubt Jim Hawkins; but we were alarmed for his safety. With the men in the temper they were in, it seemed an even chance if we should see the lad again. We ran on deck. The pitch was bubbling in the seams; the nasty stench of the place turned me sick; if ever man smelt fever and dysentery it was in that abominable anchorage. The six scoundrels were sitting grumbling under a sail in the forecastle; ashore we could see the gigs made fast, and a man sitting in each, hard by where the river runs in. One of them was whistling "Lillibullero."

Waiting was a strain; and it was decided that Hunter and I should go ashore with the jolly-boat, in quest of information. The gigs had leaned to their right; but Hunter and I pulled straight in, in the direction of the stockade upon the chart. The two who were left guarding their boats seemed in a bustle at our appearance; "Lillibullero" stopped off, and I could see the pair discussing what they ought to do. Had they gone and told Silver, all might have turned out differently; but they had their orders, I suppose, and decided to sit quietly where they were and hark back again to "Lillibullero."

There was a slight bend in the coast, and I steered so as to put it between us; even before we landed we had thus lost sight of the gigs. I jumped out, and came as near running as I durst, with a big silk handkerchief under my hat for coolness' sake, and a brace of pistols ready primed for safety.

I had not gone a hundred yards when I came on the stockade.

This was how it was: a spring of clear water rose almost at the top of a knoll. Well, on the knoll, and enclosing the spring, they had clapped a stout log-house, fit to hold two score people at a pinch, and loop-holed for musketry on every side. All round this they had cleared a wide space, and then the thing was completed by a paling six feet high, without door or opening, too strong to pull down without time and labour, and too open to shelter the besiegers. The people in the log-house had them in every way; they stood quiet in shelter and shot the others like partridges. All they wanted was a good watch and food; for, short of a complete surprise, they might have held the place against a regiment.

What particularly took my fancy was the spring. For, though we had a good enough place of it in the cabin of the *Hispaniola*, with plenty of arms and ammunition, and things to eat, and excellent wines, there had been one thing overlooked – we had no water. I was thinking this over, when there came ringing over the island the cry of a man at the point of death. I was not new to violent death – I have served his Royal Highness the Duke of Cumberland, and got a wound myself at Fontenoy – but I know my pulse went dot and carry one. "Jim Hawkins is gone" was my first thought.

It is something to have been an old soldier, but more still to have been a doctor. There is no time to dilly-dally in our work. And so now I made up my mind instantly, and with no time lost returned to the shore, and jumped on board the jolly-boat.

By good fortune Hunter pulled a good oar. We made the water fly; and the boat was soon alongside, and I aboard the schooner.

I found them all shaken, as was natural. The squire was sitting down, as white as a sheet, thinking of the harm he had led us to, the good soul! and one of the six forecastle hands was little better.

"There's a man," says Captain Smollett, nodding towards him, "new to this work. He came nigh-hand fainting, doctor, when he heard the cry. Another touch of the rudder and that man would join us."

I told my plan to the captain, and between us we settled on the details of its accomplishment.

We put old Redruth in the gallery between the cabin and the forecastle, with three or four loaded muskets and a mattress for protection. Hunter brought the boat round under the stern-port, and Joyce and I set to work loading her with powder tins, muskets, bags of biscuits, kegs of pork, a cask

' "If any one of you six make a signal of any description, that man's dead." ' (p. 93)

of cognac, and my invaluable medicine chest.

In the meantime, the squire and the captain stayed on deck, and the latter hailed the coxswain, who was the principal man aboard.

"Mr. Hands," he said, "here are two of us with a brace of pistols each. If any one of you six make a signal of any description, that man's dead."

They were a good deal taken aback; and after a little consultation, one and all tumbled down the fore companion, thinking, no doubt, to take us on the rear. But when they saw Redruth waiting for them in the sparred gallery, they went about ship at once, and a head popped out again on deck.

"Down dog!" cries the captain.

And the head popped back again; and we heard no more, for a time, of these six very faint-hearted seamen.

By this time, tumbling things in as they came, we had the jolly-boat loaded as much as we dared. Joyce and I got through the stern-port, and we made for shore again, as fast as oars could take us.

This second trip fairly aroused the watchers along shore. "Lullibullero" was dropped again; and just before we lost sight of them behind the little point, one of them whipped ashore and disappeared. I had half a mind to change my plan and destroy their boats, but I feared that Silver and the others might be close at hand, and all might very well be lost by trying for too much.

We had soon touched land in the same place as before, and set to provision the block house. All three made the first journey, heavily laden, and tossed our stores over the palisade. Then, leaving Joyce to guard them – one man, to be sure, but with half a dozen muskets – Hunter and I returned to the jolly-boat, and loaded ourselves once more. So we proceeded without pausing to take breath, till the whole cargo was bestowed when the two servants took up their position in the block house, and I, with all my power, sculled back to the *Hispaniola*.

That we should have risked a second boat load seems more daring than it really was. They had the advantage of numbers, of course, but we had the

advantage of arms. Not one of the men ashore had a musket, and before they could get within range for pistol shooting, we flattered ourselves we should be able to give a good account of a half-dozen at least.

The squire was waiting for me at the stern window, all his faintness gone from him. He caught the painter and made it fast, and we fell to loading the boat for our very lives. Pork, powder, and biscuit was the cargo, with only a musket and a cutlass apiece for squire and me and Redruth and the captain. The rest of the arms and powder we dropped overboard in two fathoms and a half of water, so that we could see the bright steel shining far below us in the sun, on the clean, sandy bottom.

By this time the tide was beginning to ebb, and the ship was swinging round to her anchor. Voices were heard faintly halloaing in the direction of the two gigs; and though this reassured us for Joyce and Hunter, who were well to the eastward, it warned our party to be off.

Redruth retreated from his place in the gallery, and dropped into the boat, which we then brought round to the ship's counter, to be handier for Captain Smollett.

"Now, men," said he, "do you hear me?"

There was no answer from the forecastle.

"It's to you, Abraham Gray – it's to you I am speaking."

Still no reply.

"Gray," resumed Mr. Smollett, a little louder, "I am leaving this ship, and I order you to follow your captain. I know you are a good man at bottom, and I dare say not one of the lot of you's as bad as he makes out. I have my watch here in my hand; I give you thirty seconds to join me in."

There was a pause.

"Come, my fine fellow," continued the captain, "don't hang so long in stays. I'm risking my life, and the lives of these good gentlemen every second."

There was a sudden scuffle, a sound of blows, and out burst Abraham Gray with a knife-cut on the side of the cheek, and came running to the captain, like a dog to the whistle.

"I'm with you, sir," said he.

And the next moment he and the captain had dropped aboard of us, and we had shoved off and given way.

We were clear out of the ship; but not yet ashore in our stockade.

CHAPTER XVII

NARRATIVE CONTINUED BY THE DOCTOR: THE JOLLY-BOAT'S LAST TRIP

THIS fifth trip was quite different from any of the others. In the first place, the little gallipot of a boat that we were in was gravely overloaded. Five grown men, and three of them – Trelawney, Redruth, and the captain – over six feet high, was already more than she was meant to carry. Add to that the powder, pork, and bread-bags. The gunwale was lipping astern. Several times we shipped a little water, and my breeches and the tails of my coat were all soaking wet before we had gone a hundred yards.

The captain made us trim the boat, and we got her to lie a little more evenly. All the same, we were afraid to breathe.

In the second place, the ebb was now making – a strong rippling current running westward through the basin, and then south'ard and seaward down the straits by which we had entered in the morning. Even the ripples were a danger to our overloaded craft; but the worst of it was that we were swept out of our true course, and away from our proper landing-place behind the point. If we let the current have its way we should come ashore beside the gigs, where the pirates might appear at any moment.

"I cannot keep her head for the stockade, sir," said I to the captain. I was steering, while he and Redruth, two fresh men, were at the oars. "The tide keeps washing her down. Could you pull a little stronger?"

"Not without swamping the boat," said he. "You must bear up, sir, if you please bear up until you see you're gaining."

I tried, and found by experiment that the tide kept sweeping us westward until I had laid her head due east, or just about right angles to the way we ought to go.

"We'll never get ashore at this rate," said I.

"If it's the only course that we can lie, sir, we must even lie it," returned the captain. "We must keep up-stream. You see, sir," he went on, "if once we dropped to leeward of the landing-place, it's hard to say where we should get ashore, besides the chance of being boarded by the gigs; whereas, the way we go the current must slacken, and then we can dodge back along the shore."

"The current's less a'ready, sir," said the man Gray, who was sitting in the fore-sheets; "you can ease her off a bit."

"Thank you, my man," said I, quite as if nothing had happened; for we had all quietly made up our minds to treat him like one of ourselves.

Suddenly the captain spoke up again, and I thought his voice was a little changed.

"The gun!" said he.

"I have thought of that," said I, for I made sure he was thinking of a bombardment of the fort. "They could never get the gun ashore, and if they did, they could never haul it through the woods."

"Look astern, doctor," replied the captain. We had entirely forgotten the long nine; and there, to our horror, were the five rogues busy about her, getting off her jacket, as they called the stout tarpaulin cover under which she sailed. Not only that, but it flashed into my mind at the same moment that the round-shot and the powder for the gun had been left behind, and a stroke with an axe would put it all into the possession of the evil ones aboard.

"Israel was Flint's gunner," said Gray hoarsely.

At any risk, we put the boat's head direct for the landing-place. By this time we had got so far out of the run of the current that we kept steerage way even at our necessarily gentle rate of rowing, and I could keep her steady for the goal. But the worst of it was, that with the course I now held, we turned our broadside instead of our stern to the *Hispaniola*, and offered a target like a barn door.

I could hear, as well as see, that brandy-faced rascal, Israel Hands, plumping down a round-shot on the deck.

"Who's the best shot?" asked the captain.

"Mr. Trelawney, out and away," said I.

"Mr. Trelawney, will you please pick me off one of these men, sir? Hands, if possible," said the captain.

Trelawney was as cool as steel. He looked to the priming of his gun.

"Now," cried the captain, "easy with that gun, sir, or you'll swamp the boat. All hands stand by to trim her when he aims."

'The Squire raised his gun, the rowing ceased, and we leaned over to the other side to keep the balance . . .' (p. 99)

'And he and Redruth backed with a great heave that sent her stern bodily under water.' (p. 99)

The squire raised his gun, the rowing ceased, and we leaned over to the other side to keep the balance, and all was so nicely contrived that we did not ship a drop.

They had the gun, by this time, slewed round upon the swivel, and Hands, who was at the muzzle with the rammer, was, in consequence, the most exposed. However, we had no luck; for just as Trelawney fired, down he stooped, the ball whistled over him, and it was one of the other four who fell.

The cry he gave was echoed, not only by his companions on board but by a great number of voices from the shore, and looking in that direction I saw the other pirates trooping out from among the trees and tumbling into their places in the boats.

"Here come the gigs, sir," said I.

"Give way, then," cried the captain. "We mustn't mind if we swamp her now. If we can't get ashore, all's up."

"Only one of the gigs is being manned, sir," I added, "the crew of the other most likely going round by shore to cut us off."

"They'll have a hot run, sir," returned the captain. "Jack's ashore, you know. It's not them I mind; it's the round-shot. Carpet-bowls! My lady's maid couldn't miss. Tell us, squire, when you see the match, and we'll hold water."

In the meanwhile we had been making headway at a good pace for a boat so overloaded, and we had shipped but little water in the process. We were now close in; thirty or forty strokes and we should beach her; for the ebb had already disclosed a narrow belt of sand below the clustering trees. The gig was no longer to be feared; the little point had already concealed it from our eyes. The ebb-tide, which had so cruelly delayed us, was now making reparation, and delaying our assailants. The one source of danger was the gun.

"If I durst," said the captain, "I'd stop and pick off another man."

But it was plain that they meant nothing should delay their shot. They had never so much as looked at their fallen comrade though he was not dead, and I could see him trying to crawl away.

"Ready!" cried the squire.

"Hold!" cried the captain, quick as an echo.

And he and Redruth backed with a great heave that sent her stern bodily under water. The report fell in at the same instant of time. This was the first that Jim heard, the sound of the squire's shot not having reached him. Where

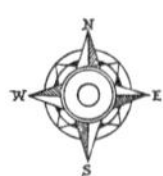

the ball passed not one of us precisely knew; but I fancy it must have been over our heads, and that the wind of it may have contributed to our disaster.

At any rate, the boat sank by the stern, quite gently, in three feet of water, leaving the captain and myself, facing each other, on our feet. The other three took complete headers, and came up again, drenched and bubbling.

So far there was no great harm. No lives were lost, and we could wade ashore in safety. But there were all our stores at the bottom, and, to make things worse, only two guns out of five remained in a state for service. Mine I had snatched from my knees and held over my head, by a sort of instinct. As for the captain, he had carried his over his shoulder by a bandoleer, and, like a wise man, lock uppermost. The other three had gone down with the boat.

To add to our concern we heard voices already drawing near us in the woods along shore; and we had not only the danger of being cut off from the stockade in our half-crippled state, but the fear before us whether, if Hunter and Joyce were attacked by half a dozen, they would have the sense and conduct to stand firm. Hunter was steady, that we knew; Joyce was a doubtful case – a pleasant, polite man for a valet, and to brush one's clothes, but not entirely fitted for a man of war.

With all this in our minds, we waded ashore as fast as we could, leaving behind us the poor jolly-boat, and a good half of all our powder and provisions.

CHAPTER XVIII

NARRATIVE CONTINUED BY THE DOCTOR: END OF THE FIRST DAY'S FIGHTING

WE made our best speed across the strip of wood that now divided us from the stockade; and at every step we took the voices of the buccaneers rang nearer. Soon we could hear their footfalls as they ran, and the cracking of the branches as they breasted across a bit of thicket.

I began to see we should have a brush for it in earnest, and looked to my priming.

"Captain," said I, "Trelawney is the dead shot. Give him your gun; his own is useless."

They exchanged guns, and Trelawney, silent and cool as he had been since the beginning of the bustle, hung a moment on his heel to see that all was fit for service. At the same time, observing Gray to be unarmed, I handed him my cutlass. It did all our hearts good to see him spit in his hand, knit his brows, and make the blade sing through the air. It was plain from every line of his body that our new hand was worth his salt.

Forty paces farther we came to the edge of the wood and saw the stockade in front of us. We struck the enclosure about the middle of the south side, and, almost at the same time, seven mutineers – Job Anderson, the boatswain, at their head, appeared in full cry at the south-western corner.

They paused, as if taken aback; and before they recovered, not only the squire and I, but Hunter and Joyce from the block house, had time to fire. The four shots came in rather a scattering volley; but they did the business; one of the enemy actually fell, and the rest, without hesitation, turned and plunged into the trees.

After reloading, we walked down the outside of the palisade to see the fallen enemy. He was stone dead – shot through the heart.

We began to rejoice over our good success, when just at that moment a

pistol cracked in the bush, a ball whistled close past my ear, and poor Tom Redruth stumbled and fell his length on the ground. Both the squire and I returned the shot; but as we had nothing to aim at, it is probable we only wasted powder. Then we reloaded, and turned our attention to poor Tom.

The captain and Gray were already examining him; and I saw with half an eye that all was over.

I believe the readiness of our return volley had scattered the mutineers once more, for we were suffered without further molestation to get the poor old gamekeeper hoisted over the stockade, and carried, groaning and bleeding, into the log-house.

Poor old fellow, he had not uttered one word of surprise, complaint, fear, or even acquiescence, from the very beginning of our troubles till now, when we had laid him down in the log-house to die. He had lain like a Trojan behind his mattress in the gallery; he had followed every order silently, doggedly, and well; he was the oldest of our party by a score of years; and now, sullen, old, serviceable servant, it was he that was to die.

The squire dropped down beside him on his knees and kissed his hand, crying like a child.

"Be I going, doctor?" he asked.

"Tom, my man," said I, "you're going home."

"I wish I had had a lick at them with the gun first," he replied.

"Tom," said the squire, "say you forgive me, won't you?"

"Would that be respectful like, from me to you, squire?" was the answer. "Howsoever, so be it, amen!"

After a little while of silence, he said he thought somebody might read a prayer. "It's the custom, sir," he added, apologetically. And not long after, without another word, he passed away.

In the meantime the captain, whom I had observed to be wonderfully swollen about the chest and pockets, had turned out a great many various stores – the British colours, a Bible, a coil of stoutish rope, pen, ink, the log-book, and pounds of tobacco. He had found a longish fir-tree lying felled

and cleared in the enclosure, and with the help of Hunter, he had set it up at the corner of the log-house where the trunks crossed and made an angle. Then, climbing on the roof, he had with his own hand bent and run up the colours.

This seemed mightily to relieve him. He re-entered the log-house and set about counting up the stores, as if nothing else existed. But he had an eye on Tom's passage for all that; and as soon as all was over, came forward with another flag, and reverently spread it on the body.

"Don't you take on, sir," he said, shaking the squire's hand. "All's well with him; no fear for a hand that's been shot down in his duty to captain and owner. It mayn't be good divinity, but it's a fact."

Then he pulled me aside.

"Dr. Livesey," he said, "in how many weeks do you and squire expect the consort?"

I told him it was a question, not of weeks, but of months; that if we were not back by the end of August, Blandly was to send to find us; but neither sooner nor later. "You can calculate for yourself," I said.

"Why, yes," returned the captain, scratching his head, "and making a large allowance, sir, for all the gifts of Providence, I should say we were pretty close hauled."

"How do you mean?" I asked.

"It's a pity, sir, we lost that second load. That's what I mean," replied the captain. "As for powder and shot, we'll do. But the rations are short, very short – so short, Dr. Livesey, that we're perhaps as well without that extra mouth."

And he pointed to the dead body under the flag.

Just then, with a roar and a whistle, a round-shot passed high above the roof of the log-house and plumped far beyond us in the wood.

"Oho!" said the captain. "Blaze away! You've little enough powder already, my lads."

At the second trial, the aim was better, and the ball descended inside the stockade, scattering a cloud of sand, but doing no further damage.

"Captain," said the squire, "the house is quite invisible from the ship. It must be the flag they are aiming at. Would it not be wiser to take it in?"

"Strike my colours!" cried the captain. "No, sir, not I;" and, as soon as he had said the words, I think we all agreed with him. For it was not only a piece of stout, seamanly, good feeling; it was good policy besides, and showed our enemies that we despised their cannonade.

All through the evening they kept thundering away. Ball after ball flew over or fell short, or kicked up the sand in the enclosure; but they had to fire so high that the shot fell dead and buried itself in the soft sand. We had no ricochet to fear; and though one popped in through the roof of the log-house and out again through the floor, we soon got used to that sort of horse-play, and minded it no more than cricket.

"There is one thing good about all this," observed the captain: "the wood in front of us is likely clear. The ebb has made a good while; our stores should be uncovered. Volunteers to go and bring in pork."

Gray and Hunter were the first to come forward. Well armed, they stole out of the stockade; but it proved a useless mission. The mutineers were bolder than we fancied, or they put more trust in Israel's gunnery. For four or five of them were busy carrying off our stores, and wading out with them to one of the gigs that lay close by, pulling an oar or so to hold her steady against the current. Silver was in the stern sheets in command; and every man of them was now provided with a musket from some secret magazine of their own.

The captain sat down to his log, and here is the beginning of the entry:—

"Alexander Smollett, master; David Livesey, ship's doctor; Abraham Gray, carpenter's mate; John Trelawney, owner; John Hunter and Richard Joyce, owner's servants, landsmen – being all that is left faithful of the ship's company – with stores for ten days at short rations, came ashore this day, and flew British colours on the log-house in Treasure Island. Thomas Redruth, owner's servant, landsman, shot by the mutineers; James Hawkins, cabin-boy—"

And at the same time I was wondering over poor Jim Hawkins's fate.

A hail on the land side.

"Somebody hailing us," said Hunter, who was on guard.

"Doctor! squire! captain! Hallo, Hunter, is that you?" came the cries.

And I ran to the door in time to see Jim Hawkins, safe and sound, come climbing over the stockade.

CHAPTER XIX

NARRATIVE RESUMED BY JIM HAWKINS: THE GARRISON IN THE STOCKADE

AS soon as Ben Gunn saw the colours he came to a halt, stopped my by the arm, and sat down. "Now," said he, "there's your friends, sure enough."

"Far more likely it's the mutineers," I answered.

"That!" he cried. "Why, in a place like this, where nobody puts in but gen'lemen of fortune, Silver would fly the Jolly Roger, you don't make no doubt of that. No; that's your friends. There's been blows, too, and I reckon your friends has had the best of it; and here they are ashore in the old stockade, as was made years and years ago by Flint. Ah, he was the man to have a headpiece, was Flint! Barring rum, his match were never seen. He was afraid of none, not he; only Silver – Silver was that genteel."

"Well," said I, "that may be so, and so be it; all the more reason that I should hurry on and join my friends."

"Nay, mate," returned Ben, "not you. You're a good boy, or I'm mistook; but you're only a boy, all told. Now, Ben Gunn is fly. Rum wouldn't bring me there, where you're going – not rum wouldn't, till I see your born gen'leman, and gets it on his word of honour. And you won't forget my words! A precious sight (that's what you'll say), a precious sight more confidence – and then nips him."

And he pinched me the third time with the same air of cleverness. "And when Ben Gunn is wanted, you know where to find him, Jim. Just where you found him to-day. And him that comes is to have a white thing in his hand: and he's to come alone. Oh! and you'll say this: 'Ben Gunn,' says you, 'has reasons of his own.' "

"Well," said I, "I believe I understand. You have something to propose, and you wish to see the squire or the doctor; and you're to be found where I found you. Is that all?"

"And when? says you," he added. "Why, from about noon observation to about six bells."

"Good," said I, "and now may I go?"

"You won't forget?" he inquired anxiously. "Precious sight, and reasons of his own, says you. Reasons of his own; that's the mainstay; as between man and man. Well, then" – still holding me – "I reckon you can go, Jim. And, Jim, if you was to see Silver, you wouldn't go for to sell Ben Gunn? wild horses wouldn't draw it from you? No, says you. And if them pirates camp ashore, Jim, what would you say but there'd be widders in the morning?"

Here he was interrupted by a loud report, and a cannon ball came tearing through the trees and pitched in the sand, not a hundred yards from where we two were talking. The next moment each of us had taken to his heels in a different direction.

For a good hour to come frequent reports shook the island, and balls kept crashing through the woods. I moved from hiding-place to hiding-place, always pursued, or so it seemed to me, by these terrifying missiles. But towards the end of the bombardment, though still I durst not venture in the direction of the stockade, where the balls fell oftenest, I had began, in a manner, to pluck up my heart again; and after a long detour to the east, crept down among the shore-side trees.

The sun had just set, the sea breeze was rustling and tumbling in the woods, and ruffling the gray surface of the anchorage; the tide, too, was far out, and great tracts of sand lay uncovered; the air, after the heat of the day, chilled me through my jacket.

The *Hispaniola* still lay where she had anchored; but, sure enough, there was the Jolly Roger, the black flag of piracy, flying from her peak. Even as I looked, there came another red flash and another report, that sent the echoes clattering, and one more round-shot whistled through the air. It was the last of the cannonade.

I lay for some time, watching the bustle which succeeded the attack. Men were demolishing something with axes on the beach near the stockade; the poor jolly-boat, I afterwards discovered. Away, near the mouth of the river, a great fire was glowing among the trees, and between that point and the ship one of the gigs kept coming and going, the men, whom I had seen so gloomy, shouting at the oars like children. But there was a sound in their voices which suggested rum.

At length I thought I might return towards the stockade. I was pretty far down on the low, sandy spit that encloses the anchorage to the east, and is joined at half-water to Skeleton Island; and now, as I rose to my feet, I saw, some distance farther down the spit, and rising from among low bushes, an isolated rock, pretty high, and peculiarly white in colour. It occurred to me that this might be the white rock of which Ben Gunn had spoken, and that some day or other a boat might be wanted, and I should know where to look for one.

Then I skirted among the woods until I had regained the rear, or shoreward side, of the stockade, and was soon warmly welcomed by the faithful party.

I had soon told my story, and began to look about me. The log house was made of unsquared trunks of pine – roof, walls, and floor. The latter stood in several places as much as a foot or a foot and a half above the surface of the sand. There was a porch at the door, and under this porch the little spring welled up into an artificial basin of a rather odd kind – no other than a great ship's kettle of iron, with the bottom knocked out, and sunk "to her bearings," as the captain said, among the sand.

Little had been left beside the framework of the house; but in one corner there was a stone slab laid down by way of hearth and an old rusty iron basket to contain the fire.

The slopes of the knoll and all the inside of the stockade had been cleared of timber to build the house, and we could see by the stumps what a fine and lofty grove had been destroyed. Most of the soil had been washed away or buried in drift after the removal of the trees; only where the streamlet ran down from the kettle a thick bed of moss and some ferns and little creeping bushes were still green among the sand. Very close around the stockade – too close for defence, they said – the wood still flourished high and dense, all of fir on the land side, but towards the sea with a large admixture of live-oaks.

The cold evening breeze, of which I have spoken, whistled through every chink of the rude building, and sprinkled the floor with a continual rain of fine sand. There was sand in our eyes, sand in our teeth, sand in our suppers, sand dancing in the spring at the bottom of the kettle, for all the world like porridge beginning to boil. Our chimney was a square hole in the roof: it was but a little part of the smoke that found its way out, and the rest eddied about the house, and kept us coughing and piping the eye.

Add to this that Gray, the new man, had his face tied up in a bandage for a cut he had got in breaking away from the mutineers; and that poor old Tom Redruth, still unburied, lay along the wall, stiff and stark, under the Union Jack.

If we had been allowed to sit idle, we should all have fallen into the blues, but Captain Smollett was never the man for that. All hands were called up before him, and he divided us into watches. The doctor, and Gray, and I, for one; the squire, Hunter, and Joyce upon the other. Tired as we all were, two were sent out for firewood; two more were set to dig a grave for Redruth; the doctor was named cook; I was put sentry at the door; and the captain himself went from one to another, keeping up our spirits, and lending a hand wherever it was wanted.

From time to time the doctor came to the door for a little air and to rest his eyes, which were almost smoked out of his head; and whenever he did so, he had a word for me.

"That man Smollett," he said once, "is a better man than I am. And when I say that it means a deal, Jim."

Another time he came and was silent for a while. Then he put his head on one side, and looked at me.

"Is this Ben Gunn a man?" he asked.

"I do not know, sir," said I. "I am not very sure whether he's sane."

"If there's any doubt about the matter, he is," returned the doctor. "A man who has been three years biting his nails on a desert island, Jim, can't expect to appear as sane as you or me. It doesn't lie in human nature. Was it cheese you said he had a fancy for?"

"Yes, sir, cheese," I answered.

"Well, Jim," says he, "just see the good that comes of being dainty in your food. You've seen my snuff-box, haven't you? And you never saw me take snuff; the reason being that in my snuff-box I carry a piece of Parmesan cheese – a cheese made in Italy, very nutritious. Well, that's for Ben Gunn!"

Before supper was eaten we buried old Tom in the sand, and stood round him for a while bare-headed in the breeze. A good deal of firewood had been got in, but not enough for the captain's fancy; and he shook his head over it, and told us we "must get back to this to-morrow rather livelier." Then, when we had eaten our pork, and each had a good stiff glass of brandy grog, the three chiefs got together in a corner to discuss our prospects.

It appears they were at their wits' end what to do, the stores being so low that we must have been starved into surrender long before help came. But our best hope, it was decided, was to kill off the buccaneers until they either hauled down their flag or ran away with the *Hispaniola*. From nineteen they were already reduced to fifteen, two others were wounded, and one, at least – the man shot beside the gun – severely wounded, if he were not dead. Every time we had a crack at them, we were to take it, saving our own lives, with the extremest care. And, besides that, we had two able allies – rum and the climate.

As for the first, though we were about half a mile away, we could hear them roaring and singing late into the night; and as for the second, the doctor staked his wig that, camped where they were in the marsh and unprovided with remedies, the half of them would be on their backs before a week.

"So," he added, "if we are not all shot down first, they'll be glad to be packing in the schooner. It's always a ship, and they can get to buccaneering again, I suppose."

"First ship that ever I lost," said Captain Smollett.

I was dead tired, as you may fancy; and when I got to sleep, which was not till after a great deal of tossing, I slept like a log of wood.

The rest had long been up, and had already breakfasted and increased the pile of firewood by about half as much again, when I was awakened by a bustle and the sound of voices.

"Flag of truce!" I heard some one say; and then, immediately after, with a cry of surprise, "Silver himself!"

And, at that, up I jumped, and, rubbing my eyes, ran to a loop-hole in the wall.

CHAPTER XX

SILVER'S EMBASSY

SURE enough, there were two men just outside the stockade, one of them waving a white cloth; the other, no less a person than Silver himself, standing placidly by.

It was still quite early, and the coldest morning that I think I ever was abroad in; a chill that pierced into the marrow. The sky was bright and cloudless overhead, and the tops of the trees shone rosily in the sun. But where Silver stood with his lieutenant all was still in shadow, and they waded knee deep in a low, white vapour, that had crawled during the night out of the morass. The chill and the vapour taken together told a poor tale of the island. It was plainly a damp, feverish, unhealthy spot.

"Keep indoors, men," said the captain. "Ten to one this is a trick."

Then he hailed the buccaneer.

"Who goes? Stand, or we fire."

"Flag of truce," cried Silver.

The captain was in the porch, keeping himself carefully out of the way of a treacherous shot should any be intended. He turned and spoke to us: –

"Doctor's watch on the look-out. Dr. Livesey, take the north side, if you please; Jim the east; Gray, west. The watch below, all hands to load muskets. Lively, men, and careful."

And then he turned again to the mutineers.

"And what do you want with your flag of truce?" he cried.

This time it was the other man who replied.

"Cap'n Silver, sir, to come on board and make terms," he shouted.

"Cap'n Silver! Don't know him. Who's he?" cries the captain. And we could hear him adding to himself: "Cap'n, is it? My heart, and here's promotion!"

Long John answered for himself.

"Me, sir. These poor lads have chosen me cap'n, after your desertion, sir" – laying a particular emphasis upon the word "desertion." "We're willing to

' "Flag of truce," cried Silver.' (p. 110)

submit, if we can come to terms, and no bones about it. All I ask is your word, Cap'n Smollett, to let me safe and sound out of this here stockade, and one minute to get out o' shot before a gun is fired."

"My man," said Captain Smollett, "I have not the slightest desire to talk to you. If you wish to talk to me, you can come, that's all. If there's any treachery, it'll be on your side, and the Lord help you."

"That's enough, cap'n," shouted Long John cheerily. "A word from you's enough. I know a gentleman, and you may lay to that."

We could see the man who carried the flag of truce attempting to hold Silver back. Nor was that wonderful, seeing how cavalier had been the captain's answer. But Silver laughed at him aloud, and slapped him on the back, as if the idea of alarm had been absurd. Then he advanced to the stockade, threw over his crutch, got a leg up, and with great vigour and skill succeeded in surmounting the fence and dropping safely to the other side.

I will confess that I was far too much taken up with what was going on to be of the slightest use as sentry; indeed, I had already deserted my eastern loophole, and crept up behind the captain, who had now seated himself on the threshold, with his elbows on his knees, his head in his hands, and his eyes fixed on the water, as it bubbled out of the old iron kettle in the sand. He was whistling to himself, "Come, Lassies and Lads."

Silver had terrible hard work getting up the knoll. What with the steepness of the incline, the thick tree stumps, and the soft sand, he and his crutch were as helpless as a ship in stays. But he stuck to it like a man in silence, and at last arrived before the captain, whom he saluted in the handsomest style. He was tricked out in his best; an immense blue coat, thick with brass buttons, hung as low as to his knees, and a fine laced hat was set on the back of his head.

"Here you are, my man," said the captain, raising his head. "You had better sit down."

"You ain't a-going to let me inside, cap'n?" complained Long John. "It's a main cold morning, to be sure, sir, to sit outside upon the sand."

"Why, Silver," said the captain, "if you had pleased to be an honest man, you might have been sitting in your galley. It's your own doing. You're either my ship's cook – and then you were treated handsome – or Cap'n Silver, a common mutineer and pirate, and then you can go hang!"

"Well, well, cap'n," returned the sea-cook, sitting down as he was bidden on the sand, "you'll have to give me a hand up again, that's all. A sweet

pretty place you have of it here. Ah, there's Jim! The top of the morning to you, Jim. Doctor, here's my service. Why, there you all are together like a happy family, in a manner of speaking."

"If you have anything to say, my man, better say it," said the captain.

"Right you were, Cap'n Smollett," replied Silver. "Dooty is dooty, to be sure. Well, now, you look here, that was a good lay of yours last night. I don't deny it was a good lay. Some of you pretty handy with a handspike-end. And I'll not deny neither but what some of my people was shook – maybe all was shook; maybe I was shook myself; maybe that's why I'm here for terms. But you mark me, cap'n, it won't do twice, by thunder! We'll have to do sentry-go, and ease off a point or so on the rum. Maybe you think we were all a sheet in the wind's eye. But I'll tell you I was sober; I was on'y dog tired; and if I'd awoke a second sooner I'd a caught you at the act, I would. He wasn't dead when I got round to him, not he."

"Well?" says Captain Smollett, as cool as can be.

All that Silver said was a riddle to him, but you would never have guessed it from his tone. As for me, I began to have an inkling. Ben Gunn's last words came back to my mind. I began to suppose that he had paid the buccaneers a visit while they all lay drunk together round their fire, and I reckoned up with glee that we had only fourteen enemies to deal with.

"Well, here it is," said Silver. "We want that treasure, and we'll have it – that's our point! You would just as soon save your lives, I reckon; and that's yours. You have a chart, haven't you?"

"That's as may be," replied the captain.

"Oh, well, you have, I know that," returned Long John. "You needn't be so husky with a man; there ain't a particle of service in that, and you may lay to it. What I mean is, we want your chart. Now, I never meant you no harm, myself."

"That won't do with me, my man," interrupted the captain. "We know exactly what you meant to do, and we don't care; for now, you see, you can't do it."

And the captain looked at him calmly, and proceeded to fill a pipe.

"If Abe Gray—" Silver broke out.

"Avast there!" cried Mr. Smollett. "Gray told me nothing and I asked him nothing; and what's more I would see you and him and this whole island blown clean out of the water into blazes first. So there's my mind for you, my man, on that."

This little whiff of temper seemed to cool Silver down. He had been growing nettled before, but now he pulled himself together.

"Like enough," said he. "I would set no limits to what gentlemen might consider shipshape, or might not, as the case were. And seein' as how you are about to take a pipe, cap'n, I'll make so free as do likewise."

And he filled a pipe and lighted it; and the two men sat silently smoking for quite a while, now looking each other in the face, now stopping their tobacco, now leaning forward to spit. It was as good as the play to see them.

"Now," resumed Silver, "here it is. You give us the chart to get the treasure by, and drop shooting poor seamen, and stoving of their heads in while asleep. You do that, and we'll offer you a choice. Either you come aboard along of us, once the treasure's shipped, and then I'll give you my affy-davy, upon my word of honour, to clap you somewhere safe ashore. Or, if that ain't to your fancy, some of my hands being rough, and having old scores, on account of hazing, then you can stay here, you can. We'll divide stores with you, man for man; and I'll give my affy-davy, as before, to speak the first ship I sight, and send 'em here to pick you up. Now you'll own that's talking. Handsomer you couldn't look to get, not you. And I hope" – raising his voice – "that all hands in this here block-house will overhaul my words, for what is spoke to one is spoke to all."

Captain Smollett rose from his seat, and knocked the ashes of his pipe in the palm of his left hand.

"Is that all?" he asked.

"Every last word, by thunder!" answered John. "Refuse that, and you've seen the last of me but musket-balls."

"Very good," said the captain. "Now you'll hear me. If you'll come up one by one, unarmed, I'll engage to clap you all in irons, and take you home to a fair trial in England. If you won't, my name is Alexander Smollett, I've

flown my sovereign's colours, and I'll see you all to Davy Jones. You can't find the treasure. You can't sail the ship – there's not a man among you fit to sail the ship. You can't fight us – Gray, there, got away from five of you. Your ship's in irons, Master Silver; you're on a lee shore, and so you'll find. I stand here and tell you so; and they're the last good words you'll get from me, for, in the name of heaven, I'll put a bullet in your back when next I meet you. Tramp, my lad. Bundle out of this, please, hand over hand, and double quick."

Silver's face was a picture; his eyes started in his head with wrath. He shook the fire out of his pipe.

"Give me a hand up!" he cried.

"Not I," returned the captain.

"Who'll give me a hand up?" he roared.

Not a man among us moved. Growling the foulest imprecations, he crawled along the sand till he got hold of the porch and could hoist himself again upon his crutch. Then he spat into the spring.

"There!" he cried, "that's what I think of ye. Before an hour's out, I'll stove in your old block-house like a rum puncheon. Laugh, by thunder, laugh! Before an hour's out ye'll laugh upon the other side. Them that die'll be the lucky ones."

And with a dreadful oath he stumbled off, ploughed down the sand, was helped across the stockade, after four or five failures, by the man with the flag of truce, and disappeared in an instant afterwards among the trees.

CHAPTER XXI

THE ATTACK

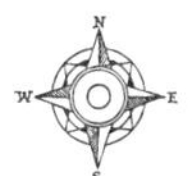

AS soon as Silver disappeared, the captain, who had been closely watching him, turned towards the interior of the house, and found not a man of us at his post but Gray. It was the first time we had ever seen him angry.

"Quarters!" he roared. And then, as we all slunk back to our places, "Gray," he said, "I'll put your name in the log; you've stood by your duty like a seaman. Mr. Trelawney, I'm surprised at you, sir. Doctor, I thought you had worn the king's coat! If that was how you served at Fontenoy, sir, you'd have been better in your berth."

The doctor's watch were all back at their loopholes, the rest were busy loading the spare muskets, and every one with a red face, you may be certain, and a flea in his ear, as the saying is.

The captain looked on for a while in silence. Then he spoke.

"My lads," said he, "I've given Silver a broadside. I pitched it in red-hot on purpose; and before the hour's out, as he said, we shall be boarded. We're outnumbered, I needn't tell you that, but we fight in shelter; and, a minute ago, I should have said we fought with discipline; I've no manner of doubt that we can drub them, if you choose."

Then he went the rounds, and saw, as he said, that all was clear.

On the two short sides of the house, east and west, there were only two loopholes; one the south side where the porch was, two again; and on the north side, five. There was a round score of muskets for the seven of us; the firewood had been built into four piles – tables, you might say – one about the middle of each side, and on each of these tables some ammunition and four loaded muskets were laid ready to the hand of the defenders. In the middle, the cutlasses lay ranged.

"Toss out the fire," said the captain; "the chill is past, and we mustn't have smoke in our eyes."

The iron fire basket was carried bodily out by Mr. Trelawney, and the embers smothered among sand.

"Hawkins hasn't had his breakfast. Hawkins, help yourself, and back to your post to eat it," continued Captain Smollett. "Lively, now, my lad; you'll want it before you've done. Hunter, serve out a round of brandy to all hands."

And while this was going on, the captain completed, in his own mind, the plan of the defence.

"Doctor, you will take the door," he resumed. "See and don't expose yourself; keep within, and fire through the porch. Hunter, take the east side, there. Joyce, you stand by the west, my man. Mr. Trelawney, you are the best shot, you and Gray will take this long north side, with the five loopholes; it's there the danger is. If they can get up to it, and fire in upon us through our own ports, things would begin to look dirty. Hawkins, neither you nor I are much account at the shooting; we'll stand by to load and bear a hand."

As the captain had said, the chill was past. As soon as the sun had climbed above our girdle of trees, it fell with all its force upon the clearing, and drank up the vapours at a draught. Soon the sand was baking, and the resin melting in the logs of the block-house. Jackets and coats were flung aside; shirts thrown open at the neck, and rolled up to the shoulders; and we stood there, each at his post, in a fever of heat and anxiety.

An hour passed away.

"Hang them!" said the captain. "This is as dull as the doldrums. Gray, whistle for a wind."

And just at that moment came the first news of the attack.

"If you please, sir," said Joyce, "if I see any one, am I to fire?"

"I told you so!" cried the captain.

"Thank you, sir," returned Joyce, with the same quiet civility.

Nothing followed for a time; but the remark had set us all on the alert, straining ears and eyes – the musketeers with their pieces balanced in their hands, the captain out in the middle of the block-house, with his mouth very tight and a frown on his face.

So some seconds passed, till suddenly Joyce whipped up his musket and fired. The report had scarcely died away ere it was repeated and repeated from without in a scattering volley, shot behind shot, like a string of geese, from every side of the enclosure. Several bullets struck the log-house, but not one entered; and, as the smoke cleared away and vanished, the stockade and the woods around it looked as quiet and empty as before. Not a bough waved, not the gleam of a musket-barrel betrayed the presence of our foes.

"Did you hit your man?" asked the captain.

"No, sir," replied Joyce. "I believe not, sir."

"Next best thing to tell the truth," muttered Captain Smollett. "Load his gun, Hawkins. How many should you say there were on your side, doctor?"

"I know precisely," said Dr. Livesey. "Three shots were fired on this side. I saw the three flashes – two close together – one farther to the west."

"Three!" repeated the captain. "And how many on yours, Mr. Trelawney?"

But this was not so easily answered. There had come many from the north – seven, by the squire's computation; eight or nine, according to Gray. From the east and west only a single shot had been fired. It was plain, therefore, that the attack would be developed from the north, and that on the other three sides we were only to be annoyed by a show of hostilities. But Captain Smollett made no change in his arrangements. If the mutineers succeeded in crossing the stockade, he argued, they would take possession of any unprotected loophole, and shoot us down like rats in our own stronghold.

Nor had we much time left to us for thought. Suddenly, with a loud huzza, a little cloud of pirates leaped from the woods on the north side, and ran straight on the stockade. At the same moment, the fire was once more opened from the woods, and a rifle ball sang through the doorway, and knocked the doctor's musket into bits.

The boarders swarmed over the fence like monkeys. Squire and Gray fired again and yet again; three men fell, one forwards into the enclosure, two back on the outside. But of these, one was evidently more frightened than hurt, for he was on his feet again in a crack, and instantly disappeared among the trees.

Two had bit the dust, one had fled, four had made good their footing inside our defences; while from the shelter of the woods seven or eight men, each evidently supplied with several muskets, kept up a hot though useless fire on the log-house.

The four who had boarded made straight before them for the building, shouting as they ran, and the men among the trees shouted back to encourage them. Several shots were fired; but, such was the hurry of the marksmen, that not one appeared to have taken effect. In a moment, the four pirates had swarmed up the mound and were upon us.

The head of Job Anderson, the boatswain, appeared at the middle loophole.

"At 'em, all hands – all hands!" he roared, in a voice of thunder.

At the same moment, another pirate grasped Hunter's musket by the muzzle, wrenched it from his hands, plucked it through the loophole, and, with one stunning blow, laid the poor fellow senseless on the floor. Meanwhile a third, running unharmed all round the house, appeared suddenly in the doorway, and fell with his cutlass on the doctor.

Our position was utterly reversed. A moment since we were firing, under cover, at an exposed enemy; now it was we who lay uncovered, and could not return a blow.

The log-house was full of smoke, to which we owed our comparative safety. Cries and confusion, the flashes and reports of pistol shots, and one loud groan, rang in my ears.

"Out, lads, out, and fight 'em in the open! Cutlasses!" cried the captain.

I snatched a cutlass from the pile, and some one, at the same time snatching another, gave me a cut across the knuckles which I hardly felt. I dashed out of the door into the clear sunlight. Some one was close behind, I knew not whom. Right in front, the doctor was pursuing his assailant down the hill, and, just as my eyes fell upon, beat down his guard, and set him sprawling on his back, with a great slash across the face.

"Round the house, lads! round the house!" cried the captain; and even in the hurly-burly I perceived a change in his voice.

Mechanically I obeyed, turned eastwards, and with my cutlass raised, ran round the corner of the house. Next moment I was face to face with Anderson. He roared aloud, and his hanger went up above his head, flashing in the sunlight. I had not time to be afraid, but, as the blow still hung impending, leaped in a trice upon one side, and missing my foot in the soft sand, rolled headlong down the slope.

When I had first sallied from the door, the other mutineers had been already swarming up the palisade to make an end of us. One Dan, in a red night-cap, with his cutlass in his mouth, had even got upon the top and thrown a leg across. Well, so short had been the interval, that when I found my feet again all was in the same posture, the fellow with the red night-cap still half-way over, another still just showing his head above the top of the stockade. And yet, in this breath of time, the fight was over, and the victory was ours.

Gray, following close behind me, had cut down the big boatswain ere he had time to recover from his lost blow. Another had been shot at a loophole in the very act of firing into the house, and now lay in agony, the pistol still smoking in his hand. A third, as I had seen, the doctor had disposed of at a blow. Of the four who had scaled the palisade, one only remained unaccounted for, and he, having left his cutlass on the field, was now clambering out again with the fear of death upon him.

"Fire – fire from the house!" cried the doctor. "And you, lads, back into cover."

But his words were unheeded, no shot was fired, and the last boarder made good his escape, and disappeared with the rest into the wood. In three seconds nothing remained of the attacking party but the five who had fallen, four on the inside, and one on the outside, of the palisade.

The doctor and Gray and I ran full speed for shelter. The survivors would soon be back where they had left their muskets, and at any moment the fire might recommence.

The house was this time somewhat cleared of smoke, and we saw at a glance the price we had paid for victory. Hunter lay beside his loophole, stunned; Joyce by his, shot through the head, never to move again; while right in the centre, the squire was supporting the captain, one as pale as the other.

"The captain's wounded," said Mr. Trelawney.

"Have they run?" asked Mr. Smollett.

"All that could, you may be bound," returned the doctor; "but there's five of them will never run again."

"Five!" cried the captain. "Come, that's better. Five against three leaves us four to nine. That's better odds than we had at starting. We were seven to nineteen then, or thought we were, and that's as bad to bear." [1]

[1] The mutineers were soon only eight in number, for the man shot by Mr. Trelawney on board the schooner died that same evening of his wound. But this was, of course, not known till after by the faithful party.

'Gray, following close behind me, had cut down the big boatswain . . .' (p. 120)

PART V MY SEA ADVENTURE

CHAPTER XXII

HOW I BEGAN MY SEA ADVENTURE

THERE was no return of the mutineers – not so much as another shot out of the woods. They had "got their rations for that day," as the captain put it, and we had the place to ourselves and a quiet time to overhaul the wounded and get dinner. Squire and I cooked outside in spite of the danger, and even outside we could hardly tell what we were at, for horror of the loud groans that reached us from the doctor's patients.

Out of the eight men who had fallen in the action, only three still breathed – that one of the pirates who had been shot at the loophole, Hunter, and Captain Smollett; and of these the first two were as good as dead; the mutineer, indeed, died under the doctor's knife, and Hunter, do what we could, never recovered consciousness in this world. He lingered all day, breathing loudly like the old buccaneer at home in his apoplectic fit; but the bones of his chest had been crushed by the blow and his skull fractured in falling, and some time in the following night, without sign or sound, he went to his Maker.

As for the captain, his wounds were grievous indeed, but not dangerous. No organ was fatally injured. Anderson's ball – for it was Job that shot him first – had broken his shoulder-blade and touched the lung, not badly; the second had only torn and displaced some muscles in the calf. He was sure to recover, the doctor said, but, in the meantime and for weeks to come, he must not walk nor move his arm, nor so much as speak when he could help it.

My own accidental cut across the knuckles was a flea-bite. Dr. Livesey patched it up with plaster, and pulled my ears for me into the bargain.

After dinner the squire and the doctor sat by the captain's side a while in consultation; and, when they had talked to their heart's content, it being then a little past noon, the doctor took up his hat and pistols, girt on a cutlass, put the chart in his pocket, and with a musket on his shoulder, crossed the palisade on the north side, and set off briskly through the trees.

Gray and I were sitting together at the far end of the block-house, to be out of earshot of our officers consulting; and Gray took his pipe out of his mouth and fairly forgot to put it back again, so thunderstruck he was at this occurrence.

"Why, in the name of Davy Jones," said he, "is Dr. Livesey mad?"

"Why, no," says I. "He's about the last of this crew for that, I take it."

"Well, shipmate," said Gray, "mad he may not be; but if he's not, you mark my words, *I* am."

"I take it," replied I, "the doctor has his idea; and if I am right, he's going now to see Ben Gunn."

I was right, as appeared later; but in the meantime, the house being stifling hot, and the little patch of sand inside the palisade ablaze with midday sun, I began to get another thought into my head, which was not by any means so right. What I began to do was to envy the doctor, walking in the cool shadow of the woods, with the birds about him, and the pleasant smell of the pines, while I sat grilling, with my clothes stuck to the hot resin, and so much blood about me, and so many poor dead bodies lying all around, that I took a disgust of the place that was almost as strong as fear.

All the time I was washing out the block-house, and then washing up the things from dinner, this disgust and envy kept growing stronger and stronger, till at last, being near a bread-bag, and no one then observing me, I took the first step towards my escapade, and filled both pockets of my coat with biscuit.

I was a fool if you like, and certainly I was going to do a foolish, over-bold act; but I was determined to do it with all the precautions in my power. These biscuits, should anything befall me, would keep me, at least, from starving till far on in the next day.

The next thing I laid hold of was a brace of pistols, and as I already had a powder-horn and bullets, I felt myself well supplied with arms.

As for the scheme I had in my head, it was not a bad one in itself. I was to go down the sandy spit that divides the anchorage on the east from the open sea, find the white rock I had observed last evening, and ascertain whether it was there or not that Ben Gunn had hidden his boat; a thing quite worth doing, as I still believe. But as I was certain I should not be allowed to leave the enclosure, my only plan was to take French leave, and slip out when nobody was watching; and that was so bad a way of doing it as made the thing itself wrong. But I was only a boy, and I had made my mind up.

Well, as things at last fell out, I found an admirable opportunity. The squire and Gray were busy helping the captain with his bandages; the coast was clear; I made a bolt for it over the stockade and into the thicket of the trees, and before my absence was observed I was out of cry of my companions.

This was my second folly, far worse than the first, as I left but two sound men to guard the house; but like the first, it was a help towards saving all of us.

I took my way straight for the east coast of the island, for I was determined to go down the sea side of the spit to avoid all chance of observation from the anchorage. It was already late in the afternoon, although still warm and sunny. As I continued to thread the tall woods I could hear from far before me not only the continuous thunder of the surf, but a certain tossing of foliage and grinding of boughs which showed me the sea breeze had set in higher than usual. Soon cool draughts of air began to reach me; and a few steps farther I came forth into the open borders of the grove, and saw the sea lying blue and sunny to the horizon, and the surf tumbling and tossing its foam along the beach.

I have never seen the sea quiet round Treasure Island. The sun might blaze overhead, the air be without a breath, the surface smooth and blue, but still these great rollers would be running along all the external coast, thundering and thundering by day and night; and I scarce believe there is one spot in the island where a man would be out of earshot of their noise.

I walked along beside the surf with great enjoyment, till, thinking I was now got far enough to the south, I took the cover of some thick bushes and crept warily up to the ridge of the spit.

Behind me was the sea, in front the anchorage. The sea breeze, as though it had the sooner blown itself out by its unusual violence, was already at an end; it had been succeeded by light, variable airs from the south and south-east, carrying great banks of fog; and the anchorage, under lee of Skeleton Island, lay still and leaden as when first we entered it. The *Hispaniola,* in that unbroken mirror, was exactly portrayed from the truck to the water line, the Jolly Roger hanging from her peak.

Alongside lay one of the gigs, Silver in the sternsheets – him I could always recognise – while a couple of men were leaning over the stern bulwarks, one of them with a red cap – the very rogue that I had seen some hours before stride-legs upon the palisade. Apparently they were talking and

laughing, though at that distance – upwards of a mile – I could, of course, hear no word of what was said. All at once, there began the most horrid, unearthly screaming, which at first startled me badly, though I soon remembered the voice of Captain Flint, and even thought I could make out the bird by her bright plumage as she sat perched upon her master's wrist.

Soon after the jolly-boat shoved off and pulled for shore, and the man with the red cap and his comrade went below by the cabin companion.

Just about the same time the sun had gone down behind the Spy-glass, and as the fog was collecting rapidly, it began to grow dark in earnest. I saw I must lose no time if I were to find the boat that evening.

The white rock, visible enough above the brush, was still some eighth of a mile farther down the spit, and it took me a goodish while to get up with it, crawling, often on all-fours, among the scrub. Night had almost come when I laid my hand on its rough sides. Right below it there was an exceedingly small hollow of green turf, hidden by banks and a thick underwood about knee-deep, that grew there very plentifully; and in the centre of the dell, sure enough, a little tent of goat-skins, like what the gipsies carry about with them in England.

I dropped into the hollow, lifted the side of the tent, and there was Ben Gunn's boat – home-made if ever anything was home-made; a rude, lop-sided framework of tough wood, and stretched upon that a covering of goatskin, with the hair inside. The thing was extremely small, even for me, and I can hardly imagine that it could have floated with a full-sized man. There was one thwart set as low as possible, a kind of stretcher in the bows, and a double paddle for propulsion.

I had not then seen a coracle, such as the ancient Britons made, but I have

"Laugh, by thunder, laugh!"
(F. Gillet)

"Hands and his companion locked together in deadly wrestle"
(M. S. Orr)

"Quick as thought, I sprang into the mizzen-shrouds..."
(M. Winter)

The coxswain loosed his grasp upon the shrouds.
(F. Gillet)

seen one since, and I can give you no fairer idea of Ben Gunn's boat than by saying it was like the first and the worst coracle ever made by man. But the great advantage of the coracle it certainly possessed, for it was exceedingly light and portable.

Well, now that I had found the boat, you would have thought I had had enough of truantry for once; but, in the meantime, I had taken another notion, and became so obstinately fond of it, that I would have carried it out, I believe, in the teeth of Captain Smollett himself. This was to slip out under cover of the night, cut the *Hispaniola* adrift, and let her go ashore where she fancied. I had quite made up my mind that the mutineers, after their repulse of the morning, had nothing nearer their hearts than to up anchor and away to sea; this, I thought, it would be a fine thing to prevent; and now that I had seen how they left their watchmen unprovided with a boat, I thought it might be done with little risk.

Down I sat to wait for darkness, and made a hearty meal of biscuit. It was a night out of ten thousand for my purpose. The fog had now buried all heaven. As the last rays of daylight dwindled and disappeared, absolute blackness settled down on Treasure Island. And when, at last, I shouldered the coracle, and groped my way stumblingly out of the hollow where I had supped, there were but two points visible on the whole anchorage.

One was the great fire on shore, by which the defeated pirates lay carousing in the swamp. The other, a mere blur of light upon the darkness, indicated the position of the anchored ship. She had swung round to the ebb – her bow was now towards me – the only lights on board were in the cabin; and what I saw was merely a reflection on the fog of the strong rays that flowed from the stern window.

The ebb had already run some time, and I had to wade through a long belt of swampy sand, where I sank several times above the ankle, before I came to the edge of the retreating water, and wading a little way in, with some strength and dexterity, set my coracle, keel downwards, on the surface.

CHAPTER XXIII

THE EBB-TIDE RUNS

THE coracle – as I had ample reason to know before I was done with her – was a very safe boat for a person of my height and weight, both buoyant and clever in a seaway; but she was the most cross-grained, lop-sided craft to manage. Do as you please, she always made more leeway than anything else, and turning round and round was the manoeuvre she was best at. Even Ben Gunn himself has admitted that she was "queer to handle till you knew her way."

Certainly I did not know her way. She turned in every direction but the one I was bound to go; the most part of the time we were broadside on, and I am very sure I never should have made the ship at all but for the tide. By good fortune, paddle as I pleased, the tide was still sweeping me down; and there lay the *Hispaniola* right in the fairway, hardly to be missed.

First she loomed before me like a blot of something yet blacker than darkness, then her spars and hull began to take shape, and the next moment, as it seemed (for the further I went, the brisker grew the current of the ebb), I was alongside of her hawser, and had laid hold.

The hawser was as taut as a bowstring – so strong she pulled upon her anchor. All round the hull, in the blackness, the rippling current bubbled and chattered like a little mountain stream. One cut with my sea-gully, and the *Hispaniola* would go humming down the tide.

So far so good; but it next occurred to my recollection that a taut hawser, suddenly cut, is a thing as dangerous as a kicking horse. Ten to one, if I were so foolhardy as to cut the *Hispaniola* from her anchor, I and the coracle would be knocked clean out of the water.

This brought me to a full stop, and if fortune had not again particularly favoured me, I should have had to abandon my design. But the light airs which had begun blowing from the south-east and south had hauled round after nightfall into the south-west. Just while I was meditating, a puff came,

caught the *Hispaniola*, and forced her up into the current; and, to my great joy, I felt the hawser slacken in my grasp, and the hand by which I held it dip for a second under water.

With that I made my mind up, took out my gully, opened it with my teeth, and cut one strand after another, till the vessel only swung by two. Then I lay quiet, waiting to sever these last when the strain should be once more lightened by a breath of wind.

All this time I had heard the sound of loud voices from the cabin; but, to say truth, my mind had been so entirely taken up with other thoughts that I had scarcely given ear. Now, however, when I had nothing else to do, I began to pay more heed.

One I recognised for the coxswain's, Israel Hands, that had been Flint's gunner in former days. The other was, of course, my friend of the red night-cap. Both men were plainly the worse for drink, and they were still drinking; for, even while I was listening, one of them, with a drunken cry, opened the stern window and threw out something, which I divined to be an empty bottle. But they were not only tipsy; it was plain that they were furiously angry. Oaths flew like hailstones, and every now and then there came forth such an explosion as I thought was sure to end in blows. But each time the quarrel passed off, and the voices grumbled lower for a while, until the next crisis came, and, in its turn, passed away without result.

On shore, I could see the glow of the great camp fire burning warmly through the shore-side trees. Some one was singing, a dull, old droning sailor's song, with a droop and a quaver at the end of every verse, and seemingly no end to it at all but the patience of the singer. I had heard it on the voyage more than once, and remembered these words:—

"But one man of her crew alive.
What put to sea with seventy-five."

And I thought it was a ditty rather too dolefully appropriate for a company that had met such cruel losses in the morning. But, indeed, from what I saw, all these buccaneers were as callous as the sea they sailed on.

At last the breeze came; the schooner sidled and drew nearer in the dark; I felt the hawser slacked once more, and with a good, tough effort, cut the last fibres through.

The breeze had but little action on the coracle, and I was almost instantly swept against the bows of the *Hispaniola*. At the same time the schooner began to turn upon her heel, spinning slowly, end for end, across the current.

I wrought like a fiend, for I expected every moment to be swamped; and since I found I could not push the coracle directly off, I now shoved straight astern. At length I was clear of my dangerous neighbour; and just as I gave the last impulsion, my hands came across a light cord that was trailing overboard across the stern bulwarks. Instantly I grasped it.

Why I should have done so I can hardly say. It was at first mere instinct; but once I had it in my hands and found it fast, curiosity began to get the upper hand, and I determined I should have one look through the cabin window. I pulled in hand over hand on the cord, and, when I judged myself near enough, rose at infinite risk to about half my height, and thus commanded the roof and a slice of the interior of the cabin.

By this time the schooner and her little consort were gliding pretty swiftly through the water; indeed, we had already fetched up level with the camp fire. The ship was talking, as sailors say, loudly, treading the innumerable ripples with an incessant weltering splash; and until I got my eye above the window-sill I could not comprehend why the watchmen had taken no alarm. One glance, however, was sufficient; and it was only one glance that I durst take from that unsteady skiff. It showed me Hands and his companion locked together in deadly wrestle, each with a hand upon the other's throat.

I dropped upon the thwart again, none too soon, for I was near overboard. I could see nothing for the moment but these two furious, encrimsoned faces, swaying together under the smoky lamp; and I shut my eyes to let them grow once more familiar with the darkness.

The endless ballad had come to an end at last, and the whole diminished company about the camp fire had broken into the chorus I had heard so often:—

"Fifteen men on The Dead Man's Chest—
Yo-ho-ho, and a bottle of rum!
Drink and the devil had done for the rest—
Yo-ho-ho, and a bottle of rum!"

I was just thinking how busy drink and the devil were at that very moment in the cabin of the *Hispaniola*, when I was surprised by a sudden lurch of the coracle. At the same moment she yawed sharply and seemed to change her course. The speed in the meantime had greatly increased.

I opened my eyes at once. All round me were little ripples, combing over with a sharp, bristling sound and slightly phosphorescent. The *Hispaniola* herself, a few yards in whose wake I was still being whirled along, seemed to stagger in her course, and I saw her spars toss a little against the blackness of the night, nay, as I looked longer, I made sure she also was wheeling to the southward.

I glanced over my shoulder, and my heart jumped against my ribs. There, right behind me, was the glow of the camp fire. The current had turned at right angles, sweeping round along with it the tall schooner and the little dancing coracle; ever quickening, ever bubbling higher, ever muttering louder, it went spinning through the narrows for the open sea.

Suddenly the schooner in front of me gave a violent yaw, turning, perhaps, through twenty degrees; and almost at the same moment one shout followed another from on board; I could hear feet pounding on the companion ladder; and I knew that the two drunkards had at last been interrupted in their quarrel and awakened to a sense of their disaster.

I lay down flat in the bottom of that wretched skiff, and devoutly recommended my spirit to its Maker. At the end of the straits, I made sure we must fall into some bar of raging breakers, where all my troubles would be ended speedily; and though I could, perhaps, bear to die, I could not bear to look upon my fate as it approached.

So I must have lain for hours, continually beaten to and fro upon the billows, now and again wetted with flying sprays, and never ceasing to expect death at the next plunge. Gradually weariness grew upon me; a numbness, an occasional stupor, fell upon my mind even in the midst of my terrors; until sleep at last supervened, and in my sea-tossed coracle I lay and dreamed of home and the old Admiral Benbow.

CHAPTER XXIV

THE CRUISE OF THE CORACLE

IT was broad day when I awoke, and found myself tossing at the south-west end of Treasure Island. The sun was up, but was still hid from me behind the great bulk of the Spy-glass, which on this side descended almost to the sea in formidable cliffs.

Haulbowline Head and Mizzen-mast Hill were at my elbow; the hill bare and dark, the head bound with cliffs forty or fifty feet high, and fringed with great masses of fallen rock. I was scarce a quarter of a mile to seaward, and it was my first thought to paddle in and land.

That notion was soon given over. Among the fallen rocks the breakers spouted and bellowed; loud reverberations, heavy sprays flying and falling, succeeded one another from second to second; and I saw myself, if I ventured nearer, dashed to death upon the rough shore, or spending my strength in vain to scale the beetling crags.

Nor was that all; for crawling together on flat tables of rock, or letting themselves drop into the sea with loud reports, I beheld huge slimy monsters – soft snails, as it were, of incredible bigness – two or three score of them together, making the rocks to echo with their barkings.

I have understood since that they were sea-lions, and entirely harmless. But the look of them, added to the difficulty of the shore and the high running of the surf, was more than enough to disgust me of that landing-place. I felt willing rather to starve at

sea than to confront such perils.

In the meantime I had a better chance, as I supposed, before me. North of Haulbowline Head, the land runs in a long way, leaving, at low tide, a long stretch of yellow sand. To the north of that, again, there comes another cape – Cape of the Woods, as it was marked upon the chart – buried in tall green pines, which descended to the margin of the sea.

I remembered what Silver had said about the current that sets northward along the whole west coast of Treasure Island; and seeing from my position that I was already under its influence, I preferred to leave Haulbowline Head behind me, and reserve my strength for an attempt to land upon the kindlier-looking Cape of the Woods.

There was a great, smooth swell upon the sea. The wind blowing steady and gentle from the south, there was no contrariety between that and the current, and the billows rose and fell unbroken.

Had it been otherwise, I must long ago have perished; but as it was, it is surprising how easily and securely my little and light boat could ride. Often, as I still lay at the bottom, and kept no more than an eye above the gunwale, I would see a big blue summit heaving close above me; yet the coracle would but bounce a little, dance as if on springs, and subside on the other side into the trough as lightly as a bird.

I began after a little to grow very bold, and sat up to try my skill at paddling. But even a small change in the disposition of the weight will produce violent changes in the behaviour of a coracle. And I had hardly moved before the boat, giving up at once her gentle dancing movement, ran straight down a slope of water so steep that it made me giddy, and struck her nose with a spout of spray, deep into the side of the next wave.

I was drenched and terrified, and fell instantly back into my old position, whereupon the coracle seemed to find her head again, and led me as softly as before among the billows. It was plain she was not to be interfered with, and at that rate, since I could in no way influence her course, what hope had I left of reaching land?

I began to be horribly frightened, but I kept my head, for all that. First, moving with all care, I gradually baled out the coracle with my sea-cap; then getting my eye once more above the gun-wale, I set myself to study how it was she managed to slip so quietly through the rollers.

I found each wave, instead of the big, smooth glossy mountain it looks from shore, or from a vessel's deck, was for all the world like any range of

hills on the dry land, full of peaks and smooth places and valleys. The coracle, left to herself, turning from side to side, threaded, so to speak, her way through these lower parts and avoided the steep slopes and higher, toppling summits of the wave.

"Well, now," thought I to myself, "it is plain I must lie where I am, and not disturb the balance; but it is plain, also, that I can put the paddle over the side, and from time to time, in smooth places, give her a shove or two towards land." No sooner thought upon than done. There I lay on my elbows, in the most trying attitude, and every now and again gave a weak stroke or two to turn her head to shore.

It was very tiring, and slow work, yet I did visibly gain ground; and, as we drew near the Cape of the Woods, though I saw I must infallibly miss that point, I had still made some hundred yards of easting. I was, indeed, close in. I could see the cool, green tree-tops swaying together in the breeze, and I felt sure I should make the next promontory without fail.

It was high time, for I now began to be tortured with thirst. The glow of the sun from above, its thousandfold reflection from the waves, the sea-water that fell and dried upon me, caking my very lips with salt, combined to make my throat burn and my brain ache. The sight of the trees so near at hand had almost made me sick with longing; but the current had soon carried me past the point; and, as the next reach of sea opened out, I beheld a sight that changed the nature of my thoughts.

Right in front of me, not half a mile away, I beheld the *Hispaniola* under sail. I made sure, of course, that I should be taken; but I was so distressed for want of water, that I scarce knew whether to be glad or sorry at the thought; and, long before I had come to a conclusion, surprise had taken entire possession of my mind, and I could do nothing but stare and wonder.

The *Hispaniola* was under her main-sail and two jibs, and the beautiful white canvas shone in the sun like snow or silver. When I first sighted her, all her sails were drawing; she was lying a course about north-west; and I presumed the men on board were going round the island on their way back to the anchorage. Presently she began to fetch more and more to the westward, so that I thought they had sighted me and were going about in chase. At last, however, she fell right into the wind's eye, was taken dead aback, and stood there a while helpless with her sails shivering.

"Clumsy fellows," said I; "they must still be drunk as owls." And I thought how Captain Smollett would have set them skipping.

'Right in front of me, not half a mile away, I beheld the Hispaniola under sail.' (p. 133)

Meanwhile, the schooner gradually fell off, and filled again upon another tack, sailed swiftly for a minute or so, and brought up once more dead in the wind's eye. Again and again was this repeated. To and fro, up and down, north, south, east and west, the *Hispaniola* sailed by swoops and dashes, and at each repetition ended as she had begun, with idly-flapping canvas. It became plain to me that nobody was steering. And, if so, where were the men? Either they were dead drunk, or had deserted her, I thought, and perhaps if I could get on board, I might return the vessel to her captain.

The current was bearing coracle and schooner southward at an equal rate. As for the latter's sailing, it was so wild and intermittent, and she hung each time so long in irons, that she certainly gained nothing, if she did not even lose. If only I dared to sit up and paddle, I made sure that I could overhaul her. The scheme had an air of adventure that inspired me, and the thought of the water breaker beside the fore companion doubled my growing courage.

Up I got, was welcomed almost instantly by another cloud of spray, but this time stuck to my purpose; and set myself, with all my strength and caution, to paddle after the unsteered *Hispaniola*. Once I shipped a sea so heavy that I had to stop and bale, with my heart fluttering like a bird; but gradually I got into the way of the thing, and guided my coracle among the waves, with only now and then a blow upon her bows and a dash of foam in my face.

I was now gaining rapidly on the schooner; I could see the brass glisten on the tiller as it banged about; and still no soul appeared upon her decks. I could not choose but suppose she was deserted. If not, the men were lying drunk below, where I might batten them down, perhaps, and do what I chose with the ship.

For some time she had been doing the worst thing possible for me – standing still. She headed nearly due south, yawing, of course, all the time. Each time she fell off her sails partly filled, and these brought her, in a moment, right to the wind again. I have said this was the worst thing possible for me; for helpless as she looked in this situation, with the canvas cracking like cannon, and the blocks trundling and banging on the deck, she still continued to run away from me, not only with the speed of the current, but by the whole amount of her leeway, which was naturally great.

But now, at last, I had my chance. The breeze fell, for some seconds, very low, and the current gradually turning her, the *Hispaniola* revolved slowly round her centre, and at last presented me her stern, with the cabin window still gaping open, and the lamp over the table still burning on into the day. The main-sail hung drooped like a banner. She was stock-still, but for the current.

For the last little while I had even lost; but now redoubling my efforts, I began once more to overhaul the chase.

I was not a hundred yards from her when the wind came again in a clap; she filled on the port tack, and was off again, stooping and skimming like a swallow.

My first impulse was one of despair, but my second was towards joy. Round she came, till she was broadside on to me – round still till she had covered a half, and then two-thirds, and then three-quarters of the distance that separated us. I could see the waves boiling white under her forefoot. Immensely tall she looked to me from my low station in the coracle.

And then, of a sudden, I began to comprehend. I had scarce time to think – scarce time to act and save myself. I was on the summit of one swell when the schooner came swooping over the next. The bowsprit was over my head. I sprang to my feet, and leaped, stamping the coracle under water. With one hand I caught the jib-boom, while my foot was lodged between the stay and the brace; and as I still clung there panting, a dull blow told me that the schooner had charged down upon and struck the coracle, and that I was left without retreat on the *Hispaniola.*

CHAPTER XXV

I STRIKE THE JOLLY ROGER

I HAD scarce gained a position on the bowsprit, when the flying jib flapped and filled upon the other tack, with a report like a gun. The schooner trembled to her keel under the reverse; but next moment, the other sails still drawing, the jib flapped back again, and hung idle.

This had nearly tossed me off into the sea; and now I lost no time, crawled back along the bowsprit, and tumbled head foremost on the deck.

I was on the lee-side of the forecastle, and the main-sail, which was still drawing, concealed from me a certain portion of the after-deck. Not a soul was to be seen. The planks, which had not been swabbed since the mutiny, bore the print of many feet; and an empty bottle, broken by the neck, tumbled to and fro like a live thing in the scuppers.

Suddenly the *Hispaniola* came right into the wind. The jibs behind me cracked aloud; the rudder slammed to; the whole ship gave a sickening heave and shudder, and at the same moment the main-boom swung inboard, the sheet groaning in the blocks, and showed me the lee after-deck.

There were the two watchmen, sure enough; red-cap on his back, as stiff as a handspike, with his arms stretched out like those of a crucifix, and his teeth showing through his open lips; Israel Hands propped against the bulwarks, his chin on his chest, his hands lying open before him on the deck, his face as white, under its tan, as a tallow candle.

For a while the ship kept bucking and sidling like a vicious horse, the sails filling, now on one tack, now on another, and the boom swinging to and fro till the mast groaned aloud under the strain. Now and again, too, there would come a cloud of light sprays over the bulwark, and a heavy blow of the ship's bows against the swell; so much heavier weather was made of it by this great rigged ship than by my home-made, lop-sided coracle, now gone to the bottom of the sea.

At every jump of the schooner, red-cap slipped to and fro; but – what was ghastly to behold – neither his attitude nor his fixed teeth-disclosing grin was anyway disturbed by this rough usage. At every jump, too, Hands appeared still more to sink into himself and settle down upon the deck, his feet sliding ever the farther out, and the whole body canting towards the stern, so that his face became, little by little, hid from me; and at last I could see nothing beyond his ear and the frayed ringlet of one whisker.

And at the same time, I observed around both of them, splashes of dark blood upon the planks, and began to feel sure that they had killed each other in their drunken wrath.

While I was thus looking and wondering, in a calm moment, when the ship was still, Israel Hands turned partly round and, with a low moan, writhed himself back to the position in which I had seen him first. The moan, which told of pain and deadly weakness and the way in which his jaw hung open, went right to my heart. But when I remembered the talk I had overheard from the apple barrel, all pity left me.

I walked aft until I reached the mainmast.

"Come aboard, Mr. Hands," I said iron-ically. He rolled his eyes round heavily; but he was too far gone to express surprise. All he could do was to utter one word, "Brandy."

It occurred to me there was no time to lose; and, dodging the boom as it once more lurched across the deck, I slipped aft, and down the companion-stairs into the cabin.

It was such a scene of confusion as you can hardly fancy. All the lock-fast places had been broken open in quest of the chart. The floor was thick with mud, where ruffians had sat down to drink or consult after wading in the marshes round their camp. The bulkheads, all painted in clear white, and beaded round with gilt, bore a pattern of dirty hands. Dozens of empty bottles clinked together in corners to the rolling of the ship. One of the doctor's medical books lay open on the table, half of the leaves gutted out, I suppose, for pipelights. In the midst of all this the lamp still cast a smoky glow, obscure and brown as umber.

I went into the cellar; all the barrels were gone, and of the bottles a most surprising number had been drunk out and thrown away. Certainly, since the mutiny began, not a man of them could ever have been sober.

Foraging about, I found a bottle with some brandy left, for Hands; and for myself I routed out some biscuit, some pickled fruits, a great bunch of raisins, and a piece of cheese. With these I came on deck, put down my own stock

'"Come aboard Mr. Hands," I said ironically.' *(p. 138)*

behind the rudder-head,, and well out of the coxswain's reach, went forward to the water-breaker, and had a good, deep drink of water, and then, and not till then, gave Hands the brandy.

He must have drunk a gill before he took the bottle from his mouth.

"Ay," said he, "by thunder, but I wanted some o' that!"

I had sat down already in my own corner and began to eat.

"Much hurt?" I asked him.

He grunted, or rather, I might say, he barked.

"If that doctor was aboard," he said, "I'd be right enough in a couple of turns; but I don't have no manner of luck, you see, and that's what's the matter with me. As for that swab, he's good as dead, he is," he added, indicating the man with the red cap. "He warn't no seaman, anyhow. And where might you have come from?"

"Well," said I, "I've come aboard to take possession of this ship, Mr. Hands; and you'll please regard me as your captain until further notice."

He looked at me sourly enough, but said nothing. Some of the colour had come back into his cheeks, though he still looked very sick, and still continued to slip out and settle down as the ship banged about.

"By the bye," I continued, "I can't have these colours, Mr. Hands; and, by your leave, I'll strike 'em. Better none than these."

And, again dodging the boom, I ran to the colour lines, handed down their cursed black flag, and chucked it overboard.

"God save the king!" said I, waving my cap; "and there's an end to Captain Silver!" He watched me keenly and slyly, his chin all the while on his breast.

"I reckon," he said at last; "I reckon Cap'n Hawkins, you'll kind of want to get ashore, now. S'pose we talks."

"Why, yes," said I, "with all my heart, Mr. Hands. Say on." And I went back to my meal with a good appetite.

"This man," he began, nodding feebly at the corpse "O'Brien were his name – a rank Irelander – this man and me got the canvas on her, meaning for to sail her back. Well, *he's* dead now, he is – as dead as bilge; and who's to sail this ship, I don't see. Without I gives you a hint, you ain't that man, as far's I can tell. Now, look here, you give me food and drink, and a old scarf or ankecher to tie my wound up, you do; and I'll tell you how to sail her; and that's about square all round, I take it."

"I'll tell you one thing," says I; "I'm not going back to Captain Kidd's anchorage. I mean to get into North Inlet, and beach her quietly there."

"To be sure you did," he cried. "Why, I ain't sich an infernal lubber, after all. I can see, can't I? I've tried my fling, I have, and I've lost, and it's you has the wind of me. North Inlet? Why, I haven't no ch'ice, not I! I'd help you sail her up to Execution Dock, by thunder! so I would."

Well, as it seemed to me, there was some sense in this. We struck our bargain on the spot. In three minutes I had the *Hispaniola* sailing easily before the wind along the coast of Treasure Island, with good hopes of turning the northern point ere noon, and beating down again as far as North Inlet before high water, when we might beach her safely, and wait till the subsiding tide permitted us to land. Then I lashed the tiller and went below to my own chest, where I got a soft silk handkerchief of my mother's. With

this, and with my aid, Hands bound up the great bleeding stab he had received in the thigh, and after he had eaten a little, and had a swallow or two more of the brandy, he began to pick up visibly, sat straighter up, spoke louder and clearer, and looked in every way another man.

The breeze served us admirably. We skimmed before it like a bird, the coast of the island flashing by, and the view changing every minute. Soon we were past the high lands and bowling beside low, sandy country, sparsely dotted with dwarf pines, and soon we were beyond that again, and had turned the corner of the rocky hill that ends the island on the north.

I was greatly elated with my new command, and pleased with the bright, sunshiny weather and these different prospects of the coast. I had now plenty of water and good things to eat, and my conscience, which had smitten me hard for my desertion, was quieted by the great conquest I had made. I should, I think, have had nothing left me to desire but for the eyes of the coxswain as they followed me derisively about the deck, and the odd smile that appeared continually on his face. It was a smile that had in it something both of pain and weakness – a haggard, old man's smile; but there was, besides that, a grain of derision, a shadow of treachery, in his expression as he craftily watched, and watched, and watched me at my work.

CHAPTER XXVI

ISRAEL HANDS

THE wind, serving us to a desire, now hauled into the west. We could run so much the easier from the north-east corner of the island to the mouth of the North Inlet. Only, as we had no power to anchor, and dared not beach her till the tide had flowed a good deal farther, time hung on our hands. The coxswain told me how to lay the ship to; after a good many trials I succeeded, and we both sat in silence, over another meal.

"Cap'n," said he at length, with that same uncomfortable smile, "here's my old shipmate, O'Brien; s'pose you was to heave him overboard. I ain't partic'lar as a rule, and I don't take no blame for settling his hash; but I don't reckon him ornamental now, do you?"

"I'm not strong enough, and I don't like the job; and there he lies, for me," said I.

"This here's an unlucky ship – this *Hispaniola*, Jim," he went on, blinking. "There's a power of men been killed in this *Hispaniola* – a sight o' poor seamen dead and gone since you and me took ship to Bristol. I never seen sich dirty luck, not I. There was this here O'Brien, now – he's dead, ain't he? Well, now, I'm no scholar, and you're a lad as can read and figure; and to put it straight, do you take it as a dead man is dead for good, or do he come alive again?"

"You can kill the body, Mr. Hands, but not the spirit; you must know that already," I replied. "O'Brien there is in another world, and maybe watching us."

"Ah !," says he. "Well, that's unfort'nate – appears as if killing parties was a waste of time. Howsomever, sperrits don't reckon for much, by what I've seen. I'll chance it with the sperrits, Jim. And now, you've spoke up free, and I'll take it kind if you'd step down into that there cabin and get me a – well, a – shiver my timbers! I can't hit the name on't; well, you get me a bottle of wine, Jim – this here brandy's too strong for my head."

Now, the coxswain's hesitation seemed to be unnatural; and as for the notion of his preferring wine to brandy, I entirely disbelieved it. The whole story was a pretext. He wanted me to leave the deck – so much was plain; but with what purpose I could in no way imagine. His eyes never met mine; they kept wandering to and fro, up and down, now with a look to the sky, now with a flitting glance upon the dead O'Brien. All the time he kept smiling, and putting his tongue out in the most guilty, embarrassed manner, so that a child could have told that he was bent on some deception. I was prompt with my answer, however, for I saw where my advantage lay; and that with a fellow so densely stupid I could easily conceal my suspicions to the end.

"Some wine?" I said. "Far better. Will you have white or red?"

"Well, I reckon it's about the blessed same to me, shipmate," he replied; "so it's strong, and plenty of it, what's the odds?"

"All right," I answered. "I'll bring you port, Mr. Hands. But I'll have to dig for it."

With that I scuttled down the companion with all the noise I could, slipped off my shoes, ran quietly along the sparred gallery, mounted the forecastle ladder, and popped my head out of the fore companion. I knew he would not expect to see me there; yet I took every precaution possible; and certainly the worst of my suspicions proved too true.

He had risen from his position to his hands and knees; and, though his leg obviously hurt him pretty sharply when he moved – for I could hear him stifle a groan – yet it was at a good, rattling rate that he trailed himself across the deck. In half a minute he had reached the port cuppers, and picked, out of a coil of rope, a long knife, or rather a short dirk, discoloured to the hilt with blood. He looked upon it for a moment, thrusting forth his under jaw, tried the point upon his hand, and then, hastily concealing it in the bosom of his jacket, trundled back again into his old place against the bulwark.

That was all that I required to know. Israel could move about; he was now armed; and if he had been at so much trouble to get rid of me, it was plain that I was meant to be the victim. What he would do afterwards – whether he would try to crawl right across the island from North Inlet to the camp among the swamps, or whether he would fire Long Tom, trusting that his own comrades might come first to help him, was, of course, more than I could say.

Yet I felt sure that I could trust him in one point, since in that our interests jumped together, and that was in the disposition of the schooner. We both desired to have her stranded safe enough, in a sheltered place, and so that, when the time came, she could be got off again with as little labour and danger as might be; and until that was done I considered that my life would certainly be spared.

While I was thus turning the business over in my mind, I had not been idle with my body. I had stolen back to the cabin, slipped once more into my shoes, and laid my hand at random on a bottle of wine, and now, with this for an excuse, I made my reappearance on the deck.

Hands lay as I had left him, all fallen together in a bundle, and with his eyelids lowered, as though he were too weak to bear the light. He looked up, however, at my coming, knocked the neck off the bottle, like a man who had done the same thing often, and took a good swig, with his favourite toast of "Here's luck!" Then he lay quiet for a little, and then, pulling out a stick of tobacco, begged me to cut him a quid.

"Cut me a junk o' that," says he, "for I haven't no knife, and hardly strength enough, so be as I had. Ah, Jim, Jim, I reckon I've missed stays! Cut me a quid, as'll likely be the last, lad; for I'm for my long home, and no mistake."

"Well," said I, "I'll cut you some tobacco; but if I was you and thought myself so badly, I would go to my prayers, like a Christian man."

"Why?" said he. "Now, you tell me why."

"Why?" I cried. "You were asking me just now about the dead. You've broken your trust; you've lived in sin and lies and blood; there's a man you killed lying at your feet this moment; and you ask me why! For God's mercy, Mr. Hands, that's why."

I spoke with a little heat, thinking of the bloody dirk he had hidden in his pocket, and designed, in his ill thoughts, to end me with. He, for his part, took a great draught of the wine, and spoke with the most unusual solemnity.

"For thirty years," he said, "I've sailed the seas, and seen good and bad, better and worse, fair weather and foul, provisions running out, knives going, and what not. Well, now, I tell you, I never seen good come o' goodness yet. Him as strikes first is my fancy; dead men don't bite; them's my views – amen, so be it. And now, you look here," he added, suddenly changing his tone, "we've had about enough of this foolery. The tide's made good enough by now. You just take my orders, Cap'n Hawkins, and we'll sail slap in and be done with it."

All told, we had scarce two miles to run; but the navigation was delicate, the entrance to this northern anchorage was not only narrow and shoal, but lay east and west, so that the schooner must be nicely handled to be got in. I think I was a good, prompt subaltern, and I am very sure that Hands was an excellent pilot; for we went about and about, and dodged in, shaving the banks, with a certainty and a neatness that were a pleasure to behold.

Scarcely had we passed the heads before the land closed around us. The shores of North Inlet were as thickly wooded as those of the southern anchorage; but the space was longer and narrower, and more like, what in truth it was, the estuary of a river. Right before us, at the southern end we saw the wreck of a ship in the last stages of dilapidation. It had been a great vessel of three masts, but had lain so long exposed to the injuries of the weather, that it was hung about with great webs of dripping seaweed, and on the deck of it shore bushes had taken root, and now flourished thick with flowers. It was a sad sight, but it showed us that the anchorage was calm.

"Now," said Hands, "look there; there's a pet bit for to beach a ship in. Fine flat sand, never a catspaw, trees all around of it, and flowers a-blooming like a garding on that old ship."

"And once beached," I inquired, "how shall we get her off again?"

"Why, so," he replied; "you take a line ashore there on the other side at low water; take a turn about one o' them big pines; bring it back, take a turn around the capstan, and lie-to for the tide. Come high water, all hands take a pull upon the line, and off she comes as sweet as natur'. And now, boy, you stand by. We're near the bit now, and she's too much way on her. Starboard a little – so – steady – starboard – larboard a little – steady – steady!"

So he issued his commands, which I breathlessly obeyed; till all of a sudden, he cried, "Now, my hearty, luff!" And I put the helm hard up, and the *Hispaniola* swung round rapidly, and ran stem on for the low wooded shore.

'I put the helm hard up, and the Hispaniola swung round rapidly, and ran stem on for the low wooded shore.' (p. 145)

The excitement of these last manoeuvres had somewhat interfered with the watch I had kept hitherto, sharply enough, upon the coxswain. Even then I was still so much interested, waiting for the ship to touch, that I had quite forgot the peril that hung over my head, and stood craning over the starboard bulwarks and watching the ripples spreading wide before the bows. I might have fallen without a struggle for my life, had not a sudden disquietude seized upon me, and made me turn my head. Perhaps I had heard a creak, or seen his shadow moving with the tail of my eye; perhaps it was an instinct like a cat's; but, sure enough, when I looked round, there was Hands, already half-way towards me, with the dirk in his right hand.

We must both have cried out aloud when our eyes met; but while mine was the shrill cry of terror, his was a roar of fury like a charging bull's. At the same instant he threw himself forward, and I leapt sideways towards the bows. As I did so, I left hold of the tiller, which sprang sharp to leeward; and I think this saved my life, for it struck Hands across the chest, and stopped him, for the moment, dead.

Before he could recover, I was safe out of the corner where he had me trapped, with all the deck to dodge about. Just forward of the mainmast I stopped, drew a pistol from my pocket, took a cool aim, though he had already turned and was once more coming directly after me, and drew the trigger. The hammer fell, but there followed neither flash nor sound; the priming was useless with sea water. I cursed myself for my neglect. Why had not I, long before, reprimed and reloaded my only weapons? Then I should not have been, as now, a mere fleeing sheep before this butcher.

Wounded as he was, it was wonderful how fast he could move, his grizzled hair tumbling over his face, and his face itself as red as a red ensign with his haste and fury. I had no time to try my other pistol, nor, indeed, much inclination, for I was sure it would be useless. One thing I saw plainly; I must not simply retreat before him, or he would speedily hold me boxed into the bows, as a moment since he had so nearly boxed me in the stern. Once so caught, and nine or ten inches of the blood-stained dirk would be my last experience on this side of eternity. I placed my palms against the mainmast, which was of a goodish bigness, and waited, every nerve upon the stretch.

Seeing that I meant to dodge, he also paused; and a moment or two passed in feints on his part, and corresponding movements upon mine. It was such a game as I had often played at home about the rocks of Black Hill Cove; but never before, you may be sure, with such a wildly beating heart as now. Still, as I say, it was a boy's game, and I thought I could hold my own at it, against an elderly seaman with a wounded thigh. Indeed, my courage had begun to rise so high, that I allowed myself a few darting thoughts on what would be the end of the affair; and while I saw certainly that I could spin it out for long, I saw no hope of any ultimate escape.

Well, while things stood thus, suddenly the *Hispaniola* struck, staggered, ground for an instant in the sand, and then, swift as a blow, canted over to the port side, till the deck stood at an angle of forty-five degrees, and about a puncheon of water splashed into the scupper holes, and lay, in a pool, between the deck and bulwark.

We were both of us capsized in a second, and both of us rolled, almost together, into the scuppers; the dead red-cap, with his arms still spread out, tumbling stiffly after us. So near were we, indeed, that my head came against the coxswain's foot with a crack that made my teeth rattle. Blow and all, I was the first afoot again; for Hands had got involved with the dead body. The sudden canting of the ship had made the deck no place for running on; I had to find some new way of escape, and that upon the instant, for my foe was almost touching me. Quick as thought I sprang into the mizzen shrouds, rattled up hand over hand, and did not draw a breath till I was seated on the cross-trees.

I had been saved by being prompt; the dirk had struck not half a foot below me, as I pursued my upward flight; and there stood Israel Hands, with his mouth open and his face upturned to mine, a perfect statue of surprise and disappointment.

Now that I had a moment to myself, I lost no time in changing the priming of my pistol, and then, having one ready for service, and to make assurance doubly sure, I proceeded to draw the load of the other, and recharge it afresh from the beginning.

My new employment struck Hands all of a heap; he began to see the dice going against him; and after an obvious hesitation, he also hauled himself heavily into the shrouds, and, with the dirk in his teeth, began slowly and painfully to mount. It cost him no end of time and groans to haul his wounded leg behind him; and I had quietly finished my arrangements before he was much more than a third of the way up. Then, with a pistol in either hand, I addressed him.

"One more step, Mr. Hands," said I, "and I'll blow your brains out! Dead men don't bite, you know," I added, with a chuckle.

' "One more step, Mr. Hands," said I, "and I'll blow your brains out." ' (p. 148)

He stopped instantly. I could see by the working of his face that he was trying to think, and the process was so slow and laborious that, in my new-found security, I laughed aloud. At last, with a swallow or two, he spoke, his face still wearing the same expression of extreme perplexity. In order to speak he had to take the dagger from his mouth, but, in all else, he remained unmoved.

"Jim," says he, "I reckon we're fouled, you and me, and we'll have to sign articles. I'd have had you but for that there lurch; but I don't have no luck, not I; and I reckon I'll have to strike, which comes hard, you see, for a master mariner to a ship's younker like you, Jim."

I was drinking in his words and smiling away, as conceited as a cock upon a wall, when, all in a breath, back went his right hand, over his shoulder. Something sang like an arrow through the air: I felt a blow and then a sharp pang, and there I was pinned by the shoulder to the mast. In the horrid pain and surprise of the moment – I scarce can say it was by my own volition, and I am sure it was without a conscious aim – both my pistols went off, and both escaped out of my hands. They did not fall alone; with a choked cry, the coxswain loosed his grasp upon the shrouds, and plunged head first into the water.

CHAPTER XXVII

"PIECES OF EIGHT!"

OWING to the cant of the vessel, the masts hung far out over the water, and from my perch on the cross-trees I had nothing below me but the surface of the bay. Hands, who was not so far up, was, in consequence, nearer to the ship, and fell between me and the bulwarks. He rose once to the surface in a lather of foam and blood, and then sank again for good. As the water settled I could see him lying huddled together on the clean, bright sand in the shadow of the vessel's sides. A fish or two whipped past his body. Sometimes, by the quivering of the water, he appeared to move a little, as if he were trying to rise. But he was dead enough, for all that, being both shot and drowned, and was food for fish in the very place where he had designed my slaughter.

I was no sooner certain of this than I began to feel sick, faint, and terrified. The hot blood was running over my back and chest. The dirk, where it had pinned my shoulder to the mast, seemed to burn like a hot iron; yet it was not so much these real sufferings that distressed me, for these, it seemed to me, I could bear without a murmur; it was the horror I had upon my mind of falling from the cross-trees into that still green water, beside the body of the coxswain.

I clung with both hands till my nails ached, and I shut my eyes as if to cover up the peril. Gradually my mind came back again, my pulses quieted down to a more natural time, and I was once more in possession of myself.

It was my first thought to pluck forth the dirk; but either it stuck too hard or my nerve failed me; and I desisted with a violent shudder. Oddly enough, that very shudder did the business. The knife, in fact, had come the nearest in the world to missing me altogether; it held me by a mere pinch of skin, and this the shudder tore away. The blood ran down the faster, to be sure; but I was my own master again, and only tacked to the mast by my coat and shirt.

'I took him by the waist as if he had been a sack of bran, and, with one good heave, tumbled him overboard.' (p. 153)

These last I broke through with a sudden jerk, and then regained the deck by the starboard shrouds. For nothing in the world would I have again ventured, shaken as I was, upon the overhanging port shrouds, from which Israel had so lately fallen.

I went below, and did what I could for my wound; it pained me a good deal, and still bled freely; but it was neither deep nor dangerous, nor did it greatly gall me when I used my arm. Then I looked around me, and as the ship was now, in a sense, my own, I began to think of clearing it from its last passenger – the dead man O'Brien.

He had pitched, as I have said, against the bulwarks, where he lay like some horrible, ungainly sort of puppet; life-sized, indeed, but how different from life's colour or life's comeliness! In that position, I could easily have my way with him; and as the habit of tragical adventures had worn off almost all my terror for the dead, I took him by the waist as if he had been a sack of bran, and, with one good heave, tumbled him overboard. He went in with a sounding plunge; the red cap came off, and remained floating on the surface; and as soon as the splash subsided, I could see him and Israel lying side by side, both wavering with the tremulous movement of the water. O'Brien, though still quite a young man, was very bald. There he lay, with that bald head across the knees of the man who had killed him, and the quick fishes steering to and fro over both.

I was now alone upon the ship; the tide had just turned. The sun was within so few degrees of setting that already the shadow of the pines upon the western shore began to reach right across the anchorage, and fall in patterns on the deck. The evening breeze had sprung up, and though it was well warded off by the hill with the two peaks upon the east, the cordage had begun to sing a little softly to itself and the idle sails to rattle to and fro.

I began to see a danger to the ship. The jibs I speedily doused and brought tumbling to the deck; but the mainsail was a harder matter. Of course, when the schooner canted over, the boom had swung out-board, and the cap of it and a foot or two of sail hung even under water. I thought this made it still more dangerous; yet the strain was so heavy that I half feared to meddle. At last, I got my knife and cut the halyards. The peak dropped instantly, a great belly of loose canvas floated broad upon the water; and since, pull as I liked, I could not budge the downhaul, that was the extent of what I could accomplish. For the rest, the *Hispaniola* must trust to luck, like myself.

By this time the whole anchorage had fallen into shadow – the last rays, I remember, falling through a glade of the wood, and shining bright as jewels, on the flowery mantle of the wreck. It began to be chill; the tide was rapidly fleeting seaward, the schooner settling more and more on her beam-ends.

I scrambled forward and looked over. It seemed shallow enough, and holding the cut hawser in both hands for a last security, I let myself drop softly overboard. The water scarcely reached my waist; the sand was firm and covered with ripple marks, and I waded ashore in great spirits, leaving the *Hispaniola* on her side, with her mainsail trailing wide upon the surface of the bay. About the same time the sun went fairly down, and the breeze whistled low in the dusk among the tossing pines.

At least, and at last, I was off the sea, nor had I returned thence empty-handed. There lay the schooner, clear at last from buccaneers and ready for our own men to board and get to sea again. I had nothing nearer my fancy than to get home to the stockade and boast of my achievements. Possibly I might be blamed a bit for my truantry, but the recapture of the *Hispaniola* was a clenching answer, and I hoped that even Captain Smollett would confess I had not lost my time.

So thinking, and in famous spirits, I began to set my face homeward for the blockhouse and my companions. I remembered that the most easterly of the rivers which drain into Captain Kidd's anchorage ran from the two-peaked hill upon my left; and I bent my course in that direction that I might pass the stream while it was small. The wood was pretty open, and keeping along the lower spurs, I had soon turned the corner of that hill, and not long after waded to the mid-calf across the water-course.

This brought me near to where I had encountered Ben Gunn, the maroon; and I walked more circumspectly, keeping an eye on every side. The dusk had come nigh hand completely, and as I opened out the cleft between the two peaks, I became aware of a wavering glow against the sky, where, as I judged, the man of the island was cooking his supper before a roaring fire. And yet I wondered, in my heart, that he should show himself so careless. For if I could see this

radiance, might it not reach the eyes of Silver himself where he camped upon the shore among the marshes?

Gradually the night fell blacker; it was all I could do to guide myself even roughly towards my destination; the double hill behind me and the Spy-glass on my right loomed faint and fainter; the stars were few and pale; and in the low ground where I wandered I kept tripping among bushes and rolling into sandy pits.

Suddenly a kind of brightness fell about me. I looked up; a pale glimmer of moonbeams had alighted on the summit of the Spy-glass, and soon after I saw something broad and silvery moving low down behind the trees, and knew the moon had risen.

With this to help me, I passed rapidly over what remained to me of my journey; and, sometimes walking, sometimes running, impatiently drew near to the stockade. Yet, as I began to thread the grove that lies before it, I was not so thoughtless but that I slacked my pace and went a trifle warily. It would have been a poor end of my adventures to get shot down by my own party in mistake.

The moon was climbing higher and higher; its light began to fall here and there in masses through the more open districts of the wood; and right in front of me a glow of a different colour appeared among the trees. It was red and hot, and now and again it was a little darkened – as it were the embers of a bonfire smouldering.

For the life of me, I could not think what it might be.

At last I came right down upon the borders of the clearing. The western end was already steeped in moonshine; the rest, and the blockhouse itself, still lay in a black shadow, chequered with long, silvery streaks of light. On the other side of the house an immense fire had burned itself into clear embers and shed a steady, red reverberation, contrasted strongly with the mellow paleness of the moon. There was not a soul stirring, nor a sound beside the noises of the breeze.

I stopped, with much wonder in my heart, and perhaps a little terror also. It had not been our way to build great fires; we were, indeed, by the captain's orders, somewhat niggardly of firewood; and I began to fear that something had gone wrong while I was absent.

I stole round by the eastern end, keeping close in shadow, and at a convenient place, where the darkness was thickest, crossed the palisade.

To make assurance surer, I got upon my hands and knees, and crawled, without a sound, towards the corner of the house. As I drew nearer, my heart was suddenly and greatly lightened. It is not a pleasant noise in itself, and I have often complained of it at other times; but just then it was like music to hear my friends snoring together so loud and peaceful in their sleep. The sea cry of the watch, that beautiful "All's well," never fell more reassuringly on my ear.

In the meantime, there was no doubt of one thing; they kept an infamous bad watch. If it had been Silver and his lads that were now creeping in on them, not a soul would have seen daybreak. That was what it was, thought I, to have the captain wounded; and again I blamed myself sharply for leaving them in that danger with so few to mount guard.

By this time I had got to the door and stood up. All was dark within, so that I could distinguish nothing by the eye. As for sounds, there was the steady drone of the snorers, and a small occasional noise, a flickering or pecking that I could in no way account for.

With my arms before me I walked steadily in. I should lie down in my own place (I thought, with a silent chuckle) and enjoy their faces when they found me in the morning.

My foot struck something yielding – it was a sleeper's leg; and he turned and groaned, but without awakening.

And then, all of a sudden, a shrill voice broke forth out of the darkness:—

"Pieces of eight! pieces of eight! pieces of eight! pieces of eight! pieces of eight!" and so forth, without pause or change, like the clacking of a tiny mill.

Silver's green parrot, Captain Flint! It was she whom I had heard pecking at a piece of bark; it was she, keeping better watch than any human being, who thus announced my arrival with her wearisome refrain.

I had no time left me to recover. At the sharp, clipping tone of the parrot, the sleepers awoke and sprang up; and with a mighty oath, the voice of Silver cried:—

"Who goes?"

I turned to run, struck violently against one person, recoiled, and ran full into the arms of a second, who, for his part, closed upon and held me tight.

"Bring a torch, Dick," said Silver, when my capture was thus assured.

And one of the men left the log-house and presently returned with a lighted brand.

PART VI CAPTAIN SILVER

CHAPTER XXVIII

IN THE ENEMY'S CAMP

THE red glare of the torch, lighting up the interior of the blockhouse, showed me the worst of my apprehensions realised. The pirates were in possession of the house and stores; there was the cask of cognac, there were the pork and bread, as before; and, what tenfold increased my horror, not a sign of any prisoner. I could only judge that all had perished, and my heart smote me sorely that I had not been there to perish with them.

There were six of the buccaneers, all told; not another man was left alive. Five of them were on their feet, flushed and swollen, suddenly called out of the first sleep of drunkenness. The sixth had only risen upon his elbow: he was deadly pale, and the blood-stained bandage round his head told that he had recently been wounded, and still more recently dressed. I remembered the man who had been shot and had run back among the woods in the great attack, and doubted not that this was he.

The parrot sat, preening her plumage, on Long John's shoulder. He himself, I thought, looked somewhat paler and more stern than I was used to. He still wore the fine broadcloth suit in which he had fulfilled his mission, but it was bitterly the worse for wear, daubed with clay and torn with the sharp briers of the wood.

"So," said he, "here's Jim Hawkins, shiver my timbers! dropped in, like, eh? Well, come, I take that friendly."

And thereupon he sat down across the brandy cask, and began to fill a pipe.

"Give me a loan of the link, Dick," said he; and then, when he had a good light, "that'll do, lad," he added; "stick the glim in the wood heap; and you, gentlemen, bring yourselves to! – you needn't stand up for Mr. Hawkins; *he'll* excuse you, you may lay to that. And so, Jim" – stopping the tobacco – "here you were, and quite a pleasant surprise for poor old John. I see you were smart when first I set my eyes on you; but this here gets away from me clean, it do."

To all this, as may be well supposed, I made no answer. They had set me with my back against the wall; and I stood there, looking Silver in the face, pluckily enough, I hope, to all outward appearance, but with black despair in my heart.

Silver took a whiff or two of his pipe with great composure, and then ran on again.

"Now, you see, Jim, so be as you are here," says he "I'll give you a piece of my mind. I've always liked you, I have, for a lad of spirit, and the picter of my own self when I was young and handsome. I always wanted you to jine and take your share, and die a gentleman, and now, my cock, you've got to. Cap'n Smollett's a fine seaman, as I'll own up to any day, but stiff on discipline. 'Dooty is dooty,' says he, and right he is. Just you keep clear of the cap'n. The doctor himself is gone dead again you – 'ungrateful scamp' was what he said; and the short and the long of the whole story is about here: you can't go back to your own lot, for they won't have you; and, without you start a third ship's company all by yourself, which might be lonely, you'll have to jine with Captain Silver."

So far so good. My friends, then, were still alive, and though I partly believed the truth of Silver's statement, that the cabin party were incensed at me for my desertion, I was more relieved than distressed by what I heard.

"I don't say nothing as to your being in our hands," continued Silver, "though there you are, and you may lay to it. I'm all for argyment; I never seen good come out o' threatening. If you like the service, well, you'll jine; and if you don't, Jim, why, you're free to answer no – free and welcome, shipmate; and if fairer can be said by mortal seaman, shiver my sides!"

"Am I to answer, then?" I asked, with a very tremulous voice. Through all this sneering talk, I was made to feel the threat of death that overhung me, and my cheeks burned and my heart beat painfully in my breast.

"Lad," said Silver, "no one's a-pressing of you. Take your bearings. None of us won't hurry you, mate; time goes so pleasant in your company, you see."

"Well," says I, growing a bit bolder, "if I'm to choose, I declare I have a right to know what's what, and why you're here, and where my friends are."

"Wot's wot?" repeated one of the buccaneers, in a deep growl. "Ah, he'd be a lucky one as knowed that!"

"You'll, perhaps, batten down your hatches till you're spoke, my friend," cried Silver truculently to this speaker. And then, in his first gracious tones,

he replied to me: "Yesterday morning, Mr. Hawkins," said he, "in the dog-watch, down came Doctor Livesey with a flag of truce. Says he, 'Cap'n Silver, you're sold out. Ship's gone.' Well, maybe we'd been taking a glass, and a song to help it round. I won't say no. Leastways none of us had looked out. We looked out, and, by thunder! the old ship was gone. I never seen a pack o' fools look fishier; and you may lay to that, if I tells you that looked the fishiest. 'Well,' says the doctor 'let's bargain.' We bargained, him and I, and here we are: stores, brandy, blockhouse, the firewood you was thoughtful enough to cut, and, in a manner of speaking, the whole blessed boat, from cross-trees to keelson. As for them, they've tramped; I don't know where's they are."

He again drew quietly at his pipe.

"And lest you should take it into that head of yours," he went on, "that you was included in the treaty, here's the last word that was said: 'How many are you,' says I, 'to leave?' 'Four,' says he – 'four, and one of us wounded. As for that boy, I don't know where he is, confound him,' says he, 'nor I don't much care. We're about sick of him.' These was his words."

"Is that all?" I asked.

"Well, it's all that you're to hear, my son," returned Silver.

"And now I am to choose?"

"And now you are to choose, and you may lay to that," said Silver.

"Well," said I, "I am not such a fool but I know pretty well what I have to look for. Let the worst come to the worst, it's little I care. I've seen too many die since I fell in with you. But there's a thing or two I have to tell you," I said, and by this time I was quite excited; "and the first is this: here you are, in a bad way: ship lost, treasure lost, men lost; your whole business gone to wreck; and if you want to know who did it – it was I! I was in the apple barrel the night we sighted land, and I heard you, John, and you, Dick Johnson, and Hands, who is now at the bottom of the sea, and told every word you said before the hour was out. And as for the schooner, it was I who cut her cable, and it was I that killed the men you had aboard of her, and it was I who brought her where you'll never see her more, not one of you. The laugh's on my side; I've had the top of this business from the first; I no more fear you than I fear a fly. Kill me, if you please, or spare me. But one thing I'll say, and no more; if you spare me, bygones are bygones, and when you fellows are in court for piracy, I'll save you all I can. It is for you to choose. Kill another and do yourselves no good, or spare me and keep a witness to save you from the gallows."

I stopped, for, I tell you, I was out of breath, and, to my wonder, not a man of them moved, but all sat staring at me like as many sheep. And while they were still staring, I broke out again:—

"And now, Mr. Silver," I said, "I believe you're the best man here, and if things go the worst, I'll take it kind of you to let the doctor know the way I took it."

"I'll bear it in mind," said Silver, with an accent so curious that I could not, for the life of me, decide whether he were laughing at my request, or had been favourably affected by my courage.

"I'll put one to that," cried the old mahogany-faced seaman – Morgan by name – whom I had seen in Long John's public-house upon the quays of Bristol. "It was him that knowed Black Dog."

"Well, and see here," added the sea-cook, "I'll put another again to that, by thunder! For it was this same boy that faked the chart from Billy Bones. First and last, we've split upon Jim Hawkins!"

"Then here goes!" said Morgan, with an oath. And he sprang up, drawing his knife as if he had been twenty.

"Avast there!" cried Silver. "Who are you, Tom Morgan? Maybe you thought you was cap'n here, perhaps. By the powers, but I'll teach you better! Cross me, and you'll go where many a good man's gone before you, first and last, these thirty year back – some to the yard-arm, shiver my sides! and some by the board, and all to feed the fishes. There's never a man looked me between the eyes and seen a good day a'terwards. Tom Morgan, you may lay to that."

Morgan paused; but a hoarse murmur rose from the others.

"Tom's right," said one.

"I stood hazing long enough from one," added another. "I'll be hanged if I'll be hazed by you, John Silver."

"Did any of you gentlemen want to have it out with *me?"* roared Silver, bending far forward from his position on the keg with his pipe still glowing in his right hand. "Put a name on what you're at; you ain't dumb, I reckon. Him that wants shall get it. Have I lived this many years, and a son of a rum puncheon cock his hat athwart my hawse at the latter end of it? You know the way; you're all gentlemen o' fortune, by your account. Well, I'm ready. Take a cutlass, him that dares, and I'll see the colour of his inside, crutch and all, before that pipe's empty."

Not a man stirred; not a man answered.

"That's your sort, is it?" he added, returning his pipe to his mouth. "Well, you're a gay lot to look at, anyway. Not much worth to fight, you ain't. P'r'aps you can understand King George's English. I'm cap'n here by 'lection. I'm cap'n here because I'm the best man by a long sea-mile. You won't fight as gentlemen o' fortune should; then, by thunder, you'll obey, and you may lay to it! I like that boy, now; I never seen a better boy than that. He's more a man than any pair of rats of you in this here house, and what I say is this: let me see him that'll lay a hand on him – that's what I say, and you may lay to it."

There was a long pause after this. I stood straight up against the wall, my heart still going like a sledge-hammer, but with a ray of hope now shining in my bosom. Silver leant back against the wall, his arms crossed, his pipe in the corner of his mouth as calm as though he had been in church; yet his eye kept wandering furtively, and he kept the tail of it on his unruly followers. They, on their part, drew gradually together towards the far end of the blockhouse, and the low hiss of their whispering sounded in my ear continuously like a stream. One after another they would look up, and the red light of the torch would fall for a second on their nervous faces; but it was not towards me, it was towards Silver that they turned their eyes.

"You seem to have a lot to say," remarked Silver, spitting far into the air. "Pipe up and let me hear it, or lay to."

"Ax your pardon, sir," returned one of the men, "you're pretty free with some of the rules; maybe you'll kindly keep an eye upon the rest. This crew's dissatisfied; this crew don't vally bullying a marlin-spike; this crew has its rights like other crews, I'll make so free as that; and by your own rules, I take it we can talk together. I ax your pardon, sir, acknowledging you to be capting at this present; but I claim my right, and steps outside for a council."

And with an elaborate sea-salute, this fellow, a long, ill-looking, yellow-eyed man of five-and-thirty, stepped coolly towards the door and disappeared out of the house. One after another, the rest followed his example; each making a salute as he passed; each adding some apology. "According to rules," said one. "Fo'c'sle council," said Morgan. And so with one remark or another, all marched out, and left Silver and me alone with the torch.

The sea-cook instantly removed his pipe.

"Now, look you here, Jim Hawkins," he said, in a steady whisper, that was

no more than audible, "you're within half a plank of death, and, what's a long sight worse, of torture. They're going to throw me off. But, you mark, I stand by you through thick and thin. I didn't mean to; no, not till you spoke up. I was about desperate to lose that much blunt, and be hanged into the bargain. But I see you was the right sort. I says to myself: "You stand by Hawkins, John, and Hawkins'll stand by you. You're his last card, and, by the living thunder, John, he's yours! Back to back, says I. You save your witness, and he'll save your neck!"

I began dimly to understand.

"You mean all's lost?" I asked.

"Ay, by gum, I do!" he answered. "Ship gone, neck gone – that's the size of it. Once I looked into that bay, Jim Hawkins, and seen no schooner – well, I'm tough, but I gave out. As for that lot and their council, mark me, they're outright fools and cowards. I'll save your life – if so be as I can – from them. But, see here, Jim – tit for tat – you save Long John from swinging."

I was bewildered; it seemed a thing so hopeless he was asking – he, the old buccaneer, the ringleader throughout.

"What I can do, that I'll do," I said.

"It's a bargain!" cried Long John. "You speak up plucky, and, by thunder! I've a chance."

He hobbled to the torch, where it stood propped among the firewood, and took a fresh light to his pipe.

"Understand me, Jim," he said, returning. "I've a head on my shoulders, I have. I'm on squire's side now. I know you've got that ship safe somewheres. How you done it, I don't know, but safe it is. I guess Hands and O'Brien turned soft. I never much believed in neither of *them*. Now, you mark me. I ask no questions, nor I won't let others. I know when a game's up, I do; and I know a lad that's staunch. Ah, you that's young – you and me might have done a power of good together!"

He drew some cognac from the cask into a tin cannikin.

"Will you taste, messmate?" he asked; and when I had refused: "Well, I'll take a drain myself, Jim," said he. "I need a caulker, for there's trouble on hand. And, talking o' trouble, why did that doctor give me the chart, Jim?"

My face expressed a wonder so unaffected that he saw the needlessness of further questions.

"Ah, well, he did, though," said he. "And there's something under that, no doubt – something surely, under that, Jim – bad or good."

And he took another swallow of the brandy, shaking his great fair head like a man who looks forward to the worst.

CHAPTER XXIX

THE BLACK SPOT AGAIN

THE council of the buccaneers had lasted some time when one of them re-entered the house, and with a repetition of the same salute, which had in my eyes an ironical air, begged for a moment's loan of the torch. Silver briefly agreed; and this emissary retired again, leaving us together in the dark.

"There's a breeze coming, Jim," said Silver, who had, by this time, adopted quite a friendly and familiar tone.

I turned to the loophole nearest me and looked out. The embers of the great fire had so far burned themselves out, and now glowed so low and duskily, that I understood why these conspirators desired a torch. About half-way down the slope to the stockade, they were collected in a group; one held the light; another was on his knees in their midst, and I saw the blade of an open knife shine in his hand with varying colours, in the moon and torchlight. The rest were all somewhat stooping, as though watching the manoeuvres of this last. I could just make out that he had a book as well as a knife in his hand; and was still wondering how anything so incongruous had come in their possession, when the kneeling figure rose once more to his feet, and the whole party began to move together towards the house.

"Here they come," said I; and I returned to my former position, for it seemed beneath my dignity that they should find me watching them.

"Well, let 'em come, lad – let 'em come," said Silver cheerily. "I've still a shot in my locker."

The door opened, and the five men, standing huddled together just inside, pushed one of their number forward. In any other circumstances it would have been comical to see his slow advance, hesitating as he set down each foot, but holding his closed right hand in front of him.

"Step up, lad," cried Silver. "I won't eat you. Hand it over, lubber. I know the rules, I do; I won't hurt a depytation."

Thus encouraged, the buccaneer steeped forth more briskly, and having passed something to Silver, from hand to hand, slipped yet more smartly back again to his companions.

The sea-cook looked at what had been given him.

"The black spot! I thought so," he observed. "Where might you have got the paper? Why, hillo! look here now: this ain't lucky! You've gone and cut this out of a Bible. What fool's cut a Bible?"

"Ah, there!" said Morgan – "there! Wot did I say? No good'll come o' that, I said."

"Well, you've about fixed it now, among you," continued Silver. "You'll all swing now, I reckon. What soft-headed lubber had a Bible?"

"It was Dick," said one.

"Dick, was it? Then Dick can get to prayers," said Silver. "He's seen his slice of luck, has Dick, and you may lay to that."

But here the long man with the yellow eyes struck in.

"Belay that talk, John Silver," he said. "This crew has tipped you the black spot in full council, as in dooty bound; just you turn it over, as in dooty bound, and see what's wrote there. Then you can talk."

"Thanky, George," replied the sea-cook. "You always was brisk for business, and has the rules by heart, George, as I'm pleased to see. Well, what is it, anyway? Ah! 'Deposed' – that's it, is it? Very pretty wrote to be sure; like print, I swear. Your hand o' write, George? Why, you was gettin' quite a leadin' man in this here crew. You'll be cap'n next, I shouldn't wonder. Just oblige me with that torch again, will you? this pipe don't draw."

"Come, now," said George, "you don't fool this crew no more. You're a funny man, by your account; but you're over now, and you'll maybe step down off that barrel, and help vote."

"I thought you said you knowed the rules," returned Silver contemptuously. "Leastways, if you don't, I do; and I wait here – I'm still your cap'n mind – till you outs with your grievances, and I reply; in the meantime, your black spot ain't worth a biscuit. After that, we'll see."

"Oh," replied George, "you don't be under no kind of apprehension; *we're* all square, we are. First, you've made a hash of this cruise – you'll be a bold man to say no to that. Second, you let the enemy out o' this here trap for nothing. Why did they want out? I dunno; but it's pretty plain they wanted it. Third, you wouldn't let us go at them upon the march. Oh, we see through you, John Silver; you want to play booty, that's what's wrong with you. And then, fourth, there's this here boy."

"Is that all?" asked Silver quietly.

"Enough, too," retorted George. "We'll all swing and sun-dry for your bungling."

"Well, now, look here, I'll answer these four p'ints, one after another I'll answer 'em. I made a hash o' this cruise, did I? Well, now, you all know what I wanted: and you all know, if that had been done, that we'd 'a' been aboard the *Hispaniola* this night as ever was, every man of us alive, and fit, and full of good plum-duff, and the treasure in the hold of her, by thunder! Well, who crossed me? Who forced my hand, as was the lawful cap'n? Who tipped me the black spot the day we landed, and began this dance? Ah, it's a fine dance – I'm with you there – and looks mighty like a hornpipe in a rope's end at Execution Dock by London town, it does. But who done it? Why, it was Anderson, and Hands, and you, George Merry! And you're the last above board of that same meddling crew; and you have the Davy Jones's insolence to up and stand for cap'n over me – you, that sank the lot of us! By the Powers! but this tops the stiffest yarn to nothing."

Silver paused, and I could see by the faces of George and his late comrades that these words had not been said in vain.

"That's for number one," cried the accused, wiping the sweat from his brow, for he had been talking with a vehemence that shook the house. "Why, I give you my word, I'm sick to speak to you. You've neither sense nor memory, and I leave it to fancy where your mothers was that let you come to sea. Sea! Gentlemen o' fortune! I reckon tailors is your trade."

"Go on, John," said Morgan. "Speak up to the others."

"Ah, the others!" returned John. "They're a nice lot, ain't they? You say this cruise is bungled. Ah! by gum, if you could understand how bad it's bungled, you would see! We're that near the gibbet that my neck's stiff with thinking on it. You've seen 'em, maybe, hanged in chains, birds about 'em, seamen p'inting 'em out as they go down with the tide. 'Who's that?' says one. 'That! Why, that's John Silver. I knowed him well,' says another. And you can hear the chains a-jangle as you go about and reach for the other buoy. Now, that's about where we are, every mother's son of us, thanks to him, and Hands, and Anderson, and other ruination fools of you. And if you want to know about number four, and that boy, why, shiver my timbers! isn't he a hostage? Are we a-going to waste a hostage? No, not us; he might be our last chance, and I shouldn't wonder. Kill that boy? not me, mates! And

' "You look there – that's why!" ' (p. 168)

number three? Ah, well, there's a deal to say to number three. Maybe you don't count it nothing to have a real college doctor come to see you every day – you, John, with your head broke – or you, George Merry, that had the ague shakes upon you not six hours agone, and has your eyes the colour of lemon peel to this same moment on the clock? And maybe, perhaps, you didn't know there was a consort coming, either? But there is; and not so long till then; and we'll see who'll be glad to have a hostage when it comes to that. And as for number two, and why I made a bargain – well, you came crawling on your knees to me to make it – on your knees you came, you was that downhearted – and you'd have starved, too, if I hadn't – but that's a trifle! you look there – that's why!"

And he cast down upon the floor a paper that I instantly recognised – none other than the chart on yellow paper, with the three red crosses, that I had found in the oilcloth at the bottom of the captain's chest. Why the doctor had given it to him was more than I could fancy.

But if it were inexplicable to me, the appearance of the chart was incredible to the surviving mutineers. They leaped upon it like cats upon a mouse. It went from hand to hand, one tearing it from another; and by the oaths and the cries and the childish laughter with which they accompanied their examination, you would have thought, not only they were fingering the very gold, but were at sea with it, besides, in safety.

"Yes," said one, "that's Flint sure enough. J. F., and a score below, with a clove hitch to it; so he done ever."

"Mighty pretty," said George. "But how are we to get away with it, and us no ship?"

Silver suddenly sprang up, and supporting himself with a hand against the wall: "Now I give you warning, George," he cried. "One more word of your sauce, and I'll call you down and fight you. How? Why, how do I know? You had ought to tell me that – you and the rest, that lost me my schooner, with your interference, burn you! But not you, you can't; you hain't got the invention of a cockroach. But civil you can speak, and shall, George Merry, you may lay to that."

"That's fair enow," said the old man Morgan.

"Fair! I reckon so," said the sea-cook. "You lost the ship; I found the treasure. Who's the better man at that? And now I resign, by thunder! Elect whom you please to be your cap'n now; I'm done with it."

"Silver!" they cried. "Barbecue for ever! Barbecue for cap'n!"

"So that's the toon, is it?" cried the cook. "George, I reckon you'll have to wait another turn, friend; and lucky for you as I'm not a revengeful man. But that was never my way. And now, shipmates, this black spot? 'Tain't much good now, is it? Dick's crossed his luck and spoiled his Bible, and that's about all."

"It'll do to kiss the book on still, won't it?" growled Dick, who was evidently uneasy at the curse he had brought upon himself.

"A Bible with a bit cut out!" returned Silver derisively. "Not it. It don't bind no more'n a ballad-book."

"Don't it, though?" cried Dick, with a sort of joy. "Well, I reckon that's worth having, too."

"Here, Jim – here's a cur'osity for you," said Silver; and he tossed me the paper.

It was a round about the size of a crown piece. One side was blank, for it had been the last leaf; the other contained a verse or two of Revelation – these words among the rest, which struck sharply home upon my mind: "Without are dogs and murderers." The printed side had been blackened with wood ash, which already began to come off and soil my fingers; on the blank side had been written with the same material the one word "Depposed." I have that curiosity beside me at this moment; but not a trace of writing now remains beyond a single scratch, such as a man might make with his thumbnail.

That was the end of the night's business. Soon after, with a drink all round, we lay down to sleep, and the outside of Silver's vengeance was to put George Merry up for sentinel, and threaten him with death if he should prove unfaithful.

It was long ere I could close an eye, and Heaven knows I had matter enough for thought in the man whom I had slain that afternoon, in my own most perilous position, and, above all, in the remarkable game that I saw Silver now engaged upon – keeping the mutineers together with one hand, and grasping, with the other, after every means, possible and impossible, to make his peace and save his miserable life. He himself slept peacefully, and snored aloud; yet my heart was sore for him, wicked as he was, to think on the dark perils that environed, and the shameful gibbet that awaited him.

CHAPTER XXX

ON PAROLE

I WAS wakened – indeed, we were all wakened, for I could see even the sentinel shake himself together from where he had fallen against the door-post – by a dear, hearty voice hailing us from the margin of the wood:—

"Blockhouse, ahoy!" it cried. "Here's the doctor."

And the doctor it was. Although I was glad to hear the sound, yet my gladness was not without admixture. I remembered with confusion my insubordinate and stealthy conduct; and when I saw where it had brought me – among what companions and surrounded by what dangers I felt ashamed to look him in the face.

He must have risen in the dark, for the day had hardly come; and when I ran to a loophole and looked out, I saw him standing, like Silver once before, up to the mid-leg in creeping vapour.

"You, doctor! Top o' the morning to you, sir!" cried Silver, broad awake and beaming with good-nature in a moment. "Bright and early, to be sure; and it's the early bird, as the saying goes, that gets the rations. George, shake up your timbers, son, and help Dr. Livesey over the ship's side. All a-doin' well, your patients was – all well and merry."

So he pattered on, standing on the hill-top, with his crutch under his elbow, and one hand upon the side of the log-house – quite the old John in voice, manner, and expression.

"We've quite a surprise for you, too, sir," he continued. "We've a little stranger here – he! he! A noo boarder and lodger, sir, and looking fit and taut as a fiddle; slep' like a supercargo, he did, right alongside of John – stem to stem, we was, all night."

Dr. Livesey was by this time across the stockade and pretty near the cook; and I could hear the alteration in his voice as he said:—

"Not Jim?"

"The very same Jim as ever was," says Silver.

The doctor stopped outright, although he did not speak, and it was some seconds before he seemed able to move on.

"Well, well," he said at last, "duty first and pleasure afterwards, as you might have said yourself, Silver. Let us overhaul these patients of yours."

A moment afterwards he had entered the blockhouse, and, with one grim nod to me, proceeded with his work among the sick. He seemed under no apprehension, though he must have known that his life, among these treacherous demons, depended on a hair; and he rattled on to his patients as if he were paying an ordinary professional visit in a quiet English family. His manner, I suppose, reacted on the men; for they behaved to him as if nothing had occurred – as if he were still ship's doctor, and they still faithful hands before the mast.

"You're doing well, my friend," he said to the fellow with the bandaged head; "and if ever any person had a close shave, it was you; your head must be as hard as iron. Well, George, how goes it? You're a pretty colour, certainly; why, your liver, man, is upside down. Did you take that medicine? Did he take that medicine, men?"

"Ay, ay, sir; he took it, sure enough," returned Morgan.

"Because, you see, since I am mutineers' doctor, or prison doctor, as I prefer to call it," says Dr. Livesey, in his pleasantest way, "I make it a point of honour not to lose a man for King George (God bless him!) and the gallows."

The rogues looked at each other, but swallowed the home-thrust in silence.

"Dick don't feel well, sir," said one.

"Don't he?" replied the doctor. "Well, step up here, Dick, and let me see your tongue. No, I should be surprised if he did! The man's tongue is fit to frighten the French. Another fever."

"Ah, there," said Morgan, "that comed of spilling Bibles."

"That comed – as you call it – of being arrant asses," retorted the doctor, "and not having sense enough to know honest air from poison, and the dry land from a vile, pestiferous slough. I think it most probable – though, of course, it's only an opinion – that you'll all have the deuce to pay before you get that malaria out of your systems. Camp in a bog, would you? Silver, I'm surprised at you. You're less of a fool than many, take you all round; but you don't appear to me to have the rudiments of a notion of the rules of health."

"Well," he added, after he had closed them round, and they had taken his prescription, with really laughable humility, more like charity school-children than blood-guilty mutineers and pirates – "well, that's done for to-day. And now I should wish to have a talk with that boy, please."

And he nodded his head in my direction carelessly.

George Merry was at the door, spitting and spluttering over some bad-tasted medicine; but at the first word of the doctor's proposal he swung round with a deep flush, and cried "No!" and swore.

Silver struck the barrel with his open hand.

"Silence!" he roared, and looked about him positively like a lion. "Doctor," he went on, in his usual tones, "I was a-thinking of that, knowing as how you had a fancy for the boy. We're all humbly grateful for your kindness, and, as you see, puts faith in you, and takes the drugs down like that much grog. And I take it, I've found a way as'll suit all. Hawkins, will you give me your word of honour as a young gentleman – for a young gentleman you are, although poor born – your word of honour not to slip your cable?"

I readily gave the pledge required.

"Then, doctor," said Silver, "you just step outside o' that stockade, and once you're there, I'll bring the boy down on the inside, and I reckon you can yarn through the spars. Good-day to you, sir, and all our dooties to the squire and Cap'n Smollett."

The explosion of disapproval, which nothing but Silver's black looks had restrained, broke out immediately the doctor had left the house. Silver was roundly accused of playing double – of trying to make a separate peace for himself – of sacrificing the interests of his accomplices and victims; and, in one word, of the identical, exact thing that he was doing. It seemed to me so obvious, in this case, that I could not imagine how he was to turn their anger. But he was twice the man the rest were; and his last night's victory had given him a huge preponderance on their minds. He called them all the fools and dolts you can imagine, said it was necessary I should talk to the doctor, fluttered the chart in their faces, asked them if they could afford to break the treaty the very day they were bound a treasure-hunting.

"No, by thunder!" he cried, "it's us must break the treaty when the time comes; and till then I'll gammon that doctor, if I have to ile his boots with brandy."

And then he bade them get the fire lit, and stalked out upon his crutch, with his hand on my shoulder, leaving them in a disarray and silenced by his volubility rather than convinced.

"Slow, lad, slow," he said. "They might round upon us in a twinkle of an eye, if we was seen to hurry."

Very deliberately, then, did we advance across the sand to where the doctor awaited us on the other side of the stockade, and as soon as we were within easy speaking distance, Silver stopped.

"You'll make a note of this here also, doctor," says he, "and the boy'll tell you how I saved his life, and were deposed for it, too, and you may lay to that. Doctor, when a man's steering as near the wind as me – playing chuck-farthing with the last breath in his body, like – you wouldn't think it too much, mayhap, to give him one good word? You'll please bear in mind it's not my life only now – it's that boy's into the bargain; and you'll speak me fair, doctor, and give me a bit o' hope to go on, for the sake of mercy."

Silver was a changed man, once he was out there and had his back to his friends and the blockhouse; his cheeks seemed to have fallen in, his voice trembled; never was a soul more dead in earnest.

"Why, John, you're not afraid?" asked Dr. Livesey.

"Doctor, I'm no coward! no, not I – not so much!" and he snapped his fingers. "If I was I wouldn't say it. But I'll own up fairly, I've the shakes upon me for the gallows. You're a good man and a true; I never seen a better man! And you'll not forget what I done good, not any more than you'll forget the bad, I know. And I step aside – see here – and leave you and Jim alone. And you'll put that down for me, too, for it's a long stretch, is that!"

So saying, he stepped back a little way, till he was out of ear-shot, and there sat down upon a tree-stump and began to whistle; spinning round now and again upon his seat so as to command a sight, sometimes of me and the doctor, and sometimes of his unruly ruffians as they went to and fro in the sand, between the fire – which they were busy rekindling – and the house, from which they brought forth pork and bread to make the breakfast.

"So, Jim," said the doctor sadly "here you are. As you have brewed, so shall you drink, my boy. Heaven knows, I cannot find it in my heart to blame you; but this much I will say, be it kind or unkind: when Captain Smollett was well, you dared not have gone off; and when he was ill, and couldn't help it, by George, it was downright cowardly!"

"At the foot of a pretty big pine, and involved in a green creeper…a human skeleton lay."
(M. S. Orr)

I HAVE NEVER SEEN MEN SO DREADFULLY AFFECTED.
(F. GILLET)

"He was brave and no mistake."
(M. S. Orr)

"NEARLY EVERY VARIETY OF MONEY IN THE WORLD MUST HAVE FOUND A PLACE IN THAT COLLECTION."
(M. WINTER)

' "So, Jim," said the doctor sadly, "here you are." ' (p. 173)

I will own that here I began to weep. "Doctor," I said, "you might spare me. I have blamed myself enough; my life's forfeit anyway, and I should have been dead by now, if Silver hadn't stood for me; and doctor, believe this, I can die – and I dare say I deserve it – but what I fear is torture. If they come to torture me—"

"Jim," the doctor interrupted, and his voice was quite changed, "Jim, I can't have this. Whip over, and we'll run for it."

"Doctor," said I, "I passed my word."

"I know, I know," he cried. "We can't help that, Jim, now. I'll take it on my shoulders, holus bolus, blame and shame, my boy; but stay here, I cannot let you. Jump! One jump, and you're out, and we'll run for it like antelopes."

"No," I replied, "you know right well you wouldn't do the thing yourself; neither you, nor squire, nor captain; and no more I. Silver trusted me; I passed my word, and back I go. But, doctor, you did not let me finish. If they come to torture me, I might let slip a word of where the ship is; for I got the ship, part by luck and part by risking, and she lies in North Inlet, on the southern beach, and just below highwater. At half tide she must be high and dry."

"The ship!" exclaimed the doctor. Rapidly I described to him my adventures, and he heard me out in silence.

"There is a kind of fate in this," he observed, when I had done. "Every step, it's you that saves our lives; and do you suppose by any chance that we are going to let you lose yours? That would be a poor return, my boy. You found out the plot; you found Ben Gunn – the best deed that ever you did, or will do, though you live to ninety. Oh, by Jupiter, and talking of Ben Gunn! why, this is the mischief in person. Silver!" he cried, "Silver! – I'll give you a piece of advice," he continued, as the cook drew near again; "don't you be in any great hurry after that treasure."

"Why, sir, I do my possible, which that ain't," said Silver. "I can only, asking your pardon, save my life and the boy's by seeking for that treasure; and you may lay to that."

"Well, Silver," replied the doctor, "if that is so, I'll go one step farther: look out for squalls when you find it."

"Sir," said Silver, "as between man and man, that's too much and too little. What you're after, why you left the blockhouse, why you've given me that there chart, I don't know, now, do I? And yet I done your bidding with my eyes shut and never a word of hope! But, no, this here's too much. If you won't tell me what you mean plain out, just say so, and I'll leave the helm."

"No," said the doctor musingly, "I've no right to say more; it's not my secret, you see, Silver, or, I give you my word, I'd tell it you. But I'll go as far with you as I dare go and a step beyond; for I'll have my wig sorted by the captain or I'm mistaken! And, first, I'll give you a bit of hope: Silver, if we both get alive out of this wolf-trap, I'll do my best to save you, short of perjury."

Silver's face was radiant. "You couldn't say more, I'm sure, sir, not if you was my mother," he cried.

"Well, that's my first concession," added the doctor. "My second is a piece of advice: Keep the boy close beside you, and when you need help, halloo. I'm off to seek it for you, and that itself will show you if I speak at random. Good-bye, Jim."

And Dr. Livesey shook hands with me through the stockade, nodded to Silver, and set off at a brisk pace into the wood.

CHAPTER XXXI

THE TREASURE HUNT – FLINT'S POINTER

"JIM," said Silver, when we were alone, "if I saved your life, you saved mine; and I'll not forget it. I seen the doctor waving you to run for it – with the tail of my eye, I did; and I seen you say no, as plain as hearing. Jim, that's one to you. This is the first glint of hope I had since the attack failed, and I owe it you. And now, Jim, we're to go in for this here treasure-hunting, with sealed orders, too, and I don't like it; and you and me must stick close, back to back like, and we'll save our necks in spite o' fate and fortune."

Just then a man hailed us from the fire that breakfast was ready, and we were soon seated here and there about the sand over biscuit and fried junk. They had lit a fire fit to roast an ox; and it was now grown so hot that they could only approach it from the wind-ward, and even there not without precaution. In the same wasteful spirit they had cooked, I suppose, three times more than we could eat; and one of them, with an empty laugh, threw what was left into the fire, which blazed and roared again over this unusual fuel. I never in my life saw men so careless of the morrow; hand to mouth is the only word that can describe their way of doing; and what with wasted food and sleeping sentries, though they were bold enough for a brush and be done with it, I could see their entire unfitness for anything like a prolonged campaign.

Even Silver, eating away, with Captain Flint upon his shoulder, had not a word of blame for their recklessness. And this the more surprised me, for I thought he had never shown himself so cunning as he did then.

"Ay, mates," said he, "it's lucky you have Barbecue to think for you with this here head. I got what I wanted, I did. Sure enough, they have the ship. Where they have it, I don't know yet; but once we hit the treasure, we'll have to jump about and find out. And then, mates, us that has the boats, I reckon, has the upper hand."

Thus he kept running on, with his mouth full of the hot bacon: thus he restored their hope and confidence, and, I more than suspect, repaired his own at the same time.

"As for hostage," he continued, "that's his last talk, I guess, with them he loves so dear. I've got my piece o' news, and thanky to him for that; but it's over and done. I'll take him in a line when we go treasure-hunting, for we'll keep him like so much gold, in case of accidents, you mark, and in the meantime. Once we got the ship and treasure both, and off to sea like jolly companions, why, then, we'll talk Mr. Hawkins over, we will, and we'll give him his share, to be sure, for all his kindness."

It was no wonder the men were in a good humour now. For my part, I was horribly cast down. Should the scheme he had now sketched prove feasible, Silver, already doubly a traitor, would not hesitate to adopt it. He had still a foot in either camp, and there was no doubt he would prefer wealth and freedom with the pirates to a bare escape from hanging, which was the best he had to hope on our side.

Nay, and even if things so fell out that he was forced to keep his faith with Dr. Livesey, even then what danger lay before us! What a moment that would be when the suspicions of his followers turned to certainty, and he and I should have to fight for dear lifc – he, a cripple, and I, a boy – against five strong and active seamen! Add to this double apprehension, the mystery that still hung over the behaviour of my friends; their unexplained desertion of the stockade; their inexplicable cession of the chart; or, harder still to understand, the doctor's last warning to Silver, "Look out for squalls when you find it"; and you will readily believe how little taste I found in my breakfast, and with how uneasy a heart I set forth behind my captors on the quest for treasure.

We made a curious figure, had any one been there to see us; all in soiled sailor clothes, and all but me armed to the teeth. Silver had two guns slung about him – one before and one behind – besides the great cutlass at his waist, and a pistol in each pocket of his square-tailed coat. To complete his strange appearance, Captain Flint sat perched upon his shoulder and gabbled odds and ends of purposeless sea-talk. I had a line about my waist, and followed obediently after the sea-cook, who held the loose end of the rope, now in his free hand, now between his powerful teeth. For all the world, I was led like a dancing bear.

The other men were variously burthened; some carrying picks and

shovels – for that had been the very first necessary they brought ashore from the *Hispaniola* – others laden with pork, bread, and brandy for the midday meal. All the stores, I observed, came from our stock; and I could see the truth of Silver's words the night before. Had he not struck a bargain with the doctor, he and his mutineers, deserted by the ship, must have been driven to subsist on clear water and the proceeds of their hunting. Water would have been little to their taste; a sailor is not usually a good shot; and besides all that, when they were so short of eatables, it was not likely they would be very flush of powder.

Well, thus equipped, we all set out – even the fellow with the broken head, who should certainly have kept in shadow – and straggled, one after another, to the beach, where the two gigs awaited us. Even these bore traces of the drunken folly of the pirates, one in a broken thwart, and both in their muddied and unbaled condition. Both were to be carried along with us, for the sake of safety; and so, with our numbers divided between them, we set forth upon the bosom of the anchorage.

As we pulled over, there was some discussion on the chart. The red cross was, of course, far too large to be a guide, and the terms of the note on the back, as you will hear, admitted of some ambiguity. They ran, the reader may remember, thus:—

> *"Tall tree, Spy-glass shoulder, bearing a point to the N. of N.N.E.*
> *"Skeleton Island E.S.E. and by E.*
> *"Ten feet."*

A tall tree was thus the principal mark. Now, right before us, the anchorage was bounded by a plateau from two to three hundred feet high, adjoining on the north the sloping southern shoulder of the Spy-glass, and rising again towards the south into the rough cliffy eminence called the Mizzen-mast Hill. The top of the plateau was dotted thickly with pine trees of varying height. Every here and there, one of a different species rose forty or fifty feet clear above its neighbours, and which of these was the particular *"tall tree"* of Captain Flint could only be decided on the spot, and by the readings of the compass.

Yet, although that was the case, every man on board the boats had picked a favourite of his own ere we were half-way over, Long John alone shrugging his shoulders and bidding them wait till they were there.

We pulled easily, by Silver's directions, not to weary the hands prematurely; and, after quite a long passage, landed at the mouth of the second river – that which runs down a woody cleft of the Spy-glass. Thence, bending to our left, we began to ascend the slope towards the plateau.

At the first outset, heavy, miry ground and a matted, marish vegetation, greatly delayed our progress; but by little and little the hill began to steepen and become stony under foot, and the wood to change its character and to grow in a more open order. It was, indeed, a most pleasant portion of the island that we were now approaching. A heavy-scented broom and many flowering shrubs had almost taken the place of grass. Thickets of green nutmeg trees were dotted here and there with the red columns and the broad shadow of the pines; and the first mingled their spice with the aroma of the others. The air, besides, was fresh and stirring, and this, under the sheer sunbeams, was a wonderful refreshment to our senses.

The party spread itself abroad, in a fan shape, shouting and leaping to and fro. About the centre, and a good way behind the rest, Silver and I followed – I tethered by my rope, he ploughing, with deep pants, among the sliding gravel. From time to time, indeed, I had to lend him a hand, or he must have missed his footing and fallen backward down the hill.

We had thus proceeded for about half a mile, and were approaching the brow of the plateau, when the man upon the farthest left began to cry aloud, as if in terror. Shout after shout came from him, and the others began to run in his direction.

"He can't 'a' found the treasure," said old Morgan, hurrying past us from the right, "for that's clean a-top."

Indeed, as we found when we also reached the spot, it was something very different. At the foot of a pretty big pine, and involved in a green creeper, which had even partly lifted some of the smaller bones, a human skeleton lay, with a few shreds of clothing, on the ground. I believe a chill struck for a moment to every heart.

"He was a seaman," said George Merry, who, bolder than the rest, had gone up close, and was examining the rags of clothing. "Leastways, this is good sea-cloth."

"Ay, ay," said Silver, "like enough; you wouldn't look to find a bishop here, I reckon. But what sort of a way is that for bones to lie? 'Tain't in natur'."

Indeed, on a second glance, it seemed impossible to fancy that the body was in a natural position. But for some disarray (the work, perhaps, of the

' "There ain't a thing left there," said Merry, still feeling round among the bones.' (p. 182)

birds that had fed upon him, or of the slow-growing creeper that had gradually enveloped his remains) the man lay perfectly straight – his feet pointing in one direction, his hands, raised above his head like a diver's, pointing directly in the opposite.

"I've taken a notion into my old numskull," observed Silver. "Here's the compass; there's the tip-top p'int o' Skeleton Island, stickin' out like a tooth. Just take a bearing, will you, along the line of them bones."

It was done. The body pointed straight in the direction of the island, and the compass read duly E.S.E. and by E.

"I thought so," cried the cook; "this here is a p'inter. Right up there is our line for the Pole Star and the jolly dollars. But, by thunder! if it don't make me cold inside to think of Flint. This is one of *his* jokes, and no mistake. Him and these six was alone here; he killed 'em, every man; and this one he hauled here and laid down by compass, shiver my timbers! They're long bones, and the hair's been yellow. Ay, that would be Allardyce. You mind Allardyce, Tom Morgan?"

"Ay, ay," returned Morgan, "I mind him; he owed me money, he did, and took my knife ashore with him."

"Speaking of knives," said another, "why don't we find his'n lying round? Flint warn't the man to pick a seaman's pocket; and the birds, I guess, would leave it be."

"By the Powers, and that's true!" cried Silver.

"There ain't a thing left here," said Merry, still feeling round among the bones, "not a copper doit nor a baccy box. It don't look nat'ral to me."

"No, by gum, it don't," agreed Silver; "not nat'ral, nor not nice, says you. Great guns! messmates, but if Flint was living, this would be a hot spot for you and me. Six they were, and six are we; and bones is what they are now."

"I saw him dead with these here deadlights," said Morgan. "Billy took me in. There he laid, with penny-pieces on his eyes."

"Dead – ay, sure enough he's dead and gone below," said the fellow with the bandage; "but if ever sperrit walked, it would be Flint's. Dear heart, but he died bad, did Flint!"

"Ay, that he did," observed another; "now he raged, and now he hollered for the rum, and now he sang. 'Fifteen Men' were his only song, mates; and I tell you true, I never rightly liked to hear it since. It was main hot, and the windy was open, and I hear that old song comin' out as clear as clear – and the death-haul on the man a'ready."

"Come, come," said Silver, "stow this talk. He's dead, and he don't walk, that I know; leastways, he won't walk by day, and you may lay to that. Care killed a cat. Fetch ahead for the doubloons."

We started, certainly; but in spite of the hot sun and the staring daylight, the pirates no longer ran separate and shouting through the wood, but kept side by side and spoke with bated breath. The terror of the dead buccaneer had fallen on their spirits.

CHAPTER XXXII

THE TREASURE HUNT – THE VOICE AMONG THE TREES

PARTLY from the damping influence of this alarm, partly to rest Silver and the sick folk, the whole party sat down as soon as they had gained the brow of the ascent.

The plateau being somewhat tilted towards the west, this spot on which we had paused commanded a wide prospect on either hand. Before us, over the tree-tops, we beheld the Cape of the Woods fringed with surf; behind, we not only looked down upon the anchorage and Skeleton Island, but saw – clear across the spit and the eastern lowlands – a great field of open sea upon the east. Sheer above us rose the Spy-glass, here dotted with single pines, there black with precipices. There was no sound but that of the distant breakers, mounting from all round, and the chirp of countless insects in the brush. Not a man, not a sail upon the sea; the very largeness of the view increased the sense of solitude.

Silver, as he sat, took certain bearings with his compass.

"There are three 'tall trees,' " said he, "about in the right line from Skeleton Island. 'Spy-glass Shoulder,' I take it, means that lower p'int there. It's child's play to find the stuff now. I've half a mind to dine first."

"I don't feel sharp," growled Morgan. "Thinkin' o' Flint – I think it were as done me."

"Ah, well, my son, you praise your stars he's dead," said Silver.

"He were an ugly devil," cried a third pirate with a shudder; "that blue in the face, too!"

"That was how the rum took him," added Merry. "Blue! well, I reckon he was blue. That's a true word."

Ever since they had found the skeleton and got upon this train of thought, they had spoken lower and lower, and they had almost got to whispering by now, so that the sound of their talk hardly interrupted the silence of the wood. All of a sudden, out of the middle of the trees in front of us, a thin, high, trembling voice struck up the well-known air and words—

"Fifteen men on The Dead Man's Chest—
Yo-ho-ho, and a bottle of rum!"

I never have seen men more dreadfully affected than the pirates. The colour went from their six faces like enchantment; some leaped to their feet, some clawed hold of others; Morgan grovelled on the ground.

"It's Flint, by—!" cried Merry.

The song had stopped as suddenly as it began – broken off, you would have said, in the middle of a note, as though some one had laid his hand upon the singer's mouth. Coming so far through the clear, sunny atmosphere among the green treetops, I thought it had sounded airily and sweetly; and the effect on my companions was the stranger.

"Come," said Silver, struggling with his ashen lips to get the word out, "this won't do. Stand by to go about. This is a rum start, and I can't name the voice; but it's some one skylarking – some one that's flesh and blood, and you may lay to that"

His courage had come back as he spoke, and some of the colour to his face along with it. Already the others had began to lend an ear to this encouragement, and were coming a little to themselves, when the same voice broke out again – not this time singing, but in a faint, distant hail, that echoed yet fainter among the clefts of the Spy-glass.

"Darby M'Graw," it wailed – for that is the word that best describes the sound – "Darby M'Graw! Darby M'Graw!" again and again and again; and then rising a little higher, and with an oath that I leave out, "Fetch aft the rum, Darby!"

The buccaneers remained rooted to the ground, their eyes starting from their heads. Long after the voice had died away they still stared in silence, dreadfully, before them.

"That fixes it!" gasped one. "Let's go."

"They was his last words," moaned Morgan, "his last words above board."

Dick had his Bible out, and was praying volubly. He had been well brought up, had Dick, before he came to sea and fell among bad companions.

Still, Silver was unconquered. I could hear his teeth rattle in his head; but he had not yet surrendered.

"Nobody in this here island ever heard of Darby," he muttered; "not one but us that's here." And then, making a great effort, "Shipmates," he cried, "I'm here to get that stuff, and I'll not be beat by man nor devil. I never was feared of Flint in his life, and, by the Powers, I'll face him dead. There's seven hundred thousand pound not a quarter of a mile from here. When did ever a gentleman o' fortune show his stern to that much dollars, for a boosy old seaman with a blue mug – and him dead, too?"

But there was no sign of re-awakening courage in his followers; rather, indeed, of growing terror at the irreverence of his words.

"Belay there, John!" said Merry. "Don't you cross a sperrit."

And the rest were all too terrified to reply. They would have run away severally had they dared; but fear kept them together, and kept them close by John, as if his daring helped them. He, on his part, had pretty well fought his weakness down.

"Sperrit? Well, maybe," he said. "But there's one thing not clear to me. There was an echo. Now, no man ever seen a sperrit with a shadow; well, then, what's he doing with an echo to him, I should like to know? That ain't in natur', surely?"

This argument seemed weak enough to me. But you can never tell what will affect the superstitious, and, to my wonder, George Merry was greatly relieved.

"Well, that's so," he said. "You've a head upon your shoulders, John, and no mistake. 'Bout ship, mates! this here crew is on a wrong tack, I do believe. And come to think on it, it was like Flint's voice, I grant you, but not just so clear-away like it, after all. It was liker somebody else's voice now – it was liker—"

"By the Powers, Ben Gunn!" roared Silver.

"Ay, and so it were," cried Morgan, springing on his knees. "Ben Gunn it were!"

"It don't make much odds, do it, now?" asked Dick. "Ben Gunn's not here in the body, any more'n Flint."

But the older hands greeted this remark with scorn.

"Why, nobody minds Benn Gunn," cried Merry; "dead or alive, nobody minds him."

It was extraordinary how their spirits had returned, and how the natural colour had revived in their faces. Soon they were chatting together, with intervals of listening; and not long after, hearing no further sound, they shouldered the tools and set forth again, Merry walking first with Silver's compass to keep them on the right line with Skeleton Island. He had said the truth: dead or alive, nobody minded Ben Gunn.

Dick alone still held his Bible, and looked around him as he went, with fearful glances; but he found no sympathy, and Silver even joked him on his precautions.

"I told you," said he; "I told you, you had sp'iled your Bible. If it ain't no good to swear by, what do you suppose a sperrit would give for it? Not that!" and he snapped his big fingers, halting a moment on his crutch.

But Dick was not to be comforted; indeed it was soon plain to me that the lad was falling sick; hastened by heat, exhaustion, and the shock of his alarm, the fever predicted by Doctor Livesey was evidently growing swiftly higher.

It was fine open walking here, upon the summit; our way lay a little downhill, for, as I have said, the plateau tilted towards the west. The pines, great and small, grew wide apart; and even between the clumps of nutmeg and azalea, wide open spaces baked in the hot sunshine. Striking, as we did, pretty near north-west across the island, we drew, on the one hand, even nearer under the shoulders of the Spy-glass, and on the other, looked ever wider over that western bay where I had once tossed and trembled in the coracle.

The first of the tall trees was reached, and by the bearing, proved the wrong one. So with the second. The third rose nearly two hundred feet in the air above a clump of underwood; a giant of a vegetable, with a red column as big as a cottage, and a wide shadow around in which a company could have manoeuvred. It was conspicuous far to sea both on the east and west, and might have been entered as a sailing mark upon the chart.

But it was not its size that now impressed my companions; it was the knowledge that seven hundred thousand pounds in gold lay somewhere buried beneath its spreading shadow. The thought of the money, as they drew nearer, swallowed up their previous terrors. Their eyes burned in their heads; their feet grew speedier and lighter; their whole soul was bound up in that fortune, that whole lifetime of extravagance and pleasure, that lay waiting there for each of them.

Silver hobbled, grunting, on his crutch; his nostrils stood out and quivered; he cursed like a madman when the flies settled on his hot and shiny countenance; he plucked furiously at the line that held me to him, and, from time to time, turned his eyes upon me with a deadly look. Certainly he took no pains to hide his thoughts; and certainly I read them like print. In

the immediate nearness of the gold, all else had been forgotten; his promise and the doctor's warning were both things of the past; and I could not doubt that he hoped to seize upon the treasure, find and board the *Hispaniola* under cover of night, cut every honest throat about that island, and sail away as he had at first intended, laden with crimes and riches.

Shaken as I was with these alarms, it was hard for me to keep up with the rapid pace of the treasure-hunters. Now and again I stumbled; and it was then that Silver plucked so roughly at the rope and launched at me his murderous glances. Dick, who had dropped behind us, and now brought up the rear, was babbling to himself both prayers and curses, as his fever kept

'On one of these boards I saw, branded with a hot iron, the name Walrus *– the name of Flint's ship.'* *(p. 190)*

rising. This also added to my wretchedness, and, to crown all, I was haunted by the thought of the tragedy that had once been acted on that plateau, when that ungodly buccaneer with the blue face – he who died at Savannah, singing and shouting for drink – had there, with his own hand, cut down his six accomplices. This grove, that was now so peaceful, must then have rung with cries, I thought; and even with the thought I could believe I heard it ringing still.

We were now at the margin of the thicket.

"Huzza, mates, all together!" shouted Merry; and the foremost broke into a run.

And suddenly, not ten yards farther, we beheld them stop. A low cry arose. Silver doubled his pace, digging away with the foot of his crutch like one possessed; and next moment he and I had come also to a dead halt.

Before us was a great excavation, not very recent, for the sides had fallen in and grass had sprouted on the bottom. In this were the shaft of a pick broken in two and the boards of several packing-cases strewn around. On one of these boards I saw, branded with a hot iron, the name *Walrus* – the name of Flint's ship.

All was clear to probation. The *cache* had been found and rifled; the seven hundred thousand pounds were gone!

CHAPTER XXXIII

THE FALL OF A CHIEFTAIN

THERE never was such an overturn in this world. Each of these six men was as though he had been struck. But with Silver the blow passed almost instantly. Every thought of his soul had been set full-stretch, like a racer, on that money; well, he was brought up in a single second, dead; and he kept his head, found his temper, and changed his plan before the others had had time to realise the disappointment.

"Jim," he whispered, "take that, and stand by for trouble."

And he passed me a double-barrelled pistol.

At the same time he began quietly moving northward, and in a few steps had put the hollow between us two and the other five. Then he looked at me and nodded, as much as to say, "Here is a narrow corner," as, indeed, I thought it was. His looks were now quite friendly; and I was so revolted at these constant changes, that I could not forbear whispering, "So you've changed sides again."

There was no time left for him to answer in. The buccaneers, with oaths and cries, began to leap, one after another, into the pit, and to dig with their fingers, throwing the boards aside as they did so. Morgan found a piece of gold. He held it up with a perfect spout of oaths. It was a two-guinea piece, and it went from hand to hand among them for a quarter of a minute.

"Two guineas!" roared Merry, shaking it at Silver. "That's your seven hundred thousand pounds, is it? You're the man for bargains, ain't you? You're him that never bungled nothing you wooden-headed lubber!"

"Dig away, boys," said Silver, with the coolest insolence; "you'll find some pig-nuts and I shouldn't wonder."

"Pig-nuts!" repeated Merry, in a scream. "Mates, do you hear that? I tell you, now, that man there knew it all along. Look in the face of him, and you'll see it wrote there."

'Before you could wink, Long John had fired two barrels of a pistol into the struggling Merry.' (p. 193)

"Ah, Merry," remarked Silver, "standing for cap'n again? You're a pushing lad, to be sure."

But this time every one was entirely in Merry's favour. They began to scramble out of the excavation, darting furious glances behind them. One thing I observed, which looked well for us: they all got out upon the opposite side from Silver.

Well, there we stood, two on one side, five on the other, the pit between us, and nobody screwed up high enough to offer the first blow. Silver never moved; he watched them, very upright on his crutch, and looked as cool as ever I saw him. He was brave, and no mistake.

At last, Merry seemed to think a speech might help matters.

"Mates," says he, "there's two of them alone there; one's the old cripple that brought us all here and blundered us down to this; the other's that cub that I mean to have the heart of. Now, mates—"

He was raising his arm and his voice, and plainly meant to lead a charge. But just then – crack! crack! crack! – three musket-shots flashed out of the thicket. Merry tumbled head foremost into the excavation; the man with the bandage spun round like a teetotum, and fell all his length upon his side, where he lay dead, but still twitching; and the other three turned and ran for it with all their might.

Before you could wink, Long John had fired two barrels of a pistol into the struggling Merry; and as the man rolled up his eyes at him in his last agony, "George," said he, "I reckon I settled you."

At the same moment the doctor, Gray, and Ben Gunn joined us, with smoking muskets, from among the nutmeg trees.

"Forward!" cried the doctor. "Double quick, my lads. We must head 'em off the boats."

And we set off, at a great pace, sometimes plunging through the bushes to the chest.

I tell you, but Silver was anxious to keep up with us. The work that man went through, leaping on his crutch till the muscles of his chest were fit to burst, was work no sound man ever equalled; and so thinks the doctor. As it was, he was already thirty yards behind us, and on the verge of strangling, when we reached the brow of the slope.

"Doctor," he hailed, "see there! no hurry!"

Sure enough there was no hurry. In a more open part of the plateau, we could see the three survivors still running in the same direction as they had started right for Mizzen-mast Hill. We were already between them and the boats; and so we four sat down to breathe, while Long John, mopping his face, came slowly up with us.

"Thank ye kindly, doctor," says he. "You came in in about the nick, I guess, for me and Hawkins. And so it's you, Ben Gunn!" he added. "Well, you're a nice one to be sure."

"I'm Ben Gunn, I am," replied the maroon, wriggling like an eel in his embarrassment. "And," he added, after a long pause, "how do, Mr. Silver. Pretty well, I thank ye, says you."

"Ben, Ben," murmured Silver, "to think as you've done me!"

The doctor sent back Gray for one of the pickaxes, deserted, in their flight, by the mutineers; and then as we proceeded leisurely downhill to where the boats were lying, related, in a few words, what had taken place. It was a story that profoundly interested Silver; and Ben Gunn, the half-idiot maroon, was the hero from beginning to end.

Ben, in his long, lonely wanderings about the island, had found the skeleton – it was he that had rifled it; he had found the treasure; he had dug it up (it was the haft of his pickaxe that lay broken in the excavation); he had carried it on his back, in many weary journeys, from the foot of a tall pine to a cave he had on the two-pointed hill at the north-east angle of the island, and there it had lain stored in safety since two months before the arrival of the *Hispaniola*.

When the doctor had wormed this secret from him, on the afternoon of the attack, and when next morning he saw the anchorage deserted, he had gone to Silver, given him the chart, which was now useless – given him the stores, for Ben Gunn's cave was well supplied with goats' meat salted by himself – given anything and everything to get a chance of moving in safety from the stockade to the two-pointed hill, there to be clear of malaria and keep a guard upon the money.

"As for you, Jim," he said, "it went against my heart, but I did what I thought best for those who had stood by their duty; and if you were not one of these, whose fault was it?"

That morning, finding that I was to be involved in the horrid disappointment he had prepared for the mutineers, he had run all the way to the cave, and, leaving squire to guard the captain, had taken Gray and the maroon, and started, making the diagonal across the island, to be at hand beside the pine. Soon, however, he saw that our party had the start of him;

and Ben Gunn, being fleet of foot, had been despatched in front to do his best alone. Then it had occurred to him to work upon the superstitions of his former shipmates; and he was so far successful that Gray and the doctor had come up and were already ambushed before the arrival of the treasure-hunters.

"Ah," said Silver, "it were fortunate for me that I had Hawkins here. You would have let old John be cut to bits, and never given it a thought, doctor."

"Not a thought," replied Doctor Livesey cheerily.

And by this time we had reached the gigs. The doctor, with the pickaxe, demolished one of them, and then we all got aboard the other and set out to go round by sea for North Inlet.

This was a run of eight or nine miles. Silver, though he was almost killed already with fatigue, was set to an oar, like the rest of us, and we were soon skimming swiftly over a smooth sea. Soon we passed out of the straits and doubled the south-east corner of the island, round which, four days ago, we had towed the *Hispaniola*.

As we passed the two-pointed hill, we could see the black mouth of Ben Gunn's cave, and a figure standing by it, leaning on a musket. It was the squire; and we waved a handkerchief and gave him three cheers, in which the voice of Silver joined as heartily as any.

Three miles farther, just inside the mouth of North Inlet, what should we meet but the *Hispaniola,* cruising by herself! The last flood had lifted her; and had there been much wind, or a strong tide current, as in the southern anchorage, we should never had found her more, or found her stranded beyond help. As it was there was little amiss, beyond the wreck of the mainsail. Another anchor was got ready, and dropped in a fathom and a half of water. We all pulled round again to Rum Cove the nearest point for Ben Gunn's treasure-house; and then Gray, single-handed, returned with the gig to the *Hispaniola,* where he was to pass the night on guard.

A gentle slope ran up from the beach to the entrance of the cave. At the top, the squire met us. To me he was cordial and kind, saying nothing of my escapade, either in the way of blame or praise. At Silver's polite salute he somewhat flushed.

"John Silver," he said, "you're a prodigious villain and impostor – a monstrous impostor, sir. I am told I am not to prosecute you. Well, then, I will not. But the dead men, sir, hang about your neck like millstones."

"Thank you kindly, sir," replied Long John, again saluting.

"I dare you to thank me!" cried the squire. "It is a gross dereliction of my duty. Stand back."

And thereupon we all entered the cave. It was a large, airy place, with a little spring and a pool of clear water, overhung with ferns. The floor was sand. Before a big fire lay Captain Smollett; and in a far corner, only duskily flickered over by the blaze, I beheld great heaps of coin and quadrilaterals built of bars of gold. That was Flint's treasure that we had come so far to seek, and that had cost already the lives of seventeen men from the *Hispaniola*. How many it had cost in the amassing, what blood and sorrow, what good ships scuttled on the deep, what brave men walking the plank blindfold, what shot of cannon, what shame and lies and cruelty, perhaps no man alive could tell. Yet there were still three upon that island – Silver, and old Morgan, and Ben Gunn – who had each taken his share in these crimes, as each had hoped in vain to share in the reward.

"Come in, Jim," said the captain. "You're a good boy in your line, Jim; but I don't think you and me'll go to sea again. You're too much of the born favourite for me. Is that you, John Silver? What brings you here, man?"

"Come back to my dooty, sir," returned Silver.

"Ah!" said the captain; and that was all he said.

What a supper I had of it that night, with all my friends around me; and what a meal it was, with Ben Gunn's salted goat, and some delicacies and a bottle of old wine from the *Hispaniola!* Never, I am sure, were people gayer or happier. And there was Silver, sitting back almost out of the firelight, but eating heartily, prompt to spring forward when anything was wanted, even joining quietly in our laughter – the same bland, polite, obsequious seaman of the voyage out.

CHAPTER XXXIV

AND LAST

THE next morning we fell early to work, for the transportation of this great mass of gold near a mile by land to the beach, and thence three miles by boat to the *Hispaniola,* was a considerable task for so small a number of workmen. The three fellows still abroad upon the island did not greatly trouble us; a single sentry on the shoulder of the hill was sufficient to ensure us against any sudden onslaught, and we thought, besides, they had had more than enough of fighting.

Therefore, the work was pushed on briskly. Gray and Ben Gunn came and went with the boat, while the rest, during their absences, piled treasure on the beach. Two of the bars, slung in a rope's end, made a good load for a grown man – one that he was glad to walk slowly with. For my part, as I was not much use at carrying, I was kept busy all day in the cave, packing the minted money into bread-bags.

It was a strange collection, like Billy Bones's hoard for the diversity of coinage, but so much larger and so much more varied that I think I never had more pleasure than in sorting them. English, French, Spanish, Portuguese, Georges, and Louises, doubloons and double guineas and moidores and sequins, the pictures of all the kings of Europe for the last hundred years, strange Oriental pieces stamped with what looked like wisps of string or bits of spider's web, round pieces and square pieces, and pieces bored through the middle, as if to wear them round your neck – nearly every variety of money in the world must, I think, have found a place in that collection; and for number, I am sure they were like autumn leaves, so that my back ached with stooping and my fingers with sorting them out.

Day after day this work went on; by every evening a fortune had been stowed aboard, but there was another fortune waiting for the morrow; and all this time we heard nothing of the three surviving mutineers.

At last – I think it was on the third night – the doctor and I were strolling

'I was kept busy all day in the cave, packing the minted money into bread-bags.' (p. 197)

on the shoulder of the hill where it overlooks the lowlands of the isle, when, from out the thick darkness below, the wind brought us a noise between shrieking and singing. It was only a snatch that reach our ears, followed by the former silence.

"Heaven forgive them," said the doctor; "'tis the mutineers!"

"All drunk, sir," struck in the voice of Silver from behind us.

Silver, I should say, was allowed his entire liberty, and, in spite of daily rebuffs, seemed to regard himself once more as quite a privileged and friendly dependent. Indeed, it was remarkable how well he bore these slights, and with what unwearying politeness he kept on trying to ingratiate himself with all. Yet, I think, none treated him better than a dog; unless it was Ben Gunn, who was still terribly afraid of his old quartermaster, or myself, who had really something to thank him for; although for that matter, I suppose, I had reason to think even worse of him than anybody else, for I had seen him meditating a fresh treachery upon the plateau. Accordingly, it was pretty gruffly that the doctor answered him.

"Drunk or raving," said he.

"Right you were, sir," replied Silver; "and precious little odds which, to you and me."

"I suppose you would hardly ask me to call you a humane man," returned the doctor with a sneer, "and so my feelings may surprise you, Master Silver. But if I were sure they were raving – as I am morally certain one, at least, of them is down with fever – I should leave this camp, and, at whatever risk to my own carcass, take them the assistance of my skill."

"Ask your pardon, sir, you would be very wrong," quoth Silver. "You would lose your precious life, and you may lay to that. I'm on your side now, hand and glove; and I shouldn't wish for to see the party weakened, let alone yourself, seeing as I know what I owes you. But these men down there, they couldn't keep their word – no, not supposing they wished to; and what's more, they couldn't believe as you could."

"No," said the doctor. "You're the man to keep your word, we know that."

Well, that was about the last news we had of the three pirates. Only once we heard a gunshot a great way off, and supposed them to be hunting. A council was held, and it was decided that we must desert them on the island – to the huge glee, I must say, of Ben Gunn, and with the strong approval of Gray. We left a good stock of powder and shot, the bulk of the salt goat, a few medicines, and some other necessaries, tools, clothing, a spare sail, a fathom or two of rope, and, by the particular desire of the doctor, a handsome present of tobacco.

That was about our last doing on the island. Before that, we had got the treasure stowed, and had shipped enough water and the remainder of the goat meat, in case of any distress; and at last, one fine morning, we weighed anchor, which was about all that we could manage, and stood out of North Inlet, the same colours flying that the captain had flown and fought under at the palisade.

The three fellows must have been watching us closer than we thought for, as we soon had proved. For, coming through the narrows, we had to lie very near the southern point, and there we saw all three of them kneeling together on a spit of sand, with their arms raised in supplication. It went to all our hearts, I think, to leave them in that wretched state; but we could not risk another mutiny; and to take them home for the gibbet would have been a cruel sort of kindness. The doctor hailed them and told them of the stores we had left, and where they were to find them. But they continued to call us by name, and appeal to us, for God's sake, to be merciful, and not leave them to die in such a place.

At last, seeing the ship still bore on her course, and was now swiftly drawing out of earshot, one of them – I know not which it was – leapt to his feet with a hoarse cry, whipped his musket to his shoulder, and sent a shot whistling over Silver's head and through the main-sail.

After that, we kept under cover of the bulwarks, and when next I looked out they had disappeared from the spit, and the spit itself had almost melted out of sight in the growing distance. That was, at least, the end of that; and before noon, to my inexpressible joy, the highest rock of Treasure Island had sunk into the blue round of sea.

We were so short of men that every one on board had to bear a hand – only the captain lying on a mattress in the stern and giving his orders; for, though greatly recovered, he was still in want of quiet. We laid her head for the nearest port in Spanish America, for we could not risk the voyage home without fresh hands; and as it was, what with baffling winds and a couple of fresh gales, we were all worn out before we reached it.

It was just at sundown when we cast anchor in a most beautiful land-locked gulf, and were immediately surrounded by shore boats full of negroes, and Mexican Indians, and half-bloods, selling fruits and vegetables, and offering to dive for bits of money. The sight of so many good-humoured

'. . . we saw all three of them kneeling together on a spit of sand, with their arms raised in supplication.' *(p. 200)*

faces (especially the blacks), the taste of the tropical fruits, and, above all, the lights that began to shine in the town, made a most charming contrast to our dark and bloody sojourn on the island; and the doctor and the squire, taking me alone with them, went ashore to pass the early part of the night. Here they met the captain of an English man-of-war, fell in talk with him, went on board his ship, and, in short, had so agreeable a time, that day was breaking when we came alongside the *Hispaniola.*

Ben Gunn was on deck alone, and, as soon as we came on board, he began, with wonderful contortions, to make us a confession. Silver was gone. The maroon had connived at his escape in a shore boat some hours ago, and he now assured us he had only done so to preserve our lives, which would certainly have been forfeit if "that man with the one leg had stayed aboard." But this was not all. The sea-cook had not gone empty handed. He had cut through a bulkhead unobserved, and had removed one of the sacks of coin, worth, perhaps, three or four hundred guineas, to help him on his further wanderings.

I think we were all pleased to be so cheaply quit of him.

Well, to make a long story short, we got a few hands on board, made a good cruise home, and the *Hispaniola* reached Bristol just as Mr. Blandly was beginning to think of fitting out her consort. Five men only of those who had sailed returned with her. "Drink and the devil had done for the rest," with a vengeance; although, to be sure, we were not quite in so bad a case as that other ship they sang about:—

"But one man of her crew alive.
What put to sea with seventy-five."

All of us had an ample share of the treasure, and used it wisely or foolishly, according to our natures. Captain Smollett is now retired from the sea. Gray not only saved his money, but, being suddenly smit with the desire to rise, also studied his profession; and he is now mate and part owner of a fine full-rigged ship; married besides, and father of a family. As for Ben Gunn, he got a thousand pounds, which he spent or lost in three weeks, or, to be more exact, in nineteen days, for he was back begging on the twentieth. Then he was given a lodge to keep, exactly as he had feared upon the island; and he still lives, a great favourite, though something of a butt, with the country boys, and a notable singer in church on Sundays and saints' days.

Of Silver we have heard no more. That formidable seafaring man with one leg has at last gone clean out of my life; but I dare say he met his old negress, and perhaps still lives in comfort with her and Captain Flint. It is to be hoped so, I suppose, for his chances of comfort in another world are very small.

The bar silver and the arms still lie, for all that I know, where Flint buried them; and certainly they shall lie there for me. Oxen and wain-ropes would not bring me back again to that accursed island; and the worst dreams that ever I have are when I hear the surf booming about its coasts, or start upright in bed, with the sharp voice of Captain Flint still ringing in my ears: "Pieces of eight! pieces of eight!"

THE

LIFE

AND

STRANGE SURPRIZING

ADVENTURES

OF

ROBINSON CRUSOE,

Of *YORK*, MARINER:

Who lived Eight and Twenty Years, all alone in an un-inhabited Island on the Coast of AMERICA, near the Mouth of the Great River of OROONOQUE;

Having been cast on Shore by Shipwreck, wherein all the Men perished but himself.

WITH

An Account how he was at last as strangely deliver'd by PYRATES.

Written by Himself.

THE LIFE AND ADVENTURES OF ROBINSON CRUSOE

CHAPTER ONE

I WAS born in the year 1632, in the city of York, of a good family, though not of that country, my father being a foreigner of Bremen, who settled first at Hull. He got a good estate by merchandise, and leaving off his trade, lived afterward at York, from whence he had married my mother, whose relations were named Robinson, a very good family in that country, and from whom I was called Robinson Kreutznaer; but by the usual corruption of words in England we are now called, nay, we call ourselves, and write our name, Crusoe, and so my companions always called me.

I had two elder brothers, one of whom was lieutenant-colonel to an English regiment of foot in Flanders, formerly commanded by the famous Colonel Lockhart, and was killed at the battle near Dunkirk against the Spaniards. What became of my second brother, I never knew, any more than my father and mother did know what was become of me.

Being the third son of the family, and not bred to any trade, my head began to be filled very early with rambling thoughts. My father, who was very ancient, had given me a competent share of learning, as far as house-education and a country free-school generally goes, and designed me for the law; but I would be satisfied with nothing but going to sea; and my inclination to this led me so strongly against the will, nay, the commands of my father, and against all the entreaties and persuasions of my mother and other friends, that there seemed to be something fatal in that propension of nature tending directly to the life of misery which was to befall me.

My father, a wise and grave man, gave me serious and excellent counsel against what he foresaw was my design. He called me one morning into his chamber, where he was confined by the gout, and expostulated very warmly with me upon this subject: he asked me what reasons, more than a mere wandering inclination, I had for leaving my father's house, and my native country, where I might be well introduced, and had a prospect of raising my fortunes by application and industry, with a life of ease and pleasure. He told me it was for men of desperate fortunes, on

one hand, or of aspiring, superior fortunes, on the other, who went abroad upon adventures, to rise by enterprise, and make themselves famous in undertakings of a nature out of the common road; that these things were all either too far above me, or too far below me; that mine was the middle state, or what might be called the upper station of low life, which he had found, by long experience, was the best state in the world, the most suited to human happiness; not exposed to the miseries and hardships, the labour and sufferings, of the mechanic part of mankind, and not embarrassed with the pride, luxury, ambition, and envy of the upper part of mankind. He told me, I might judge of the happiness of this state by one thing, viz. that this was the state of life which all other people envied; that kings have frequently lamented the miserable consequences of being born to great things, and wished they had been placed in the middle of the two extremes, between the mean and the great; that the wise man gave his testimony to this as the just standard of true felicity, when he prayed to have neither poverty or riches.

He bid me observe it, and I should always find, that the calamities of life were shared among the upper and lower part of mankind; but that the middle station had the fewest disasters, and was not exposed to so many vicissitudes as the higher or lower part of mankind: nay, they were not subjected to so many distempers and uneasinesses, either of body or mind, as those were, who, by vicious living, luxury, and extravagancies, on one hand, or by hard labour, want of necessaries, and mean and insufficient diet, on the other hand, bring distempers upon themselves by the natural consequences of their way of living; that the middle station,of life was calculated for all kind of virtues, and all kind of enjoyments; that peace and plenty were the handmaids of a middle fortune; that temperance, moderation, quietness, health, society, all agreeable diversions, and all desirable pleasures were the blessings attending the middle station of life; that this way men went silently and smoothly through the world, and comfortably out of it, not embarrassed with the labours of the hands or of the head, not sold to the life of slavery for daily bread, or harassed with perplexed circumstances, which rob the soul of peace, and the body of rest; not enraged with the passion of envy, or secret burning lust of ambition for great things; but, in easy circumstances, sliding gently through the world, and sensibly tasting the sweets of living, without the bitter; feeling that they are happy, and learning by every day's experience to know it more sensibly.

After this he pressed me earnestly, and in the most affectionate manner, not to play the young man, not to precipitate myself into miseries which Nature and the station of life I was born in seemed to have provided against; that I was under no necessity of seeking my bread; that he would do well for me, and endeavour to enter me fairly into

the station of life which he had been just recommending to me; and that if I was not very easy and happy in the world it must be my mere fate or fault that must hinder it, and that he should have nothing to answer for, having thus discharged his duty in warn-ing me against measures which he knew would be to my hurt; in a word, that as he would do very kind things for me if I would stay and settle at home as he directed, so he would not have so much hand in my misfortunes, as to give me any encouragement to go away. And to close all, he told me I had my elder brother for an example, to whom he had used the same earnest persuasions to keep him from going into the Low Country wars, but could not prevail, his young desires prompting him to run into the army, where he was killed; and though he said he would not cease to pray for me, yet he would venture to say to me, that if I did take this foolish step, God would not bless me, and I would have leisure hereafter to reflect upon having neglected his counsel when there might be none to assist in my recovery.

I observed, in this last part of his discourse, which was truly prophetic, though I suppose my father did not know it to be so himself; I say, I observed the tears run down his face very plentifully, and especially when he spoke of my brother who was killed; and that, when he spoke of my having leisure to repent, and none to assist me, he was so moved, that he broke off the discourse, and told me his heart was so full, he could say no more to me.

I was sincerely affected with this discourse, as indeed who could be otherwise? and I resolved not to think of going abroad any more, but to settle at home according to my father's desire. But alas! a few days wore it all off; and, in short, to prevent any of my father's farther importunities, in a few weeks after I resolved to run quite away from him. However, I did not act so hastily neither as my first heat of resolution prompted, but I took my mother, at a time when I thought her a little pleasanter than ordinary, and told her that my thoughts were so entirely bent upon seeing the world, that I should never settle to anything with resolution enough to go through with it, and my father had better give me his consent than force me to go without it; that I was now eighteen years old, which was too late to go apprentice to a trade, or clerk to an attorney; that I was sure if I did, I should never serve out my time, and I should certainly run away from my master before my time was out, and go to sea; and if she would speak to my father to let me go but one voyage abroad, if I came home again and did not like it, I would go no more, and I would promise by a double diligence to recover that time I had lost.

This put my mother into a great passion. She told me, she knew it would be to no purpose to speak to my father upon any such subject; that he knew too well what was my interest to give his consent to anything so much for my hurt, and that she wondered how I could think of any such thing after such a discourse as I had had with my father, and such kind and tender expressions as she knew my father had used to me; and that, in short, if I would ruin myself there was no help for me; but I might depend I should never have their consent to it; that for her part, she would not have so much hand in my destruction, and I should never have it to say, that my mother was willing when my father was not.

Though my mother refused to move it to my father, yet, as I have heard afterwards, she reported all the discourse to him, and that my father, after showing a great concern at it, said to her with a sigh, "that boy might be happy if he would stay at home, but if he goes abroad he will be the miserablest wretch that was ever born: I can give no consent to it."

It was not till almost a year after this that I broke loose, though in the meantime I continued obstinately deaf to all proposals of settling to business, and frequently expostulating with my father and mother about their being so positively determined against what they knew my inclinations prompted me to. But being one day at Hull, where I went casually, and without any purpose of making an elopement that time; but I say, being there, and one of my companions being going by sea to London, in his father's ship, and prompting me to go with them, with the common allurement of seafaring men, viz. that it should cost me nothing for my passage, I consulted neither father or mother any more, nor so much as sent them word of it; but leaving them to hear of it as they might, without asking God's blessing, or my father's, without any consideration of circumstances or consequences, and in an ill hour, God knows, on the 1st of September, 1651, I went on board a ship bound for London. Never any young adventurer's misfortunes, I believe, began sooner, or continued longer than mine. The ship was no sooner gotten out of the Humber, but the wind began to blow, and the waves to rise in a most frightful manner; and as I had never been at sea before, I was most inexpressibly sick in body, and terrified in my mind. I began now seriously to reflect upon what I had done, and how justly I was overtaken by the judgment of Heaven for my wicked leaving my father's house, and abandoning my duty. All the good counsel of my parents, my father's tears, and my mother's entreaties, came now fresh into my mind; and my conscience, which was not yet come to the pitch of hardness to which it has been since, reproached me with the contempt of advice, and the breach of my duty to God and my father.

All this while the storm increased, and the sea, which I had never been upon before, went very high, though nothing like what I have seen many times since; no, nor like what I saw a few days after. But it was enough to affect me then, who was but a young sailor, and had never known anything of the matter. I expected every wave would have swallowed us up, and that every time the ship fell down, as I thought, in the trough, or hollow of the sea, we should never rise more; and in this agony of mind I made many vows and resolutions, that if it would please God here to spare my life this one voyage, if ever I got once my foot upon dry land again, I would go directly home to my father, and never set it into a ship again while I lived; that I would take his advice, and never run myself into such miseries as these any more. Now I saw plainly the goodness of his observations about the middle station of life, how easy, how comfortably he had lived all his days, and never had been exposed to tempests at sea, or troubles on shore; and I resolved that I would, like a true repenting prodigal, go home to my father.

These wise and sober thoughts continued all the while the storm continued, and indeed some time after; but the next day the wind was abated and the sea calmer, and

I began to be a little inured to it. However, I was very grave for all that day, being also a little sea-sick still; but towards night the weather cleared up, the wind was quite over, and a charming fine evening followed; the sun went down perfectly clear, and rose so the next morning; and having little or no wind, and a smooth sea, the sun shining upon it, the sight was, as I thought, the most delightful that ever I saw.

I had slept well in the night, and was now no more sea-sick but very cheerful, looking with wonder upon the sea that was so rough and terrible the day before, and could be so calm and so pleasant in so little time after. And now lest my good resolutions should continue, my companion, who had indeed enticed me away, comes to me: "Well, Bob," says he, clapping me on the shoulder, "how do you do after it? I warrant you were frighted, wa'n't you, last night, when it blew but a capful of wind?" "A capful, d'you call it?" said I; "'twas a terrible storm." "A storm, you fool you," replies he; "do you call that a storm? Why, it was nothing at all; give us but a good ship and sea-room, and we think nothing of such a squall of wind as that; but you're but a fresh-water sailor, Bob. Come, let us make a bowl of punch, and we'll forget all that; d'ye see what charming weather 'tis now?" To make short this sad part of my story, we went the old way of all sailors; the punch was made, and I was made drunk with it, and in that one night's wickedness I drowned all my repentance, all my reflections upon my past conduct, and all my resolutions for my future. In a word, as the sea was returned to its smoothness of surface and settled calmness by the abatement of that storm, so the hurry of my thoughts being over, my fears and apprehensions of being swallowed up by the sea being forgotten, and the current of my former desires returned, I entirely forgot the vows and promises that I made in my distress. I found indeed some intervals of reflection, and the serious thoughts did, as it were, endeavour to return again sometimes; but I shook them off, and roused myself from them as it were from a

distemper, and applying myself to drink and company, soon mastered the return of those fits, for so I called them, and I had in five or six days got as complete a victory over conscience as any young fellow that resolved not to be troubled with it could desire. But I was to have another trial for it still; and Providence, as in such cases generally it does, resolved to leave me entirely without excuse. For if I would not take this for a deliverance, the next was to be such a one as the worst and most hardened wretch among us would confess both the danger and the mercy.

The sixth day of our being at sea we came into Yarmouth roads; the wind having been contrary and the weather calm, we had made but little way since the storm. Here we were obliged to come to an anchor, and here we lay, the wind continuing contrary, viz. at south-west, for seven or eight days, during which time a great many ships from Newcastle came into the same roads, as the common harbour where the ships might wait for a wind for the river.

We had not, however, rid here so long, but should have tided it up the river, but that the wind blew too fresh; and after we had lain four or five days, blew very hard. However, the roads being reckoned as good as a harbour, the anchorage good, and our ground-tackle very strong, our men were unconcerned, and not in the least apprehensive of danger, but spent the time in rest and mirth, after the manner of the sea; but the eighth day in the morning the wind increased, and we had all hands at work to strike our topmasts, and make everything snug and close, that the ship might ride as easy as possible. By noon the sea went very high indeed, and our ship rid forecastle in, shipped several seas, and we thought once or twice our anchor had come home; upon which our master ordered out the sheet-anchor, so that we rode with two anchors ahead, and the cables veered out to the better end.

By this time it blew a terrible storm indeed, and now I began to see terror and amazement in the faces even of the seamen themselves. The master, though vigilant to the business of preserving the ship, yet as he went in and out of his cabin by me, I could hear him softly to himself say several times, "Lord be merciful to us, we shall be all lost, we shall be all undone"; and the like. During these first hurries I was stupid, lying still in my cabin, which was in the steerage, and cannot describe my temper; I could ill reassume the first penitence, which I had so apparently trampled upon, and hardened myself against; I thought the bitterness of death had been passed, and that this would be nothing too, like the first. But when the master himself came by me, as I said just now, and said we should be all lost, I was dreadfully frighted; I got up out of my cabin, and looked out. But such a dismal sight I never saw; the sea went mountains high, and broke upon us every three or four minutes; when I could look about, I could see nothing but distress round us. Two ships that rid near us we found had cut their masts by the board, being deep loaden; and our men cried out, that a ship which rid about a mile ahead of us was foundered. Two more ships being driven from their anchors, were run out of the roads to sea at all adventures, and that with not a mast standing. The light ships fared the best, as not so much labouring in the sea; but two or three of them drove, and came close by us, running away with only their sprit-sail out before the wind.

Towards evening the mate and boatswain begged the master of our ship to let them cut away the foremast, which he was very unwilling to. But the boatswain protesting to him that if he did not the ship would founder, he consented; and when they had cut away the foremast, the mainmast stood so loose, and shook the ship so much, they were obliged to cut her away also, and make a clear deck.

Any one may judge what a condition I must be in at all this, who was but a young sailor, and who had been in such a fright before at but a little. But if I can express at this distance the thoughts I had about me at that time, I was in tenfold more horror of mind upon account of my former convictions, and the having returned from them to the resolutions I had wickedly taken at first, than I was at death itself; and these, added to the terror of the storm, put me into such a condition, that I can by no words describe it. But the worst was not come yet; the storm continued with such fury, that the seamen themselves acknowledged they had never known a worse. We had a good ship, but she was deep loaden, and wallowed in the sea, that the seamen every now and then cried out she would founder. It was my advantage in one respect, that I did not know what they meant by founder till I inquired. However, the storm was so violent, that I saw what is not often seen, the master, the boatswain, and some others more sensible than the rest, at their prayers, and expecting every moment when the ship would go to the bottom. In the middle of the night, and under all the rest of our distresses, one of the men that had been down on purpose to see, cried out we had sprung a leak; another said there was four foot water in the hold. Then all hands were called to the pump. At that very word my heart, as I thought, died within me, and I fell backwards upon the side of my bed where I sat, into the cabin. However, the men roused me, and told me, that I, that was able to do nothing before, was as well able to pump as another; at which I stirred up and went to the pump and worked very heartily. While this was doing, the master seeing some light colliers, who, not able to ride out the storm, were obliged to slip and run away to sea, and would come near us, ordered to fire a gun as a signal of distress. I, who knew nothing what that meant, was so surprised that I thought the ship had broke, or some dreadful thing had happened. In a word, I was so surprised that I fell down in a swoon. As this was a time when everybody had his own life to think of, nobody minded me, or what was become of me; but another man stepped up to the pump, and thrusting me aside with his foot, let me lie, thinking I had been dead; and it was a great while before I came to myself

We worked on, but the water increasing in the hold, it was apparent that the ship would founder, and though the storm began to abate a little, yet as it was not possible she could swim till we might run into a port, so the master continued firing guns for help; and a light ship, who had rid it out just ahead of us, ventured a boat out to help us. It was with the utmost hazard the boat came near us, but it was impossible for us to get on board, or for the boat to lie near the ship's side, till at last the men rowing very heartily, and venturing their lives to save ours, our men cast them a rope over the stern with a buoy to it, and then veered it out a great length, which they after great labour and hazard took hold of, and we hauled them close under our stern, and got

all into their boat. It was to no purpose for them or us after we were in the boat to think of reaching to their own ship, so all agreed to let her drive and only to pull her in towards shore as much as we could, and our master promised them that if the boat was staved upon shore he would make it good to their master; so partly rowing and partly driving, our boat went away to the northward, sloping towards the shore almost as far as Winterton Ness.

We were not much more than a quarter of an hour out of our ship but we saw her sink; and then I understood, for the first time, what was meant by a ship foundering in the sea. I must acknowledge, I had hardly eyes to look up when the seamen told me she was sinking; for, from that moment they rather put me into the boat than that I might be said to go in, my heart was, as it were, dead within me, partly with fright, partly with horror of mind and the thoughts of what was yet before me.

While we were in this condition, the men yet labouring at the oar to bring the boat near the shore, we could see, when, our boat mounting the waves, we were able to see the shore, a great many people running along the shore to assist us when we should come near. But we made but slow way towards the shore, nor were we able to reach the shore, till being past the lighthouse at Winterton, the shore falls off to the westward towards Cromer, and so the land broke off a little the violence of the wind. Here we got in, and though not without much difficulty got all safe on shore, and walked afterwards on foot to Yarmouth, where, as unfortunate men, we were used with great humanity as well by the magistrates of the town, who assigned us good quarters, as by particular merchants and owners of ships, and had money given us sufficient to carry us either to London or back to Hull, as we thought fit.

Had I now had the sense to have gone back to Hull, and have gone home, I had been happy, and my father, an emblem of our blessed Saviour's parable, had even killed the fatted calf for me; for hearing the ship I went away in was cast away in Yarmouth road, it was a great while before he had any assurance that I was not drowned.

But my ill fate pushed me on now with an obstinacy that nothing could resist; and though I had several times loud calls from my reason and my more composed judgment to go home, yet I had no power to do it. I know not what to call this, nor will I urge that it is a secret overruling decree that hurries us on to be the instruments of our own destruction, even though it be before us, and that we rush upon it with our eyes open. Certainly nothing but some such decreed unavoidable misery attending, and which it was impossible for me to escape, could have pushed me forward against the calm reasonings and persuasions of my most retired thoughts, and against two such visible instructions as I had met with in my first attempt.

My comrade, who had helped to harden me before, and who was the master's son, was now less forward than I. The first time he spoke to me after we were at Yarmouth, which was not till two or three days, for we were separated in the town to several quarters; I say, the first time he saw me, it appeared his tone was altered, and looking very melancholy and shaking his head, asked me how I did, and telling his father who I was, and how I had come this voyage only for a trial in order to go farther abroad, his father turning to me with a very grave and concerned tone, "Young man," says he, "you ought never to go to sea any more, you ought to take this for a plain and visible token, that you are not to be a seafaring man." "Why, sir?" said I; "will you go to sea no more?" "That is another case," said he; "it is my calling, and therefore my duty; but as you made this voyage for a trial, you see what a taste Heaven has given you of what you are to expect if you persist. Perhaps this has all befallen us on your account, like Jonah in the ship of Tarshish. Pray," continues he, "what are you, and on what account did you go to sea?" Upon that I told him some of my story; at the end of which he burst out with a strange kind of passion. "What had I done," says he, "that such an unhappy wretch should come into my ship? I would not set my foot in the same ship with thee again for a thousand pounds." This indeed was, as I said, an excursion of his spirits, which were yet agitated by the sense of his loss, and was farther than he could have authority to go. However, he afterwards talked very gravely to me; exhorted me to go back to my father, and not tempt Providence to my ruin; told me, I might see a visible hand of Heaven against me; "and, young man," said he, "depend upon it, if you do not go back, wherever you go you will meet with nothing but disasters and disappointments, till your father's words are fulfilled upon you."

We parted soon after; for I made him little answer, and I saw him no more; which way he went, I know not. As for me, having some money in my pocket, I travelled to London by land; and there, as well as on the road, had many struggles with myself

what course of life I should take, and whether I should go home, or go to sea.

As to going home, shame opposed the best motions that offered to my thoughts; and it immediately occurred to me how I should be laughed at among the neighbours, and should be ashamed to see, not my father and mother only, but even everybody else; from whence I have since often ob-served how incongruous and irrational the common temper of mankind is, especially of youth, to that reason which ought to guide them in such cases, viz. that they are not ashamed to sin, and yet are ashamed to repent; not ashamed of the action for which they ought justly to be esteemed fools, but are ashamed of the returning, which only can make them be esteemed wise men.

In this state of life, however, I remained some time, uncertain what measures to take, and what course of life to lead. An irresistible reluctance continued to going home; and as I stayed awhile, the remembrance of the distress I had been in wore off; and as that abated, the little motion I had in my desires to a return wore off with it, till at last I quite laid aside the thoughts of it, and looked out for a voyage.

That evil influence which carried me first away from my father's house, that hurried me into the wild and indigested notion of raising my fortune, and that impressed those conceits so forcibly upon me, as to make me deaf to all good advice, and to the entreaties, and even command of my father; I say, the same influence, whatever it was, presented the most unfortunate of all enterprises to my view; and I went on board a vessel bound to the coast of Africa; or, as our sailors vulgarly call it, a voyage to Guinea.

It was my great misfortune, that in all these adventures I did not ship myself as a sailor; whereby, though I might indeed have worked a little harder than ordinary, yet, at the same time, I had learned the duty and office of a foremastman, and in time might have qualified myself for a mate or lieutenant, if not for a master. But as it was always my fate to choose for the worse, so I did here; for having money in my pocket, and good clothes upon my back, I would always go on board in the habit of a gentleman; and so I neither had any business in the ship, or learned to do any.

CHAPTER TWO

It was my lot first of all to fall into pretty good company in London, which does not always happen to such loose and misguided young fellows as I then was; the devil generally not omitting to lay some snare for them very early. But it was not so with me. I first fell acquainted with the master of a ship who had been on the coast of Guinea, and who, having had very good success there, was resolved to go again; and who, taking a fancy to my conversation, which was not at all disagreeable at that time, hearing me say I had a mind to see the world, told me if I would go the voyage with him I should be at no expense; I should be his messmate and his companion; and if I could carry anything with me, I should have all the advantage of it that trade would admit, and perhaps I might meet with some encouragement.

I embraced the offer; and, entering into a strict friendship with this captain, who was an honest and plain-dealing man, I went the voyage with him, and carried a small adventure with me, which, by the disinterested honesty of my friend the captain, I increased very considerably; for I carried about £40 in such toys and trifles as the captain directed me to buy. This £40 I had mustered together by the assistance of some of my relations whom I corresponded with, and who, I believe, got my father, or at least my mother, to contribute so much as that to my first adventure.

This was the only voyage which I may say was successful in all my adventures, and which I owe to the integrity and honesty of my friend the captain; under whom also I got a competent knowledge of the mathematics and the rules of navigation, learned how to keep an account of the ship's course, take an observation, and, in short, to understand some things that were needful to be understood by a sailor. For, as he took delight to introduce me, I took delight to learn; and, in a word, this voyage made me both a sailor and a merchant; for I brought home five pounds nine ounces of gold dust for my adventure, which yielded me in London at my return almost £300, and this filled me with those aspiring thoughts which have since so completed my ruin.

Yet even in this voyage I had my misfortunes too; particularly, that I was continually sick, being thrown into a violent calenture by the excessive heat of the

climate; our principal trading being upon the coast, from the latitude of 15 degrees north even to the line itself.

I was now set up for a Guinea trader; and my friend, to my great misfortune, dying soon after his arrival, I resolved to go the same voyage again, and I embarked in the same vessel with one who was his mate in the former voyage, and had now got the command of the ship. This was the unhappiest voyage that ever man made; for though I did not carry quite £100 of my new-gained wealth, so that I had £200 left, and which I lodged with my friend's widow, who was very just to me, yet I fell into terrible misfortunes in this voyage; and the first was this, viz. our ship making her course towards the Canary Islands, or rather between those islands and the African

shore, was surprised in the grey of the morning by a Turkish rover of Sallee, who gave chase to us with all the sail she could make. We crowded also as much canvas as our yards would spread, or our masts carry, to have got clear; but finding the pirate gained upon us, and would certainly come up with us in a few hours, we prepared to fight, our ship having twelve guns, and the rogue eighteen. About three in the afternoon he came up with us, and bringing to, by mistake, just athwart our quarter, instead of athwart our stern, as he intended, we brought eight of our guns to bear on that side, and poured in a broadside upon him, which made him sheer off again, after returning our fire and pouring in also his small-shot from near 200 men which he had on board. However, we had not a man touched, all our men keeping close. He prepared to attack us again, and we to defend ourselves; but laying us on board the next time upon our other quarter, he entered sixty men upon our decks, who immediately fell to cutting and hacking the decks and rigging. We plied them with small-shot, half-pikes, powder-chests,and such like, and cleared our deck of them twice. However, to cut short this melancholy part of our story, our ship being disabled, and three of our men killed and eight wounded, we were obliged to yield, and were carried all prisoners into Sallee, a port belonging to the Moors.

The usage I had there was not so dreadful as at first I apprehended, nor was I carried up the country to the emperor's court, as the rest of our men were, but was kept by the captain of the rover as his proper prize, and made his slave, being young and nimble, and fit for his business. At this surprising change of my circumstances, from a merchant to a miserable slave, I was perfectly overwhelmed; and now I looked back upon my father's prophetic discourse to me, that I should be miserable, and have none to relieve me; which I thought was now so effectually brought to pass, that it could not be worse; that now the hand of Heaven had overtaken me, and I was undone, without redemption. But, alas! this was but a taste of the misery I was to go through, as will appear in the sequel of this story.

As my new patron, or master, had taken me home to his house, so I was in hopes that he would take me with him when he went to sea again, believing that it would some time or other be his fate to be taken by a Spanish or Portugal man-of-war; and that then I should be set at liberty. But this hope of mine was soon taken away; for when he went to sea, he left me on shore to look after his little garden, and do the common drudgery of slaves about his house; and when he came home again from his cruise, he ordered me to lie in the cabin to look after the ship.

Here I meditated nothing but my escape, and what method I might take to effect it, but found no way that had the least probability in it. Nothing presented to make the supposition of it rational; for I had nobody to communicate it to that would embark with me; no fellow-slave, no Englishman, Irishman, or Scotsman there but myself; so that for two years, though I often pleased myself with the imagination, yet I never had the least encouraging prospect of putting it in practice.

After about two years an odd circumstance presented itself, which put the old thought of making some attempt for my liberty again in my head. My patron lying at home longer than usual without fitting out his ship, which, as I heard, was for want of money, he used constantly, once or twice a week, sometimes oftener, if the weather was fair, to take the ship's pinnace, and go out into the road a-fishing; and as he always took me and a young Maresco with him to row the boat, we made him very merry, and I proved very dexterous in catching fish; insomuch, that sometimes he would send me with a Moor, one of his kinsmen, and the youth the Maresco, as they called him, to catch a dish of fish for him.

It happened one time that, going a-fishing in a stark calm morning, a fog rose so thick, that though we were not half a league from the shore we lost sight of it; and rowing we knew not whither or

which way, we laboured all day, and all the next night, and when the morning came we found we had pulled off to sea instead of pulling in for the shore; and that we were at least two leagues from the shore. However, we got well in again, though with a great deal of labour, and some danger, for the wind began to blow pretty fresh in the morning; but particularly we were all very hungry.

But our patron, warned by this disaster, resolved to take more care of himself for the future; and having lying by him the long-boat of our English ship which he had taken, he resolved he would not go a-fishing any more without a compass and some provision; so he ordered the carpenter of his ship, who also was an English slave, to build a little stateroom, or cabin, in the middle of the long-boat, like that of a barge, with a place to stand behind it to steer and haul home the mainsheet, and room before for a hand or two to stand and work the sails. She sailed with what we call a shoulder-of-mutton sail; and the boom jibbed over the top of the cabin, which lay very snug and low, and had in it room for him to lie, with a slave or two, and a table to eat on, with some small lockers to put in some bottles of such liquor as he thought fit to drink; particularly his bread, rice, and coffee.

We went frequently out with this boat a-fishing, and as I was most dexterous to catch fish for him, he never went without me. It happened that he had appointed to go out in this boat, either for pleasure or for fish, with two or three Moors of some distinction in that place, and for whom he had provided extraordinarily; and had therefore sent on board the boat overnight a larger store of provisions than ordinary; and had ordered me to get ready three fuzees with powder and shot, which were on board his ship, for that they designed some sport of fowling as well as fishing.

I got all things ready as he had directed, and waited the next morning with the boat, washed clean, her ancient and pendants out, and everything to accommodate his guests; when by-and-by my patron came on board alone, and told me his guests had put off going, upon some business that fell out, and ordered me with the man and boy, as usual, to go out with the boat and catch them some fish, for that his friends were to sup at his house; and commanded that as soon as I had got some fish I should bring it home to his house; all which I prepared to do.

This moment my former notions of deliverance darted into my thoughts, for now I found I was like to have a little ship at my command; and my master being gone, I prepared to furnish myself, not for a fishing business, but for a voyage; though I knew not, neither did I so much as consider, whither I should steer; for anywhere, to get out of that place, was my way.

My first contrivance was to make a pretence to speak to this Moor, to get something for our subsistence on board; for I told him we must not presume to eat of our patron's bread. He said that was true; so he brought a large basket of rusk or biscuit of their kind, and three jars with fresh water, into the boat. I knew where my patron's case of bottles stood, which it was evident by the make were taken out of some English prize; and I conveyed them into the boat while the Moor was on shore, as if they had been there before for our master. I conveyed also a great lump of beeswax into the boat, which weighed about half a hundredweight, with a parcel of twine or thread, a hatchet, a saw, and a hammer, all which were of great use to us afterwards, especially the wax to make candles. Another trick I tried upon him, which he innocently came into also: his name was Ismael, who they call Muley, or Moley: so I called to him; "Moley," said I, "our patron's guns are on board the boat, can you not get a little powder and shot? it may be we may kill some alcamies (a fowl like our curlews) for ourselves, for I know he keeps the gunner's stores in the ship." "Yes," says he, "I'll bring some;" and accordingly he brought a great leather pouch, which held about a pound and half of powder, or rather more, and another with shot, that had five or six pound, with some bullets, and put all into the boat. At the same time I had found some powder of my master's in the great cabin, with which I filled one of the large bottles in the case, which was almost empty, pouring what was in it into another; and thus furnished with everything needful, we sailed out of the port to fish. The castle, which is at the entrance of the port, knew who we were, and took no notice of us; and we were not above a mile out of the port before we hauled in our sail, and set us down to fish. The wind blew from the N. N . E., which was contrary to my desire; for had it blown southerly I had been sure to have made the coast of Spain, and at least reached to the bay of Cadiz; but my resolutions were, blow which way it would, I would be gone from the horrid place where I was, and leave the rest to Fate.

After we had fished some time and catched nothing, for, when I had fish on my hook I would not pull them up that he might not see them, I said to the Moor, "This will not do; our master will not be thus served; we must stand farther off." He, thinking no harm, agreed, and being in the head of the boat set the sails; and as I had the helm I run the boat out near a league farther, and then brought her to as if I would fish; when giving the boy the helm, I stepped forward to where the Moor was, and making as if I stooped for something behind him, I took him by surprise with my arm under his twist, and tossed him clear overboard into the sea. He rose immediately, for he swam like a cork, and called to me, begged to be taken in, told me he would go all the world over with me. He swam so strong after the boat, that he would have reached me very quickly, there being but little wind; upon which I stepped into the cabin, and fetching one of the fowling-pieces, I presented it at him, and told him I had done him no hurt, and if he would be quiet I would do him none. "But," said I, "you swim well enough to reach to the shore, and the sea is calm; make the best of your way to shore, and I will do you no harm; but if you come near the boat I'll shoot you through the head, for I am resolved to have my liberty." So he turned himself about, and swam for the shore, and I make no doubt but he reached it with ease, for he was an excellent swimmer.

I could have been content to have taken this Moor with me, and have drowned the boy, but there was no venturing to trust him. When he was gone I turned to the boy, whom they called Xury, and said to him, "Xury, if you will be faithful to me I'll make you a great man; but if you will not stroke your face to be true to me," that is, swear by Mahomet and his father's beard, "I must throw you into the sea too." The boy smiled in my face, and spoke so innocently, that I could not mistrust him, and swore to be faithful to me, and go all over the world with me.

' "If you come near the boat, I'll shoot you . . . " ' (p. 17)

While I was in view of the Moor that was swimming, I stood out directly to sea with the boat, rather stretching to windward, that they might think me gone towards the straits' mouth (as indeed any one that had been in their wits must have been supposed to do); for who would have supposed we were sailed on to the southward, to the truly Barbarian coast, where whole nations of negroes were sure to surround us with their canoes, and destroy us; where we could never once go on shore but we should be devoured by savage beasts, or more merciless savages of human kind?

But as soon as it grew dusk in the evening, I changed my course, and steered directly south and by east, bending my course a little toward the east, that I might keep in with the shore; and having a fair, fresh gale of wind, and a smooth, quiet sea, I made such sail that I believe by the next day at three o'clock in the afternoon, when I first made the land, I could not be less than 150 miles south of Sallee; quite beyond the Emperor of Morocco's dominions, or indeed of any other king thereabouts, for we saw no people.

Yet such was the fright I had taken at the Moors, and the dreadful apprehensions I had of falling into their hands, that I would not stop, or go on shore, or come to an anchor, the wind continuing fair, till I had sailed in that manner five days; and then the wind shifting to the southward, I concluded also that if any of our vessels were in chase of me, they also would now give over; so I ventured to make to the coast, and came to an anchor in the mouth of a little river, I knew not what, or where; neither what latitude, what country, what nation, or what river. I neither saw, or desired to see, any people; the principal thing I wanted was fresh water. We came into this creek in the evening, resolving to swim on shore as soon as it was dark, and discover the country; but as soon as it was quite dark we heard such dreadful noises of the barking, roaring, and howling of wild creatures, of we knew not what kinds, that the poor boy was ready to die with fear, and begged of me not to go on shore till day. "Well, Xury," said I, "then I will not; but it may be, we may see men by day, who will be as bad to us as those lions." "Then we give them the shoot-gun," says Xury, laughing; "make them run way." Such English Xury spoke by conversing among us slaves. However, I was glad to see the boy so cheerful, and I gave him a dram (out of our patron's case of bottles) to cheer him up. After all, Xury's advice was good, and I took it. We dropped our little anchor, and lay still all night: I say still, for we slept none! for in two or three hours we saw vast great creatures (we knew not what to call them), of many sorts, come down to the seashore, and run into the water, wallowing and washing themselves, for the pleasure of cooling themselves; and they made such hideous howlings and yellings, that I never indeed heard the like.

Xury was dreadfully frighted, and indeed so was I too; but we were both more frighted when we heard one of these mighty creatures come swimming towards our boat; we could not see him, but we might hear him by his blowing to be a monstrous huge and furious beast. Xury said it was a lion, and it might be so for aught I know; but poor Xury cried to me to weigh the anchor and row away. "No," says I, "Xury; we can slip our cable with the buoy to it, and go off to sea; they cannot follow us far." I had no sooner said so but I perceived the creature (whatever it was) within

two oars' length, which something surprised me; however, I immediately stepped to the cabin door, and taking up my gun, fired at him, upon which he immediately turned about and swam towards the shore again.

But it is impossible to describe the horrible noises, and hideous cries and howlings, that were raised, as well upon the edge of the shore as higher within the country, upon the noise or report of the gun, a thing I have some reason to believe those creatures had never heard before. This convinced me that there was no going on shore for us in the night upon that coast; and how to venture on shore in the day was another question too; for to have fallen into the hands of any of the savages, had been as bad as to have fallen into the hands of lions and tigers; at least we were equally apprehensive of the danger of it.

Be that as it would, we were obliged to go on shore somewhere or other for water, for we had not a pint left in the boat; when or where to get to it, was the point. Xury said if I would let him go on shore with one of the jars, he would find if there was any water and bring some to me. I asked him why he would go? why I should not go and he stay in the boat? The boy answered with so much affection, that made me love him ever after. Says he, "If wild mans come, they eat me, you go way." "Well, Xury," said I, "we will both go; and if the wild mans come, we will kill them, they shall eat neither of us." So I gave Xury a piece of rusk bread to eat, and a dram out of our patron's case of bottles which I mentioned before; and we hauled in the boat as near the shore as we thought was proper, and so waded on shore, carrying nothing but our arms and two jars for water

I did not care to go out of sight of the boat, fearing the coming of canoes with savages down the river; but the boy seeing a low place about a mile up the country, rambled to it, and by-and-by I saw him come running towards me. I thought he was pursued by some savage, or frighted with some wild beast, and I ran forward towards him to help him; but when I came nearer to him, I saw something hanging over his shoulders, which was a creature that he had shot, like a hare, but different in colour, and longer legs. However, we were very glad of it, and it was very good meat; but the great joy that poor Xury came with was to tell me he had found good water, and seen no wild mans.

But we found afterwards that we need not take such pains for water; for a little higher up the creek where we were, we found the water fresh when the tide was out, which flowed but a little way up; so we filled our jars, and feasted on the

hare we had killed; and prepared to go on our way, having seen no footsteps of any human creature in that part of the country.

As I had been one voyage to this coast before, I knew very well that the islands of the Canaries, and the Cape de Verde Islands also, lay not far off from the coast. But as I had no instruments to take an observation to know what latitude we were in, and did not exactly know, or at least remember, what latitude they were in, I knew not where to look for them, or when to stand off to sea towards them; otherwise I might now easily have found some of these islands. But my hope was, that if I stood along this coast till I came to that part where the English traded, I should find some of their vessels upon their usual design of trade, that would relieve and take us in.

By the best of my calculation, that place where I now was, must be that country which, lying between the Emperor of Morocco's dominions and the Negroes, lies waste, and uninhabited, except by wild beasts; the Negroes having abandoned it, and gone farther south, for fear of the Moors, and the Moors not thinking it worth inhabiting, by reason of its barrenness; and, indeed, both forsaking it because of the prodigious numbers of tigers, lions, leopards, and other furious creatures which harbour there: so that the Moors use it for their hunting only, where they go like an army, two or three thousand men at a time: and, indeed, for near an hundred miles together upon this coast, we saw nothing but a waste, uninhabited country by day, and heard nothing but howlings and roaring of wild beasts by night.

One or twice in the daytime I thought I saw the Pico of Teneriffe, being the high top of the Mountain Teneriffe in the Canaries, and had a great mind to venture out, in hopes of reaching thither; but having tried twice, I was forced in again by contrary winds, the sea also going too high for my little vessel; so I resolved to pursue my first design, and keep along the shore.

Several times I was obliged to land for fresh water after we had left this place; and once in particular, being early in the morning, we came to an anchor under a little point of land which was pretty high; and the tide beginning to flow, we lay still to go farther in. Xury, whose eyes were more about him than it seems mine were, calls softly to me, and tells me that we had best go farther off the shore; "For," says he, "look, yonder lies a dreadful monster on the side of that hillock fast asleep." I looked where he pointed, and saw a dreadful monster indeed, for it was a terrible great lion that lay on the side of the shore, under the shade of a piece of the hill that hung as it were a little over him. "Xury," says I, "you shall go on shore and kill him." Xury looked frighted, and said, "Me kill! he eat me at one mouth"; one mouthful he meant. However, I said no more to the boy, but bade him lie still, and I took our biggest gun, which was almost musket-bore, and loaded it with a good charge of powder, and with two slugs, and laid it down; then I loaded another gun with two bullets; and the third (for we had three pieces) I loaded with five smaller bullets. I took the best aim I could with the first piece to have shot him into the head, but he lay so with his leg raised a little above his nose that the slugs hit his leg about the knee, and broke the bone. He started up growling at first, but finding his leg broke, fell down again, and then got up upon three legs and gave the most hideous roar that ever I heard. I was

a little surprised that I had not hit him on the head. However, I took up the second piece immediately, and, though he began to move off, fired again, and shot him into the head, and had the pleasure to see him drop, and make but little noise, but lay struggling for life. Then Xury took heart, and would have me let him go on shore. "Well, go," said I; so the boy jumped into the water, and taking a little gun in one hand, swam to shore with the other hand, and coming close to the creature, put the muzzle of the piece to his ear, and shot him into the head again, which despatched him quite.

This was game indeed to us, but this was no food; and I was very sorry to loose three charges of powder and shot upon a creature that was good for nothing to us. However, Xury said he would have some of him; so he comes on board, and asked me to give him the hatchet. "For what, Xury?" said I. "Me cut off his head," said he. However, Xury could not cut off his head, but he cut off a foot, and brought it with him, and it was a monstrous great one.

I bethought myself, however, that perhaps the skin of him might one way or other be of some value to us; and I resolved to take off his skin if I could. So Xury and I went to work with him; but Xury was much the better workman at it, for I knew very ill how to do it. Indeed, it took us up both the whole day, but at last we got off the hide of him, and spreading it on the top of our cabin, the sun effectually dried it in two days' time, and it afterwards served me to lie upon.

CHAPTER THREE

After this stop we made on to the southward continually for ten or twelve days, living very sparing on our provisions, which began to abate very much, and going no oftener into the shore than we were obliged to for fresh water. My design in this was to make the river Gambia or Senegal – that is to say, anywhere about the Cape de Verde – where I was in hopes to meet with some European ship; and if I did not, I knew not what course I had to take, but to seek out for the islands, or perish there among the negroes. I knew that all the ships from Europe, which sailed either to the coast of Guinea, or to Brazil, or to the East Indies, made this cape, or those islands; and in a word, I put the whole of my fortune upon this single point, either that I must meet with some ship, or must perish.

When I had pursued this resolution for about ten days longer, as I have said, I began to see that the land was inhabited; and in two or three places, as we sailed by,

'This was game indeed . . .' (p. 22)

we saw people stand upon the shore to look at us; we could also perceive they were quite black, and stark naked. I was once inclined to have gone on shore to them; but Xury was my better counsellor, and said to me, "No go, no go." However, I hauled in nearer the shore that I might talk to them, and I found they ran along the shore by me a good way. I observed they had no weapons in their hands, except one, who had a long slender stick, which Xury said was a lance, and that they would throw them a great way with good aim. So I kept at a distance, but talked with them by signs as well as I could, and particularly made signs for something to eat; they beckoned to me to stop my boat, and that they would fetch me some meat. Upon this I lowered the top of my sail, and lay by, and two of them ran up into the country and in less than half an hour came back, and brought with them two pieces of dried flesh and some corn, such as is the produce of their country; but we neither knew what the one or the other was. However, we were willing to accept it, but how to come at it was our next dispute, for I was not for venturing on shore to them, and they were as much afraid of us; but they took a safe way for us all, for they brought it to the shore and laid it down, and went and stood a great way off till we fetched it on board, and then came close to us again.

We made signs of thanks to them, for we had nothing to make them amends; but an opportunity offered that very instant to oblige them wonderfully; for while we were lying by the shore, came two mighty creatures, one pursuing the other (as we took it) with great fury, from the mountains towards the sea; whether it was the male pursuing the female, or whether they were in sport or in rage, we could not tell, any more than we could tell whether it was usual or strange; but I believe it was the latter, because, in the first place, those ravenous creatures seldom appear but in the night; and, in the second place we found the people terribly frighted, especially the women. The man that had the lance, or dart, did not fly from them, but the rest did; however, as the two creatures ran directly into the water, they did not seem to offer to fall upon any of the negroes, but plunged themselves into the sea, and swam about, as if they had come for their diversion; at last, one of them began to come nearer our boat than at first I expected; but I lay ready for him, for I had loaded my gun with all possible expedition, and bade Xury load both the other. As soon as he came fairly within my reach, I fired, and shot him directly into the head: immediately he sunk down into the water, but rose instantly, and plunged up and down, as if he was struggling for life, and so indeed he was: he immediately made to the shore, but between the wound which was his mortal hurt, and the strangling of the water, he died just before he reached the shore.

It is impossible to express the astonishment of these poor creatures, at the noise and fire of my gun; some of them were even ready to die for fear, and fell down as dead with the very terror. But when they saw the creature dead, and sunk in the water, and that I made signs to them to come to the shore, they took heart and came to the shore, and began to search for the creature. I found him by his blood staining the water; and by the help of a rope, which I slung round him, and gave the negroes to haul, they dragged him on shore, and found that it was a most curious leopard, spotted, and fine to an admirable degree; and the negroes held up their hands with admiration, to think what it was I had killed him with.

The other creature, frighted with the flash of fire, and the noise of the gun, swam on shore, and ran up directly to the mountains from whence they came; nor could I, at that distance, know what it was. I found quickly the Negroes were for eating the flesh of this creature, so I was willing to have them take it as a favour from me; which, when I made signs to them that they might take him, they were very thankful for. Immediately they fell to work with him; and though they had no knife, yet with a sharpened piece of wood, they took off his skin as readily, and much more readily, than we could have done with a knife. They offered me some of the flesh, which I declined, making as if I would give it them, but made signs for the skin, which they gave me very freely, and brought me a great deal more of their provision, which, though I did not understand, yet I accepted. Then I made signs to them for some water, and held out one of my jars to them, turning it bottom upward, to show that it was empty, and that I wanted to have it filled. They called immediately to some of their friends, and there came two women, and brought a great vessel made of earth, and burnt, as I suppose, in the sun; this they set down for me, as before, and I sent Xury on shore with my jars, and filled them all three. The women were as stark naked as the men.

I was now furnished with roots and corn, such as it was, and water; and leaving my friendly negroes, I made forward for about eleven days more, without offering to go near the shore, till I saw the land run out a great length into the sea, at about the distance of four or five leagues before me; and the sea being very calm, I kept a large offing, to make this point. At length, doubling the point, at about two leagues from the land, I saw plainly land on the other side, to seaward; then I concluded, as it was most certain indeed, that this was the Cape de Verde, and those the islands, called from thence Cape de Verde Islands. However, they were at a great distance, and I could not well tell what I had best to do; for, if I should be taken with a fresh of wind, I might neither reach one nor the other.

In this dilemma, as I was very pensive, I stepped into the cabin, and sat me down, Xury having the helm; when, on a sudden, the boy cried out, "Master, master, a ship with a sail!" and the foolish boy was frighted out of his wits, thinking it must needs be some of his master's ships sent to pursue us, when I knew we were gotten far enough out of their reach. I jumped out of the cabin, and immediately saw, not only the ship, but what she was, viz. that it was a Portuguese ship, and, as I thought, was bound to the coast of Guinea, for negroes. But when I observed the course she steered, I was soon convinced they were bound some other way, and did not design to come any nearer to the shore; upon which I stretched out to sea as much as I could, resolving to speak with them if possible.

With all the sail I could make, I found I should not be able to come in their way, but that they would be gone by before I could make any signal to them; but after I had crowded to the utmost, and began to despair, they, it seems, saw me by the help of their perspective glasses, and that it was some European boat, which, as they

supposed, must belong to some ship that was lost, so they shortened sail to let me come up. I was encouraged with this; and as I had my patron's ancient on board, I made a waft of it to them for a signal of distress, and fired a gun, both which they saw; for they told me they saw the smoke, though they did not hear the gun. Upon these signals they were kindly brought to, and lay by for me; and in about three hours' time I came up with them.

They asked me what I was, in Portuguese, and in Spanish, and in French, but I understood none of them; but at last a Scots sailor, who was on board, called to me, and I answered him, and told him I was an Englishman, that I had made my escape out of slavery from the Moors, at Sallee. Then they bade me come on board, and very kindly took me in, and all my goods.

It was an inexpressible joy to me, that any one will believe, that I was thus delivered, as I esteemed it, from such a miserable, and almost hopeless, condition as I was in; and immediately offered all I had to the captain of the ship, as a return for my deliverance. But he generously told me he would take nothing from me, but that all I had should be delivered safe to me when I came to the Brazils. "For," says he, "I have saved your life on no other terms than I would be glad to be saved myself, and it may, one time or other, be my lot to be taken up in the same condition. Besides," says he, "when I carry you to the Brazils, so great a way from your own country, if I should take from you what you have, you will be starved there, and then I only take away that life I have given. No, no, Seignor Inglese," says he, "Mr. Englishman, I will carry you thither in charity, and those things will help you to buy your subsistence there, and your passage home again."

As he was charitable in his proposal, so he was just in the performance to a tittle; for he ordered the seamen that none should offer to touch anything I had; then he took everything into his own possession, and gave me back an exact inventory of them, that I might have them, even so much as my three earthen jars.

As to my boat, it was a very good one, and that he saw, and told me he would buy it of me for the ship's use, and asked me what I would have for it? I told him he had been so generous to me in everything, that I could not offer to make any price of the boat, but left it entirely to him; upon which he told me he would give me a note of his hand to pay me eighty pieces of eight for it at Brazil, and when it came there, if any one offered to give more, he would make it up. He offered me also sixty pieces of eight more for my boy Xury, which I was loth to take; not that I was not willing to let the captain have him, but I was very loth to sell the poor boy's liberty, who had assisted me so faithfully in procuring my own. However, when I let him know my reason, he owned it to be just, and offered me this medium, that he would give the boy an obligation to set him free in ten years if he turned Christian. Upon this, and Xury saying he was willing to go to him, I let the captain have him.

We had a very good voyage to the Brazils, and arrived in the Bay de Todos los Santos, or All Saints' Bay, in about twenty-two days after. And now I was once more delivered from the most miserable of all conditions of life; and what to do next with myself I was now to consider.

The generous treatment the captain gave, I can never enough remember. He would take nothing of me for my passage, gave me twenty ducats for the leopard's skin, and forty for the lion's skin, which I had in my boat, and caused everything I had in the ship to be punctually delivered me; and what I was willing to sell he bought, such as the case of bottles, two of my guns, and a piece of the lump of beeswax – for I had made candles of the rest; in a word, I made about 220 pieces of eight of all my cargo, and with this stock I went on shore in the Brazils.

I had not been long here, but being recommended to the house of a good honest man like himself who had an ingenio as they call it, that is, a plantation and a sugar-house, I lived with him some time, and acquainted myself by that means with the manner of their planting and making of sugar; and seeing how well the planters lived, and how they grew rich suddenly, I resolved, if I could get licence to settle there, I would turn planter among them, resolving in the meantime to find out some way to get my money which I had left in London remitted to me. To this purpose, getting a kind of a letter of naturalisation, I purchased as much land that was uncured as my money would reach, and formed a plan for my plantation and settlement, and such a one as might be suitable to the stock which I proposed to myself to receive from England.

I had a neighbour, a Portuguese of Lisbon, but born of English parents, whose name was Wells, and in much such circumstances as I was. I call him my neighbour, because his plantation lay next to mine, and we went on very sociably together. My stock was but low, as well as his; and we rather planted for food than anything else, for about two years. However, we began to increase, and our land began to come into order; so that the third year we planted some tobacco, and made each of us a large piece of ground ready for planting canes in the year to come. But we both wanted help; and now I found more than before, I had done wrong in parting with my boy Xury.

But, alas! for me to do wrong, that never did right, was no great wonder. I had no remedy, but to go on: I was gotten into an employment quite remote to my genius, and directly contrary to the life I delighted in, and for which I forsook my father's house, and broke through all his good advice: nay, I was coming into the very middle station, or upper degree of low life, which my father advised me to before; and which, if I resolved to go on with, I might as well have staid at home, and never have fatigued myself in the world, as I had done: and I used often to say to myself, I could have done this as well in England, among my friends, as have gone five thousand miles off to do it among strangers and savages, in a wilderness, and at such a distance as never to hear from any part of the world that had the least knowledge of me.

In this manner, I used to look upon my condition with the utmost regret. I had nobody to converse with, but now and then this neighbour; no work to be done, but by the labour of my hands: and I used to say, I lived just like a man cast away upon some desolate island, that had nobody there but himself. But how just has it been, and how should all men reflect, that when they compare their present conditions with others that are worse, Heaven may oblige them to make the exchange, and be convinced of their former felicity by their experience: I say, how just has it been, that

the truly solitary life I reflected on, in an island of mere desolation, should be my lot, who had so often unjustly compared it with the life which I then led, in which, had I continued, I had, in all probability, been exceeding prosperous and rich.

I was in some degree settled in my measures for carrying on the plantation before my kind friend, the captain of the ship that took me up at sea, went back; for the ship remained there in providing his loading, and preparing for his voyage, near three months; when telling him what little stock I had left behind me in London, he gave me this friendly and sincere advice: "Seignor Inglese," says he, for so he always called me, "if you will give me letters, and a procuration here in form to me, with orders to the person who has your money in London to send your effects to Lisbon, to such persons as I shall direct, and in such goods as are proper for this country, I will bring you the produce of them, God willing, at my return. But since human affairs are all subject to changes and disasters, I would have you give orders but for one hundred pounds sterling, which, you say, is half your stock, and let the hazard be run for the first; so that if it come safe, you may order the rest the same way; and if it miscarry, you may have the other half to have recourse to for your supply."

This was so wholesome advice, and looked so friendly, that I could not but be convinced it was the best course I could take; so I accordingly prepared letters to the gentlewoman with whom I had left my money, and a procuration to the Portuguese captain, as he desired.

I wrote the English captain's widow a full account of all my adventures; my slavery, escape, and how I had met with the Portugal captain at sea, the humanity of his behaviour, and in what condition I was now in, with all other necessary directions for my supply. And when this honest captain came to Lisbon, he found means, by some of the English merchants there, to send over not the order only, but a full account of my story to a merchant at London, who represented it effectually to her; whereupon, she not only delivered the money, but out of her own pocket sent the Portugal captain a very handsome present for his humanity and charity to me.

The merchant in London vesting this hundred pounds in English goods, such as the captain had writ for, sent them directly to him at Lisbon, and he brought them all safe to me to the Brazils; among which, without my direction (for I was too young in my business to think of them), he had taken care to have all sorts of tools, iron-work, and utensils necessary for my plantation, and which were of great use to me.

When this cargo arrived, I thought my fortune made, for I was surprised with joy of it; and my good steward, the captain, had laid out the five pounds, which my friend had sent him for a present for himself, to purchase and bring me over a servant under bond for six years' service, and would not accept of any consideration, except a little tobacco, which I would have him accept, being of my own produce.

Neither was this all; but my goods being all English manufactures, such as cloth, stuffs, baize, and things particularly valuable and desirable in the country, I found means to sell them to a very great advantage; so that I may say I had more than four times the value of my first cargo, and was now infinitely beyond my poor neighbour, I mean in the advancement of my plantation; for the first thing I did, I bought me a negro slave, and an European servant also; I mean another besides that which the captain brought me from Lisbon.

But as abused prosperity is oftentimes made the very means of our greatest adversity, so was it with me. I went on the next year with great success in my plantation. I raised fifty great rolls of tobacco on my own ground, more than I had disposed of for necessaries among my neighbours; and these fifty rolls, being each of above an hundredweight, were well cured, and laid by against the return of the fleet from Lisbon. And now, increasing in business and in wealth, my head began to be full of projects and undertakings beyond my reach, such as are, indeed, often the ruin of the best heads in business.

Had I continued in the station I was now in, I had room for all the happy things to have yet befallen me, for which my father so earnestly recommended a quiet, retired life, and which he had so sensibly described the middle station of life to be full of: but other things attended me, and I was still to be the wilful agent of all my own miseries; and, particularly, to increase my fault, and double the reflections upon myself, which in my future sorrows I should have leisure to make, all these miscarriages were procured by my apparent obstinate adhering to my foolish inclination of wandering about, and pursuing that inclination, in contradiction to the clearest views of doing myself good in a fair and plain pursuit of those prospects, and those measures of life, which nature and Providence concurred to present me with, and to make my duty.

As I had once done thus in my breaking away from my parents, so I could not be content now, but I must go and leave the happy view I had of being a rich and thriving man in my new plantation, only to pursue a rash and immoderate desire of rising faster than the nature of the thing admitted; and thus I cast myself down again into the deepest gulf of human misery that ever man fell into, or perhaps could be consistent with life, and a state of health in the world.

To come then, by the just degrees, to the particulars of this part of my story. You may suppose, that having now lived almost four years in the Brazils, and beginning to thrive and prosper very well upon my plantation, I had not only learned the

language, but had contracted acquaintance and friendship among my fellow-planters, as well as among the merchants at St. Salvador, which was our port, and that in my discourses among them I had frequently given them an account of my two voyages to the Coast of Guinea, the manner of trading with the negroes there, and how easy it was to purchase upon the coast for trifles, such as beads, toys, knives, scissors, hatchets, bits of glass, and the like, not only gold-dust, Guinea grains, elephants' teeth, etc., but negroes, for the service of the Brazils, in great numbers.

They listened always very attentively to my discourses on these heads, but especially to that part which related to the buying negroes; which was a trade, at that time, not only not far entered into, but, as far as it was, had been carried on by the assientos, or permission, of the Kings of Spain and Portugal, and engrossed in the public, so that few negroes were brought, and those excessive dear.

It happened, being in company with some merchants and planters of my acquaintance, and talking of those things very earnestly, three of them came to me the next morning, and told me they had been musing very much upon what I had discoursed with them of, the last night, and they came to make a secret proposal to me. And after enjoining me secrecy, they told me that they had a mind to fit out a ship to go to Guinea; that they had all plantations as well as I, and were straitened for nothing so much as servants; that as it was a trade that could not be carried on because they could not publicly sell the negroes when they came home, so they desired to make but one voyage, to bring the negroes on shore privately, and divide them among their own plantations; and, in a word, the question was, whether I would go their supercargo in the ship, to manage the trading part upon the coast of Guinea? And they offered me that I should have my equal share of the negroes without providing any part of the stock.

This was a fair proposal, it must be confessed, had it been made to any one that had not had a settlement and plantation of his own to look after, which was in a fair way of coming to be very considerable, and with a good stock upon it. But for me, that was thus entered and established, and had nothing to do but go on as I had begun, for three or four years more, and to have sent for the other hundred pounds from England; and who, in that time, and with that little addition, could scarce have failed of being worth three or four thousand pounds sterling, and that increasing too; for me to think of such a voyage, was the most preposterous thing that ever man, in such circumstances, could be guilty of.

But I, that was born to be my own destroyer, could no more resist the offer than

I could restrain my first rambling designs, when my father's good counsel was lost upon me. In a word, I told them I would go with all my heart, if they would undertake to look after my plantation in my absence, and would dispose of it to such as I should direct if I miscarried. This they all engaged to do, and entered into writings or covenants to do so; and I made a formal will, disposing of my plantation and effects, in case of my death; making the captain of the ship that had saved my life, as before, my universal heir, but obliging him to dispose of my effects as I had directed in my will; one half of the produce being to himself, and the other to be shipped to England.

In short, I took all possible caution to preserve my effects, and keep up my plantation. Had I used half as much prudence to have looked into my own interest, and have made a judgment of what I ought to have done and not to have done, I had certainly never gone away from so prosperous an undertaking, leaving all the probable views of a thriving circumstance, and gone upon a voyage to sea, attended with all its common hazards; to say nothing of the reasons I had to expect particular misfortunes to myself.

But I was hurried on, and obeyed blindly the dictates of my fancy rather than my reason; and accordingly, the ship being fitted out, and the cargo furnished, and all things done as by agreement by my partners in the voyage, I went on board in an evil hour, the first of September, 1659 being the same day eight year that I went from my father and mother at Hull, in order to act the rebel to their authority, and the fool to my own interest.

Our ship was about 120 ton burthen, carried six guns and fourteen men, besides the master, his boy, and myself. We had on board no large cargo of goods, except of such toys as were fit for our trade with the negroes, such as beads, bits of glass, shells, and odd trifles, especially little looking glasses, knives, scissors, hatchets, and the like.

The same day I went on board we set sail, standing away to the northward upon our own coast, with design to stretch over for the African coast, when they came about ten or twelve degrees of northern latitude, which, it seems, was the manner of their course in those days. We had very good weather, only excessive hot, all the way upon our own coast, till we came to the height of Cape St. Augustino; from whence, keeping farther off at sea, we lost sight of land, and steered as if we was bound for the isle Fernando de Noronha, holding our course N.E. by N. and leaving those isles on the east. In this course we passed the line in about twelve days' time, and were, by our last observation, in seven degrees twenty-two minutes northern latitude, when a violent tornado, or hurricane, took us quite out of our knowledge. It began from the south-east, came about to the north-west, and then settled into the north-east, from whence it blew in such a terrible manner, that for twelve days together we could do nothing but drive, and, scudding away before it, let it carry us wherever fate and the fury of the winds directed; and during these twelve days, I need not say that I expected every day to be swallowed up, nor, indeed, did any in the ship expect to save their lives.

In this distress we had, besides the terror of the storm, one of our men died of the calenture, and one man and the boy washed overboard. About the twelfth day, the weather abating a little, the master made an observation as well as he could, and found that he was in about eleven degrees north latitude, but that he was twenty-two degrees of longitude difference, west from Cape St. Augustino; so that he found he was gotten upon the coast of Guiana, or the north part of Brazil, beyond the river Amazon, toward that of the river Orinoco, commonly called the Great River, and began to consult with me what course he should take, for the ship was leaky and very much disabled, and he was going directly back to the coast of Brazil.

I was positively against that; and looking over the charts of the sea-coast of America with him, we concluded there was no inhabited country for us to have recourse to till we came within the circle of the Caribbee Islands, and therefore resolved to stand away for Barbadoes, which by keeping off at sea, to avoid the indraft of the Bay or Gulf of Mexico, we might easily perform, as we hoped, in about fifteen days' sail; whereas we could not possibly make our voyage to the coast of Africa without some assistance, both to our ship and to ourselves.

With this design we changed our course, and steered away N.W. by W. in order to reach some of our English islands, where I hoped for relief; but our voyage was otherwise determined; for being in the latitude of twelve degrees eighteen minutes a second storm came upon us, which carried us away with the same impetuosity westward, and drove us so out of the very way of all human commerce, that had all our lives been saved, as to the sea, we were rather in danger of being devoured by savages than ever returning to our own country.

In this distress, the wind still blowing very hard, one of our men early in the morning cried out, "Land!" and we had no sooner run out of the cabin to look out, in hopes of seeing whereabouts in the world we were, but the ship struck upon a sand, and in a moment, her motion being so stopped, the sea broke over her in such a manner, that we expected we should all have perished immediately; and we were immediately driven into our close quarters, to shelter us from the very foam and spray of the sea.

It is not easy for any one, who has not been in the like condition, to describe or conceive the consternation of men in such circumstances. We knew nothing where we were, or upon what land it was we were driven, whether an island or the main, whether inhabited or not inhabited; and as the rage of the wind was still great, though rather less than at first, we could not so much as hope to have the ship hold many minutes without breaking in pieces, unless the winds, by a kind of miracle, should turn immediately about. In a word, we sat looking one upon another, and expecting death every moment, and every man acting accordingly, as preparing for another world; for there was little or nothing more for us to do in this. That which was our present comfort, and all the comfort we had, was that, contrary to our expectation, the ship did not break yet, and that the master said the wind began to abate.

Now, though we thought that the wind did a little abate, yet the ship having thus struck upon the sand, and sticking too fast for us to expect her getting off, we were in a dreadful condition indeed, and had nothing to do but to think of saving our lives as well as we could. We had a boat at our stern just before the storm, but she was first staved by dashing against the ship's rudder, and in the next place, she broke away, and either sunk, or was driven off to sea, so there was no hope from her; we had another boat on board, but how to get her off into the sea was a doubtful thing. However, there was no room to debate, for we fancied the ship would break in pieces every minute, and some told us she was actually broken already.

In this distress, the mate of our vessel lays hold of the boat, and with the help of the rest of the men they got her slung over the ship's side; and getting all into her, let go, and committed ourselves, being eleven in number, to God's mercy, and the wild sea; for though the storm was abated considerably, yet the sea went dreadful high upon the shore, and might be well called den wild Zee, as the Dutch call the sea in a storm.

And now our case was very dismal indeed, for we all saw plainly that the sea went so high, that the boat could not live, and that we should be inevitably drowned. As to making sail, we had none; nor, if we had, could we have done anything with it; so we worked at the oar towards the land, though with heavy hearts, like men going to execution; for we all knew that when the boat came nearer the shore, she would be dashed in a thousand pieces by the breach of the sea. However, we

committed our souls to God in the most earnest manner; and the wind driving us towards the shore, we hastened our destruction with our own hands, pulling as well as we could towards land.

What the shore was, whether rock or sand, whether steep or shoal, we knew not; the only hope that could rationally give us the least shadow of expectation was, if we might happen into some bay or gulf, or the mouth of some river, where by great chance we might have run our boat in, or got under the lee of the land, and perhaps made smooth water. But there was nothing of this appeared; but as we made nearer and nearer the shore, the land looked more frightful than the sea.

After we had rowed, or rather driven, about a league and a half, as we reckoned it, a raging wave, mountain-like, came rolling astern of us, and plainly bade us expect the coup de grace. In a word, it took us with such a fury, that it overset the boat at once; and separating us, as well from the boat as from one another, gave us not time hardly to say: "O God!" for we were all swallowed up in a moment.

Nothing can describe the confusion of thought which I felt when I sunk into the water; for though I swam very well, yet I could not deliver myself from the waves so as to draw breath, till that wave having driven me, or rather carried me, a vast way on towards the shore, and having spent itself, went back, and left me upon the land almost dry, but half dead with the water I took in. I had so much presence of mind, as well as breath left, that seeing myself nearer the mainland than I expected, I got upon my feet, and endeavoured to make on towards the land as fast as I could, before another wave should return and take me up again. But I soon found it was impossible to avoid it; for I saw the sea come after me as high as a great hill, and as furious as an enemy, which I had no means or strength to contend with. My business was to hold my breath, and raise myself upon the water, if I could; and so by swimming, to preserve my breathing, and pilot myself towards the shore, if possible; my greatest concern now being, that the sea, as it would carry me a great way towards the shore when it came on, might not carry me back again with it when it gave back towards the sea.

The wave that came upon me again, buried me at once 20 or 30 feet deep in its own body, and I could feel myself carried with a mighty force and swiftness towards the shore a very great way; but I held my breath, and assisted myself to swim still forward with all my might. I was ready to burst with holding my breath, when, as I felt myself rising up, so, to my immediate relief, I found my head and hands shoot out above the surface of the water; and though it was not two seconds of time that I could keep myself so, yet it relieved me greatly, gave me breath and new courage. I was covered again with water a good while, but not so long but I held it out; and finding the water had spent itself, and began to return, I struck forward against the return of the waves, and felt ground again with my feet. I stood still a few moments to recover breath, and till the water went from me, and then took to my heels, and ran with what strength I had farther towards the shore. But neither would this deliver me from the fury of the sea, which came pouring in after me again, and twice more I was lifted up by the waves and carried forwards as before, the shore being very flat.

The last time of these two had well near been fatal to me; for the sea, having hurried me along as before, landed me, or rather dashed me, against a piece of a rock, and that with such force, as it left me senseless, and indeed helpless, as to my own deliverance; for the blow taking my side and breast, beat the breath as it were quite out of my body; and had it returned again immediately, I must have been strangled in the water. But I recovered a little before the return of the waves, and seeing I should be covered again with the water, I resolved to hold fast by a piece of the rock, and so to hold my breath, if possible, till the wave went back. Now as the waves were not so high as at first, being near land, I held my hold till the wave abated, and then fetched another run, which brought me so near the shore, that the next wave, though it went over me, yet did not so swallow me up as to carry me away, and the next run I took I got to the mainland, where, to my great comfort, I clambered up the cliffs of the shore, and sat me down upon the grass, free from danger, and quite out of the reach of the water.

I was now landed, and safe on shore, and began to look up and thank God that my life was saved in a case wherein there was some minutes before scarce any room to hope. I believe it is impossible to express, to the life, what the ecstasies and transports of the soul are, when it is so saved, as I may say, out of the very grave: and I do not wonder now at that custom, viz. that when a malefactor, who has the halter about his neck, is tied up, and just going to be turned off, and has a reprieve brought to him; I say, I do not wonder that they bring a surgeon with it, to let him blood that very moment they tell him of it, that the surprise may not drive the animal spirits from the heart, and overwhelm him.

For sudden joys, like griefs, confound at first.

I walked about on the shore, lifting up my hands, and my whole being, as I may say, wrapt up in the contemplation of my deliverance, making a thousand gestures and motions which I cannot describe, reflecting upon all my comrades that were drowned, and that there should not be one soul saved but myself; for, as for them, I never saw them afterwards, or any sign of them, except three of their hats, one cap, and two shoes that were not fellows.

I cast my eyes to the stranded vessel, when the breach and froth of the sea being so big, I could hardly see it, it lay so far off, and considered, Lord! how was it possible I could get on shore?

After I had solaced my mind with the comfortable part of my condition, I began

to look round me to see what kind of place I was in, and what was next to be done, and I soon found my comforts abate, and that, in a word, I had a dreadful deliverance; for I was wet, had no clothes to shift me, nor anything either to eat or drink to comfort me, neither did I see any prospect before me but that of perishing with hunger, or being devoured by wild beasts; and that which was particularly afflicting to me was, that I had no weapon either to hunt and kill any creature for my sustenance, or to defend myself against any other creature that might desire to kill me for theirs. In a word, I had nothing about me but a knife, a tobacco-pipe, and a little tobacco in a box. This was all my provision; and this threw me into terrible agonies of mind, that for a while I ran about like a madman. Night coming upon me, I began, with a heavy heart, to consider what would be my lot if there were any ravenous beasts in that country, seeing at night they always come abroad for their prey.

All the remedy that offered to my thoughts at that time was, to get up into a thick bushy tree like a fir, but thorny, which grew near me, and where I resolved to sit all night, and consider the next day what death I should die, for as yet I saw no prospect of life. I walked about a furlong from the shore, to see if I could find any fresh water to drink, which I did, to my great joy; and having drank, and put a little tobacco in my mouth to prevent hunger, I went to the tree, and getting up into it, endeavoured to place myself so, as that if I should sleep I might not fall; and having cut me a short stick, like a truncheon, for my defence, I took up my lodging, and having been excessively fatigued, I fell fast asleep, and slept as comfortably as, I believe, few could have done in my condition, and found myself the most refreshed with it that I think I ever was on such an occasion.

CHAPTER FOUR

When I waked it was broad day, the weather clear, and the storm abated, so that the sea did not rage and swell as before. But that which surprised me most was, that the ship was lifted off in the night from the sand where she lay, by the swelling of the tide, and was driven up almost as far as the rock which I first mentioned, where I had been so bruised by the dashing me against it. This being within about a mile from the shore where I was, and the ship seeming to stand upright still, I wished myself on board, that, at least, I might have some necessary things for my use.

When I came down from my apartment in the tree I looked about me again, and the first thing I found was the boat, which lay as the wind and the sea had tossed her up upon the land, about two miles on my right hand. I walked as far as I could upon the shore to have got to her, but found a neck or inlet of water between me and the boat, which was about half a mile broad; so I came back for the present, being more intent upon getting at the ship, where I hoped to find something for my present subsistence.

A little after noon I found the sea very calm, and the tide ebbed so far out, that I could come within a quarter of a mile of the ship; and here I found a fresh renewing of my grief, for I saw evidently, that if we had kept on board we had been all safe, that is to say, we had all got safe on shore, and I had not been so miserable as to be left entirely destitute of all comfort and company, as I now was. This forced tears from my eyes again; but as there was little relief in that, I resolved, if possible, to get to the ship; so I pulled off my clothes, for the weather was hot to extremity, and took the water. But when I came to the ship, my difficulty was still greater to know how to get on board; for as she lay aground, and high out of the water, there was nothing within my reach to lay hold of. I swam round her twice, and the second time I spied a small piece of a rope, which I wondered I did not see at first, hang down by the fore-chains so low, as that with great difficulty I got hold of it, and by the help of that rope got up into the forecastle of the ship. Here I found that the ship was bulged, and had a great deal of water in her hold, but that she lay so on the side of a bank

of hard sand, or rather earth, that her stern lay lifted up upon the bank, and her head low almost to the water. By this means all her quarter was free, and all that was in that part was dry; for you may be sure my first work was to search and to see what was spoiled and what was free. And first I found that all the ship's provisions were dry and untouched by the water; and being very well disposed to eat, I went to the bread-room and filled my pockets with biscuit, and eat it as I went about other things, for I had no time to lose. I also found some rum in the great cabin, of which I took a large dram, and which I had indeed need enough of to spirit me for what was before me. Now I wanted nothing but a boat, to furnish myself with many things which I foresaw would be very necessary to me.

It was in vain to sit still and wish for what was not to be had, and this extremity roused my application. We had several spare yards, and two or three large spars of wood, and a spare top-mast or two in the ship. I resolved to fall to work with these, and flung as many of them overboard as I could manage for their weight, tying every one with a rope, that they might not drive away. When this was done I went down the ship's side, and, pulling them to me, I tied four of them fast together at both ends as well as I could, in the form of a raft; and laying two or three short pieces of plank upon them crossways, I found I could walk upon it very well, but that it was not able to bear any great weight, the pieces being too light. So I went to work, and with the carpenter's saw I cut a spare top-mast into three lengths, and added them to my raft, with a great deal of labour and pains; but hope of furnishing myself with necessaries encouraged me to go beyond what I should have been able to have done upon another occasion.

My raft was now strong enough to bear any reasonable weight. My next care was what to load it with, and how to preserve what I laid upon it from the surf of the sea; but I was not long considering this. I first laid all the planks or boards upon it that I could get, and having considered well what I most wanted, I first got three of the seamen's chests, which I had broken open, and emptied, and lowered them down upon my raft. The first of these I filled with provisions, viz. bread, rice, three Dutch cheeses, five pieces of dried goat's flesh, which we lived much upon, and a little remainder of European corn, which had been laid by for some fowls which we brought to sea with us, but the fowls were killed. There had been some barley and wheat together, but, to my great disappointment, I found afterwards that the rats had eaten or spoiled it all. As for liquors, I found several cases of bottles belonging to our skipper, in which were some cordial waters, and, in all, about five or six gallons of rack. These I stowed by themselves, there being no need to put them into the chest, nor no room for them. While I was doing this, I found the tide began to flow, though very calm, and I had the mortification to see my coat, shirt, and waistcoat, which I had left on shore upon the sand, swim away; as for my breeches, which were only linen, and open-kneed, I swam on board in them, and my stockings. However, this put me upon rummaging for clothes, of which I found enough, but took no more than I wanted for present use; for I had other things which my eye was more upon, as first tools to work with on shore; and it was after long searching that I found out the carpenter's chest, which was indeed a very useful prize to me, and much more valuable than a shiploading of gold would have been at that time. I got it down to my raft, even whole as it was, without losing time to look into it, for I knew in general what it contained.

My next care was for some ammunition and arms; there were two very good fowling-pieces in the great cabin, and two pistols; these I secured first, with some powder-horns, and a small bag of shot, and two old rusty swords. I knew there were three barrels of powder in the ship, but knew not where our gunner had stowed them; but with much search I found them, two of them dry and good, the third had taken water; those two I got to my raft with the arms. And now I thought myself pretty well freighted, and began to think how I should get to shore with them, having neither sail, oar or rudder; and the least capful of wind would have overset all my navigation.

I had three encouragements. 1. A smooth calm sea. 2. The tide rising and setting in to the shore. 3. What little wind there was blew me towards the land. And thus, having found two or three broken oars belonging to the boat, and besides the tools which were in the chest, I found two saws, an axe, and a hammer, and with this cargo I put to sea. For a mile or thereabouts my raft went very well, only that I found it drive a little distant from the place where I had landed before, by which I perceived that there was some indraft of the water, and consequently I hoped to find some creek or river there, which I might make use of as a port to get to land with my cargo.

As I imagined, so it was; there appeared before me a little opening of the land, and I found a strong current of the tide set into it, so I guided my raft as well as I could to keep in the middle of the stream. But here I had like to have suffered a second shipwreck, which, if I had, I think verily would have broke my heart; for knowing nothing of the coast, my raft ran aground at one end of it upon a shoal, and

"I WENT ON BOARD A SHIP BOUND FOR LONDON."
(J. MATTHEW)

"...WE WENT THE OLD WAY OF ALL SAILORS; THE PUNCH WAS MADE, AND I WAS MADE DRUNK WITH IT..."
(G. LEESE)

“...WE COMMITTED OURSELVES, BEING ELEVEN IN NUMBER, TO GOD’S MERCY AND THE WILD SEA.”
(F. N. J. MOODY)

"I BELIEVE IT WAS THE FIRST GUN THAT HAD BEEN FIRED THERE SINCE THE CREATION OF THE WORLD."
(N. POCOCK)

not being aground at the other end, it wanted but a little that all my cargo had slipped off towards that end that was afloat, and so fallen into the water. I did my utmost by setting my back against the chests to keep them in their places, but could not thrust off the raft with all my strength, neither durst I stir from the posture I was in, but holding up the chests with all my might, stood in that manner near half-an-hour, in which time the rising of the water brought me a little more upon a level; and a little after, the water still rising, my raft floated again, and I thrust her off with the oar I had into the channel, and then driving up higher, I at length found myself in the mouth of a little river, with land on both sides, and a strong current or tide running up. I looked on both sides for a proper place to get to shore, for I was not willing to be driven too high up the river, hoping in time to see some ship at sea, and therefore resolved to place myself as near the coast as I could.

At length I spied a little cove on the right shore of the creek, to which, with great pain and difficulty, I guided my raft, and at last got so near, as that, reaching ground with my oar, I could thrust her directly in; but here I had like to have dipped all my cargo in the sea again; for that shore lying pretty steep, that is to say, sloping, there was no place to land but where one end of my float, if it run on shore, would lie so high and the other sink lower, as before, that it would endanger my cargo again. All that I could do was to wait till the tide was at the highest, keeping the raft with my oar like an anchor to hold the side of it fast to the shore, near a flat piece of ground, which I expected the water would flow over; and so it did. As soon as I found water enough, for my raft drew about a foot of water, I thrust her on upon that flat piece of ground, and there fastened or moored her by sticking my two broken oars into the ground; one on one side near one end, and one on the other side near the other end; and thus I lay till the water ebbed away, and left my raft and all my cargo safe on shore.

My next work was to view the country and seek a proper place for my habitation,

and where to stow my goods to secure them from whatever might happen. Where I was, I yet knew not; whether on the continent, or on an island; whether inhabited, or not inhabited; whether in danger of wild beasts, or not. There was a hill, not above a mile from me, which rose up very steep and high, and which seemed to overtop some other hills, which lay as in a ridge from it, northward. I took out one of the fowling-pieces and one of the pistols, and an horn of powder; and thus armed, I travelled for discovery up to the top of that hill, where, after I had with great labour and difficulty got to the top, I saw my fate to my great affliction, viz. that I was in an island environed every way with the sea, no land to be seen, except some rocks which lay a great way off, and two small islands less than this, which lay about three leagues to the west.

I found also that the island I was in was barren, and, as I saw good reason to believe, uninhabited, except by wild beasts, of whom, however, I saw none; yet I saw abundance of fowls, but knew not their kinds; neither, when I killed them, could I tell what was fit for food, and what not. At my coming back, I shot at a great bird which I saw sitting upon a tree on the side of a great wood. I believe it was the first gun that had been fired there since the creation of the world. I had no sooner fired, but from all the parts of the wood there arose an innumerable number of fowls of many sorts, making a confused screaming, and crying everyone according to his usual note; but not one of them of any kind that I knew. As for the creature I killed, I took it to be a kind of a hawk, its colour and beak resembling it, but had no talons or claws more than common; its flesh was carrion, and fit for nothing.

Contented with this discovery, I came back to my raft, and fell to work to bring my cargo on shore, which took me up the rest of that day; and what to do with myself at night I knew not, nor indeed where to rest; for I was afraid to lie down on the ground, not knowing but some wild beast might devour me, though, as I afterwards found, there was really no need for those fears. However, as well as I could, I barricaded myself round with the chests and boards that I had brought on shore, and made a kind of a hut for that night's lodging; as for food, I yet saw not which way to supply myself, except that I had seen two or three creatures like hares run out of the wood where I shot the fowl.

I now began to consider, that I might yet get a great many things out of the ship, which would be useful to me, and particularly some of the rigging and sails, and such other things as might come to land; and I resolved to make another voyage on board the vessel, if possible. And as I knew that the first storm that blew must necessarily break her all in pieces, I resolved to set all other things apart till I got everything out of the ship that I could get. Then I called a council, that is to say, in my thoughts, whether I should take back the raft, but this appeared impracticable; so I resolved to go as before, when the tide was down; and I did so, only that I stripped before I went from my hut, having nothing on but a chequered shirt and a pair of linen drawers, and a pair of pumps on my feet.

I got on board the ship as before, and prepared a second raft, and having had experience of the first, I neither made this so unwieldy, nor loaded it so hard; but yet

I brought away several things very useful to me; as, first, in the carpenter's stores I found two or three bags full of nails and spikes, a great screw-jack, a dozen or two of hatchets, and above all, that most useful thing called a grindstone. All these I secured together, with several things belonging to the gunner, particularly two or three iron crows, and two barrels of musket bullets, seven muskets, and another fowling-piece, with some small quantity of powder more; a large bag full of small-shot, and a great roll of sheet lead; but this last was so heavy, I could not hoist it up to get it over the ship's side. Besides these things, I took all the men's clothes that I could find, and a spare fore-top-sail, a hammock, and some bedding; and with this I loaded my second raft, and brought them all safe on shore, to my very great comfort.

I was under some apprehensions during my absence from the land, that at least my provisions might be devoured on shore; but when I came back, I found no sign of any visitor, only there sat a creature like a wild cat upon one of the chests, which, when I came towards it, ran away a little distance, and then stood still. She sat very composed and unconcerned, and looked full in my face, as if she had a mind to be acquainted with me. I presented my gun at her; but as she did not understand it, she was perfectly unconcerned at it, nor did she offer to stir away; upon which I tossed her a bit of biscuit, though, by the way, I was not very free of it, for my store was not great. However, I spared her a bit, I say, and she went to it, smelled of it, and ate it, and looked (as pleased) for more; but I thanked her, and could spare no more, so she marched off.

Having got my second cargo on shore, though I was fain to open the barrels of powder and bring them by parcels, for they were too heavy, being large casks, I went to work to make me a little tent with the sail and some poles which I cut for that purpose; and into this tent I brought everything that I knew would spoil either with rain or sun; and I piled all the empty chests and casks up in a circle round the tent, to fortify it from any sudden attempt, either from man or beast.

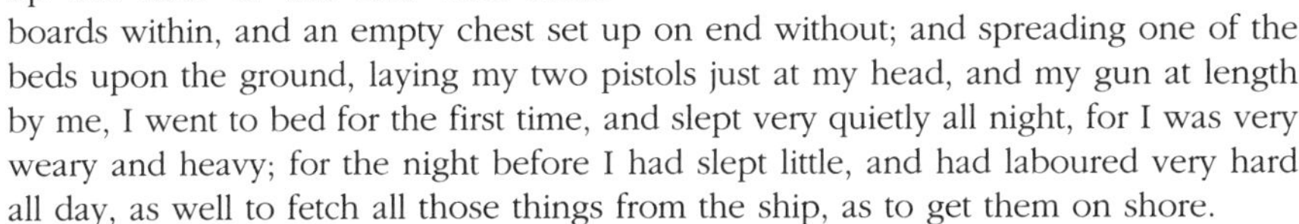

When I had done this I blocked up the door of the tent with some boards within, and an empty chest set up on end without; and spreading one of the beds upon the ground, laying my two pistols just at my head, and my gun at length by me, I went to bed for the first time, and slept very quietly all night, for I was very weary and heavy; for the night before I had slept little, and had laboured very hard all day, as well to fetch all those things from the ship, as to get them on shore.

I had the biggest magazine of all kinds now that ever were laid up, I believe, for one man; but I was not satisfied still, for while the ship sat upright in that posture, I thought I ought to get everything out of her that I could. So every day at low water I went on board, and brought away something or other; but, particularly, the third time I went I brought away as much of the rigging as I could, as also all the small ropes and rope-twine I could get, with a piece of spare canvas, which was to mend the sails upon occasion, the barrel of wet gunpowder; in a word, I brought away all the sails first and last, only that I was fain to cut them in pieces, and bring as much at a time as I could; for they were no more useful to be sails, but as mere canvas only.

But that which comforted me more still was, that at last of all, after I had made five or six such voyages as these, and thought I had nothing more to expect from the ship that was worth my meddling with; I say, after all this, I found a great hogshead of bread, and three large runlets of rum or spirits, and a box of sugar, and a barrel of fine flour; this was surprising to me, because I had given over expecting any more provisions, except what was spoilt by the water. I soon emptied the hogshead of that bread, and wrapped it up parcel by parcel in pieces of the sails, which I cut out; and, in a word, I got all this safe on shore also.

The next day I made another voyage; and now, having plundered the ship of what was portable and fit to hand out, I began with the cables; and cutting the great cable into pieces, such as I could move, I got two cables and a hawser on shore, with all the iron-work I could get; and having cut down the sprit-sailyard, and the mizen-yard, and everything I could to make a large raft, I loaded it with all those heavy goods, and came away. But my good luck began now to leave me; for this raft was so unwieldy, and so overloaden, that after I was entered the little cove where I had landed the rest of my goods, not being able to guide it so handily as I did the other, it overset, and threw me and all my cargo into the water. As for myself, it was no great harm, for I was near the shore; but as to my cargo, it was great part of it lost, especially the iron, which I expected would have been of great use to me. However, when the tide was out I got most of the pieces of cable ashore, and some of the iron, though with infinite labour; for I was fain to dip for it into the water, a work which fatigued me very much. After this I went every day on board, and brought away what I could get.

I had been now thirteen days on shore, and had been eleven times on board the ship; in which time I had brought away all that one pair of hands could well be supposed capable to bring, though I believe verily, had the calm weather held, I should have brought away the whole ship piece by piece. But preparing the twelfth time to go on board, I found the wind begin to rise. However, at low water I went on board, and though I thought I had rummaged the cabin so effectually as that nothing more could be found, yet I discovered a locker with drawers in it, in one of which I found two or three razors, and one pair of large scissors, with some ten or a dozen of good knives and forks; in another I found about thirty-six pounds value in money, some European coin, some Brazil, some pieces of eight, some gold, some silver.

I smiled to myself at the sight of this money. "O drug!" said I aloud, "what art thou good for? Thou art not worth to me, no, not the taking off of the ground; one of those knives is worth all this heap. I have no manner of use for thee; e'en remain

where thou art, and go to the bottom as a creature whose life is not worth saving." However, upon second thoughts, I took it away; and wrapping all this in a piece of canvas, I began to think of making another raft; but while I was preparing this, I found the sky overcast, and the wind began to rise, and in a quarter of an hour it blew a fresh gale from the shore. It presently occurred to me that it was in vain to pretend to make a raft with the wind off shore, and that it was my business to be gone before the tide of flood began, otherwise I might not be able to reach the shore at all. Accordingly I let myself down into the water, and swam across the channel, which lay between the ship and the sands, and even that with difficulty enough, partly with the weight of the things I had about me, and partly the roughness of the water; for the wind rose very hastily, and before it was quite high water it blew a storm.

But I was gotten home to my little tent, where I lay with all my wealth about me very secure. It blew very hard all that night, and in the morning, when I looked out, behold, no more ship was to be seen. I was a little surprised, but recovered myself with this satisfactory reflection, viz. that I had lost no time, nor abated no diligence, to get everything out of her that could be useful to me, and that indeed there was little left in her that I was able to bring away if I had had more time.

I now gave over any more thoughts of the ship, or of anything out of her, except what might drive on shore from her wreck, as indeed divers pieces of her afterwards did; but those things were of small use to me.

My thoughts were now wholly employed about securing myself against either savages, if any should appear, or wild beasts, if any were in the island; and I had many thoughts of the method how to do this, and what kind of dwelling to make, whether I should make me a cave in the earth, or a tent upon the earth; and, in short, I resolved upon both, the manner and description of which it may not be improper to give an account of.

I soon found the place I was in was not for my settlement, particularly because it was upon a low moorish ground near the sea, and I believed would not be wholesome; and more particularly because there was no fresh water near it. So I resolved to find a more healthy and more convenient spot of ground.

I consulted several things in my situation, which I found would be proper for me. First, health and fresh water, I just now mentioned. Secondly, shelter from the heat of the sun. Thirdly, security from ravenous creatures, whether men or beasts. Fourthly, a view to the sea, that if God sent any ship in sight I might not lose any advantage for my deliverance, of which I was not willing to banish all my expectation yet.

In search of a place proper for this, I found a little plain on the side of a rising hill, whose front towards this little plain was steep as a house-side, so that nothing could come down upon me from the top; on the side of this rock there was a hollow place, worn a little way in, like the entrance or door of a cave; but there was not really any cave, or way into the rock at all.

On the flat of the green, just before this hollow place, I resolved to pitch my tent. This plain was not above an hundred yards broad, and about twice as long, and lay like a green before my door, and at the end of it descended irregularly every way down into the low grounds by the seaside. It was on the N.N.W. side of the hill, so that I was sheltered from the heat every day, till it came to a W. and by S. sun, or thereabouts, which in those countries is near the setting.

Before I set up my tent, I drew a half circle before the hollow place, which took in about ten yards in its semidiameter from the rock, and twenty yards in its diameter from its beginning and ending. In this half-circle I pitched two rows of strong stakes, driving them into the ground till they stood very firm like piles, the biggest end being out of the ground about five feet and a half, and sharpened on the top. The two rows did not stand above six inches from one another.

Then I took the pieces of cable which I had cut in the ship, and laid them in rows one upon another, within the circle, between these two rows of stakes, up to the top, placing other stakes in the inside leaning against them, about two feet and a half high, like a spur to a post; and this fence was so strong, that neither man or beast could get into it, or over it. This cost me a great deal of time and labour, especially to cut the piles in the woods, bring them to the place, and drive them into the earth.

The entrance into this place I made to be not by a door, but by a short ladder to go over the top; which ladder, when I was in, I lifted over after me, and so I was completely fenced in, and fortified, as I thought, from all the world, and consequently slept secure in the night, which otherwise I could not have done; though as it appeared afterward, there was no need of all this caution from the enemies that I apprehended danger from.

Into this fence or fortress, with infinite labour, I carried all my riches, all my provisions, ammunition, and stores, of which you have the account above; and I made me a large tent, which, to preserve me from the rains that in one part of the year are very violent there, I made double, viz. one smaller tent within, and one larger tent above it, and covered the uppermost with a large tarpaulin, which I had saved among the sails. And now I lay no more for a while in the bed which I had brought on shore, but in a hammock, which was indeed a very good one, and belonged to the mate of the ship.

Into this tent I brought all my provisions, and everything that would spoil by the wet; and having thus enclosed all my goods, I made up the entrance, which, till now, I had left open, and so passed and repassed, as I said, by a short ladder.

When I had done this, I began to work my way into the rock; and bringing all the earth and stones that I dug down out through my tent, I laid them up within my fence in the nature of a terrace, so that it raised the ground within about a foot and a half; and thus I made me a cave just behind my tent, which served me like a cellar to my house.

It cost me much labour, and many days, before all these things were brought to perfection, and therefore I must go back to some other things which took up some of my thoughts. At the same time it happened, after I had laid my scheme for the setting up my tent, and making the cave, that a storm of rain falling from a thick dark cloud, a sudden flash of lightning happened, and after that a great clap of thunder, as is naturally the effect of it. I was not so much surprised with the lightning, as I was

with a thought which darted into my mind as swift as the lightning itself. O my powder. My very heart sunk within me when I thought, that at one blast all my powder might be destroyed, on which, not my defence only, but the providing me food, as I thought, entirely depended. I was nothing near so anxious about my own danger; though had the powder took fire, I had never known who had hurt me.

Such impression did this make upon me, that after the storm was over I laid aside all my works, my building, and fortifying, and applied myself to make bags and boxes to separate the powder, and keep it a little and a little in a parcel, in hope that whatever might come it might not all take fire at once, and to keep it so apart, that it should not be possible to make one part fire another. I finished this work in about a fortnight, and I think my powder, which in all was about 240 pound weight, was divided in not less than a hundred parcels. As to the barrel that had been wet, I did not apprehend any danger from that, so I placed it in my new cave which in my fancy I called my kitchen, and the rest I hid up and down in holes among the rocks, so that no wet might come to it, marking very carefully where I laid it.

In the interval of time while this was doing, I went out once, at least, every day with my gun, as well to divert myself, as to see if I could kill anything fit for food, and as near as I could to acquaint myself with what the island produced. The first time I went out, I presently discovered that there were goats in the island, which was a great satisfaction to me; but then it was attended with this misfortune to me, viz. that they were so shy, so subtle, and so swift of foot, that it was the difficultest thing in the world to come at them. But I was not discouraged at this, not doubting but I might now and then shoot one, as it soon happened; for after I had found their haunts a little, I laid wait in this manner for them. I observed if they saw me in the valleys, though they were upon the rocks, they would run away as in a terrible fright; but if they were feeding in the valleys, and I was upon the rocks, they took no notice of me, from whence I concluded that, by the position of their optics, their sight was so directed downward, that they did not readily see objects that were above them. So afterward I took this method; I always climbed the rocks first to get above them, and then had frequently a fair mark. The first shot I made among these creatures I killed a she-goat, which had a little kid by her, which she gave suck to, which grieved me heartily; but when the old one fell, the kid stood stock still by her till I came and took her up; and not only so, but when I carried the old one with me upon my shoulders, the kid followed me quite to my enclosure; upon which I laid down the dam, and took the kid in my arms, and carried it over my pale, in hopes to have bred it up tame; but it would not eat, so I was forced to kill it, and eat it myself. These two supplied me with flesh a great while, for I eat sparingly, and saved my provisions, my bread especially, as much as possibly I could.

Having now fixed my habitation, I found it absolutely necessary to provide a place to make a fire in, and fuel to burn; and what I did for that, as also how I enlarged my cave, and what conveniences I made, I shall give a full account of in its place: but I must first give some little account of myself, and of my thoughts about living, which, it may well be supposed, were not a few.

I had a dismal prospect of my condition; for as I was not cast away upon that island without being driven, as is said, by a violent storm quite out of the course of our intended voyage; and a great way, viz. some hundreds of leagues, out of the ordinary course of the trade of mankind, I had great reason to consider it as a determination of Heaven, that in this desolate place, and in this desolate manner, I should end my life. The tears would run plentifully down my face when I made these reflections; and sometimes I would expostulate with myself, why Providence should thus completely ruin its creatures, and render them so absolutely miserable; so without help abandoned, so entirely depressed, that it could hardly be rational to be thankful for such a life.

But something always returned swift upon me to check these thoughts, and to reprove me; and particularly, one day walking with my gun in my hand, by the sea-side, I was very pensive upon the subject of my present condition, when reason, as it were, expostulated with me the other way, thus: "Well, you are in a desolate condition 'tis true; but, pray remember, where are the rest of you? Did not you come eleven of you into the boat? Where are the ten? Why were not they saved, and you lost? Why were you singled out? Is it better to be here or there?" and then I pointed to the sea. All evils are to be considered with the good that is in them, and with what worse attends them.

Then it occurred to me again, how well I was furnished for my subsistence, and what would have been my case if it had not happened (which was an hundred thousand to one) that the ship floated from the place where she first struck, and was driven so near to the shore, that I had time to get all these things out of her; what would have been my case, if I had been to have lived in the condition in which I at first came on shore, without necessaries of life, or necessaries to supply and procure them? Particularly, said I aloud (though to myself, what should I have done without a gun, without ammunition, without any tools to make anything, or to work with, without clothes, bedding, a tent, or any manner of covering? and that now I had all these to a sufficient quantity, and was in a fair way to provide myself in such a manner as to live without my gun, when my ammunition was spent: so that I had a tolerable view of subsisting, without any want, as long as I lived; for I considered, from the beginning, how I would provide for the accidents that might happen, and for the time that was to come, not only after my ammunition should be spent, but even after my health or strength should decay.

I confess, I had not entertained any notion of my ammunition being destroyed at one blast, I mean my powder being blown up by lightning; and this made the thoughts of it so surprising to me, when it lightened and thundered, as I observed just now.

Chapter Four

And now being to enter into a melancholy relation of a scene of silent life, such, perhaps, as was never heard of in the world before, I shall take it from its beginning, and continue it in its order. It was, by my account, the 30th of September when, in the manner as above said, I first set foot upon this horrid island, when the sun being to us in its autumnal equinox, was almost just over my head, for I reckoned myself, by observation, to be in the latitude of 9 degrees 22 minutes north of the line.

After I had been there about ten or twelve days, it came into my thoughts that I should lose my reckoning of time for want of books and pen and ink, and should even forget the Sabbath days from the working days; but to prevent this, I cut it with my knife upon a large post, in capital letters; and making it into a great cross, I set it up on the shore where I first landed, viz. "I came on shore here on the 30th September 1659." Upon the sides of this square post I cut every day a notch with my knife, and every seventh notch was as long again as the rest, and every first day of the month as long again as that long one; and thus I kept my calendar, or weekly, monthly, and yearly reckoning of time.

In the next place we are to observe, that among the many things which I brought out of the ship in the several voyages, which, as above mentioned, I made to it, I got several things of less value, but not all less useful to me, which I omitted setting down before; as in particular, pens, ink, and paper, several parcels in the captain's, mate's, gunner's, and carpenter's keeping, three or four compasses, some mathematical instruments, dials, perspectives, charts, and books of navigation, all which I huddled together, whether I might want them or no. Also I found three very good Bibles, which came to me in my cargo from England, and which I had packed up among my things; some Portuguese books also, and among them two or three Popish prayer-books, and several other books, all which I carefully secured. And I must not forget, that we had in the ship a dog and two cats, of whose eminent history I may have occasion to say something in its place; for I carried both the cats with me; and as for the dog, he jumped out of the ship of himself, and swam on shore to me the day after I went on shore with my first cargo, and was a trusty servant to me many years. I wanted nothing that he could fetch me, nor any company that he could make up to me; I only wanted to have him talk to me, but that would not do. As I observed before, I found pen, ink, and paper, and I husbanded them to the utmost; and I shall show that while my ink lasted, I kept things very exact; but after that was gone, I could not, for I could not make any ink by any means that I could devise.

And this put me in mind that I wanted many things, notwithstanding all that I had amassed together; and of these, this of ink was one, as also spade, pick-axe, and shovel, to dig or remove the earth, needles, pins, and thread; as for linen, I soon learned to want that without much difficulty.

This want of tools made every work I did go on heavily; and it was near a whole year before I had entirely finished my little pale or surrounded habitation. The piles or stakes, which were as heavy as I could well lift, were a long time in cutting and preparing in the woods, and more by far in bringing home; so that I spent sometimes two days in cutting and bringing home one of those posts, and a third day in driving it into the ground; for which purpose I got a heavy piece of wood at first, but at last bethought myself of one of the iron crows, which, however, though I found it, yet it made driving those posts or piles very laborious and tedious work.

But what need I have been concerned at the tediousness of anything I had to do, seeing I had time enough to do it in? nor had I any other employment, if that had been over, at least, that I could foresee, except the ranging the island to seek for food, which I did more or less every day.

I now began to consider seriously my condition, and the circumstance I was reduced to; and I drew up the state of my affairs in writing; not so much to leave them to any that were to come after me, for I was like to have but few heirs, as to deliver my thoughts from daily poring upon them, and afflicting my mind. And as my reason began now to master my despondency, I began to comfort myself as well as I could, and to set the good against the evil, that I might have something to distinguish my case from worse; and I stated it very impartially, like debtor and creditor, the comforts I enjoyed against the miseries I suffered, thus:

Evil	***Good***
I am cast upon a horrible desolate island, void of all hope of recovery.	*But I am alive, and not drowned, as all my ship's company was.*
I am singled out and separated, as it were, from all the world to be miserable.	*But I am singled out, too, from all the ship's crew to be spared from death; and He that miraculously saved me from death, can deliver me from this condition.*
I am divided from mankind, a solitaire, one banished from human society.	*But I am not starved and perishing on a barren place, affording no sustenance.*
I have not clothes to cover me.	*But I am in a hot climate, where if I had clothes I could hardly wear them.*
I am without any defence or means to resist any violence of man or beast.	*But I am cast on an island, where I see no wild beasts to hurt me, as I saw on the coast of Africa; and what if I had been shipwrecked there?*

Evil	***Good***
I have no soul to speak to, or relieve me.	*But God wonderfully sent the ship in near enough to the shore, that I have gotten out so many necessary things as will either supply my wants, or enable me to supply myself even as long as I live.*

Upon the whole, here was an undoubted testimony, that there was scarce any condition in the world so miserable, but there was something negative, or something positive, to be thankful for in it: and let this stand as a direction, from the experience of the most miserable of all conditions in this world, that we may always find in it something to comfort ourselves from, and to set, in the description of good and evil, on the credit side of the account.

Having now brought my mind a little to relish my condition, and given over looking out to sea, to see if I could spy a ship; I say, giving over these things, I began to apply myself to accommodate my way of living, and to make things as easy to me as I could.

I have already described my habitation, which was a tent under the side of a rock, surrounded with a strong pale of posts and cables; but I might now rather call it a wall, for I raised a kind of wall up against it of turfs, about two feet thick on the outside, and after some time – I think it was a year and a half – I raised rafters from it leaning to the rock, and thatched or covered it with boughs of trees and such things as I could get to keep out the rain, which I found at some times of the year very violent.

I have already observed how I brought all my goods into this pale, and into the cave which I had made behind me. But I must observe, too, that at first this was a confused heap of goods, which as they lay in no order, so they took up all my place; I had no room to turn myself. So I set myself to enlarge my cave and works farther into the earth; for it was a loose sandy rock, which yielded easily to the labour I bestowed on it. And so, when I found I was pretty safe as to beasts of prey, I worked sideways to the right hand into the rock; and then, turning to the right again, worked quite out, and made me a door to come out on the outside of my pale or fortification. This gave me not only egress and regress, as it were a back-way to my tent and to my storehouse, but gave me room to stow my goods.

And now I began to apply myself to make such necessary things as I found I most wanted, as particularly a chair and a table; for without these I was not able to enjoy the few comforts I had in the world. I could not write or eat, or do several things with so much pleasure without a table.

So I went to work. And here I must needs observe, that as reason is the substance and original of the mathematics, so by stating and squaring everything by reason, and by making the most rational judgment of things, every man may be, in time, master of every mechanic art.

I had never handled a tool in my life; and yet in time, by labour, application, and contrivance, I found at last that I wanted nothing but I could have made it, especially if I had had tools. However, I made abundance of things even without tools, and some with no more tools than an adze and a hatchet, which, perhaps were never made that way before, and that with infinite labour. For example, if I wanted a board, I had no other way but to cut down a tree, set it on an edge before me, and hew it flat on either side with my axe, till I had brought it to be thin as a plank, and then dub it smooth with my adze. It is true, by this method I could make but one board out of a whole tree; but this I had no remedy for but patience, any more than I had for the prodigious deal of time and labour which it took me up to make a plank or board. But my time or labour was little worth, and so it was as well employed one way as another.

However, I made me a table and a chair, as I observed above, in the first place, and this I did out of the short pieces of boards that I brought on my raft from the ship. But when I had wrought out some boards, as above, I made large shelves of the breadth of a foot and a half one over another, all along one side of my cave, to lay all my tools, nails, and iron-work; and, in a word, to separate everything at large in their places, that I might come easily at them. I knocked pieces into the wall of the rock to hang my guns and all things that would hang up; so that had my cave been to be seen, it looked like a general magazine of all necessary things; and I had everything so ready at my hand, that it was a great pleasure to me to see all my goods in such order, and especially to find my stock of all necessaries so great.

And now it was when I began to keep a journal of every day's employment; for, indeed, at first, I was in too much hurry, and not only hurry as to labour, but in too much discomposure of mind; and my journal would have been full of many dull things. For example, I must have said thus: Sept. 30th.—After I got to shore, and had escaped drowning, instead of being thankful to God for my deliverance, having first vomited, with the great quantity of salt water which was gotten into my stomach, and recovering myself a little, I ran about the shore, wringing my hands, and beating my head and face, exclaiming at my misery, and crying out I was undone, undone! till, tired and faint, I was forced to lie down on the ground to repose; but durst not sleep, for fear of being devoured.

Some days after this, and after I had been on board the ship and got all that I could out of her, yet I could not forbear getting up to the top of a little mountain, and looking out to sea, in hopes of seeing a ship: then fancy at a vast distance I spied a sail, please myself with the hopes of it, and then after looking steadily till I was almost blind, lose it quite, and sit down and weep like a child, and thus increase my misery by my folly.

But having gotten over these things in some measure, and having settled my household stuff and habitation, made me a table and a chair, and all as handsome about me as I could, I began to keep my Journal, of which I shall here give you the copy (though in it will be told all these particulars over again) as long as it lasted; for, having no more ink, I was forced to leave it off.

CHAPTER FIVE

THE JOURNAL

September 30, 1659.

I, poor miserable Robinson Crusoe, being shipwrecked, during a dreadful storm, in the offing, came on shore on this dismal unfortunate island, which I called the Island of Despair; all the rest of the ship's company being drowned, and myself almost dead.

All the rest of that day I spent in afflicting myself at the dismal circumstances I was brought to, viz. I had neither food, house, clothes, weapon, or place to fly to: and in despair of any relief, saw nothing but death before me; either that I should be devoured by wild beasts, murdered by savages, or starved to death for want of food. At the approach of night I slept in a tree, for fear of wild creatures; but slept soundly, though it rained all night.

October 1.—In the morning I saw, to my great surprise, the ship had floated with the high tide, and was driven on shore again much nearer the island; which, as it was some comfort on one hand (for seeing her sit upright, and not broken in pieces, I hoped, if the wind abated, I might get on board, and get some food and necessaries out of her for my relief), so, on the other hand, it renewed my grief at the loss of my comrades, who, I imagined, if we had all staid on board, might have saved the ship, or, at least, that they would not have been all drowned, as they were: and that, had the men been saved, we might perhaps have built us a boat, out of the ruins of the ship, to have carried us to some other part of the world. I spent great part of this day in perplexing myself on these things; but, at length, seeing the ship almost dry, I went upon the sand as near as I could, and then swam on board. This day also it continued raining, though with no wind at all.

From the 1st of October to the 24th. All these days entirely spent in many several voyages to get all I could out of the ship; which I brought on shore, every tide of

flood, upon rafts. Much rain also in these days, though with some intervals of fair weather: but, it seems, this was the rainy season.

Oct. 20.—I overset my raft, and all the goods I had got upon it; but being in shoal water, and the things being chiefly heavy, I recovered many of them when the tide was out.

Oct. 25.—It rained all night and all day, with some gusts of wind; during which time the ship broke in pieces, the wind blowing a little harder than before, and was no more to be seen, except the wreck of her, and that only at low water. I spent this day in covering and securing the goods which I had saved, that the rain might not spoil them.

Oct. 26.—I walked about the shore almost all day, to find out a place to fix my habitation; greatly concerned to secure myself from any attack in the night, either from wild beasts or men. Towards night I fixed upon a proper place, under a rock, and marked out a semicircle for my encampment; which I resolved to strengthen with a work, wall, or fortification, made of double piles, lined within with cables, and without with turf.

From the 26th to the 30th, I worked very hard in carrying all my goods to my new habitation, though some part of the time it rained exceeding hard.

The 31st, in the morning, I went out into the island with my gun, to see for some food, and discover the country; when I killed a she-goat, and her kid followed me home, which I afterwards killed also, because it would not feed.

November 1—I set up my tent under a rock, and lay there for the first night; making it as large as I could, with stakes driven in to swing my hammock upon.

Nov. 2.—I set up all my chests and boards, and the pieces of timber which made my rafts; and with them formed a fence round me, a little within the place I had marked out for my fortification.

Nov. 3.—I went out with my gun, and killed two fowls like ducks, which were very good food. In the afternoon went to work to make me a table.

Nov. 4.—This morning I began to order my times of work, of going out with my gun, time of sleep, and time of diversion, viz. every morning I walked out with my gun for two or three hours, if it did not rain; then employed myself to work till about eleven o'clock; then eat what I had to live on; and from twelve to two I lay down to sleep, the weather being excessive hot; and then in the evening to work again. The working part of this day and of the next were wholly employed in making my table; for I was yet but a very sorry workman, though time and necessity made me a complete natural mechanic soon after, as I believe it would do any one else.

Nov. 5.—This day went abroad with my gun and my dog, and killed a wild cat; her skin pretty soft, but her flesh good for nothing. Every creature I killed, I took off the skins and preserved them. Coming back by the sea-shore, I saw many sorts of sea-fowls, which I did not understand; but was surprised, and almost frighted, with two or three seals, while I was gazing at, not well knowing what they were, got into the sea, and escaped me for that time.

Nov. 6.—After my morning walk I went to work with my table again, and finished it, though not to my liking; nor was it long before I learnt to mend it.

Nov. 7.—Now it began to be settled fair weather. The 7th, 8th, 9th, 10th, and part of the 12th (for the 11th was Sunday) I took wholly up to make me a chair, and with much ado, brought it to a tolerable shape, but never to please me; and even in the making, I pulled it in pieces several times. Note, soon neglected my keeping Sundays; for, omitting my mark for them on my post, I forgot which was which.

Nov. 13.—This day it rained; which refreshed me exceedingly, and cooled the earth: but it was accompanied with terrible thunder and lightning, which frighted me dreadfully, for fear of my powder. As soon as it was over, I resolved to separate my stock of powder into as many little parcels as possible, that it might not be in danger.

Nov. 14, 15, 16.—These three days I spent in making little square chests or boxes, which might hold about a pound, or two pound at most, of powder: and so, putting the powder in, I stowed it in places as secure and as remote from one another as possible. On one of these three days I killed a large bird that was good to eat; but I know not what to call it.

Nov. 17.—This day I began to dig behind my tent into the rock, to make room for my farther conveniency. Note, Three things I wanted exceedingly for this work, viz. a pick-axe, a shovel, and a wheelbarrow or basket; so I desisted from my work, and began to consider how to supply that want, and make me some tools. As for a pick-axe, I made use of the iron crows, which were proper enough, though heavy; but the next thing was a shovel or spade. This was so absolutely necessary, that indeed I could do nothing effectually without it; but what kind of one to make, I knew not.

Nov. 18.—The next day, in searching the woods, I found a tree of that wood, or like it, which in the Brazils they call the iron-tree, for its exceeding hardness; of this, with great labour, and almost spoiling my axe, I cut a piece, and brought it home, too, with difficulty enough, for it was exceeding heavy.

The excessive hardness of the wood, and having no other way, made me a long while upon this machine, for I worked it effectually, by little and little, into the form of a shovel or spade, the handle exactly shaped like ours in England, only that the broad part having no iron shod upon it at bottom, it would not last me so long.

However, it served well enough for the uses which I had occasion to put it to; but never was a shovel, I believe, made after that fashion, or so long a-making.

I was still deficient, for I wanted a basket or a wheelbarrow. A basket I could not make by any means, having no such things as twigs that would bend to make wicker ware, at least none yet found out. And as to a wheelbarrow, I fancied I could make all but the wheel, but that I had no notion of, neither did I know how to go about it; besides, I had no possible way to make the iron gudgeons for the spindle or axis of the wheel to run in, so I gave it over; and so for carrying away the earth which I dug out of the cave, I made me a thing like a hod which the labourers carry mortar in, when they serve the bricklayers.

This was not so difficult to me as the making the shovel: and yet this and the shovel, and the attempt which I made in vain to make a wheelbarrow, took me up no less than four days; I mean always, excepting my morning walk with my gun, which I seldom failed, and very seldom failed also bringing home something fit to eat.

Nov. 23.—My other work having now stood still because of my making these tools, when they were finished I went on, and working every day, as my strength and time allowed, I spent eighteen days entirely in widening and deepening my cave, that it might hold my goods commodiously.

Note, During all this time I worked to make this room or cave spacious enough to accommodate me as a warehouse or magazine, a kitchen, a dining-room, and a cellar; as for my lodging, I kept to the tent, except that sometimes in the wet season of the year it rained so hard, that I could not keep myself dry, which caused me afterwards to cover all my place within my pale with long poles, in the form of rafters, leaning against the rock, and load them with flags and large leaves of trees, like a thatch.

December 10th.—I began now to think my cave or vault finished, when on a sudden (it seems I had made it too large) a great quantity of earth fell down from the top and one side, so much, that, in short, it frighted me, and not without reason too; for if I had been under it, I had never wanted a gravedigger. Upon this disaster I had a great deal of work to do over again; for I had the loose earth to carry out; and, which was of more importance, I had the ceiling to prop up, so that I might be sure no more would come down.

Dec. 11.—This day I went to work with it accordingly, and got two shores or posts pitched upright to the top, with two pieces of boards across over each post. This I finished the next day; and setting more posts up with boards, in about a week more I had the roof secured; and the posts standing in rows, served me for partitions to part of my house.

Dec. 17.—From this day to the twentieth I placed shelves, and knocked up nails on the posts to hang everything up that could be hung up; and now I began to be in some order within doors.

Dec. 20.—Now I carried everything into the cave, and began to furnish my house, and set up some pieces of boards, like a dresser, to order my victuals upon; but boards began to be very scarce with me; also I made me another table.

Dec. 24.—Much rain all night and all day; no stirring out.

Dec. 25.—Rain all day.

Dec. 26.—No rain, and the earth much cooler than before, and pleasanter.

Dec. 27.—Killed a young goat, and lamed another, so that I catched it, and led it home in a string. When I had it home, I bound and splintered up its leg, which was broke. *N.B.* – I took such care of it, that it lived, and the leg grew well and as strong as ever; but by my nursing it so long it grew tame, and fed upon the little green at my door, and would not go away. This was the first time that I entertained a thought of breeding up some tame creatures, that I might have food when my powder and shot was all spent.

Dec. 28, 29, 30.—Great heats and no breeze, so that there was no stirring abroad, except in the evening, for food. This time I spent in putting all my things in order within doors.

January 1.—Very hot still, but I went abroad early and late with my gun, and lay still in the middle of the day. This evening, going farther into the valleys which lay towards the centre of the island, I found there was plenty of goats, though exceeding shy, and hard to come at. However, I resolved to try if I could not bring my dog to hunt them down.

Jan. 2.—Accordingly, the next day, I went out with my dog, and set him upon the goats; but I was mistaken, for they all faced about upon the dog; and he knew his danger too well, for he would not come near them.

Jan. 3.—I began my fence or wall; which, being still jealous of my being attacked by somebody, I resolved to make very thick and strong.

N.B.—This wall being described before, I purposely omit what was said in the Journal. It is sufficient to observe that I was no less time than from the 3rd of January to the 14th of April working, finishing, and perfecting this wall, though it was no more than about twenty-four yards in length, being a half circle from one place in the rock to another place about eight yards from it, the door of the cave being in the centre behind it.

All this time I worked very hard, the rains hindering me many days, nay, sometimes weeks together; but I thought I should never be perfectly secure till this wall was finished. And it was scarce credible what inexpressible labour everything was done with, especially the bringing piles out of the woods, and driving them into the ground; for I made them much bigger than I need to have done.

When this wall was finished, and the outside doublefenced with a turf-wall raised up close to it, I persuaded myself that if any people were to come on shore there, they would not perceive anything like a habitation; and it was very well I did so, as may be observed hereafter upon a very remarkable occasion.

During this time, I made my rounds in the woods for game every day, when the rain admitted me, and made frequent discoveries in these walks of something or other

to my advantage; particularly I found a kind of wild pigeons, who built, not as wood pigeons in a tree, but rather as house pigeons, in the holes of the rocks. And taking some young ones, I endeavoured to breed them up tame, and did so; but when they grew older they flew all away, which, perhaps, was at first for want of feeding them, for I had nothing to give them. However, I frequently found their nests, and got their young ones, which were very good meat.

And now in the managing my household affairs I found myself wanting in many things, which I thought at first it was impossible for me to make, as indeed, as to some of them, it was. For instance, I could never make a cask to be hooped; I had a small runlet or two, as I observed before, but I could never arrive to the capacity of making one by them, though I spent many weeks about it. I could neither put in the heads, or joint the staves so true to one another, as to make them hold water; so I gave that also over.

In the next place, I was at a great loss for candle; so that as soon as ever it was dark, which was generally by seven o'clock, I was obliged to go to bed. I remembered the lump of beeswax with which I made candles in my African adventure, but I had none of that now. The only remedy I had was, that when I had killed a goat I saved the tallow, and with a little dish made of clay, which I baked in the sun, to which I added a wick of some oakum, I made me a lamp; and this gave me light, though not a clear steady light like a candle.

In the middle of all my labours it happened, that rummaging my things, I found a little bag, which, as I hinted before, had been filled with corn for the feeding of poultry, not for this voyage, but before, as I suppose, when the ship came from Lisbon. What little remainder of corn had been in the bag was all devoured with the rats, and I saw nothing in the bag but husks and dust; and being willing to have the bag for some other use, I think it was to put powder in, when I divided it for fear of the lightning, or some such use, I shook the husks of corn out of it on one side of my fortification, under the rock. It was a little before the great rains, just now mentioned, that I threw this stuff a way, taking no notice of anything, and not so much as remembering that I had thrown anything there; when, about a month after, or thereabout, I saw some few stalks of something green shooting out of the ground, which I fancied might be some plant I had not seen; but I was surprised, and perfectly astonished, when, after a little longer time, I saw about ten or twelve ears come out, which were perfect green barley of the same kind as our European, nay, as our English barley.

It is impossible to express the astonishment and confusion of my thoughts on this occasion. I had hitherto acted upon no religious foundation at all: indeed, I had very few notions of religion in my head, or had entertained any sense of any thing that had befallen me, otherwise than as a chance, or, as we lightly say, what pleases God; without so much as inquiring into the end of Providence in these things, or his order in governing events in the world. But after I saw barley grow there, in a climate which I know was not proper for corn, and especially that I knew not how it came there, it startled me strangely; and I began to suggest, that God had miraculously caused this grain to grow without any help of seed sown, and that it was so directed purely for my sustenance, on that wild miserable place.

This touched my heart a little, and brought tears out of my eyes; and I began to bless myself that such a prodigy of nature should happen upon my account: and this was the more strange to me, because I saw near it still, all along by the side of the rock, some other straggling stalks, which proved to be stalks of rice, and which I knew, because I had seen it grow in Africa, when I was ashore there.

I not only thought these the pure productions of Providence for my support, but, not doubting but that there was more in the place, I went over all that part of the island where I had been before, peering in every corner, and under every rock, to see for more of it; but I could not find any. At last it occurred to my thoughts, that I had shook a bag of chicken's-meat out in that place, and then the wonder began to cease; and I must confess, my religious thankfulness to God's providence began to abate too, upon the discovering that all this was nothing but what was common; though I ought to have been as thankful for so strange and unforeseen providence, as if it had been miraculous: for it was really the work of Providence, as to me, that should order or appoint that ten or twelve grains of corn should remain unspoiled (when the rats had destroyed all the rest), as if it had been dropped from heaven; as also, that I should throw it out in that particular place, where, it being in the shade of a high rock, it sprang up immediately whereas, if I had thrown it anywhere else, at that time, it would have been burnt up and destroyed.

I carefully saved the ears of this corn, you may be sure, in their season, which was about the end of June; and laying up every corn, I resolved to sow them all again, hoping in time to have some quantity sufficient to supply me with bread. But it was not till the fourth year that I could allow myself the least grain of this corn to eat, and even then but sparingly, as I shall say afterwards in its order; for I lost all that I sowed the first season, by not observing the proper time; for I sowed it just before the dry season, so that it never came up at all, at least not as it would have done; of which in its place.

Besides this barley, there was, as above, twenty or thirty stalks of rice, which I preserved with the same care, and whose use was of the same kind, or to the same purpose, viz. to make me bread, or rather food; for I found ways to cook it up without baking, though I did that also after some time. But to return to my Journal.

I worked excessive hard these three or four months to get my wall done; and the 14th of April I closed it up, contriving to go into it, not by a door, but over the wall

by a ladder, that there might be no sign in the outside of my habitation.

April 16.—I finished the ladder, so I went up with the ladder to the top, and then pulled it up after me, and let it down on the inside. This was a complete enclosure to me; for within I had room enough, and nothing could come at me from without, unless it could first mount my wall.

The very next day after this wall was finished, I had almost had all my labour overthrown at once, and myself killed. The case was thus: As I was busy in the inside of it, behind my tent, just in the entrance into my cave, I was terribly frighted with a most dreadful surprising thing indeed; for all on a sudden I found the earth come crumbling down from the roof of my cave, and from the edge of the hill over my head, and two of the posts I had set up in the cave cracked in a frightful manner. I was heartily scared, but thought nothing of what was really the cause, only thinking that the top of my cave was falling in, as some of it had done before; and for fear I should be buried in it, I ran forward to my ladder; and not thinking myself safe there neither, I got over my wall for fear of the pieces of the hill which I expected might roll down upon me. I was no sooner stepped down upon the firm ground, but I plainly saw it was a terrible earthquake; for the ground I stood on shook three times at about eight minutes' distance, with three such shocks, as would have overturned the strongest building that could be supposed to have stood on the earth; and a great piece of the top of a rock, which stood about half a mile from me next the sea, fell down with such a terrible noise, as I never heard in all my life. I perceived also the very sea was put into violent motion by it; and I believe the shocks were stronger under the water than on the island.

I was so much amazed with the thing itself (having never felt the like, or discoursed with any one that had) that I was like one dead or stupefied; and the motion of the earth made my stomach sick, like one that was tossed at sea: but the noise of the falling of the rock awaked me, as it were, and rousing me from the stupefied condition I was in, filled me with horror, and I thought of nothing then but the hill falling upon my tent and all my household goods, and burying all at once; and this sunk my very soul within me a second time.

After the third shock was over, and I felt no more for some time, I began to take courage; and yet I had not heart enough to go over my wall again, for fear of being buried alive, but sat still upon the ground, greatly cast down and disconsolate, not knowing what to do. All this while I had not the least serious religious thought, nothing but the common, "Lord, have mercy upon me!" and when it was over, that went away too.

While I sat thus, I found the air overcast, and grow cloudy, as if it would rain. Soon after that the wind rose by little and little, so that in less than half-an-hour it blew a most dreadful hurricane. The sea was all on a sudden covered over with foam and froth; the shore was covered with the breach of the water; the trees were torn up by the roots; and a terrible storm it was: and this held about three hours, and then began to abate; and in two hours more it was stark calm, and began to rain very hard.

All this while I sat upon the ground, very much terrified and dejected; when, on a sudden, it came into my thoughts that these winds and rain being the consequence of the earthquake, the earthquake itself was spent and over, and I might venture into my cave again. With this thought my spirits began to revive; and the rain also helping to persuade me, I went in, and sat down in my tent; but the rain was so violent, that my tent was ready to be beaten down with it; and I was forced to go into my cave, though very much afraid and uneasy, for fear it should fall on my head.

This violent rain forced me to a new work, viz. to cut a hole through my new fortification, like a sink, to let the water go out, which would else have drowned my cave. After I had been in my cave some time, and found still no more shocks of the earthquake follow, I began to be more composed. And now to support my spirits, which indeed wanted it very much, I went to my little store, and took a small sup of rum which however, I did then, and always, very sparingly, knowing I could have no more when that was gone.

It continued raining all that night and great part of the next day, so that I could not stir abroad; but my mind being more composed, I began to think of what I had best do, concluding that if the island was subject to these earthquakes, there would be no living for me in a cave, but I must consider of building me some little hut in an open place, which I might surround with a wall, as I had done here, and so make myself secure from wild beasts or men; but concluded, if I staid where I was, I should certainly, one time or other, be buried alive.

With these thoughts I resolved to remove my tent from the place where it stood, which was just under the hanging precipice of the hill, and which, if it should be shaken again, would certainly fall upon my tent; and I spent the two next days, being the 19th and 20th of April, in contriving where and how to remove my habitation.

The fear of being swallowed up alive made me that I never slept in quiet; and yet the apprehension of lying abroad without any fence was almost equal to it. But still, when I looked about and saw how everything was put in order, how pleasantly concealed I was, and how safe from danger, it made me very loth to remove.

In the meantime it occurred to me that it would require a vast deal of time for me to do this, and that I must be contented to run the venture where I was, till I had formed a camp for myself, and had secured it so as to remove to it. So with this resolution I composed myself for a time, and resolved that I would go to work with all speed to build me a wall with piles and cables, etc., in a circle as before, and set

my tent up in it when it was finished, but that I would venture to stay where I was till it was finished, and fit to remove to. This was the 21st.

April 22.—The next morning I began to consider of means to put this resolve in execution; but I was at a great loss about my tools. I had three large axes, and abundance of hatchets (for we carried the hatchets for traffic with the Indians), but with much chopping and cutting knotty hard wood, they were all full of notches and dull; and though I had a grindstone, I could not turn it and grind my tools too. This cost me as much thought as a statesman would have bestowed upon a grand point of politics, or a judge upon the life and death of a man. At length I contrived a wheel with a string, to turn it with my foot, that I might have both my hands at liberty. Note, I had never seen any such thing in England, or at least not to take notice how it was done, though since I have observed it is very common there; besides that, my grindstone was very large and heavy. This machine cost me a full week's work to bring it to perfection.

April 28, 29.—These two whole days I took up in grinding my tools, my machine for turning my grindstone performing very well.

April 30.—Having perceived that my bread had been low a great while, now I took a survey of it, and reduced myself to one biscuit-cake a day, which made my heart very heavy.

CHAPTER SIX

May 1.—In the morning, looking towards the seaside, the tide being low, I saw something lie on the shore bigger than ordinary, and it looked like a cask. When I came to it, I found a small barrel, and two or three pieces of the wreck of the ship, which were driven on shore by the late hurricane; and looking towards the wreck itself, I thought it seemed to lie higher out of the water than it used to do. I examined the barrel which was driven on shore, and soon found it was a barrel of gunpowder; but it had taken water, and the powder was caked as hard as a stone. However, I rolled it farther on shore for the present, and went on upon the sands as near as I could to the wreck of the ship to look for more.

When I came down to the ship I found it strangely removed. The forecastle, which lay before buried in sand, was heaved up at least six foot; and the stern, which was broken to pieces, and parted from the rest by the force of the sea, soon after I had left rummaging her, was tossed, as it were, up, and cast on one side, and the sand was thrown so high on that side next her stern, that whereas there was a great place of water before, so that I could not come within a quarter of a mile of the wreck without swimming, I could now walk quite up to her when the tide was out. I was surprised with this at first, but soon concluded it must be done by the earthquake. And as by this violence the ship was more broken open than formerly, so many things came daily on shore, which the sea had loosened, and which the winds and water rolled by degrees to the land.

This wholly diverted my thoughts from the design of removing my habitation; and I busied myself mightily, that day especially, in searching whether I could make any way into the ship. But I found nothing was to be expected of that kind, for that all the inside of the ship was choked up with sand. However, as I had learned not to despair of anything, I resolved to pull everything to pieces that I could of the ship, concluding, that everything I could get from her would be of some use or other to me.

May 3.—I began with my saw, and cut a piece of a beam through, which I thought held some of the upper part or quarter-deck together; and when I had cut it through, I cleared away the sand as well as I could from the side which lay highest; but the tide coming in, I was obliged to give over for that time.

May 4.—I went a fishing, but caught not one fish that I durst eat of, till I was weary of my sport; when, just going to leave off, I caught a young dolphin. I had made me a long line of some rope-yarn, but I had no hooks; yet I frequently caught fish enough, as much as I cared to eat; all which I dried in the sun, and eat them dry.

May 5.—Worked on the wreck: cut another beam asunder, and brought three great fir planks off from the decks, which I tied together, and made swim on shore when the tide of flood came on.

May 6.—Worked on the wreck: got several iron bolts out of her, and other pieces of iron work: worked very hard, and came home very much tired, and had thoughts of giving it over.

May 7.—Went to the wreck again, but with an intent not to work; but found the weight of the wreck had broke itself down, the beams being cut; that several pieces of the ship seemed to lie loose; and the inside of the hold lay so open that I could see into it; but almost full of water and sand.

May 8.—Went to the wreck, and carried an iron crow to wrench up the deck, which lay now quite clear of the water or sand. I wrenched open two planks, and brought them on shore also with the tide. I left the iron crow in the wreck for next day.

May 9.—Went to the wreck, and with the crow made way into the body of the wreck, and felt several casks, and loosened them with the crow, but could not break them up. I felt also the roll of English lead, and could stir it; but it was too heavy to remove.

May 10, 12, 13, 14.—Went every day to the wreck, and got a great deal of pieces of timber, and boards, or plank, and two or three hundredweight of iron.

May 15.—I carried two hatchets, to try if I could not cut a piece off of the roll of lead, by placing the edge of one hatchet, and driving it with the other; but as it lay about a foot and a half in the water, I could not make any blow to drive the hatchet.

May 16.—It had blowed hard in the night, and the wreck appeared more broken by the force of the water; but I stayed so long in the woods, to get pigeons for food, that the tide prevented my going to the wreck that day.

May 17.—I saw some pieces of the wreck blown on shore, at a great distance, near two miles off me, but resolved to see what they were, and found it was a piece of the head, but too heavy for me to bring away.

May 24.—Every day to this day I worked on the wreck, and with hard labour I loosened some things so much with the crow, that the first blowing tide several casks floated out, and two of the seamen's chests. But the wind blowing from the shore, nothing came to land that day but pieces of timber, and a hogshead, which had some Brazil pork in it, but the salt water and the sand had spoiled it.

I continued this work every day to the 15th of June, except the time necessary to get food, which I always appointed, during this part of my employment, to be when the tide was up, that I might be ready when it was ebbed out. And by this time I had gotten timber, and plank, and ironwork enough to have builded a good boat, if I had known how; and also, I got at several times, and in several pieces, near one hundredweight of the sheet lead.

June 16.—Going down to the seaside, I found a large tortoise or turtle. This was the first I had seen, which it seems was only my misfortune, not any defect of the place, or scarcity; for had I happened to be on the other side of the island, I might have had hundreds of them every day, as I found afterwards; but, perhaps, had paid dear enough for them.

June 17.—I spent in cooking the turtle. I found in her three score eggs; and her flesh was to me, at that time, the most savoury and pleasant that ever I tasted in my life, having had no flesh but of goats and fowls, since I landed in this horrid place.

June 18.—Rained all day, and I stayed within. I thought at this time the rain felt cold, and I was something chilly, which I knew was not usual in that latitude.

June 19.—Very ill, and shivering, as if the weather had been cold.

June 20.—No rest all night; violent pains in my head, and feverish.

June 21.—Very ill, frighted almost to death with the apprehensions of my sad condition, to be sick, and no help. Prayed to God for the first time since the storm off of Hull, but scarce knew what I said, or why; my thoughts being all confused.

June 22.—A little better, but under dreadful apprehensions of sickness.

June 23.—Very bad again; cold and shivering, and then a violent headache.

June 24.—Much better.

June 25.—An ague very violent; the fit held me seven hours; cold fit, and hot with faint sweats after it.

June 26.—Better; and having no victuals to eat, took my gun, but found myself very weak. However, I killed a shegoat, and with much difficulty got it home, and broiled some of it, and eat. I would fain have stewed it, and made some broth, but had no pot.

June 27.—The ague again so violent that I lay abed all day, and neither eat or drink. I was ready to perish for thirst; but so weak, I had not strength to stand up, or to get myself any water to drink. Prayed to God again, but was light-headed; and when I was not, I was so ignorant that I knew not what to say; only I lay and cried, "Lord, look upon me! Lord, pity me! Lord, have mercy upon me!" I suppose I did nothing else for two or three hours, till the fit wearing off, I fell asleep, and did not wake till far in the night. When I waked, I found myself much refreshed, but weak, and exceeding thirsty. However, as I had no water in my whole habitation, I was forced to lie till morning, and went to sleep again. In this second sleep I had this terrible dream.

I thought that I was sitting on the ground, on the outside of my wall, where I sat when the storm blew after the earthquake, and that I saw a man descend from a great black cloud, in a bright flame of fire, and light upon the ground. He was all over as bright as a flame, so that I could but just bear to look towards him. His countenance was most inexpressibly dreadful, impossible for words to describe. When he stepped upon the ground with his feet, I thought the earth trembled, just as it had done before in the earthquake, and all the air looked, to my apprehension, as if it had been filled with flashes of fire.

He was no sooner landed upon the earth, but he moved forward towards me, with a long spear or weapon in his hand, to kill me; and when he came to a rising ground, at some distance, he spoke to me, or I heard a voice so terrible, that it is impossible to express the terror of it. All that I can say I understood was this: "Seeing all these things have not brought thee to repentance, now thou shalt die;" at which words I thought he lifted up the spear that was in his hand to kill me.

No one that shall ever read this account, will expect that I should be able to describe

the horrors of my soul at this terrible vision: I mean, that even while it was a dream, I even dreamed of those horrors; nor is it any more possible to describe the impression that remained upon my mind when I awaked, and found it was but a dream.

I had, alas! no divine knowledge; what I had received by the good instruction of my father was then worn out, by an uninterrupted series, for eight years, of seafaring wickedness, and a constant conversation with nothing but such as were, like myself, wicked and profane to the last degree. I do not remember that I had, in all that time, one thought that so much as tended either to looking upwards towards God, or inwards towards a reflection upon my own ways; but a certain stupidity of soul, without desire of good, or consciousness of evil, had entirely overwhelmed me; and I was all that the most hardened, unthinking, wicked creature among our common sailors can be supposed to be; not having the least sense, either of the fear of God in danger, or of thankfulness to Him in deliverances.

In the relating what is already past of my story, this will be the more easily believed, when I shall add, that through all the variety of miseries that had to this day befallen me, I never had so much as one thought of it being the hand of God, or that it was a just punishment for my sin; my rebellious behaviour against my father, or my present sins, which were great; or so much as a punishment for the general course of my wicked life. When I was on the desperate expedition on the desert shores of Africa, I never had so much as one thought of what would become of me; or one wish to God to direct me whither I should go, or to keep me from the danger which apparently surrounded me as well from voracious creatures as cruel savages: but I was merely thoughtless of a God or a Providence; acted like a mere brute, from the principles of nature, and by the dictates of common sense only; and indeed hardly that.

When I was delivered and taken up at sea by the Portugal captain, well used, and dealt justly and honourably with, as well as charitably, I had not the least thankfulness in my thoughts. When, again, I was shipwrecked, ruined, and in danger of drowning on this island, I was as far from remorse, or looking on it as a judgment: I only said to myself often, that I was an unfortunate dog, and born to be always miserable.

It is true, when I got on shore first here, and found all my ship's crew drowned, and myself spared, I was surprised with a kind of ecstasy, and some transports of soul, which, had the grace of God assisted, might have come up to true thankfulness; but it ended where it begun, in a mere common flight of joy, or, as I may say, being glad I was alive, without the least reflection upon the distinguishing goodness of the hand which had preserved me, and had singled me out to be preserved, when all the rest were destroyed; or an inquiry why Providence had been thus merciful to me; even just the same common sort of joy which seamen generally have after they are got safe ashore from a shipwreck, which they drown all in the next bowl of punch, and forget almost as soon as it is over, and all the rest of my life was like it.

Even when I was afterwards, on due consideration, made sensible of my condition, how I was cast on this dreadful place, out of the reach of human kind, out of all hope of relief, or prospect of redemption, as soon as I saw but a prospect of living, and that I should not starve and perish for hunger, all the sense of my affliction wore off, and I began to be very easy, applied myself to the works proper for my preservation and supply, and was far enough from being afflicted at my condition, as a judgment from Heaven, or as the hand of God against me: these were thoughts which very seldom entered into my head.

The growing up of the corn, as is hinted in my Journal, had, at first, some little influence upon me, and began to affect me with seriousness, as long as I thought it had something miraculous in it; but as soon as ever that part of the thought was removed, all the impression which was raised from it wore off also, as I have noted already.

Even the earthquake, though nothing could be more terrible in its nature, or more immediately directing to the invisible Power, which alone directs such things, yet no sooner was the first fright over, but the impression it had made went off also. I had no more sense of God or His judgments, much less of the present affliction of my circumstances being from His hand, than if I had been in the most prosperous condition of life.

But now, when I began to be sick, and a leisurely view of the miseries of death came to place itself before me; when my spirits began to sink under the burthen of a strong distemper, and Nature was exhausted with the violence of the fever; conscience, that had slept so long, began to awake, and I began to reproach myself with my past life, in which I had so evidently, by uncommon wickedness, provoked the justice of God to lay me under uncommon strokes, and to deal with me in so vindictive a manner.

These reflections oppressed me for the second or third day of my distemper; and, in the violence as well of the fever as of the dreadful reproaches of my conscience, extorted some words from me like praying to God: though I cannot say they were either a prayer attended with desires or with hopes; it was rather the voice of mere fright and distress. My thoughts were confused; the convictions great upon my mind; and the horror of dying in such a miserable condition, raised vapours in my head with the mere apprehensions: and, in these hurries of my soul, I know not what my tongue might express; but it was rather exclamation, such as, "Lord, what a miserable creature am I! If I should be sick, I shall certainly die for want of help; and what will become of me?" Then the tears burst out of my eyes, and I could say no more for a good while.

In this interval, the good advice of my father came to my mind, and presently his prediction, which I mentioned at the beginning of this story, viz. that if I did take this foolish step, God would not bless me; and I would have leisure hereafter to reflect upon having neglected his counsel, when there might be none to assist in my recovery.

"Now," said I aloud, "my dear father's words are come to pass; God's justice has overtaken me, and I have none to help or hear me. I rejected the voice of Providence, which had mercifully put me in a posture or station of life wherein I might have been happy and easy; but I would neither see it myself, or learn to know the blessing of it from my parents. I left them to mourn over my folly, and now I am left to mourn under the consequences of it. I refused their help and assistance, who would have

lifted me into the world, and would have made everything easy to me; and now I have difficulties to struggle with, too great for even Nature itself to support, and no assistance, no help, no comfort, no advice." Then I cried out, "Lord, be my help, for I am in great distress."

This was the first prayer, if I may call it so, that I had made for many years. But I return to my Journal.

June 28.—Having been somewhat refreshed with the sleep I had had, and the fit being entirely off, I got up; and though the fright and terror of my dream was very great, yet I considered that the fit of the ague would return again the next day, and now was my time to get something to refresh and support myself when I should be ill. And the first thing I did, I filled a large square case-bottle with water, and set it upon my table, in reach of my bed; and to take off the chill or aguish disposition of the water, I put about a quarter of a pint of rum into it, and mixed them together. Then I got me a piece of the goat's flesh, and broiled it on the coals, but could eat very little. I walked about, but was very weak, and withal very sad and heavy-hearted in the sense of my miserable condition, dreading the return of my distemper the next day. At night I made my supper of three of the turtle's eggs, which I roasted in the ashes, and eat, as we call it, in the shell; and this was the first bit of meat I had ever asked God's blessing to, even as I could remember, in my whole life.

After I had eaten, I tried to walk, but found myself so weak, that I could hardly carry the gun (for I never went out without that); so I went but a little way, and sat down upon the ground, looking out upon the sea, which was just before me, and very calm and smooth. As I sat here, some such thoughts as these occurred to me.

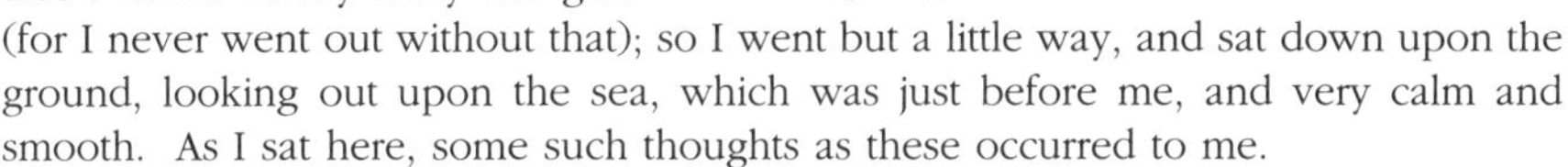

What is this earth and sea, of which I have seen so much? Whence is it produced? And what am I, and all the other creatures, wild and tame, human and brutal? Whence are we? Sure we are all made by some secret Power, who formed the earth and sea, the air and sky. And who is that? Then it followed most naturally, It is God that has made it all. Well, but then it came on strangely, if God has made all these things, He guides and governs them all, and all things that concern them; for the Power that could make all things, must certainly have power to guide and direct them. If so, nothing can happen in the great circuit of His works, either without His knowledge or appointment.

And if nothing happens without His knowledge, He knows that I am here, and am in this dreadful condition: and if nothing happens without his appointment, He has appointed all this to befall me. Nothing occurred to my thoughts to contradict any of these conclusions; and therefore it rested upon me with the greater force, that it must needs be that God had appointed all this to befall me; that I was brought to this miserable circumstance by His direction, He having the sole power, not of me only, but of everything that happened in the world. Immediately it followed, Why has God done this to me? What have I done to be thus used?

My conscience presently checked me in that inquiry, as if I had blasphemed, and methought it spoke to me like a voice: "Wretch! dost thou ask what thou hast done? Look back upon a dreadful misspent life, and ask thyself what thou hast not done? Ask, why is it that thou wert not long ago destroyed? Why wert thou not drowned in Yarmouth Roads? killed in the fight when the ship was taken by the Sallee man-of-war? devoured by the wild beasts on the coast of Africa? or drowned here, when all the crew perished but thyself? Dost thou ask, What have I done?"

I was struck dumb with these reflections, as one astonished, and had not a word to say, no, not to answer to myself, but rose up pensive and sad, walked back to my retreat, and went up over my wall, as if I had been going to bed. But my thoughts were sadly disturbed, and I had no inclination to sleep; so I sat down in my chair, and lighted my lamp, for it began to be dark. Now, as the apprehension of the return of my distemper terrified me very much, it occurred to my thought that the Brazilians take no physic but their tobacco for almost all distempers; and I had a piece of a roll of tobacco in one of the chests, which was quite cured, and some also that was green, and not quite cured.

I went, directed by Heaven no doubt; for in this chest I found a cure both for soul and body. I opened the chest, and found what I looked for, viz. the tobacco; and as the few books I had saved lay there too, I took out one of the Bibles which I mentioned before, and which to this time I had not found leisure, or so much as inclination, to look into. I say, I took it out, and brought both that and the tobacco with me to the table.

What use to make of the tobacco I knew not, as to my distemper, or whether it was good for it or no; but I tried several experiments with it, as if I was resolved it should hit one way or other. I first took a piece of a leaf, and chewed it in my mouth, which indeed at first almost stupefied my brain, the tobacco being green and strong, and that I had not been much used to it. Then I took some and steeped it an hour or two in some rum, and resolved to take a dose of it when I lay down. And lastly, I burnt some upon a pan of coals, and held my nose close over the smoke of it as long as I could bear it, as well for the heat, as almost for suffocation.

In the interval of this operation, I took up the Bible, and began to read, but my head was too much disturbed with the tobacco to bear reading, at least that time; only having opened the book casually, the first words that occurred to me were these, "Call on Me in the day of trouble, and I will deliver, and thou shalt glorify Me."

The words were very apt to my case; and made some impression upon my

thoughts at the time of reading them, though not so much as they did afterwards; for, as for being delivered, the word had no sound, as I may say, to me; the thing was so remote, so impossible in my apprehension of things, that I began to say, as the children of Israel did when they were promised flesh to eat, "Can God spread a table in the wilderness?" so I began to say, "Can God himself deliver me from this place?" And as it was not for many years that any hope appeared, this prevailed very often upon my thoughts: but, however the words made a great impression upon me, and I mused upon them very often.

It grew now late, and the tobacco had, as I said, dozed my head so much, that I inclined to sleep; so I left my lamp burning in the cave, lest I should want anything in the night, and went to bed. But before I lay down, I did what I never had done in all my life; I kneeled down, and prayed to God to fulfil the promise to me, that if I called upon Him in the day of trouble, He would deliver me. After my broken and imperfect prayer was over, I drunk the rum in which I had steeped the tobacco; which was so strong and rank of the tobacco, that indeed I could scarce get it down. Immediately upon this I went to bed. I found presently it flew up in my head violently; but I fell into a sound sleep, and waked no more, till, by the sun, it must necessarily be near three o'clock in the afternoon the next day. Nay, to this hour I am partly of the opinion that I slept all the next day and night, and till almost three that day after; for otherwise I knew not how I should lose a day out of my reckoning in the days of the week, as it appeared some years after I had done. For if I had lost it by crossing and recrossing the line, I should have lost more than one day. But certainly I lost a day in my account, and never knew which way.

Be that, however, one way or the other, when I awaked I found myself exceedingly refreshed, and my spirits lively and cheerful. When I got up, I was stronger than I was the day before, and my stomach better, for I was hungry; and, in short, I had no fit the next day, but continued much altered for the better. This was the 29th.

The 30th was my well day, of course, and I went abroad with my gun, but did not care to travel too far. I killed a sea-fowl or two, something like a brand-goose, and brought them home, but was not very forward to eat them; so I eat some more of the turtle's eggs, which were very good. This evening I renewed the medicine, which I had supposed did me good the day before, viz. the tobacco steeped in rum; only I did not take so much as before, nor did I chew any of the leaf, or hold my head over the smoke. However, I was not so well the next day, which was the first of July, as I hoped I should have been; for I had a little spice of the cold fit, but it was not much.

July 2.—I renewed the medicine all the three ways, and dosed myself with it as at first, and doubled the quantity which I drank.

July 3.—I missed the fit for good and all, though I did not recover my full strength for some weeks after. While I was thus gathering strength, my thoughts ran exceedingly upon this Scripture, "I will deliver thee;" and the impossibility of my deliverance lay much upon my mind, in bar of my ever expecting it: but as I was discouraging myself with such thoughts, it occurred to my mind that I pored so much

upon my deliverance from the main affliction, that I disregarded the deliverance I had received; and I was, as it were, made to ask myself such questions as these, viz. Have I not been delivered, and wonderfully, too, from sickness; from the most distressed condition that could be, and that was so frightful to me, and what notice I had taken of it? Had I done my part? "God had delivered me, but I had not glorified Him;" that is to say, I had not owned and been thankful for that as a deliverance, and how could I expect greater deliverance? This touched my heart very much; and immediately I kneeled down, and gave God thanks aloud for my recovery from my sickness.

July 4.—In the morning I took the Bible; and beginning at the New Testament, I began seriously to read it, and imposed upon myself to read awhile every morning and every night, not tying myself to the number of chapters, but as long as my thoughts should engage me. It was not long after I set seriously to this work, that I found my heart more deeply and sincerely affected with the wickedness of my past life. The impression of my dream revived; and the words, "All these things have not brought thee to repentance," ran seriously in my thought. I was earnestly begging of God to give me repentance, when it happened providentially, the very same day, that, reading the scripture, I came to these words, "He is exalted a Prince and a Saviour, to give repentance and to give remission." I threw down the book; and with my heart as well as my hands lifted up to heaven, in a kind of ecstasy of joy, I cried out aloud, "Jesus, thou son of David! Jesus, thou exalted Prince and Saviour! give me repentance!" This was the first time that I could say, in the true sense of the words, that I prayed in all my life; for now I prayed with a sense of my condition, and with a true scripture view of hope, founded on the encouragement of the word of God: and from this time, I may say, I began to have hope that God would hear me.

Now I began to construe the words mentioned above, "Call on Me, and I will deliver you," in a different sense from what I had ever done before; for then I had no notion of anything being called deliverance but my being delivered from the captivity I was in; for though I was indeed at large in the place, yet the island was certainly a prison to me, and that in the worst sense in the world. But now I learned to take it in another sense; now I looked back upon my past life with such horror, and my sins appeared so dreadful, that my soul sought nothing of God but deliverance from the load of guilt that bore down all my comfort. As for my solitary life, it was nothing; I did not so much as pray to be delivered from it, or think of it; it was all of no consideration, in comparison with this. And I add this part here, to hint to whoever shall read it, that whenever they come to a true sense of things, they will find deliverance from sin a much greater blessing than deliverance from affliction.

But leaving this part, I return to my Journal.

My condition began now to be, though not less miserable as to my way of living, yet much easier to my mind; and my thoughts being directed, by a constant reading the Scripture, and praying to God, to things of a higher nature, I had a great deal of comfort within, which, till now, I knew nothing of. Also, as my health and strength returned, I bestirred myself to furnish myself with everything that I wanted, and make my way of living as regular as I could.

From the 4th of July to the 14th, I was chiefly employed in walking about with my gun in my hand, a little and a little at a time, as a man that was gathering up his strength after a fit of sickness; for it is hardly to be imagined how low I was, and to what weakness I was reduced. The application which I made use of was perfectly new, and perhaps what had never cured an ague before; neither can I recommend it to any one to practise, by this experiment; and though it did carry off the fit, yet it rather contributed to weakening me; for I had frequent convulsions in my nerves and limbs for some time.

I learnt from it also this, in particular; that being abroad in the rainy season was the most pernicious thing to my health that could be, especially in those rains which came attended with storms and hurricanes of wind; for as the rain which came in the dry season was almost always accompanied with such storms, so I found that rain was much more dangerous than the rain which fell in September and October.

I had been now in this unhappy island above ten months, all possibility of deliverance from this condition seemed to be entirely taken from me; and I firmly believed that no human shape had ever set foot upon that place. Having now secured my habitation, as I thought, fully to my mind, I had a great desire to make a more perfect discovery of the island, and to see what other productions I might find, which I yet knew nothing of.

CHAPTER SEVEN

It was the 15th of July that I began to take a more particular survey of the island itself. I went up the creek first, where, as I hinted, I brought my rafts on shore. I found, after I came about two miles up, that the tide did not flow any higher, and that it was no more than a little brook of running water, and very fresh and good; but this being the dry season, there was hardly any water in some parts of it, at least, not enough to run in any stream, so as it could be perceived.

On the bank of this brook I found many pleasant savannas or meadows, plain, smooth, and covered with grass; and on the rising parts of them, next to the higher grounds, where the water, as might be supposed, never overflowed, I found a great deal of tobacco, green, and growing to a great and very strong stalk. There were divers other plants, which I had no notion of, or understanding about, and might perhaps have virtues of their own which I could not find out.

I searched for the cassava root, which the Indians, in all that climate, make their bread of, but I could find none. I saw large plants of aloes, but did not then understand them. I saw several sugar-canes, but wild, and, for want of cultivation, imperfect. I contented myself with these discoveries for this time, and came back, musing with myself what course I might take to know the virtue and goodness of any of the fruits or plants which I should discover; but could bring it to no conclusion; for, in short, I had made so little observation while I was in the Brazils, that I knew little of the plants in the field, at least very little that might serve me to any purpose now in my distress.

The next day, the 16th, I went up the same way again; and after going something farther than I had gone the day before, I found the brook and the savannas began to cease, and the country became more woody than before. In this part I found different fruits, and particularly I found melons upon the ground in great abundance, and grapes upon the trees. The vines had spread indeed over the trees, and the clusters of grapes were just now in their prime, very ripe and rich. This was a surprising discovery, and I was exceeding glad of them; but I was warned by my experience to eat sparingly of them, remembering that when I was ashore in Barbary the eating of grapes killed several of our Englishmen, who were slaves there, by throwing them into fluxes and fevers. But I found an excellent use for these grapes; and that was, to cure or dry them in the sun, and keep them as dried grapes or raisins are kept, which I thought would be, as indeed they were, as wholesome as agreeable to eat, when no grapes might be to be had.

I spent all that evening there, and went not back to my habitation; which, by the way, was the first night, as I might say, I had lain from home. In the night, I took my first contrivance, and got up into a tree, where I slept well; and the next morning proceeded upon my discovery, travelling near four miles, as I might judge by the length of the valley, keeping still due north, with a ridge of hills on the south and north side of me.

'I descended a little on the side of that delicious vale . . .' (p. 74)

At the end of this march I came to an opening, where the country seemed to descend to the west; and a little spring of fresh water, which issued out of the side of the hill by me, ran the other way, that is, due east; and the country appeared so fresh, so green, so flourishing, everything being in a constant verdure or flourish of spring, that it looked like a planted garden.

I descended a little on the side of that delicious vale, surveying it with a secret kind of pleasure, though mixed with my other afflicting thoughts, to think that this was all my own; that I was king and lord of all this country indefeasibly, and had a right of possession; and, if I could convey it, I might have it in inheritance as completely as any lord of a manor in England. I saw here abundance of cocoa trees, orange, and lemon, and citron trees; but all wild, and very few bearing any fruit, at least not then. However, the green limes that I gathered were not only pleasant to eat, but very wholesome; and I mixed their juice afterwards with water, which made it very wholesome, and very cool and refreshing.

I found now I had business enough to gather and carry home; and I resolved to lay up a store, as well of grapes as limes and lemons, to furnish myself for the wet season, which I knew was approaching.

In order to this, I gathered a great heap of grapes in one place, and a lesser heap in another place, and a great parcel of limes and lemons in another place; and, taking a few of each with me, I travelled homeward; and resolved to come again, and bring a bag or sack, or what I could make, to carry the rest home.

Accordingly, having spent three days in this journey, I came home (so I must now call my tent and my cave); but before I got thither, the grapes were spoiled; the richness of the fruits, and the weight of the juice, having broken them and bruised them; they were good for little or nothing: as to the limes, they were good, but I could bring but a few.

The next day, being the 19th, I went back, having made me two small bags to bring home my harvest; but I was surprised, when, coming to my heap of grapes, which were so rich and fine when I gathered them, I found them all spread about, trod to pieces, and dragged about, some here, some there, and abundance eaten and devoured. By this I concluded there were some wild creatures thereabouts, which had done this; but what they were, I knew not.

However, as I found that there was no laying them up on heaps, no carrying them away in a sack, but that one way they would be destroyed, and the other way they would be crushed with their own weight, I took another course; for I gathered a large quantity of the grapes, and hung them up upon the out-branches of the trees, that they might cure and dry in the sun; and as for the limes and lemons, I carried as many back as I could well stand under.

When I came home from this journey, I contemplated with great pleasure the fruitfulness of that valley, and the pleasantness of the situation; the security from storms on that side, the water and the wood; and concluded that I had pitched upon a place to fix my abode, which was by far the worst part of the country. Upon the whole, I began to consider of removing my habitation, and to look out for a place equally safe

as where I now was situate, if possible, in that pleasant fruitful part of the island.

This thought ran long in my head, and I was exceeding fond of it for some time, the pleasantness of the place tempting me; but when I came to a nearer view of it, and to consider that I was now by the seaside, where it was at least possible that something might happen to my advantage, and, by the same ill fate that brought me hither, might bring some other unhappy wretches to the same place; and though it was scarce probable that any such thing should ever happen, yet to enclose myself among the hills and woods in the centre of the island, was to anticipate my bondage, and to render such an affair not only improbable, but impossible; and that therefore I ought not by any means to remove.

However, I was so enamoured of this place, that I spent much of my time there for the whole remaining part of the month of July; and though, upon second thoughts, I resolved, as above, not to remove, yet I built me a little kind of a bower, and surrounded it at a distance with a strong fence, being a double hedge as high as I could reach, well staked, and filled between with brushwood. And here I lay very secure, sometimes two or three nights together, always going over it with a ladder, as before; so that I fancied now I had my country house and my sea-coast house; and this work took me up to the beginning of August.

I had but newly finished my fence, and began to enjoy my labour, but the rains came on, and made me stick close to my first habitation; for though I had made me a tent like the other, with a piece of a sail, and spread it very well, yet I had not the shelter of a hill to keep me from storms, nor a cave behind me to retreat into, when the rains were extraordinary.

About the beginning of August, as I said, I had finished my bower, and began to enjoy myself. The 3rd of August, I found the grapes I had hung up were perfectly dried, and indeed were excellent good raisins of the sun; so I began to take them down from the trees. And it was very happy that I did so, for the rains which followed would have spoiled them, and I had lost the best part of my winter food; for I had above two hundred large bunches of them. No sooner had I taken them all down, and carried most of them home to my cave, but it began to rain; and from hence, which was the 14th of August, it rained, more or less, every day till the middle of October, and sometimes so violently, that I could not stir out of my cave for several days.

In this season, I was much surprised with the increase of my family. I had been concerned for the loss of one of my cats, who run away from me, or, as I thought, had been dead, and I heard no more tale or tidings of her, till, to my astonishment, she came home about the end of August with three kittens. This was the more strange to me, because, though I had killed a wild cat, as I called it, with my gun, yet I thought it was quite a different kind from our European cats: yet the young cats were the same kind of house-breed like the old one; and both of my cats being females, I thought it very strange. But from these three cats I afterwards came to be so pestered with cats, that I was forced to kill them like vermin, or wild beasts, and to drive them from my house as much as possible.

From the 14th of August to the 26th, incessant rain, so that I could not stir, and was now very careful not to be much wet. In this confinement, I began to be straitened for food; but venturing out twice, I one day killed a goat, and the last day, which was the 26th, found a very large tortoise, which was a treat to me, and my food was regulated thus: I eat a bunch of raisins for my breakfast, a piece of the goat's flesh, or of the turtle, for my dinner, broiled; for, to my great misfortune, I had no vessel to boil or stew anything; and two or three of the turtle's eggs for my supper.

During this confinement in my cover by the rain, I worked daily two or three hours at enlarging my cave, and by degrees worked it on towards one side, till I came to the outside of the hill, and made a door, or way out, which came beyond my fence or wall; and so I came in and out this way. But I was not perfectly easy at lying so open; for as I had managed myself before, I was in a perfect enclosure; whereas now I thought I lay exposed, and open for anything to come in upon me; and yet I could not perceive that there was any living thing to fear, the biggest creature that I had yet seen upon the island being a goat.

September 30th.—I was now come to the unhappy anniversary of my landing. I cast up the notches on my post, and found I had been on shore three hundred and sixty-five days. I kept this day as a solemn fast, setting it apart to religious exercise, prostrating myself on the ground with the most serious humiliation, confessing my sins to God, acknowledging his righteous judgments upon me, and praying to him to have mercy on me through Jesus Christ; and having not tasted the least refreshment for twelve hours, even till the going down of the sun, I then ate a biscuit cake and a bunch of grapes, and went to bed, finishing the day as I began it.

I had all this time observed no Sabbath day, for as at first I had no sense of religion upon my mind, I had, after some time, omitted to distinguish the weeks, by making a longer notch than ordinary for the Sabbath day, and so did not really know what any of the days were. But now, having cast up the days, as above, I found I had been there a year, so I divided it into weeks, and set apart every seventh day for a Sabbath; though I found at the end of my account, I had lost a day or two in my reckoning.

A little after this my ink began to fail me, and so I contented myself to use it more sparingly, and to write down only the most remarkable events of my life, without continuing a daily memorandum of other things.

The rainy season and the dry season began now to appear regular to me, and I learned to divide them so as to provide for them accordingly; but I bought all my experience before I had it, and this I am going to relate was one of the most discouraging experiments that I made at all. I have mentioned that I had saved the few ears of barley and rice, which I had so surprisingly found spring up, as I thought, of themselves, and believe there were about thirty stalks of rice, and about twenty of barley; and now I thought it a proper time to sow it after the rains, the sun being in its southern position, going from me.

Accordingly I dug up a piece of ground as well as I could with my wooden spade,

and dividing it into two parts, I sowed my grain; but as I was sowing, it casually occurred to my thoughts that I would not sow it all at first, because I did not know when was the proper time for it, so I sowed about two-thirds of the seed, leaving about a handful of each.

It was a great comfort to me afterwards that I did so, for not one grain of that I sowed this time came to anything, for the dry months following, the earth having had no rain after the seed was sown, it had no moisture to assist its growth, and never came up at all, till the wet season had come again, and then it grew as if it had been but newly sown.

Finding my first seed did not grow, which I easily imagined was by the drought, I sought for a moister piece of ground to make another trial in, and I dug up a piece of ground near my new bower, and sowed the rest of my seed in February, a little before the vernal equinox. And this having the rainy months of March and April to water it, sprung up very pleasantly, and yielded a very good crop; but having part of the seed left only, and not daring to sow all that I had, I had but a small quantity at last, my whole crop not amounting to above half a peck of each kind. But by this experiment I was made master of my business, and knew exactly when the proper season was to sow, and that I might expect two seedtimes and two harvests every year.

While this corn was growing, I made a little discovery, which was of use to me afterwards. As soon as the rains were over, and the weather began to settle, which was about the month of November, I made a visit up the country to my bower, where, though I had not been some months, yet I found all things just as I left them. The circle or double hedge that I had made was not only firm and entire, but the stakes which I had cut out of some trees that grew thereabouts were all shot out, and grown with long branches, as much as a willow-tree usually shoots the first year after lopping its head. I could not tell what tree to call it that these stakes were cut from. I was surprised, and yet very well pleased to see the young trees grow, and I pruned them, and led them up to grow as much alike as I could; and it is scarce credible how beautiful a figure they grew into in three years; so that though the hedge made a circle of about twenty-five yards in diameter, yet the trees, for such I might now call them, soon covered it, and it was a complete shade, sufficient to lodge under all the dry season.

This made me resolve to cut some more stakes, and make me a hedge like this, in a semicircle round my wall (I mean that of my first dwelling), which I did; and placing the trees or stakes in a double row, at about eight yards' distance from my first fence, they grew presently, and were at first a fine cover to my habitation, and afterwards served for a defence also, as I shall observe in its order.

I found now that the seasons of the year might generally be divided, not into summer and winter, as in Europe, but into the rainy seasons and the dry seasons, which were generally thus:

Half February, *March,* *Half April,*	*Rainy, the Sun being then on, or near the Equinox.*
Half April, *May,* *June,* *July,* *Half August,*	*Dry, the Sun being then to the North of the Line.*
Half August, *September,* *Half October,*	*Rainy, the Sun being then come back.*
Half October, *November,* *December,* *January,* *Half February,*	*Dry, the Sun being then to the South of the Line.*

The rainy season sometimes held longer or shorter, as the winds happened to blow; but this was the general observation I made. After I had found by experience the ill consequence of being abroad in the rain, I took care to furnish myself with provisions beforehand, that I might not be obliged to go out; and I sat within doors as much as possible during the wet months.

In this time I found much employment, and very suitable also to the time, for I found great occasion of many things which I had no way to furnish myself with but by hard labour and constant application; particularly, I tried many ways to make myself a basket; but all the twigs I could get for the purpose proved so brittle, that they would do nothing. It proved of excellent advantage to me now, that when I was a boy I used to take a great delight in standing at a basket-maker's in the town where my father lived, to see them make their wicker-ware; and being, as boys usually are, very officious to help, and a great observer of the manner how they worked those things, and sometimes lending a hand, I had by this means full knowledge of the

methods of it, that I wanted nothing but the materials; when it came into my mind that the twigs of that tree from whence I cut my stakes that grew might possibly be as tough as the sallows, and willows, and osiers in England, and I resolved to try.

Accordingly, the next day, I went to my country-house, as I called it; and cutting some of the smaller twigs, I found them to my purpose as much as I could desire; whereupon I came the next time prepared with a hatchet to cut down a quantity, which I soon found, for there was great plenty of them. These I set up to dry within my circle or hedge, and when they were fit for use, I carried them to my cave; and here during the next season I employed myself in making, as well as I could, a great many baskets, both to carry earth, or to carry or lay up anything as I had occasion. And though I did not finish them very handsomely, yet I made them sufficiently serviceable for my purpose. And thus, afterwards, I took care never to be without them; and as my wicker-ware decayed, I made more, especially I made strong deep baskets to place my corn in, instead of sacks, when I should come to have any quantity of it.

Having mastered this difficulty, and employed a world of time about it, I bestirred myself to see, if possible, how to supply two wants. I had no vessels to hold anything that was liquid, except two runlets, which were almost full of rum, and some glass bottles, some of the common size, and others which were case-bottles square, for the holding of waters, spirits, etc. I had not so much as a pot to boil anything, except a great kettle, which I saved out of the ship, and which was too big for such use as I desired it, viz. to make broth, and stew a bit of meat by itself. The second thing I would fain have had was a tobacco-pipe; but it was impossible to me to make one. However, I found a contrivance for that, too, at last.

I employed myself in planting my second rows of stakes or piles and in this wicker-working all the summer or dry season, when another business took me up more time than it could be imagined I could spare.

CHAPTER EIGHT

I mentioned before that I had a great mind to see the whole island, and that I had travelled up the brook, and so on to where I built my bower, and where I had an opening quite to the sea, on the other side of the island. I now resolved to travel quite across to the seashore on that side; so taking my gun, a hatchet, and my dog, and a larger quantity of powder and shot than usual, with two biscuit-cakes and a great

bunch of raisins in my pouch for my store, I began my journey. When I had passed the vale where my bower stood, as above, I came within view of the sea to the west; and it being a very clear day, I fairly descried land, whether an island or a continent I could not tell; but it lay very high, extending from the west to the W.S.W. at a very great distance; by my guess, it could not be less than fifteen or twenty leagues off.

I could not tell what part of the world this might be; otherwise than that I know it must be part of America; and, as I concluded by all my observations, must be near the Spanish dominions; and perhaps was all inhabited by savages, where, if I should have landed, I had been in a worse condition than I was now. And therefore I acquiesced in the dispositions of Providence, which I began now to own and to believe ordered everything for the best; I say, I quieted my mind with this, and left afflicting myself with fruitless wishes of being there. Besides, after some pause upon this affair, I considered that if this land was the Spanish coast, I should certainly, one time or other, see some vessel pass or repass one way or other; but if not, then it was the savage coast between the Spanish country and the Brazils, whose inhabitants are indeed the worst of savages; for they are cannibals, or meneaters, and fail not to murder and devour all the human bodies that fall into their hands.

With these considerations, I walked very leisurely forward. I found that side of the island, where I now was, much pleasanter than mine; the open or savanna fields sweet, adorned with flowers and grass, and full of very fine woods. I saw abundance of parrots; and fain I would have caught one, if possible, to have kept it to be tame, and taught it to speak to me. I did, after some painstaking, catch a young parrot; for I knocked it down with a stick, and, having recovered it, I brought it home; but it was some years before I could make him speak. However, at last I taught him to call me by my name very familiarly; but the accident that followed, though it be a trifle, will be very diverting in its place.

I was exceedingly diverted with this journey. I found in the low grounds hares, as I thought them to be, and foxes; but they differed greatly from all the other kinds I had met with, nor could I satisfy myself to eat them, though I killed several. But I had no need to be venturous, for I had no want of food, and of that which was very good too; especially these three sorts, viz. goats, pigeons, and turtle, or tortoise; which, added to my grapes, Leadenhall Market could not have furnished a table better than I, in proportion to the company. And though my case was deplorable enough, yet I had great cause for thankfulness, and that I was not driven to any extremities for food, but rather plenty, even to dainties.

I never travelled in this journey above two miles outright in a day, or thereabouts; but I took so many turns and returns, to see what discoveries I could make, that I came weary enough to the place where I resolved to sit down for all night; and then I either reposed myself in a tree, or surrounded myself with a row of stakes, set

upright in the ground, either from one tree to another, or so as no wild creature could come at me without waking me.

As soon as I came to the seashore, I was surprised to see that I had taken up my lot on the worst side of the island; for here indeed the shore was covered with innumerable turtles, whereas, on the other side, I had found but three in a year and a half. Here was also an infinite number of fowls of many kinds, some which I had seen, and some which I had not seen of before, and many of them very good meat; but such as I knew not the names of, except those called penguins.

I could have shot as many as I pleased, but was very sparing of my powder and shot, and therefore had more mind to kill a she-goat, if I could, which I could better feed on; and though there were many goats here, more than on my side the island, yet it was with much more difficulty that I could come near them, the country being flat and even, and they saw me much sooner than when I was on the hill.

I confess this side of the country was much pleasanter than mine; but yet I had not the least inclination to remove, for as I was fixed in my habitation, it became natural to me, and I seemed all the while I was here to be as it were upon a journey, and from home. However, I travelled along the shore of the sea towards the east, I suppose about twelve miles, and then setting up a great pole upon the shore for a mark, I concluded I would go home again; and that the next journey I took should be on the other side of the island, east from my dwelling, and so round till I came to my post again; of which in its place.

I took another way to come back than that I went, thinking I could easily keep all the island so much in my view, that I could not miss finding my first dwelling by viewing the country. But I found myself mistaken; for being come about two or three miles, I found myself descended into a very large valley, but so surrounded with hills, and those hills covered with wood, that I could not see which was my way by any direction but that of the sun, nor even then, unless I knew very well the position of the sun at that time of the day. It happened to my farther misfortune, that the weather proved hazy for three or four days while I was in this valley; and not being able to see the sun, I wandered about very uncomfortably, and at last was obliged to find out the seaside, look for my post, and come back the same way I went; and then by easy journeys I turned homeward, the weather being exceeding hot, and my gun, ammunition, hatchet, and other things very heavy.

In this journey my dog surprised a young kid, and seized upon it, and I running in to take hold of it, caught it, and saved it alive from the dog. I had a great mind to bring it home if I could, for I had often been musing whether it might not be possible to get a kid or two, and so raise a breed of tame goats, which might supply me when my powder and shot should be all spent.

I made a collar to this little creature, and with a string, which I made of some rope-yarn, which I always carried about me, I led him along, though with some difficulty, till I came to my bower, and there I enclosed him and left him, for I was very impatient to be at home, from whence I had been absent above a month.

I cannot express what a satisfaction it was to me to come into my old hutch, and lie down in my hammock-bed. This little wandering journey, without settled place of abode, had been so unpleasant to me, that my own house, as I called it to myself, was a perfect settlement to me compared to that; and it rendered everything about me so comfortable, that I resolved I would never go a great way from it again, while it should be my lot to stay on the island.

I reposed myself here a week, to rest and regale myself after my long journey; during which most of the time was taken up in the weighty affair of making a cage for my Poll, who began now to be a mere domestic, and to be mighty well acquainted with me. Then I began to think of the poor kid which I had penned in within my little circle, and resolved to go and fetch it home, or give it some food. Accordingly I went, and found it where I left it, for indeed it could not get out, but almost starved for want of food. I went and cut boughs of trees, and branches of such shrubs as I could find, and threw it over, and having fed it, I tied it as I did before, to lead it away; but it was so tame with being hungry, that I had no need to have tied it, for it followed me like a dog. And as I continually fed it, the creature became so loving, so gentle, and so fond, that it became from that time one of my domestics also, and would never leave me afterwards.

The rainy season of the autumnal equinox was now come, and I kept the 30th of September in the same solemn manner as before, being the anniversary of my landing on the island, having now been there two years, and no more prospect of being delivered than the first day I came there. I spent the whole day in humble and thankful acknowledgments of the many wonderful mercies which my solitary condition was attended with, and without which it might have been infinitely more miserable. I gave humble and hearty thanks that God had been pleased to discover to me, even that it was possible I might be more happy in this solitary condition, than I should have been in a liberty of society, and in all the pleasures of the world; that He could fully make up to me the deficiencies of my solitary state, and the want of human society, by His presence, and the communications of His grace to my soul; supporting, comforting, and encouraging me to depend upon His providence here, and to hope for His eternal presence hereafter.

It was now that I began sensibly to feel how much more happy this life I now led was, with all its miserable circumstances, than the wicked, cursed, abominable life I led all the past part of my days. And now I changed both my sorrows and my joys; my very desires altered, my affections changed their gusts, and my delights were perfectly new from what they were at my first coming, or indeed for the two years past.

Before, as I walked about, either on my hunting, or for viewing the country, the anguish of my soul at my condition would break out upon me on a sudden, and my very heart would die within me, to think of the woods, the mountains, the deserts I was in; and how I was a prisoner, locked up with the eternal bars and bolts of the ocean, in an uninhabited wilderness, without redemption. In the midst of the greatest composures of my mind, this would break out upon me like a storm, and make me wring my hands and weep like a child: sometimes it would take me in the middle of

my work, and I would immediately sit down and sigh, and look upon the ground for an hour or two together: and this was still worse to me; for if I could burst out into tears, or vent myself by words, it would go off; and the grief having exhausted itself, would abate.

But now I began to exercise myself with new thoughts; I daily read the word of God, and applied all the comforts of it to my present state. One morning, being very sad, I opened the Bible upon these words, "I will never, never leave thee, nor forsake thee:" immediately it occurred, that these words were to me; why else should they be directed in such a manner, just at the moment when I was mourning over my condition, as one forsaken of God and man? "Well then," said I, "if God does not forsake me, of what ill consequence can it be, or what matters it, though the world should all forsake me; seeing, on the other hand, if I had all the world, and should lose the favour and blessing of God, there would be no comparison in the loss?"

From this moment I began to conclude in my mind that it was possible for me to be more happy in this forsaken, solitary condition, than it was probable I should ever have been in any other particular state in the world; and with this thought I was going to give thanks to God for bringing me to this place. I know not what it was, but something shocked my mind at that thought, and I durst not speak the words. "How canst thou be such a hypocrite," said I, even audibly, "to pretend to be thankful for a condition, which, however thou mayst endeavour to be contented with, thou wouldst rather pray heartily to be delivered from?" So I stopped there; but though I could not say I thanked God for being here, yet I sincerely gave thanks to God for opening my eyes, by whatever afflicting providences, to see the former condition of my life, and to mourn for my wickedness, and repent. I never opened the Bible, or shut it, but my very soul within me blessed God for directing my friend in England, without any order of mine, to pack it up among my goods; and for assisting me afterwards to save it out of the wreck of the ship.

Thus, and in this disposition of mind, I began my third year; and though I have not given the reader the trouble of so particular account of my works this year as the first, yet in general it may be observed, that I was very seldom idle, but having regularly divided my time, according to the several daily employments that were before me, such as, first, my duty to God, and the reading the Scriptures, which I constantly set apart some time for, thrice every day; secondly, the going abroad with my gun for food, which generally took me up three hours in every morning, when it did not rain; thirdly, the ordering, curing, preserving, and cooking what I had killed or catched for my supply; these took up great part of the day; also, it is to be considered that the middle of the day, when the sun was in the zenith, the violence of the heat was too great to stir out; so that about four hours in the evening was all the time I could be supposed to work in, with this exception, that sometimes I changed my hours of hunting and working, and went to work in the morning, and abroad with my gun in the afternoon.

To this short time allowed for labour, I desire may be added the exceeding laboriousness of my work; the many hours which, for want of tools, want of help, and want of skill, everything I did took up out of my time. For example, I was full two and forty days making me a board for a long shelf, which I wanted in my cave; whereas two sawyers, with their tools and a sawpit, would have cut six of them out of the same tree in half a day.

My case was this: it was to be a large tree which was to be cut down, because my board was to be a broad one. This tree I was three days a-cutting down, and two more cutting off the boughs, and reducing it to a log, or piece of timber. With inexpressible hacking and hewing, I reduced both the sides of it into chips till it began to be light enough to move; then I turned it, and made one side of it smooth and flat as a board from end to end; then turning that side downward, cut the other side, till I brought the plank to be about three inches thick, and smooth on both sides. Anyone may judge the labour of my hands in such a piece of work; but labour and patience carried me through that, and many other things. I only observe this in particular, to show the reason why so much of my time went away with so little work, viz. that what might be a little to be done with help and tools, was a vast labour, and required a prodigious time to do alone, and by hand. But notwithstanding this, with patience and labour, I went through many things, and, indeed, everything that my circumstances made necessary to me to do, as will appear by what follows.

I was now, in the months of November and December, expecting my crop of barley and rice. The ground I had manured or dug up for them was not great; for as I observed, my seed of each was not above the quantity of half a peck; for I had lost one whole crop by sowing in the dry season. But now my crop promised very well, when on a sudden I found I was in danger of losing it all again by enemies of several sorts, which it was scarce possible to keep from it; as, first, the goats and wild creatures which I called hares, who, tasting the sweetness of the blade, lay in it night and day, as soon as it came up, and eat it so close, that it could get no time to shoot up into stalk.

This I saw no remedy for but by making an enclosure about it with a hedge, which I did with a great deal of toil, and the more, because it required speed. However, as my arable land was but small, suited to my crop, I got it totally well fenced in about three weeks' time, and shooting some of the creatures in the daytime, I set my dog to guard it in the night, tying him up to a stake at the gate, where he would stand and bark all night long; so in a little time the enemies forsook the place, and the corn grew very strong and well, and began to ripen apace.

But as the beasts ruined me before while my corn was in the blade, so the birds were as likely to ruin me now when it was in the ear; for going along by the place to see how it throve, I saw my little crop surrounded with fowls, of I know not how many sorts, who stood, as it were, watching till I should be gone. I immediately let fly among them, for I always had my gun with me. I had no sooner shot, but there rose up a little cloud of fowls, which I had not seen at all, from among the corn itself.

This touched me sensibly, for I foresaw that in a few days they would devour all my hopes, that I should be starved, and never be able to raise a crop at all, and what to do I could not tell. However, I resolved not to lose my corn, if possible, though I should watch it night and day. In the first place, I went among it to see what damage was already done, and found they had spoiled a good deal of it; but that as it was yet too green for them, the loss was not so great, but that the remainder was like to be a good crop if it could be saved.

I staid by it to load my gun, and then coming away, I could easily see the thieves sitting upon all the trees about me, as if they only waited till I was gone away. And the event proved it to be so; for as I walked off, as if I was gone, I was no sooner out of their sight but they dropped down, one by one, into the corn again. I was so provoked, that I could not have patience to stay till more came on, knowing that every grain that they eat now was, as it might be said, a peckloaf to me in the consequence; but coming up to the hedge, I fired again, and killed three of them. This was what I wished for; so I took them up, and served them as we serve notorious thieves in England, viz. hanged them in chains, for a terror to others. It is impossible to imagine almost that this should have such an effect as it had, for the fowls would not only not come at the corn, but, in short, they forsook all that part of the island, and I could never see a bird near the place as long as my scarecrows hung there.

This I was very glad of, you may be sure; and about the latter end of December, which was our second harvest of the year, I reaped my crop.

I was sadly put to it for a scythe or a sickle to cut it down, and all I could do was to make one as well as I could out of one of the broadswords, or cutlasses, which I saved among the arms out of the ship. However, as my first crop was but small, I had no great difficulty to cut it down; in short, I reaped it my way; for I cut nothing off but the ears, and carried it away in a great basket which I had made, and so rubbed it out with my hands; and at the end of all my harvesting, I found that out of my half peck of seed I had near two bushels of rice, and above two bushels and a half of barley, that is to say, by my guess, for I had no measure at that time.

However, this was a great encouragement to me, and I foresaw that, in time, it would please God to supply me with bread. And yet here I was perplexed again, for I neither knew how to grind or make meal of my corn, or indeed how to clean it and part it; nor, if made into meal, how to make bread of it, and if how to make it, yet I knew not how to bake it. These things being added to my desire of having a good quantity for store, and to secure a constant supply, I resolved not to taste any of this crop, but to preserve it all for seed against the next season, and, in the meantime, to employ all my study and hours of working to accomplish this great work of providing myself with corn and bread.

It might be truly said, that now I worked for my bread. 'Tis a little wonderful, and what I believe few people have thought much upon, viz. the strange multitude of little things necessary in the providing, producing, curing, dressing, making, and finishing this one article of bread. I, that was reduced to a mere state of nature, found this to my daily discouragement, and was made more and more sensible of it every hour, even after I had got the first handful of seed-corn, which, as I have said, came up unexpectedly, and indeed to a surprise.

First, I had no plough to turn up the earth; no spade or shovel to dig it. Well, this I conquered, by making a wooden spade, as I observed before; but this did my work in but a wooden manner; and though it cost me a great many days to make it, yet, for want of iron, it not only wore out the sooner, but made my work the harder, and made it be performed much worse. However, this I bore with, and was content to work it out with patience, and bear with the badness of the performance. When the corn was sowed, I had no harrow, but was forced to go over it myself, and drag a great heavy bough of a tree over it, to scratch it, as it may be called, rather than rake or harrow it. When it was growing and grown, I have observed already how many things I wanted to fence it, secure it, mow or reap it, cure and carry it home, thrash, part it from the chaff, and save it. Then I wanted a mill to grind it, sieves to dress it, yeast and salt to make it into bread, and an oven to bake it; and yet all these things I did without, as shall be observed; and yet the corn was an inestimable comfort and advantage to me too. All this, as I said, made everything laborious and tedious to me, but that there was no help for; neither was my time so much loss to me, because, as I had divided it, a certain part of it was every day appointed to these works; and as I resolved to use none of the corn for bread till I had a greater quantity by me, I had the next six months to apply myself wholly, by labour and invention, to furnish myself with utensils proper for the performing all the operations necessary for the making the corn (when I had it) fit for my use.

But first I was to prepare more land; for I had now seed enough to sow above an acre of ground. Before I did this, I had a week's work at least to make me a spade; which, when it was done, was but a sorry one indeed, and very heavy, and required double labour to work with it: however, I went through that, and sowed my seed in two large flat pieces of ground, as near my house as I could find them to my mind, and fenced them in with a good hedge, the stakes of which were all cut of that wood which I had set before, and knew it would grow; so that, in one year's time, I knew I should have a quick or living hedge, that would want but little repair. This work was not so little as to take me up less than three months; because great part of that time was of the wet season, when I could not go abroad.

Within doors, that is, when it rained and I could not go out, I found employment on the following occasions; always observing, that all the while I was at work, I diverted myself with talking to my parrot, and teaching him to speak, and I quickly learned him to know his own name, and at last to speak it out pretty loud, "Poll," which was the first word I ever heard spoken in the island by any mouth but my own.

"I BROUGHT AWAY SEVERAL THINGS VERY USEFUL TO ME..."
(J. MATTHEW)

"I WAS A PRISONER, LOCKED UP WITH THE ETERNAL BARS AND BOLTS OF THE OCEAN..."
(N. POCOCK)

"I made me a suit of clothes wholly of these skins..."
(G. Leese)

"It would have made a stoic smile to have seen me and my family sit down to dinner."
(F. N. J. Moody)

This, therefore, was not my work, but an assistant to my work; for now, as I said, I had a great employment upon my hands, as follows, viz. I had long studied, by some means or other, to make myself some earthen vessels, which indeed I wanted sorely, but knew not where to come at them. However, considering the heat of the climate, I did not doubt but if I could find out any such clay, I might botch up some such pot as might, being dried in the sun, be hard enough and strong enough to bear handling, and to hold anything that was dry, and required to be kept so; and as this was necessary in the preparing corn, meal, etc., which was the thing I was upon, I resolved to make some as large as I could, and fit only to stand like jars, to hold what should be put into them.

CHAPTER NINE

It would make the reader pity me, or rather laugh at me, to tell how many awkward ways I took to raise this paste; what odd, misshapen, ugly things I made; how many of them fell in, and how many fell out, the clay not being stiff enough to bear its own weight; how many cracked by the over-violent heat of the sun, being set out too hastily; and how many fell in pieces with only removing, as well before as after they were dried; and, in a word, how, after having laboured hard to find the clay, to dig it, to temper it, to bring it home, and work it, I could not make above two large earthen ugly things (I cannot call them jars) in about two months' labour.

However, as the sun baked these two very dry and hard, I lifted them very gently up, and set them down again in two great wicker baskets, which I had made on purpose for them that they might not break; and as between the pot and the basket there was a little room to spare, I stuffed it full of the rice and barley straw, and these two pots being to stand always dry, I thought would hold my dry corn, and perhaps the meal, when the corn was bruised.

Though I miscarried so much in my design for large pots, yet I made several smaller things with better success; such as little round pots, flat dishes, pitchers, and pipkins, and any things my hand turned to; and the heat of the sun baked them strangely hard. But all this would not answer my end, which was to get an earthen pot to hold what was liquid, and bear the fire, which none of these could do. It happened after some time, making a pretty large fire for cooking my meat, when I went to put it out after I had done with it, I found a broken piece of one of my earthenware vessels in the fire, burnt as hard as a stone, and red as a tile. I was agreeably surprised to see it, and said to myself, that certainly they might be made to burn whole, if they would burn broken.

This set me to studying how to order my fire, so as to make it burn me some pots. I had no notion of a kiln, such as the potters burn in, or of glazing them with lead, though I had some lead to do it with; but I placed three large pipkins, and two or three pots in a pile, one upon another, and placed my firewood all round it, with a great heap of embers under them. I plied the fire with fresh fuel round the outside, and upon the top, till I saw the pots in the inside red-hot quite through, and observed that they did not crack at all. When I saw them clear red, I let them stand in that heat about five or six hours, till I found one of them, though it did not crack, did melt or run, for the sand which was mixed with the clay melted by the violence of the heat, and would have run into glass, if I had gone on; so I slacked my fire gradually till the pots began to abate of the red colour; and watching them all night, that I might not let the fire abate too fast, in the morning I had three very good, I will not say handsome, pipkins, and two other earthen pots, as hard burnt as could be desired, and one of them perfectly glazed with the running of the sand.

After this experiment, I need not say that I wanted no sort of earthenware for my use; but I must needs say, as to the shapes of them, they were very indifferent, as anyone may suppose, when I had no way of making them but as the children make dirt pies, or as a woman would make pies that never learned to raise paste.

No joy at a thing of so mean a nature was ever equal to mine, when I found I had made an earthen pot that would bear the fire; and I had hardly patience to stay till they were cold, before I set one upon the fire again, with some water in it, to boil me some meat, which it did admirably well; and with a piece of a kid I made some very good broth, though I wanted oatmeal and several other ingredients requisite to make it so good as I would have had it been.

My next concern was to get me a stone mortar to stamp or beat some corn in; for as to the mill, there was no thought at arriving to that perfection of art with one pair of hands. To supply this want I was at a great loss; for of all trades in the world I was as perfectly unqualified for a stone-cutter as for any whatever; neither had I any tools to go about it with. I spent many a day to find out a great stone big enough to cut hollow, and make fit for a mortar, and could find none at all, except what was in the solid rock, and which I had no way to dig or cut out; nor indeed were the rocks in the island of hardness sufficient, but were all of a sandy crumbling stone, which neither would bear the weight of a heavy pestle, or would break the corn without filling it with sand. So, after a great deal of time lost in searching for a stone, I gave it over, and resolved to look out for a great block of hard wood, which I found indeed much easier; and getting one as big as I had strength to stir, I rounded it, and formed it in the outside with my axe and hatchet, and then, with the help of fire, and infinite labour, made a hollow place in it, as the Indians in Brazil make their canoes. After this, I made a great heavy pestle, or beater, of the wood called the iron-wood; and this I prepared and laid by against I had my next crop of corn, when I proposed to myself to grind, or rather pound, my corn into meal, to make my bread.

My next difficulty was to make a sieve, or search, to dress my meal, and to part it from the bran and the husk, without which I did not see it possible I could have any bread. This was a most difficult thing, so much as but to think on, for to be sure I had nothing like the necessary thing to make it; I mean fine thin canvas or stuff to search the meal through. And here I was at a full stop for many months, nor did I really know what to do; linen I had none left, but what was mere rags; I had goats'-hair, but neither knew I how to weave it or spin it; and had I known how, here was no tools to work it with. All the remedy that I found for this was, that at last I did remember I had, among the seamen's clothes which were saved out of the ship, some neckcloths of calico or muslin; and with some pieces of these I made three small sieves, but proper enough for the work; and thus I made shift for some years. How I did afterwards, I shall show in its place.

The baking part was the next thing to be considered, and how I should make bread when I came to have corn; for, first, I had no yeast. As to that part, as there was no supplying the want, so I did not concern myself much about it; but for an oven I was indeed in great pain. At length I found out an experiment for that also, which was this: I made some earthen vessels very broad, but not deep, that is to say, about two foot diameter, and not above nine inches deep; these I burnt in the fire, as I had done the other, and laid them by; and when I wanted to bake, I made a great fire upon my hearth, which I had paved with some square tiles, of my own making and burning also; but I should not call them square.

When the firewood was burned pretty much into embers, or live coals, I drew them forward upon this hearth, so as to cover it all over, and there I let them lie till the hearth was very hot; then sweeping away all the embers, I set down my loaf, or loaves, and whelming down the earthen pot upon them, drew the embers all round the outside of the pot, to keep in and add to the heat. And thus, as well as in the

best oven in the world, I baked my barley-loaves, and became, in little time, a mere pastry-cook into the bargain; for I made myself several cakes of the rice, and puddings; indeed I made no pies, neither had I anything to put into them, supposing I had, except the flesh either of fowls or goats.

It need not be wondered at, if all these things took me up most part of the third year of my abode here; for it is to be observed, that in the intervals of these things I had my new harvest and husbandry to manage; for I reaped my corn in its season, and carried it home as well as I could, and laid it up in the ear, in my large baskets, till I had time to rub it out, for I had no floor to thrash it on, or instrument to thrash it with.

And now, indeed, my stock of corn increasing, I really wanted to build my barns bigger. I wanted a place to lay it up in, for the increase of the corn now yielded me so much, that I had of the barley about twenty bushels, and of the rice as much, or more, insomuch that now I resolved to begin to use it freely; for my bread had been quite gone a great while; also, I resolved to see what quantity would be sufficient for me a whole year, and to sow but once a year.

Upon the whole, I found that the forty bushels of barley and rice was much more than I could consume in a year; so I resolved to sow just the same quantity every year that I sowed the last, in hopes that such a quantity would fully provide me with bread, etc.

All the while these things were doing, you may be sure my thoughts run many times upon the prospect of land which I had seen from the other side of the island, and I was not without secret wishes that I were on shore there, fancying the seeing the mainland, and in an inhabited country, I might find some way or other to convey myself farther, and perhaps at last find some means of escape.

But all this while I made no allowance for the dangers of such a condition, and how I might fall into the hands of savages, and perhaps such as I might have reason to think far worse than the lions and tigers of Africa; that if I once came into their power, I should run a hazard more than a thousand to one of being killed, and perhaps of being eaten; for I had heard that the people of the Caribbean coasts were cannibals, or man-eaters, and I knew by the latitude that I could not be far off from that shore. That suppose they were not cannibals, yet that they might kill me, as many Europeans who had fallen into their hands had been served, even when they had been ten or twenty together, much more I, that was but one, and could make little or no defence; all these things, I say, which I ought to have considered well of, and did cast up in my thoughts afterwards, yet took up none of my apprehensions at first, but my head ran mightily upon the thought of getting over to the shore.

Now I wished for my boy Xury, and the long-boat with the shoulder-of-mutton sail, with which I sailed above a thousand miles on the coast of Africa; but this was in vain. Then I thought I would go and look at our ship's boat, which as I have said, was blown up upon the shore a great way, in the storm, when we were first cast away. She lay almost where she did at first, but not quite; and was turned, by the force of the waves and the winds, almost bottom upward, against a high ridge of beachy rough sand, but no water about her, as before.

If I had had hands to have refitted her, and to have launched her into the water, the boat would have done well enough, and I might have gone back into the Brazils with her easily enough; but I might have foreseen that I could no more turn her and set her upright upon her bottom, than I could remove the island. However, I went to the woods, and cut levers and rollers, and brought them to the boat, resolved to try what I could do; suggesting to myself that if I could but turn her down, I might easily repair the damage she had received, and she would be a very good boat, and I might go to sea in her very easily.

I spared no pains, indeed, in this piece of fruitless toil, and spent, I think, three or four weeks about it. At last, finding it impossible to heave it up with my little strength, I fell to digging away the sand, to undermine it, and so to make it fall down, setting pieces of wood to thrust and guide it right in the fall. But when I had done this, I was unable to stir it up again, or to get under it, much less to move it forward towards the water; so I was forced to give it over. And yet, though I gave over the hopes of the boat, my desire to venture over for the main increased, rather than decreased, as the means for it seemed impossible.

This at length put me upon thinking whether it was not possible to make myself a canoe, or periagua, such as the natives of those climates make, even without tools, or, as I might say, without hands, viz. of the trunk of a great tree. This I not only thought possible but easy, and pleased myself extremely with the thoughts of making it, and with my having much more convenience for it than any of the negroes or Indians; but not at all considering the particular inconveniences which I lay under, more than the Indians did, viz. want of hands to move it, when it was made, into the water, a difficulty much harder for me to surmount than all the consequences of want of tools could be to them. For what was it to me, that when I had chosen a vast tree in the woods, I might with much trouble cut it down, if, after I might be able with my tools to hew and dub the outside into the proper shape of a boat, and burn or cut out the inside to make it hollow, so to make a boat of it; if, after all this, I must leave it just there where I found it, and was not able to launch it into the water?

One would have thought I could not have had the least reflection upon my mind of my circumstance, while I was making this boat, but I should have immediately thought how I should get it into the sea; but my thoughts were so intent upon my voyage over the sea in it, that I never once considered how I should get it off of the land; and it was really, in its own nature, more easy for me to guide it over forty-five miles of sea, than about forty-five fathoms of land, where it lay, to set it afloat in the water.

I went to work upon this boat the most like a fool that ever man did who had any of his senses awake. I pleased myself with the design, without determining whether I was ever able to undertake it. Not but that the difficulty of launching my boat came often into my head; but I put a stop to my own inquiries into it, by this foolish answer which I gave myself, "Let's first make it; I'll warrant I'll find some way or other to get it along when 'tis done."

This was a most preposterous method; but the eagerness of my fancy prevailed, and to work I went. I felled a cedar tree: I question much whether Solomon ever had such a one for the building of the Temple at Jerusalem. It was five foot ten inches diameter at the lower part next the stump, and four foot eleven inches diameter at the end of twenty-two foot, after which it lessened for a while, and then parted into branches. It was not without infinite labour that I felled this tree. I was twenty days hacking and hewing at it at the bottom; I was fourteen more getting the branches and limbs, and the vast spreading head of it cut off, which I hacked and hewed through with axe and hatchet, and inexpressible labour. After this, it cost me a month to shape it and dub it to a proportion, and to something like the bottom of a boat, that it might swim upright as it ought to do. It cost me near three months more to clear the inside, and work it so as to make an exact boat of it. This I did, indeed, without fire, by mere mallet and chisel, and by the dint of hard labour, till I had brought it to be a very handsome periagua, and big enough to have carried six and twenty men, and consequently big enough to have carried me and all my cargo.

When I had gone through this work, I was extremely delighted with it. The boat was really much bigger than I ever saw a canoe or periagua, that was made of one tree, in my life. Many a weary stroke it had cost, you may be sure; and there remained nothing but to get it into the water; and had I gotten it into the water, I make no question but I should have begun the maddest voyage, and the most unlikely to be performed, that ever was undertaken.

But all my devices to get it into the water failed me, though they cost me infinite labour too. It lay about one hundred yards from the water, and not more; but the first inconvenience was, it was uphill towards the creek. Well, to take away this discouragement, I resolved to dig into the surface of the earth, and so make a declivity. This I began, and it cost

me a prodigious deal of pains; but who grudges pains, that have their deliverance in view? But when this was worked through, and this difficulty managed, it was still much at one, for I could no more stir the canoe than I could the other boat.

Then I measured the distance of ground, and resolved to cut a dock or canal, to bring the water up to the canoe, seeing I could not bring the canoe down to the water. Well, I began this work; and when I began to enter into it, and calculate how deep it was to be dug, how broad, how the stuff to be thrown out, I found that by the number of hands I had, being none but my own, it must have been ten or twelve years before I should have gone through with it; for the shore lay high, so that at the upper end it must have been at least twenty foot deep; so at length, though with great reluctancy, I gave this attempt over also.

This grieved me heartily; and now I saw, though too late, the folly of beginning a work before we count the cost, and before we judge rightly of our own strength to go through with it.

In the middle of this work I finished my fourth year in this place, and kept my anniversary with the same devotion, and with as much comfort as ever before; for, by a constant study and serious application of the Word of God, and by the assistance of His grace, I gained a different knowledge from what I had before. I entertained different notions of things. I looked now upon the world as a thing remote, which I had nothing to do with, no expectation from, and, indeed, no desires about. In a word, I had nothing indeed to do with it, nor was ever like to have; so I thought it looked, as we may perhaps look upon it hereafter, viz. as a place I had lived in, but was come out of it; and well might I say, as father Abraham to Dives, "Between me and thee is a great gulf fixed."

In the first place, I was removed from all the wickedness of the world here; I had neither the lust of the flesh, the lust of the eye, or the pride of life. I had nothing to covet, for I had all that I was now capable of enjoying: I was lord of the whole manor; or, if I pleased, I might call myself king or emperor over the whole country which I had possession of. There were no rivals; I had no competitor, none to dispute sovereignty or command with me. I might have raised shiploadings of corn, but I had no use for it; so I let as little grow as I thought enough for my occasion. I had tortoise or turtle enough, but now and then one was as much as I could put to any use. I had timber enough to have built a fleet of ships. I had grapes enough to have made wine, or to have cured into raisins, to have loaded that fleet when they had been built.

But all I could make use of was all that was valuable. I had enough to eat and to supply my wants, and what was all the rest to me? If I killed more flesh than I could eat, the dog must eat it, or the vermin. If I sowed more corn than I could eat, it must be spoiled. The trees that I cut down were lying to rot on the ground; I could make no more use of them than for fuel, and that I had no other occasion for, but to dress my food.

In a word, the nature and experience of things dictated to me, upon just reflection, that all the good things of this world are of no farther good to us than they are for our use; and that whatever we may heap up indeed to give others, we enjoy just as much as we can use, and no more. The most covetous griping miser in the world would have been cured of the vice of covetousness, if he had been in my case; for I possessed infinitely more than I knew what to do with. I had no room for desire, except it was of things which I had not, and they were but trifles, though indeed of great use to me. I had, as I hinted before, a parcel of money, as well gold as silver, about thirty-six pounds sterling. Alas! there the nasty, sorry, useless stuff lay: I had no manner of business for it; and I often thought with myself, that I would have given a handful of it for a gross of tobacco-pipes, or for a hand-mill to grind my corn; nay, I would have given it all for sixpenny-worth of turnip and carrot seed out of England, or for a handful of peas and beans, and a bottle of ink. As it was, I had not the least advantage by it, or benefit from it; but there it lay in a drawer, and grew mouldy with the damp of the cave in the wet season; and if I had had the drawer full of diamonds, it had been the same case, and they had been of no manner of value to me, because of no use.

I had now brought my state of life to be much easier in itself than it was at first, and much easier to my mind, as well as to my body. I frequently sat down to my meat with thankfulness, and admired the hand of God's providence, which had thus spread my table in the wilderness. I learned to look more upon the bright side of my condition, and less upon the dark side, and to consider what I enjoyed, rather than what I wanted; and this gave me sometimes such secret comforts, that I cannot express them; and which I take notice of here, to put those discontented people in mind of it, who cannot enjoy comfortably what God has given them, because they see and covet something that He has not given them. All our discontents about what we want, appeared to me to spring from the want of thankfulness for what we have.

Another reflection was of great use to me, and doubtless would be so to any one that should fall into such distress as mine was; and this was, to compare my present condition with what I at first expected it should be: nay, with what it would certainly have been, if the good providence of God had not wonderfully ordered the ship to be cast up nearer to the shore, where I not only could come at her, but could bring what I got out of her to the shore, for my relief and comfort; without which, I had wanted for tools to work, weapons for defence, and gunpowder and shot for getting my food.

I spent whole hours, I may say whole days, in representing to myself, in the most lively colours, how I must have acted if I had got nothing out of the ship. How I could not have so much as got any food, except fish and turtles; and that as it was long before I found any of them, I must have perished first; that I should have lived, if I had not perished, like a mere savage; that if I had killed a goat or a fowl, by any contrivance, I had no way to flay or open them, or part the flesh from the skin and the bowels, or to cut it up; but must gnaw it with my teeth, and pull it with my claws, like a beast.

These reflections made me very sensible of the goodness of Providence to me, and very thankful for my present condition, with all its hardships and misfortunes; and this part also I cannot but recommend to the reflection of those who are apt, in their misery,

to say, "Is any affliction like mine?" Let them consider how much worse the cases of some people are, and their case might have been, if Providence had thought fit.

I had another reflection, which assisted me also to comfort my mind with hopes; and this was, comparing my present condition with what I had deserved, and had therefore reason to expect from the hand of Providence. I had lived a dreadful life, perfectly destitute of the knowledge and fear of God. I had been well instructed by father and mother; neither had they been wanting to me, in their early endeavours to infuse a religious awe of God into my mind, a sense of my duty, and of what the nature and end of my being required of me. But, alas! falling early into the seafaring life, which of all the lives is the most destitute of the fear of God, though his terrors are always before them; I say, falling early into the seafaring life, and into seafaring company, all that little sense of religion which I had entertained was laughed out of me by my messmates; by a hardened despising of dangers, and the views of death, which grew habitual to me; by my long absence from all manner of opportunities to converse with anything but what was like myself, or to hear anything that was good, or tended towards it.

So void was I of everything that was good, or of the least sense of what I was, or was to be, that in the greatest deliverances I enjoyed, such as my escape from Sallee; my being taken up by the Portuguese master of the ship; my being planted so well in the Brazils; my receiving the cargo from England, and the like; I never had once the words, "Thank God," so much as on my mind, or in my mouth; nor in the greatest distress had I so much as a thought to pray to Him, or so much as to say, "Lord, have mercy upon me!" no, nor to mention the name of God, unless it was to swear by, and blaspheme it.

I had terrible reflections upon my mind for many months, as I have already observed, on the account of my wicked and hardened life past; and when I looked about me, and considered what particular providences had attended me since my coming into this place, and how God had dealt bountifully with me; had not only punished me less than my iniquity had deserved, but had so plentifully provided for me; this gave me great hopes that my repentance was accepted, and that God had yet mercy in store for me.

With these reflections I worked my mind up, not only to resignation to the will of God in the present disposition of my circumstances, but even to a sincere thankfulness for my condition; and that I, who was yet a living man, ought not to complain, seeing I had not the due punishment of my sins; that I enjoyed so many mercies which I had no reason to have expected in that place, that I ought never more to repine at my condition, but to rejoice, and to give daily thanks for that daily bread, which nothing but a crowd of wonders could have brought; that I ought to consider I had been fed even by miracle, even as great as that of feeding Elijah by ravens; nay, by a long series of miracles: and that I could hardly have named a place in the unhabitable part of the world where I could have been cast more to my advantage; a place where, as I had no society, which was my affliction on one hand, so I found no ravenous beasts, no furious wolves or tigers, to threaten my life; no venomous creatures or poisonous, which I might feed on to my hurt; no savages, to murder and devour me.

In a word, as my life was a life of sorrow one way, so it was a life of mercy another; and I wanted nothing to make it a life of comfort, but to be able to make my sense of God's goodness to me, and care over me in this condition, be my daily consolation; and after I did make a just improvement of these things, I went away, and was no more sad.

I had now been here so long, that many things which I brought on shore for my help were either quite gone, or very much wasted, and near spent. My ink, as I observed, had been gone for some time, all but a very little, which I eked out with water, a little and a little, till it was so pale it scarce left any appearance of black upon the paper. As long as it lasted, I made use of it to minute down the days of the month on which any remarkable thing happened to me. And, first, by casting up times past, I remember that there was a strange concurrence of days in the various providences which befell me, and which, if I had been superstitiously inclined to observe days as fatal or fortunate, I might have had reason to have looked upon with a great deal of curiosity.

First, I had observed that the same day that I broke away from my father and my friends, and run away to Hull, in order to go to sea, the same day afterwards I was taken by the Sallee man-of-war, and made a slave.

The same day of the year that I escaped out of the wreck of that ship in Yarmouth Roads, that same day-year afterwards I made my escape from Sallee in the boat.

The same day of the year I was born on, viz. the 30th of September, that same day I had my life so miraculously saved twenty-six years after, when I was cast on shore in this island; so that my wicked life and my solitary life began both on a day.

The next thing to my ink's being wasted, was that of my bread; I mean the biscuit, which I brought out of the ship. This I had husbanded to the last degree, allowing myself but one cake of bread a day for above a year; and yet I was quite without bread for near a year before I got any corn of my own; and great reason I had to be thankful that I had any at all, the getting it being, as has been already observed, next to miraculous.

My clothes began to decay, too, mightily. As to linen, I had none a good while, except some chequered shirts which I found in the chests of the other seamen, and which I carefully preserved, because many times I could bear no other clothes on but a shirt; and it was a very great help to me that I had, among all the men's clothes of the ship, almost three dozen of shirts. There were also several thick watchcoats of the seamen's which were left indeed, but they were too hot to wear; and though it is true that the weather was so violent hot that there was no need of clothes, yet I could not go quite naked; no, though I had been inclined to it, which I was not, nor could abide the thoughts of it, though I was all alone

The reason why I could not go quite naked was, I could not bear the heat of the sun so well when quite naked as with some clothes on; nay, the very heat frequently blistered my skin; whereas, with a shirt on, the air itself made some motion, and

whistling under that shirt, was twofold cooler than without it. No more could I ever bring myself to go out in the heat of the sun without a cap or a hat. The heat of the sun beating with such violence, as it does in that place, would give me the headache presently, by darting so directly on my head, without a cap or hat on, so that I could not bear it; whereas, if I put on my hat, it would presently go away.

Upon those views, I began to consider about putting the few rags I had, which I called clothes, into some order. I had worn out all the waistcoats I had, and my business was now to try if I could not make jackets out of the great watchcoats which I had by me, and with such other materials as I had; so I set to work a-tailoring, or rather, indeed, a-botching, for I made most piteous work of it. However, I made shift to make two or three new waistcoats, which I hoped would serve me a great while. As for breeches, or drawers, I made but a very sorry shift indeed till afterward.

I have mentioned that I saved the skins of all the creatures that I killed, I mean four-footed ones, and I had hung them up stretched out with sticks in the sun, by which means some of them were so dry and hard that they were fit for little, but others it seems were very useful. The first thing I made of these was a great cap for my head, with the hair on the outside, to shoot off the rain; and this I performed so well, that after this I made me a suit of clothes wholly of these skins, that is to say, a waistcoat, and breeches open at knees, and both loose, for they were rather wanting to keep me cool than to keep me warm. I must not omit to acknowledge that they were wretchedly made; for if I was a bad carpenter, I was a worse tailor. However, they were such as I made very good shift with; and when I was abroad, if it happened to rain, the hair of my waistcoat and cap being outermost, I was kept very dry.

After this I spent a great deal of time and pains to make me an umbrella. I was indeed in great want of one, and had a great mind to make one. I had seen them made in the Brazils, where they are very useful in the great heats, which are there; and I felt the heats every jot as great here, and greater too, being nearer the equinox. Besides, as I was obliged to be much abroad, it was a most useful thing to me, as well for the rains as the heats. I took a world of pains at it, and was a great while before I could m. anything likely to hold: nay, after I thought I had hit the way, I spoiled two or three before I made one to my mind; but at last I made one that answered indifferently well.

The main difficulty I found was to make it to let down. I could make it to spread; but if it did not let down too, and draw in, it was not portable for me any way but just over my head, which would not do.

However, at last, as I said, I made one to answer, and covered it with skins, the hair upwards, so that it cast off the rains like a pent-house, and kept off the sun so effectually, that I could walk out in the hottest of the weather with greater advantage than I could before in the coolest; and when I had no need of it, could close it, and carry it under my arm.

Thus I lived mighty comfortably, my mind being entirely composed by resigning to the will of God, and throwing myself wholly upon the disposal of His providence. This made my life better than sociable; for when I began to regret the want of conversation, I would ask myself, whether thus conversing mutually with my own thoughts, and, as I hope I may say, with even God Himself, by ejaculations, was not better than the utmost enjoyment of human society in the world?

I cannot say that after this, for five years, any extraordinary thing happened to me; but I lived on in the same course, in the same posture and place, just as before. The chief things I was employed in, besides my yearly labour of planting my barley and rice, and curing my raisins, of both which I always kept up just enough to have sufficient stock of one year's provisions beforehand; I say, besides this yearly labour, and my daily labour of going out with my gun, I had one labour, to make me a canoe, which at last I finished; so that by digging a canal to it of six foot wide, and four foot deep, I brought into the creek, almost half a mile. As for the first, which was so vastly big, as I made it without considering beforehand, as I ought to do, how I should be able to launch it; so, never being able to bring it to the water, or bring the water to it, I was obliged to let it lie where it was, as a memorandum to teach me to be wiser next time. Indeed, the next time, though I could not get a tree proper for it, and in a place where I could not get the water to it at any less distance than, as I have said, near half a mile, yet as I saw it was practicable at last, I never gave it over; and though I was near two years about it, yet I never grudged my labour, in hopes of having a boat to go off to sea at last.

CHAPTER TEN

However, though my little periagua was finished, yet the size of it was not at all answerable to the design which I had in view when I made the first; I mean, of venturing over to the terra firma where it was about forty miles broad. Accordingly, the smallness of my boat assisted to put an end to that design, and now I thought no more of it. But as I had a boat, my next design was to make a tour round the island; for as I had been on the other side in one place, crossing, as I have already described it, over the land, so the discoveries I made in that little journey made me very eager to see other parts of the coast; and now I had a boat, I thought of nothing but sailing round the island.

For this purpose, that I might do everything with discretion and consideration, I fitted up a little mast to my boat, and made a sail to it out of some of the pieces of the ship's sail, which lay in store, and of which I had a great stock by me.

Having fitted my mast and sail, and tried the boat, I found she would sail very well. Then I made little lockers, or boxes, at either end of my boat, to put provisions, necessaries, and ammunition, etc., into, to be kept dry, either from rain or the spray of the sea; and a little long hollow place I cut in the inside of the boat, where I could lay my gun, making a flap to hang down over it to keep it dry.

I fixed my umbrella also in a step at the stern, like a mast, to stand over my head, and keep the heat of the sun off of me, like an awning; and thus I every now and then took a little voyage upon the sea, but never went far out, not far from the little creek. But at last, being eager to view the circumference of my little kingdom, I resolved upon my tour; and accordingly I victualled my ship for the voyage, putting in two dozen of my loaves (cakes I should rather call them) of barley bread, an earthen pot full of parched rice, a food I eat a great deal of, a little bottle of rum, half a goat, and powder and shot for killing more, and two large watch-coats, of those which, as I mentioned before, I had saved out of the seamen's chests; these I took, one to lie upon, and the other to cover me in the night.

It was the 6th of November, in the sixth year of my reign, or my captivity, which you please, that I set out on this voyage, and I found it much longer than I expected;

for though the island itself was not very large, yet when I came to the east side of it I found a great ledge of rocks lie out above two leagues into the sea, some above water, some under it, and beyond that a shoal of sand, lying dry half a league more; so that I was obliged to go a great way out to sea to double the point.

When first I discovered them, I was going to give over my enterprise and come back again, not knowing how far it might oblige me to go out to sea, and, above all, doubting how I should get back again, so I came to an anchor; for I had made me a kind of an anchor with a piece of a broken grappling which I got out of the ship.

Having secured my boat, I took my gun and went on shore, climbing up upon a hill, which seemed to overlook that point, where I saw the full extent of it, and resolved to venture.

In my viewing the sea from that hill, where I stood, I perceived a strong, and indeed a most furious current, which run to the east, and even came close to the point; and I took the more notice of it, because I saw there might be some danger that when I came into it I might be carried out to sea by the strength of it, and not be able to make the island again. And indeed, had I not gotten first up upon this hill, I believe it would have been so; for there was the same current on the other side the island, only that it set off at a farther distance; and I saw there was a strong eddy under the shore; so I had nothing to do but to get in out of the first current, and I should presently be in an eddy.

I lay here, however, two days; because the wind, blowing pretty fresh at E.S.E., and that being just contrary to the said current, made a great breach of the sea upon the point; so that it was not safe for me to keep too close to the shore for the breach, nor to go too far off because of the stream.

The third day, in the morning, the wind having abated overnight, the sea was calm, and I ventured. But I am a warning piece again to all rash and ignorant pilots; for no sooner was I come to the point, when even I was not my boat's length from the shore, but I found myself in a great depth of water, and a current like the sluice of a mill. It carried my boat along with it with such violence, that all I could do could not keep her so much as on the edge of it, but I found it hurried me farther and farther out from the eddy, which was on my left hand. There was no wind stirring to help me, and all I could do with my paddlers signified nothing. And now I began to give myself over for lost; for, as the current was on both sides the island, I knew in a few leagues' distance they must join again, and then I was irrecoverably gone.

Nor did I see any possibility of avoiding it; so that I had no prospect before me but of perishing; not by the sea, for that was calm enough, but of starving for hunger. I had indeed found a tortoise on the shore, as big almost as I could lift, and had tossed it into the boat; and I had a great jar of fresh water, that is to say, one of my earthen pots; but what was all this to being driven into the vast ocean, where, to be sure, there was no shore, no mainland or island, for a thousand leagues at least.

And now I saw how easy it was for the providence of God to make the most miserable condition mankind could be in, worse. Now I looked back upon my desolate solitary island as the most pleasant place in the world, and all the happiness my heart could wish for was to be but there again. I stretched out my hands to it, with eager wishes. "O happy desert!" said I, "I shall never see thee more. O miserable creature!" said I, "whither am I going!" Then I reproached myself with my unthankful temper, and how I had repined at my solitary condition; and now what would I give to be on shore there again! Thus we never see the true state of our condition till it is illustrated to us by its contraries, nor know how to value what we enjoy, but by the want of it. It is scarce possible to imagine the consternation I was now in, being driven from my beloved island (for so it appeared to me now to be) into the wide ocean, almost two leagues, and in the utmost despair of ever recovering it again. However, I worked hard, till indeed my strength was almost exhausted, and kept my boat as much to the northward, that is, towards the side of the current which the eddy lay on, as possibly I could; when about noon, as the sun passed the meridian, I thought I felt a little breeze of wind in my face, springing up from the S.S.E. This cheered my heart a little, and especially when, in about half-an-hour more, it blew a pretty small gentle gale. By this time I was gotten at a frightful distance from the island; and had the least cloud or hazy weather intervened, I had been undone another way too; for I had no compass on board, and should never have known how to have steered towards the island if I had but once lost sight of it. But the weather continuing clear, I applied myself to get up my mast again, and spread my sail, standing away to the north as much as possible, to get out of the current.

Just as I had set my mast and sail, and the boat began to stretch away, I saw even by the clearness of the water some alteration of the current was near; for where the current was so strong, the water was foul; but perceiving the water clear, I found the current abate; and presently I found to the east, at about half a mile, a breach of the sea upon some rocks: these rocks I found caused the current to part again, and as the main stress of it ran away more southerly, leaving the rocks to the north-east, so the other returned by the repulse of the rocks, and made a strong eddy, which ran back again to the north-west, with a very sharp stream.

They who know what it is to have a reprieve brought to them upon the ladder, or to be rescued from thieves just going to murder them, or who have been in such-like extremities, may guess what my present surprise of joy was, and how gladly I put my boat into the stream of this eddy; and the wind also freshening, how gladly I spread my sail to it, running cheerfully before the wind, and with a strong tide or eddy under foot.

This eddy carried me about a league in my way back again, directly towards the island, but about two leagues more to the northward than the current which carried me away at first: so that when I came near the island, I found myself open to the northern shore of it, that is to say, the other end of the island, opposite to that which I went out from.

When I had made something more than a league of way by the help of this current or eddy, I found it was spent, and served me no farther. However, I found that being between two great currents, viz. that on the south side, which had hurried me away, and that on the north, which lay about a league on the other side; I say, between these two, in the wake of the island, I found the water at least still, and running no way; and having still a breeze of wind fair for me, I kept on steering directly for the island, though not making such fresh way as I did before.

About four o'clock in the evening, being then within a league of the island, I found the point of the rocks which occasioned this disaster stretching out, as is described before, to the southward, and casting off the current more southerly, had, of course, made another eddy to the north; and this I found very strong, but not directly setting the way my course lay, which was due west, but almost full north. However, having a fresh gale I stretched across this eddy, slanting northwest; and in about an hour came within about a mile of the shore, where, it being smooth water, I soon got to land.

When I was on shore, I fell on my knees, and gave God thanks for my deliverance, resolving to lay aside all thoughts of my deliverance by my boat; and refreshing myself with such things as I had, I brought my boat close to the shore, in a little cove that I had spied under some trees, and laid me down to sleep, being quite spent with the labour and fatigue of the voyage.

I was now at a great loss which way to get home with my boat. I had run so much hazard, and knew too much the case, to think of attempting it by the way I went out; and what might be at the other side (I mean the west side) I knew not, nor had I any mind to run any more ventures. So I only resolved in the morning to make my way westward along the shore, and to see if there was no creek where I might lay up my frigate in safety, so as to have her again if I wanted her. In about three mile, or thereabouts, coasting the shore, I came to a very good inlet or bay, about a mile

over, which narrowed till it came to a very little rivulet or brook, where I found a very convenient harbour for my boat, and where she lay as if she had been in a little dock made on purpose for her. Here I put in, and having stowed my boat very safe, I went on shore to look about me, and see where I was.

I soon found I had but a little passed by the place where I had been before, when I travelled on foot to that shore; so taking nothing out of my boat but my gun and my umbrella, for it was exceedingly hot, I began my march. The way was comfortable enough after such a voyage as I had been upon, and I reached my old bower in the evening, where I found everything standing as I left it; for I always kept it in good order, being, as I said before, my country house.

I got over the fence, and laid me down in the shade to rest my limbs, for I was very weary, and fell asleep. But judge you, if you can, that read my story, what a surprise I must be in, when I was waked out of my sleep by a voice calling me by my name several times, "Robin, Robin, Robin Crusoe, poor Robin Crusoe! Where are you, Robin Crusoe? Where are you? Where have you been?"

I was so dead asleep at first, being fatigued with rowing, or paddling, as it is called, the first part of the day, and with walking the latter part, that I did not wake thoroughly; but dozing between sleeping and waking, thought I dreamed that somebody spoke to me. But as the voice continued to repeat "Robin Crusoe, Robin Crusoe," at last I began to wake more perfectly, and was at first dreadfully frighted, and started up in the utmost consternation. But no sooner were my eyes open, but I saw my Poll sitting on the top of the hedge, and immediately knew that it was he that spoke to me; for just in such bemoaning language I had used to talk to him, and teach him; and he had learned it so perfectly, that he would sit upon my finger, and lay his bill close to my face, and cry, "Poor Robin Crusoe! Where are you? Where have you been? How come you here?" and such things as I had taught him.

However, even though I knew it was the parrot, and that indeed it could be nobody else, it was a good while before I could compose myself. First, I was amazed how the creature got thither, and then, how he should just keep about the place, and nowhere else. But as I was well satisfied it could be nobody but honest Poll, I got it over; and holding out my hand, and calling him by his name, Poll, the sociable creature came to me, and sat upon my thumb, as he used to do, and continued talking to me, "Poor Robin Crusoe!" and how did I come here? and where had I been? just as if he had been overjoyed to see me again; and so I carried him home along with me.

I had now had enough of rambling to sea for some time, and had enough to do for many days to sit still, and reflect upon the danger I had been in. I would have been very glad to have had my boat again on my side of the island; but I knew not how it was practicable to get it about. As to the east side of the island, which I had gone round, I knew well enough there was no venturing that way; my very heart would shrink, and my very blood run chill, but to think of it. And as to the other side of the island, I did not know how it might be there; but supposing the current ran with the same force against the shore at the east as it passed by it on the other, I might run the same risk of being driven down the stream, and carried by the island, as I had

been before of being carried away from it. So, with these thoughts, I contented myself to be without any boat, though it had been the product of so many months' labour to make it, and of so many more to get it unto the sea.

In this government of my temper I remained near a year, lived a very sedate, retired life, as you may well suppose; and my thoughts being very much composed as to my condition, and fully comforted in resigning myself to the dispositions of Providence, I thought I lived really very happily in all things, except that of society.

I improved myself in this time in all the mechanic exercises which my necessities put me upon applying myself to, and I believe could, upon occasion, make a very good carpenter, especially considering how few tools I had. Besides this, I arrived at an unexpected perfection in my earthenware, and contrived well enough to make them with a wheel, which I found infinitely easier and better, because I made things round and shapable which before were filthy things indeed to look on. But I think I was never more vain of my own performance, or more joyful for anything I found out, than for my being able to make a tobacco-pipe. And though it was a very ugly clumsy thing when it was done, and only burnt red, like other earthenware, yet as it was hard and firm, and would draw the smoke, I was exceedingly comforted with it; for I had been always used to smoke, and there were pipes in the ship, but I forgot them at first, not knowing that there was tobacco in the island; and afterwards, when I searched the ship again, I could not come at any pipes at all.

In my wicker-ware also I improved much, and made abundance of necessary baskets, as well as my invention showed me; though not very handsome, yet they were such as were very handy and convenient for my laying things up in, or fetching things home in. For example, if I killed a goat abroad, I could hang it up in a tree, flay it, and dress it, and cut it in pieces, and bring it home in a basket; and the like by a turtle; I could cut it up, take out the eggs, and a piece or two of the flesh, which was enough for me, and bring them home in a basket, and leave the rest behind me. Also large deep baskets were my receivers for my corn, which I always rubbed out as soon as it was dry, and cured, and kept it in great baskets.

I began now to perceive my powder abated considerably, and this was a want which it was impossible for me to supply, and I began seriously to consider what I must do when I should have no more powder; that is to say, how I should do to kill any goat. I had, as is observed, in the third year of my being here kept a young kid, and bred her up tame, and I was in hope of getting a he-goat, but I could not by any means bring it to pass, till my kid grew an old goat; and I could never find in my heart to kill her, till she died at last of mere age.

But being now in the eleventh year of my residence, and, as I have said, my ammunition growing low, I set myself to study some art to trap and snare the goats, to see whether I could not catch some of them alive; and particularly I wanted a she-goat great with young.

To this purpose, I made snares to hamper them, and I do believe they were more than once taken in them; but my tackle was not good, for I had no wire, and I always found them broken, and my bait devoured. At length I resolved to try a pitfall; so I

dug several large pits in the earth, in places where I had observed the goats used to feed, and over these pits I placed hurdles, of my own making too, with a great weight upon them; and several times I put ears of barley and dry rice, without setting the trap, and I could easily perceive that the goats had gone in and eaten up the corn, for I could see the mark of their feet. At length I set three traps in one night, and going the next morning, I found them all standing, and yet the bait eaten and gone; this was very discouraging. However, I altered my trap; and, not to trouble you with particulars, going one morning to see my trap, I found in one of them a large old he-goat, and in one of the other three kids, a male and two females.

As to the old one, I knew not what to do with him, he was so fierce I durst not go into the pit to him; that is to say, to go about to bring him away alive, which was what I wanted. I could have killed him, but that was not my business, nor would it answer my end. So I e'en let him out, and he ran away, as if he had been frighted out of his wits. But I had forgot then what I learned afterwards, that hunger will tame a lion. If I had let him stay there three or four days without food, and then have carried him some water to drink, and then a little corn, he would have been as tame as one of the kids, for they are mighty sagacious, tractable creatures where they are well used.

However, for the present I let him go, knowing no better at that time. Then I went to the three kids, and taking them one by one, I tied them with strings together, and with some difficulty brought them all home.

It was a good while before they would feed, but throwing them some sweet corn, it tempted them, and they began to be tame. And now I found that if I expected to supply myself with goat-flesh when I had no powder or shot left, breeding some up tame was my only way, when perhaps I might have them about my house like a flock of sheep.

But then it presently occurred to me that I must keep the tame from the wild, or else they would always run wild when they grew up; and the only way for this was to have some enclosed piece of ground, well fenced either with hedge or pale, to keep them in so effectually, that those within might not break out, or those without break in.

This was a great undertaking for one pair of hands; yet as I saw there was an absolute necessity of doing it, my first piece of work was to find out a proper piece of ground, viz. where there was likely to be herbage for them to eat, water for them to drink, and cover to keep them from the sun.

Those who understand such enclosures will think I had very little contrivance, when I pitched upon a place very proper for all these, being a plain open piece of meadow land, or savanna, (as our people call it in the western colonies), which had two or three little drills of fresh water in it, and at one end was very woody; I say, they will smile at my forecast, when I shall tell them, I began my enclosing this piece of ground in such a manner, that my hedge or pale must have been at least two mile about. Nor was the madness of it so great as to the compass, for if it was ten mile about, I was like to have time enough to do it in. But I did not consider that my goats would be as wild in so much compass as if they had had the whole island, and I should have so much room to chase them in, that I should never catch them.

My hedge was begun and carried on, I believe about fifty yards, when this thought occurred to me; so I presently stopped short, and, for the first beginning, I resolved to enclose a piece of about 150 yards in length, and 100 yards in breadth; which, as it would maintain as many as I should have in any reasonable time, so, as my flock increased, I could add more ground to my enclosure.

This was acting with some prudence, and I went to work with courage. I was about three months hedging in the first piece, and, till I had done it, I tethered the three kids in the best part of it, and used them to feed as near me as possible, to make them familiar; and very often I would go and carry them some ears of barley, or a handful of rice, and feed them out of my hand; so that after my enclosure was finished, and I let them loose, they would follow me up and down, bleating after me for a handful of corn.

This answered my end, and in about a year and half I had a flock of about twelve goats, kids, and all; and in two years more I had three and forty, besides several that I took and killed for my food. And after that I enclosed five several pieces of ground to feed them in, with little pens to drive them into, to take them as I wanted, and gates out of one piece of ground into another.

But this was not all, for now I not only had goat's flesh to feed on when I pleased, but milk too, a thing which, indeed, in my beginning, I did not so much as think of, and which, when it came into my thoughts, was really an agreeable surprise. For now I set up my dairy, and had sometimes a gallon or two of milk in a day; and as Nature, who gives supplies of food to every creature, dictates even naturally how to make use of it, so I, that had never milked a cow, much less a goat, or seen butter or cheese made, very readily and handily, though after a great many essays and miscarriages, made me both butter and cheese at last, and never wanted it afterwards.

How mercifully can our great Creator treat His creatures, even in those conditions in which they seemed to be overwhelmed in destruction! How can He sweeten the bitterest providences, and give us cause to praise Him for dungeons and prisons! What a table was here spread for me in a wilderness, where I saw nothing, at first, but to perish for hunger!

It would have made a stoic smile, to have seen me and my little family sit down to dinner. There was my majesty, the prince and lord of the whole island; I had the lives of all my subjects at my absolute command. I could hang, draw, give liberty, and take it away; and no rebels among all my subjects.

Then to see how like a king I dined, too, all alone, attended by my servants, Poll,

as if he had been my favourite, was the only person permitted to talk to me. My dog, who was now grown very old and crazy, and had found no species to multiply his kind upon, sat always at my right hand, and two cats, one on one side the table, and one on the other, expecting now and then a bit from my hand, as a mark of special favour.

But these were not the two cats which I brought on shore at first, for they were both of them dead, and had been interred near my habitation by my own hand; but one of them having multiplied by I know not what kind of creature, these were two which I had preserved tame; whereas the rest run wild in the woods, and became indeed troublesome to me at last; for they would often come into my house, and plunder me too, till at last I was obliged to shoot them, and did kill a great many; at length they left me. With this attendance, and in this plentiful manner, I lived: neither could I be said to want anything but society; and of that in some time after this, I was like to have too much.

CHAPTER ELEVEN

I was something impatient, as I have observed, to have the use of my boat, though very loth to run any more hazards; and therefore sometimes I sat contriving ways to get her about the island, and at other times I sat myself down contented enough without her. But I had a strange uneasiness in my mind to go down to the point of the island where, as I have said, in my last ramble, I went up the hill to see how the shore lay, and how the current set, that I might see what I had to do. This inclination increased upon me every day, and at length I resolved to travel thither by land, following the edge of the shore. I did so; but had anyone in England been to meet such a man as I was, it must either have frighted them, or raised a great deal of laughter; and as I frequently stood still to look at myself, I could not but smile at the notion of my travelling through Yorkshire, with such an equipage, and in such a dress. Be pleased to take a sketch of my figure, as follows.

I had a great high shapeless cap, made of a goat's skin, with a flap hanging down behind, as well to keep the sun from me, as to shoot the rain off from running into my neck; nothing being so hurtful in these climates as the rain upon the flesh, under the clothes.

I had a short jacket of goat-skin, the skirts coming down to about the middle of my thighs; and a pair of open-kneed breeches of the same. The breeches were made of the skin of an old he-goat, whose hair hung down such a length on either side, that, like pantaloons, it reached to the middle of my legs. Stockings and shoes I had none, but had made me a pair of somethings, I scarce know what to call them, like buskins, to flap over my legs, and lace on either side like spatterdashes; but of a most barbarous shape, as indeed were all the rest of my clothes.

I had on a broad belt of goat's skin dried, which I drew together with two thongs of the same, instead of buckles; and in a kind of a frog on either side of this, instead of a sword and a dagger, hung a little saw and a hatchet, one on one side, one on the other. I had another belt, not so broad, and fastened in the same manner, which hung over my shoulder; and at the end of it, under my left arm, hung two pouches, both made of goat's skin too; in one of which hung my powder, in the other my shot. At my back I carried my basket, on my shoulder my gun, and over my head a great clumsy ugly goat-skin umbrella, but which, after all, was the most necessary thing I had about me, next to my gun. As for my face, the colour of it was really not so mulatto-like as one might expect from a man not at all careful of it, and living within nineteen degrees of the equinox. My beard I had once suffered to grow till it was about a quarter of a yard long; but as I had both scissors and razors sufficient, I had cut it pretty short, except what grew on my upper lip, which I had trimmed into a large pair of Mahometan whiskers, such as I had seen worn by some Turks whom I saw at Sallee; for the Moors did not wear such, though the Turks did. Of these mustachios or whiskers, I will not say they were long enough to hang my hat upon them, but they were of a length and shape monstrous enough, and such as, in England, would have passed for frightful.

But all this is by-the-bye; for, as to my figure, I had so few to observe me, that it was of no manner of consequence; so I say no more to that part. In this kind of figure I went my new journey, and was out five or six days. I travelled first along the sea-shore, directly to the place where I first brought my boat to an anchor, to get up upon the rocks. And having no boat now to take care of, I went over the land, a nearer way, to the same height that I was upon before; when, looking forward to the point of the rocks which lay out, and which I was obliged to double with my boat, as is said above, I was surprised to see the sea all smooth and quiet, no rippling, no motion, no current, any more there than in other places.

I was at a strange loss to understand this, and resolved to spend some time in the observing it, to see if nothing from the sets of the tide had occasioned it; but I was presently convinced how it was, viz. that the tide of ebb, setting from the west, and joining with the current of waters from some great river on the shore, must be the occasion of this current; and that according as the wind blew more forcibly from the west, or from the north, this current came near, or went farther from the shore: for waiting thereabouts till evening, I went up to the rock again, and then the tide of ebb being made, I plainly saw the current again as before, only that it ran farther off, being near half a league from the shore; whereas, in my case, it set close upon the shore, and hurried me and my canoe along with it, which, at another time, it would not have done.

This observation convinced me that I had nothing to do but to observe the ebbing and the flowing of the tide, and I might very easily bring my boat about the island again. But when I began to think of putting it in practice, I had such a terror upon my spirits at the remembrance of the danger I had been in, that I could not think of it again with any patience; but, on the contrary, I took up another resolution, which was more safe, though more laborious; and this was that I would build, or rather make me another periagua or canoe; and so have one for one side of the island, and one for the other.

You are to understand that now I had, as I may call it, two plantations in the island; one, my little fortification or tent, with the wall about it, under the rock, with the cave behind me, which, by this time, I had enlarged into several apartments or caves, one within another. One of these, which was the driest and largest, and had a door out beyond my wall or fortification, that is to say, beyond where my wall joined to the rock, was all filled up with the large earthen pots, of which I have given an account, and with fourteen or fifteen great baskets, which would hold five or six bushels each, where I laid up my stores of provision, especially my corn, some in the ear, cut off short from the straw, and the other rubbed out with my hand.

As for my wall, made, as before, with long stakes or piles, those piles grew all like trees, and were by this time grown so big, and spread so very much, that there was not the least appearance, to any one's view, of any habitation behind them.

Near this dwelling of mine, but a little farther within the land, and upon lower ground, lay my two pieces of corn ground, which I kept duly cultivated and sowed, and which duly yielded me their harvest in its season; and whenever I had occasion for more corn, I had more land adjoining as fit as that.

Besides this, I had my country seat, and I had now a tolerable plantation there also; for, first, I had my little bower, as I called it, which I kept in repair; that is to say, I kept the hedge which circled it in constantly fitted up to its usual height, the ladder standing always in the inside. I kept the trees, which at first were no more than my stakes, but were now grown very firm and tall, I kept them always so cut, that they might spread and grow thick and wild, and make the more agreeable shade, which they did effectually to my mind. In the middle of this, I had my tent always standing, being a piece of a sail spread over poles, set up for that purpose, and which never wanted any repair or renewing; and under this I had made me a squab or couch, with the skins of the creatures I had killed, and with other soft things, and a blanket laid on them, such as belonged to our sea-bedding, which I had saved, and a great watch-coat to cover me; and here, whenever I had occasion to be absent from my chief seat, I took up my country habitation.

Adjoining to this I had my enclosures for my cattle, that is to say, my goats. And as I had taken an inconceivable deal of pains to fence and enclose this ground, so I was so uneasy to see it kept entire, lest the goats should break through, that I never left off till, with infinite labour, I had stuck the outside of the hedge so full of small stakes, and so near to one another, that it was rather a pale than a hedge, and there was scarce room to put a hand through between them; which afterwards, when those stakes grew, as they all did in the next rainy season, made the enclosure strong like a wall, indeed, stronger than any wall.

This will testify for me that I was not idle, and that I spared no pains to bring to pass whatever appeared necessary for my comfortable support; for I considered the keeping up a breed of tame creatures thus at my hand would be a living magazine of flesh, milk, butter, and cheese for me as long as I lived in the place, if it were to be forty years; and that keeping them in my reach depended entirely upon my perfecting my enclosures to such a degree, that I might be sure of keeping them together; which, by this method, indeed, I so effectually secured, that when these little stakes began to grow, I had planted them so very thick, I was forced to pull some of them up again.

In this place also I had my grapes growing, which I principally depended on for my winter store of raisins, and which I never failed to preserve very carefully, as the best and most agreeable dainty of my whole diet. And indeed they were not agreeable only, but physical, wholesome, nourishing, and refreshing to the last degree.

As this was also about half-way between my other habitation and the place where I had laid up my boat, I generally staid and lay here in my way thither; for I used frequently to visit my boat, and I kept all things about or belonging to her in very good order. Sometimes I went out in her to divert myself, but no more hazardous

voyages would I go, nor scarce ever above a stone's cast or two from the shore, I was so apprehensive of being hurried out of my knowledge again by the currents or winds, or any other accident. But now I come to a new scene of my life.

It happened one day, about noon, going towards my boat, I was exceedingly surprised with the print of a man's naked foot on the shore, which was very plain to be seen in the sand. I stood like one thunderstruck, or as if I had seen an apparition. I listened, I looked round me, I could hear nothing, nor see anything. I went up to a rising ground, to look farther. I went up the shore, and down the shore, but it was all one; I could see no other impression but that one. I went to it again to see if there were any more, and to observe if it might not be my fancy; but there was no room for that, for there was exactly the very print of a foot – toes, heel, and every part of a foot. How it came thither I knew not, nor could in the least imagine. But after innumerable fluttering thoughts, like a man perfectly confused and out of myself, I came home to my fortification, not feeling, as we say, the ground I went on, but terrified to the last degree, looking behind me at every two or three steps, mistaking every bush and tree, and fancying every stump at a distance to be a man; nor is it possible to describe how many various shapes affrighted imagination represented things to me in, how many wild ideas were found every moment in my fancy, and what strange unaccountable whimsies came into my thoughts, by the way.

When I came to my castle, for so I think I called it ever after this, I fled into it like one pursued. Whether I went over by the ladder, as first contrived, or went in at the hole in the rock, which I called a door, I cannot remember; no, nor could I remember the next morning, for never frighted hare fled to cover, or fox to earth, with more terror of mind than I to this retreat.

I slept none that night. The farther I was from the occasion of my fright, the greater my apprehensions were; which is something contrary to the nature of such things, and especially to the usual practice of all creatures in fear. But I was so embarrassed with my own frightful ideas of the thing, that I formed nothing but dismal imaginations to myself, even though I was now a great way off it. Sometimes I fancied it must be the devil, and reason joined in with me upon this supposition; for how should any other thing in human shape come into the place? Where was the vessel that brought them? What marks was there of any other footsteps? And how was it possible a man should come there? But then to think that Satan should take human shape upon him in such a place, where there could be no manner of occasion for it, but to leave the print of his foot behind him, and that even for no purpose too, for he could not be sure I should see it, this was an amusement the other way. I considered that the devil might have found out abundance of other ways to have terrified me than this of the single print of a foot; that as I live quite on the other side of the island, he would never have been so simple to leave a mark in a place where

'I stood like one thunderstruck . . .' (p. 111)

it was ten thousand to one whether I should ever see it or not, and in the sand too, which the first surge of the sea, upon a high wind, would have defaced entirely. All this seemed inconsistent with the thing itself, and with all the notions we usually entertain of the subtlety of the devil.

Abundance of such things as these assisted to argue me out of all apprehensions of its being the devil; and I presently concluded then, that it must be some more dangerous creature, viz. that it must be some of the savages of the mainland over against me, who had wandered out to sea in their canoes, and, either driven by the currents or by contrary winds, had made the island, and had been on shore, but were gone away again to sea, being as loth, perhaps, to have staid in this desolate island as I would have been to have had them.

While these reflections were rolling upon my mind, I was very thankful in my thoughts that I was so happy as not to be thereabouts at that time, or that they did not see my boat, by which they would have concluded that some inhabitants had been in the place, and perhaps have searched farther for me. Then terrible thoughts racked my imagination about their having found my boat, and that there were people here; and that if so, I should certainly have them come again in greater numbers, and devour me; that if it should happen so that they should not find me, yet they would find my enclosure, destroy all my corn, carry away all my flock of tame goats, and I should perish at last for mere want.

Thus my fear banished all my religious hope. All that former confidence in God, which was founded upon such wonderful experience as I had had of His goodness, now vanished, as if He that had fed me by miracle hitherto could not preserve, by His power, the provision which He had made for me by His goodness. I reproached myself with my easiness, that would not sow any more corn one year than would just serve me till the next season, as if no accident could intervene to prevent my enjoying the crop that was upon the ground. And this I thought so just a reproof, that I resolved for the future to have two or three years' corn beforehand, so that, whatever might come, I might not perish for want of bread.

How strange a chequer-work of Providence is the life of man and by what secret differing springs are the affections hurried about, as differing circumstances present! To-day we love what to-morrow we hate; to-day we seek what to-morrow we shun; to-day we desire what to-morrow we fear, nay, even tremble at the apprehensions of. This was exemplified in me, at this time, in the most lively manner imaginable; for I, whose only affliction was that I seemed banished from human society, that I was alone, circumscribed by the boundless ocean, cut off from mankind, and condemned to what I called silent life; that I was as one whom Heaven thought not worthy to be numbered among the living, or to appear among the rest of His creatures; that to have seen one of my own species would have seemed to me a raising me from death to life, and the greatest blessing that Heaven itself, next to the supreme blessing of salvation, could bestow; I say, that I should now tremble at the very apprehensions of seeing a man, and was ready to sink into the ground at but the shadow or silent appearance of a man's having set his foot in the island.

Such is the uneven state of human life; and it afforded me a great many curious speculations afterwards, when I had a little recovered my first surprise. I considered that this was the station of life the infinitely wise and good providence of God had determined for me; that as I could not foresee what the ends of divine wisdom might be in all this, so I was not to dispute His sovereignty, who, as I was His creature, had an undoubted right, by creation, to govern and dispose of me absolutely as He thought fit; and who, as I was a creature who had offended Him, had likewise a judicial right to condemn me to what punishment He thought fit; and that it was my part to submit to bear His indignation, because I had sinned against Him.

I then reflected that God, who was not only righteous, but omnipotent, as He had thought fit thus to punish and afflict me, so He was able to deliver me; that if He did not think fit to do it, 'twas my unquestioned duty to resign myself absolutely and entirely to His will; and, on the other hand, it was my duty also to hope in Him, pray to Him, and quietly to attend the dictates and directions of His daily providence.

These thoughts took me up many hours, days, nay, I may say, weeks and months; and one particular effect of my cogitations on this occasion I cannot omit, viz. one morning early, lying in my bed, and filled with thought about my danger from the appearance of savages, I found it discomposed me very much; upon which those words of the Scripture come into my thoughts, "Call upon Me in the day of trouble, and I will deliver, and thou shalt glorify Me."

Upon this, rising cheerfully out of my bed, my heart was not only comforted, but I was guided and encouraged to pray earnestly to God for deliverance. When I had done praying, I took up my Bible, and opening it to read, the first words that presented to me were, "Wait on the Lord, and be of good cheer, and He shall strengthen thy heart; wait, I say, on the Lord." It is impossible to express the comfort this gave me. In answer, I thankfully laid down the book, and was no more sad, at least on that occasion.

In the middle of these cogitations, apprehensions, and reflections, it came into my thought one day, that all this might be a mere chimera of my own; and that this foot might be the print of my own foot, when I came on shore from my boat. This cheered me up a little too, and I began to persuade myself it was all a delusion, that it was nothing else but my own foot; and why might not I come that way from the boat, as well as I was going that way to the boat? Again, I considered also, that I could by no means tell, for certain, where I had trod, and where I had not; and that if, at last, this was only the print of my own foot, I had played the part of those fools who strive to make stories of spectres and apparitions, and then are frighted at them more than anybody.

Now I began to take courage, and to peep abroad again, for I had not stirred out of my castle for three days and nights, so that I began to starve for provision; for I had little or nothing within doors but some barley-cakes and water. Then I knew that my goats wanted to be milked too, which usually was my evening diversion; and the poor creatures were in great pain and inconvenience for want of it; and, indeed, it almost spoiled some of them, and almost dried up their milk.

Heartening myself, therefore, with the belief that this was nothing but the print of one of my own feet, and so I might be truly said to start at my own shadow, I began to go abroad again, and went to my country house to milk my flock. But to see with what fear I went forward, how often I looked behind me, how I was ready, every now and then, to lay down my basket, and run for my life, it would have made any one have thought I was haunted with an evil conscience, or that I had been lately most terribly frighted; and so, indeed, I had.

However, as I went down thus two or three days, and having seen nothing, I began to be a little bolder, and to think there was really nothing in it but my own imagination. But I could not persuade myself fully of this till I should go down to the shore again, and see this print of a foot, and measure it by my own, and see if there was any similitude or fitness, that I might be assured it was my own foot. But when I came to the place, first, it appeared evidently to me, that when I laid up my boat, I could not possibly be on shore anywhere thereabout; secondly, when I came to measure the mark with my own foot, I found my foot not so large by a great deal. Both these things filled my head with new imaginations, and gave me the vapours again to the highest degree; so that I shook with cold, like one in an ague; and I went home again, filled with the belief that some man or men had been on shore there; or, in short, that the island was inhabited, and I might be surprised before I was aware. And what course to take for my security, I knew not.

O what ridiculous resolutions men take when possessed with fear! It deprives them of the use of those means which reason offers for their relief. The first thing I proposed to myself was, to throw down my enclosures, and turn all my tame cattle wild into the woods, that the enemy might not find them, and then frequent the island in prospect of the same or the like booty: then to the simple thing of digging up my two corn fields, that they might not find such a grain there, and still be prompted to frequent the island: then to demolish my bower and tent, that they might not see any vestiges of habitation, and be prompted to look farther, in order to find out the persons inhabiting.

These were the subject of the first night's cogitation, after I was come home again, while the apprehensions which had so overrun my mind were fresh upon me, and my head was full of vapours, as above. Thus fear of danger is ten thousand times more terrifying than danger itself when apparent to the eyes; and we find the burden of anxiety greater, by much, than the evil which we are anxious about: and, which was worse than all this, I had not that relief in this trouble from the resignation I used to practise, that I hoped to have. I looked, I thought, like Saul, who complained not only that the Philistines were upon him, but that God had forsaken him; for I did not now take due ways to compose my mind, by crying to God in my distress, and resting upon His providence, as I had done before, for my defence and deliverance; which, if I had done, I had at least been more cheerfully supported under this new surprise, and perhaps carried through it with more resolution.

This confusion of my thoughts kept me waking all night, but in the morning I fell asleep; and having, by the amusement of my mind, been, as it were, tired, and my spirits exhausted, I slept very soundly, and waked much better composed than I had ever been before. And now I began to think sedately; and upon the utmost debate with myself, I concluded that this island, which was so exceeding pleasant, fruitful, and no farther from the mainland than as I had seen, was not so entirely abandoned as I might imagine; that although there were no stated inhabitants who lived on the spot, yet that there might sometimes come boats off from the shore, who, either with design, or perhaps never but when they were driven by cross winds, might come to this place; that I had lived here fifteen years now, and had not met with the least shadow or figure of any people yet; and that if at any time they should be driven here, it was probable they went away again as soon as ever they could, seeing they had never thought fit to fix there upon any occasion to this time; that the most I could suggest any danger from, was from any such casual accidental landing of straggling people from the main, who, as it was likely, if they were driven hither, were here against their wills; so they made no stay here, but went off again with all possible speed, seldom staying one night on shore, lest they should not have the help of the tides and daylight back again; and that, therefore, I had nothing to do but to consider of some safe retreat, in case I should see any savages land upon the spot.

Now I began sorely to repent that I had dug my cave so large as to bring a door through again, which door, as I said, came out beyond where my fortification joined to the rock. Upon maturely considering this, therefore, I resolved to draw me a second fortification, in the same manner of a semicircle, at a distance from my wall, just where I had planted a double row of trees about twelve years before, of which I made mention. These trees having been planted so thick before, they wanted but a few piles to be driven between them, that they should be thicker and stronger, and my wall would be soon finished.

So that I had now a double wall; and my outer wall was thickened with pieces of timber, old cables, and everything I could think of, to make it strong, having in it seven little holes, about as big as I might put my arm out at. In the inside of this I thickened my wall to above ten foot thick with continual bringing earth out of my cave, and laying it at the foot of the wall, and walking upon it; and through the seven holes I contrived to plant the muskets, of which I took notice that I got seven on shore out of the ship. These, I say, I planted like my cannon, and fitted them into frames, that held them like a carriage, that so I could fire all the seven guns in two minutes' time. This wall I was many a weary month a-finishing, and yet never thought myself safe till it was done.

When this was done, I stuck all the ground without my wall, for a great way every way, as full with stakes, or sticks, of the osier-like wood, which I found so apt to grow, as they could well stand; insomuch, that I believe I might set in near twenty thousand of them, leaving a pretty large space between them and my wall, that I might have room to see an enemy, and they might have no shelter from the young trees, if they attempted to approach my outer wall.

Thus in two years' time I had a thick grove; and in five or six years' time I had a wood before my dwelling, growing so monstrous thick and strong, that it was indeed perfectly impassable; and no men, of what kind soever, would ever imagine that there was anything beyond it, much less a habitation. As for the way which I proposed to myself to go in and out, for I left no avenue, it was by setting two ladders, one to a part of the rock which was low, and then broke in, and left room to place another ladder upon that; so when the two ladders were taken down, no man living could come down to me without mischieving himself; and if they had come down, they were still on the outside of my outer wall.

Thus I took all the measures human prudence could suggest for my own preservation; and it will be seen, at length, that they were not altogether without just reason; though I foresaw nothing at that time more than my mere fear suggested to me.

While this was doing, I was not altogether careless of my other affairs; for I had a great concern upon me for my little herd of goats. They were not only a present supply to me upon every occasion, and began to be sufficient to me, without the expense of powder and shot, but also without the fatigue of hunting after the wild ones; and I was loth to lose the advantage of them, and to have them all to nurse up over again.

To this purpose, after long consideration, I could think of but two ways to preserve them. One was, to find another convenient place to dig a cave under ground, and to drive them into it every night; and the other was, to enclose two or three little bits of land, remote from one another, and as much concealed as I could, where I might keep about half-a-dozen young goats in each place; so that if any disaster happened to the flock in general, I might be able to raise them again with little trouble and time. And this, though it would require a great deal of time and labour, I thought was the most rational design.

Accordingly I spent some time to find out the most retired parts of the island; and I pitched upon one which was as private indeed as my heart could wish for. It was a little damp piece of ground in the middle of the hollow and thick woods, where, as is observed, I almost lost myself once before, endeavouring to come back that way from the eastern part of the island. Here I found a clear piece of land, near three acres, so surrounded with woods, that it was almost an enclosure by Nature; at least, it did not want near so much labour to make it so as the other pieces of ground I had worked so hard at.

I immediately went to work with this piece of ground, and in less than a month's time I had so fenced it round, that my flock, or herd, call it which you please, who were not so wild now as at first they might be supposed to be, were well enough secured in it. So, without any farther delay, I removed ten young she-goats and two he-goats to this piece. And when they were there, I continued to perfect the fence, till I had made it as secure as the other, which, however, I did at more leisure, and it took me up more time by a great deal.

CHAPTER TWELVE

All this labour I was at the expense of, purely from my apprehensions on the account of the print of a man's foot which I had seen; for, as yet, I never saw any human creature come near the island. And I had now lived two years under these uneasinesses, which, indeed, made my life much less comfortable than it was before, as may well be imagined by any who know what it is to live in the constant snare of the fear of man. And this I must observe, with grief too, that the discomposure of my mind had too great impressions also upon the religious part of my thoughts; for the dread and terror of falling into the hands of savages and cannibals lay so upon my spirits, that I seldom found myself in a due temper for application to my Maker, at least not with the sedate calmness and resignation of soul which I was wont to do. I rather prayed to God as under great affliction and pressure of mind, surrounded with danger, and in expectation every night of being murdered and devoured before morning; and I must testify from my experience, that a temper of peace, thankfulness, love and affection, is much more the proper frame for prayer than that of terror and discomposure; and that under the dread of mischief impending, a man is no more fit for a comforting performance of the duty of praying to God, than he is for a repentance on a sick-bed; for these discomposures affect the mind, as the others do the body; and the discomposure of the mind must necessarily be as great a disability as that of the body, and much greater, praying to God being properly an act of the mind, not of the body.

But to go on. After I had thus secured one part of my little living stock, I went about the whole island, searching for another private place to make such another deposit; when, wandering more to the west point of the island than I had ever done yet, and looking out to sea, I thought I saw a boat upon the sea, at a great distance. I had found a prospective glass or two in one of the seamen's chests, which I saved out of our ship, but I had it not about me; and this was so remote, that I could not tell what to make of it, though I looked at it till my eyes were not able to hold to look any longer. Whether it was a boat or not, I do not know; but as I descended from the hill, I could see no more of it, so I gave it over; only I resolved to go no more out without a prospective glass in my pocket.

When I was come down the hill to the end of the island, where, indeed, I had never been before, I was presently convinced that the seeing of the print of a man's foot was not such a strange thing in the island as I imagined. And, but that it was a special providence that I was cast upon the side of the island where the savages never came, I should easily have known that nothing was more frequent than for the canoes from the main, when they happened to be a little too far out at sea, to shoot over to that side of the island for harbour; likewise, as they often met and fought in their canoes, the victors having taken any prisoners would bring them over to this shore, where, according to their dreadful customs, being all cannibals, they would kill and eat them; of which hereafter.

When I was come down the hill to the shore, as I said above, being the S. W. point of the island, I was perfectly confounded and amazed; nor is it possible for me to express the horror of my mind at seeing the shore spread with skulls, hands, feet, and other bones of human bodies; and particularly I observed a place where there had been a fire made, and a circle dug in the earth, like a cockpit, where it is supposed the savage wretches had sat down to their inhuman feastings upon the bodies of their fellow-creatures.

I was so astonished with the sight of these things, that I entertained no notion of any danger to myself from it for a long while. All my apprehensions were buried in the thoughts of such a pitch of inhuman, hellish brutality, and the horror of the degeneracy of human nature, which, though I had heard of often, yet I never had so near a view of before. In short, I turned away my face from the horrid spectacle; my stomach grew sick, and I was just at the point of fainting, when nature discharged the disorder from my stomach: and having vomited with an uncommon violence, I was a little relieved, but could not bear to stay in the place a moment; so I gat me up the hill again with all the speed I could, and walked on towards my own habitation.

When I came a little out of that part of the island, I stood still awhile, as amazed; and then recovering myself, I looked up with the utmost affection of my soul, and with a flood of tears in my eyes, gave God thanks, that had cast my first lot in a part of the world where I was distinguished from such dreadful creatures as these; and that, though I had esteemed my present condition very miserable, had yet given me so many comforts in it, that I had still more to give thanks for than to complain of: and this, above all, that I had, even in this miserable condition, been comforted with the knowledge of Himself, and the hope of His blessing, which was a felicity more than sufficiently equivalent to all the misery which I had suffered or could suffer.

In this frame of thankfulness I went home to my castle, and began to be much easier now, as to the safety of my circumstances, than ever I was before; for I observed that these wretches never came to this island in search of what they could get; perhaps not seeking, not wanting, or not expecting, anything here; and having often, no doubt, been up in the covered, woody part of it, without finding anything to their purpose. I knew I had been here now almost eighteen years, and never saw the least footsteps of human creature there before; and I might be here eighteen more as entirely concealed as I was now, if I did not discover myself to them, which I had no manner of occasion to do; it being my only business to keep myself entirely concealed where I was, unless I found a better sort of creatures than cannibals to make myself known to.

Yet I entertained such an abhorrence of the savage wretches that I have been speaking of, and of the wretched inhuman custom of their devouring and eating one another up, that I continued pensive and sad, and kept close within my own circle for almost two years after this. When I say my own circle, I mean by it my three plantations, viz. my castle, my country seat, which I called my bower, and my enclosure in the woods. Nor did I look after this for any other use than as an enclosure for my goats; for the aversion which Nature gave me to these hellish wretches was such, that I was fearful of seeing them as of seeing the devil himself. Nor did I so much as go to look after my boat in all this time, but began rather to think of making me another; for I could not think of ever making any more attempts to bring the other boat round the island to me, lest I should meet with some of these creatures at sea: in which if I had happened to have fallen into their hands, I knew what would have been my lot.

Time, however, and the satisfaction I had that I was in no danger of being discovered by these people, began to wear off my uneasiness about them; and I began to live just in the same composed manner as before; only with this difference, that I used more caution, and kept my eyes more about me, than I did before, lest I should happen to be seen by any of them; and particularly, I was more cautious of firing my gun, lest any of them being on the island should happen to hear of it. And

it was, therefore, a very good providence to me that I had furnished myself with a tame breed of goats, that I needed not hunt any more about the woods, or shoot at them. And if I did catch any of them after this, it was by traps and snares, as I had done before; so that for two years after this I believe I never fired my gun once off, though I never went out without it; and, which was more, as I had saved three pistols out of the ship, I always carried them out with me, or at least two of them, sticking them in my goat-skin belt. Also I furbished up one of the great cutlasses that I had out of the ship, and made me a belt to put it on also; so that I was now a most formidable fellow to look at when I went abroad, if you add to the former description of myself the particular of two pistols and a great broadsword hanging at my side in a belt, but without a scabbard.

Things going on thus, as I have said, for some time, I seemed, excepting these cautions, to be reduced to my former calm, sedate way of living. All these things tended to showing me, more and more, how far my condition was from being miserable, compared to some others; nay, to many other particulars of life, which it might have pleased God to have made my lot. It put me upon reflecting how little repining there would be among mankind at any condition of life, if people would rather compare their condition with those that are worse, in order to be thankful, than be always comparing them with those which are better, to assist their murmurings and complainings.

As in my present condition there were not really many things which I wanted, so indeed I thought that the frights I had been in about these savage wretches, and the concern I had been in for my own preservation, had taken off the edge of my invention for my own conveniences. And I had dropped a good design, which I had once bent my thoughts too much upon; and that was, to try if l could not make some of my barley into malt, and then try to brew myself some beer. This was really a whimsical thought, and I reproved myself often for the simplicity of it; for I presently saw there would be the want of several things necessary to the making my beer, that it would be impossible for me to supply; as, first, casks to preserve it in, which was a thing that, as I had observed already, I could never compass; no, though I spent not only many days, but weeks, nay, months, in attempting it, but to no purpose. In the next place, I had no hops to make it keep, no yeast to make it work, no copper or kettle to make it boil; and yet, all these things notwithstanding, I verily believe, had not these things intervened, I mean the frights and terrors I was in about the savages, I had undertaken it, and perhaps brought it to pass too; for I seldom gave anything over without accomplishing it, when once I had it in my head enough to begin it.

But my invention now run quite another way; for, night and day, I could think of nothing but how I might destroy some of these monsters in their cruel, bloody entertainment, and, if possible, save the victim they should bring hither to destroy. It would take up a larger volume than this whole work is intended to be, to set down all the contrivances I hatched, or rather brooded upon, in my thought, for the destroying these creatures, or at least frighting them so as to prevent their coming hither any more. But all was abortive; nothing could be possible to take effect, unless

I was to be there to do it myself. And what could one man do among them, when perhaps there might be twenty or thirty of them together, with their darts, or their bows and arrows, with which they could shoot as true to a mark as I could with my gun?

Sometimes I contrived to dig a hole under the place where they made their fire, and put in five or six pound of gunpowder, which, when they kindled their fire, would consequently take fire, and blow up all that was near it. But as, in the first place, I should be very loth to waste so much powder upon them, my store being now within the quantity of one barrel, so neither could I be sure of its going off at any certain time, when it might surprise them; and, at best, that it would do little more than just blow the fire about their ears, and fright them, but not sufficient to make them forsake the place. So I laid it aside, and then proposed that I would place myself in ambush in some convenient place, with my three guns all double-loaded, and, in the middle of their bloody ceremony, let fly at them, when I should be sure to kill or wound perhaps two or three at every shoot; and then falling in upon them with my three pistols and my sword, I made no doubt but that if there was twenty I should kill them all. This fancy pleased my thoughts for some weeks; and I was so full of it, that I often dreamed of it, and sometimes that I was just going to let fly at them in my sleep.

I went so far with it in my imagination, that I employed myself several days to find out proper places to put myself in ambuscade, as I said, to watch for them; and I went frequently to the place itself, which was now grown more familiar to me; and especially while my mind was thus filled with thoughts of revenge, and of a bloody putting twenty or thirty of them to the sword, as I may call it, the horror I had at the place, and at the signals of the barbarous wretches devouring one another, abated my malice.

Well, at length I found a place in the side of the hill, where I was satisfied I might securely wait till I saw any of their boats coming; and might then, even before they would be ready to come on shore, convey myself, unseen, into thickets of trees, in one of which there was a hollow large enough to conceal me entirely; and where I might sit and observe all their bloody doings, and take my full aim at their heads, when they were so close together, as that it would be next to impossible that I should miss my shoot, or that I could fail wounding three or four of them at the first shoot.

In this place, then, I resolved to fix my design; and, accordingly, I prepared two muskets and my ordinary fowling-piece. The two muskets I loaded with a brace of slugs each, and four or five smaller bullets, about the size of pistol-bullets; and the fowling-piece I loaded with near a handful of swanshot, of the largest size. I also loaded my pistols with about four bullets each; and in this posture, well provided with ammunition for a second or third charge, I prepared myself for my expedition.

After I had thus laid the scheme of my design, and in my imagination put it in practice, I continually made my tour every morning up to the top of the hill, which was from my castle, as I called it, about three miles, or more, to see if I could observe any boats upon the sea coming near the island, or standing over towards it. But I began to tire of this hard duty, after I had, for two or three months, constantly kept my watch, but came always back without any discovery; there having not, in all that

time, been the least appearance, not only on or near the shore, but not on the whole ocean, so far as my eyes or glasses could reach every way.

As long as I kept up my daily tour to the hill to look out, so long also I kept up the vigour of my design, and my spirits seemed to be all the while in a suitable form for so outrageous an execution as the killing twenty or thirty naked savages for an offence which I had not at all entered into a discussion of in my thoughts, any farther than my passions were at first fired by the horror I conceived at the unnatural custom of that people of the country; who, it seems, had been suffered by Providence, in His wise disposition of the world, to have no other guide than that of their own abominable and vitiated passions; and consequently were left, and perhaps had been so for some ages, to act such horrid things, and receive such dreadful customs, as nothing but Nature, entirely abandoned of Heaven, and acted by some hellish degeneracy, could have run them into. But now, when, as I have said, I began to be weary of the fruitless excursion, which I had made so long and so far every morning in vain, so my opinion of the action itself began to alter; and I began, with cooler and calmer thoughts, to consider what it was I was going to engage in: what authority or call I had to pretend to be judge and executioner upon these men as criminals, whom Heaven had thought fit, for so many ages, to suffer, unpunished, to go on, and to be, as it were, the executioners of His judgments one upon another: how far these people were offenders against me, and what right I had to engage in the quarrel of that blood which they shed promiscuously one upon another. I debated this very often with myself, thus: How do I know what God Himself judges in this particular case? It is certain these people do not commit this as a crime; it is not against their own consciences reproving, or their light reproaching them; they do not know it to be an offence, and then commit it in defiance of divine justice, as we do in almost all the sins we commit. They think it no more a crime to kill a captive taken in war, than we do to kill an ox; nor to eat human flesh, than we do to eat mutton.

When I had considered a little, it followed necessarily that I was certainly in the wrong in it; that these people were not murderers in the sense that I had before condemned them in my thoughts, any more than those Christians were murderers who often put to death the prisoners taken in battle; or more frequently, upon many occasions, put whole troops of men to the sword, without giving quarter, though they threw down their arms and submitted.

In the next place it occurred to me, that albeit the usage they thus gave one another was thus brutish and inhuman, yet it was really nothing to me; these people had done me no injury. That if they attempted me, or I saw it necessary for my immediate preservation to fall upon them, something might be said for it; but that as I was yet out of their power, and they had really no knowledge of me, and consequently no design upon me, and therefore it could not be just for me to fall upon them. That this would justify the conduct of the Spaniards in all their barbarities practised in America, and where they destroyed millions of these people: who, however they were idolaters and barbarians, and had several bloody and barbarous rites in their customs, such as sacrificing human bodies to their idols, were yet, as to the Spaniards, very innocent people; and that the rooting them out of the country is spoken of with the utmost abhorrence and detestation by even the Spaniards themselves at this time, and by all other Christian nations in Europe, as a mere butchery, a bloody and unnatural piece of cruelty, unjustifiable either to God or man; and such as for which the very name of a Spaniard is reckoned to be frightful and terrible to all people of humanity, or of Christian compassion: as if the kingdom of Spain were particularly eminent for the produce of a race of men who were without principles of tenderness, or the common bowels of pity to the miserable, which is reckoned to be a mark of generous temper in the mind.

These considerations really put me to a pause, and to a kind of a full stop; and I began, by little and little, to be off of my design, and to conclude I had taken wrong measures in my resolutions to attack the savages; that it was not my business to meddle with them, unless they first attacked me; and this it was my business, if possible, to prevent; but that if I were discovered and attacked, then I knew my duty.

On the other hand, I argued with myself that this really was the way not to deliver myself, but entirely to ruin and destroy myself; for unless I was sure to kill every one that not only should be on shore at that time, but that should ever come on shore afterwards, if but one of them escaped to tell their country people what had happened, they would come over again by thousands to revenge the death of their fellows, and I should only bring upon myself a certain destruction, which, at present, I had no manner of occasion for.

Upon the whole, I concluded that neither in principles nor in policy I ought, one way or other, to concern myself in this affair. That my business was, by all possible means, to conceal myself from them, and not to leave the least signal to them to guess by that there were any living creatures upon the island; I mean of human shape.

Religion joined in with this prudential, and I was convinced now, many ways, that I was perfectly out of my duty when I was laying all my bloody schemes for the destruction of innocent creatures; I mean innocent as to me. As to the crimes they were guilty of towards one another, I had nothing to do with them. They were national, and I ought to leave them to the justice of God, who is the Governor of nations, and knows how, by national punishments, to make a just retribution for national offences, and to bring public judgments upon those who offend in a public manner, by such ways as best pleases Him.

This appeared so clear to me now, that nothing was a greater satisfaction to me than that I had not been suffered to do a thing which I now saw so much reason to

believe would have been no less a sin than that of wilful murder, if I had committed it; and I gave most humble thanks on my knees to God, that had thus delivered me from blood-guiltiness; beseeching Him to grant me the protection of His providence, that I might not fall into the hands of the barbarians, or that I might not lay my hands upon them, unless I had a more clear call from Heaven to do it, in defence of my own life.

In this disposition I continued for near a year after this; and so far was I from desiring an occasion for falling upon these wretches, that in all that time I never once went up the hill to see whether there were any of them in sight, or to know whether any of them had been on shore there or not, that I might not be tempted to renew any of my contrivances against them, or be provoked, by any advantage which might present itself, to fall upon them. Only this I did, I went and removed my boat, which I had on the other side the island, and carried it down to the east end of the whole island, where I ran it into a little cove, which I found under some high rocks and where I knew, by reason of the currents, the savage durst not, at least would not come, with their boats, upon any account whatsoever.

With my boat I carried away everything that I had left there belonging to her, though not necessary for the bare going thither, viz. a mast and a sail which I had made for her and a thing like an anchor, but indeed which could not be called either anchor or grappling; however, it was the best I could make of its kind. All these I removed, that there might not be the least shadow of any discovery, or any appearance of any boat, or of any human habitation, upon the island.

Besides this, I kept myself, as I said, more retired than ever, and seldom went from my cell, other than upon my constant employment, viz. to milk my she-goats, and manage my little flock in the wood, which, as it was quite on the other part of the island, was quite out of danger; for certain it is, that these savage people, who sometimes haunted this island, never came with any thoughts of finding anything here, and consequently never wandered off from the coast; and I doubt not but they might have been several times on shore after my apprehensions of them had made me cautious, as well as before; and indeed, I looked back with some horror upon the thoughts of what my condition would have been if I had chopped upon them and been discovered before that, when, naked and unarmed, except with one gun, and that loaded often only with small shot, I walked everywhere, peeping and peeping about the island to see what I could get. What a surprise should I have been in if, when I discovered the print of a man's foot, I had, instead of that, seen fifteen or twenty savages and found them pursuing me, and by the swiftness of their running, no possibility of my escaping them!

The thoughts of this sometimes sunk my very soul within me, and distressed my mind so much, that I could not soon recover it, to think what I should have done, and how I should not only have been unable to resist them, but even should not have had presence of mind enough to do what I might have done, much less what now, after so much consideration and preparation, I might be able to do. Indeed, after serious thinking of these things, I would be very melancholy, and sometimes it would last a great while; but I resolved it, at last, all into thankfulness to that Providence which had delivered me from so many unseen dangers, and had kept me from those mischiefs which I could no way have been the agent in delivering myself from; because I had not the least notion of any such thing depending, or the least supposition of it being possible.

This renewed a contemplation which often had come to my thoughts in former time, when first I began to see the merciful dispositions of Heaven, in the dangers we run through in this life; how wonderfully we are delivered when we know nothing of it; how, when we are in (a quandary, as we call it) a doubt or hesitation, whether to go this way, or that way, a secret hint shall direct us this way, when we intended to go that way: nay, when sense, our own inclination, and perhaps business, has called to go the other way, yet a strange impression upon the mind, from we know not what springs, and by we know not what power, shall overrule us to go this way; and it shall afterwards appear, that had we gone that way which we should have gone, and even to our imagination ought to have gone, we should have been ruined and lost. Upon these, and many like reflections, I afterwards made it a certain rule with me, that whenever I found those secret hints or pressings of mind, to doing or not doing any thing that presented, or to going this way or that way, I never failed to obey the secret dictate; though I knew no other reason for it than that such a pressure, or such a hint, hung upon my mind. I could give many examples of the success of this conduct in the course of my life, but more especially in the latter part of my inhabiting this unhappy island; besides many occasions which it is very likely I might have taken notice of, if I had seen with the same eyes then that I saw with now. But 'tis never too late to be wise; and I cannot but advise all considering men, whose lives are attended with such extraordinary incidents as mine, or even though not so extraordinary, not to slight such secret intimations of Providence, let them come from what invisible intelligence they will. That I shall not discuss, and perhaps cannot account for; but certainly they are a proof of the converse of spirits, and the secret communication between those embodied and those unembodied, and such a proof as can never be withstood; of which I shall have occasion to give some very remarkable instances in the remainder of my solitary residence in this dismal place.

I believe the reader of this will not think strange if I confess that these anxieties, these constant dangers I lived in, and the concern that was now upon me, put an end to all invention, and to all the contrivances that I had laid for my future accommodations and conveniences. I had the care of my safety more now upon my hands than that of my food. I cared not to drive a nail, or chop a stick of wood now, for fear the noise I should make should be heard; much less would I fire a gun, for the same reason; and, above all, I was intolerably uneasy at making any fire, lest the smoke, which is visible at a great distance in the day, should betray me; and for this reason I removed that part of my business which required fire, such as burning of pots and pipes, etc., into my new apartment in the woods; where, after I had been some time, I found, to my unspeakable consolation, a mere natural cave in the earth, which went in a vast way, and where, I dare say, no savage, had he been at the mouth

of it, would be so hardy as to venture in; nor, indeed, would any man else, but one who, like me, wanted nothing so much as a safe retreat.

The mouth of this hollow was at the bottom of a great rock, where, by mere accident, (I would say, if I did not see abundant reason to ascribe all such things now to Providence), I was cutting down some thick branches of trees to make charcoal; and before I go on, I must observe the reason of my making this charcoal, which was thus:

I was afraid of making a smoke about my habitation, as I said before; and yet I could not live there without baking my bread, cooking my meat, etc. So I contrived to burn some wood here, as I had seen done in England under turf, till it became chark, or dry coal; and then putting the fire out, I preserved the coal to carry home, and perform the other services which fire was wanting for at home, without danger of smoke.

But this is by-the-bye. While I was cutting down some wood here, I perceived that behind a very thick branch of low brushwood, or underwood, there was a kind of hollow place. I was curious to look into it; and getting with difficulty into the mouth of it, I found it was pretty large; that is to say, sufficient for me to stand upright in it, and perhaps another with me. But I must confess to you I made more haste out than I did in, when, looking farther into the place, and which was perfectly dark, I saw two broad shining eyes of some creature, whether devil or man I knew not, which twinkled like two stars, the dim light from the cave's mouth shining directly in, and making the reflection.

However, after some pause, I recovered myself, and began to call myself a thousand fools, and tell myself, that he that was afraid to see the devil was not fit to live twenty years in an island all alone; and that I durst to believe there was nothing in this cave that was more frightful than myself. Upon this, plucking up my courage, I took up a great firebrand, and in I rushed again, with the stick flaming in my hand: I had not gone three steps in, but I was almost as much frighted as I was before; for I heard a very loud sigh, like that of a man in some pain, and it was followed by a broken noise, as of words half expressed, and then a deep sigh again. I stepped back, and was indeed struck with such a surprise, that it put me into a cold sweat; and if I had had a hat on my head, I will not answer for it, that my hair might not have lifted it off. But still plucking up my spirits as well as I could, and encouraging myself a little with considering that the power and presence of God was everywhere, and was able to protect me, upon this I stepped forward again, and by the light of the firebrand, holding it up a little over my head, I saw lying on the ground a most monstrous, frightful, old he-goat, just making his will, as we say, and gasping for life; and dying indeed, of mere old age.

I stirred him a little to see if I could get him out, and he essayed to get up, but was not able to raise himself; and I thought with myself he might even lie there; for if he had frighted me so, he would certainly fright any of the savages, if any of them should be so hardy as to come in there while he had any life in him.

I was now recovered from my surprise, and began to look round me when I found the cave was but very small; that is to say, it might be about twelve foot over, but in no manner of shape, either round or square, no hands having ever been employed in making it but those of mere Nature. I observed also that there was a place at the farther side of it that went in farther, but was so low, that it required me to creep upon my hands and knees to go into it, and whither I went I knew not; so having no candle, I gave it over for some time, but resolved to come again the next day, provided with candles and a tinder-box, which I had made of the lock of one of the muskets, with some wild-fire in the pan.

Accordingly the next day I came provided with six large candles of my own making, for I made very good candles now of goat's tallow; and going into this low place, I was obliged to creep upon all fours, as I have said, almost ten yards; which, by the way, I thought was a venture bold enough, considering that I knew not how far it might go, nor what was beyond it. When I was got through the straight, I found the roof rose higher up, I believe near twenty foot. But never was such a glorious sight seen in the island, I dare say, as it was, to look round the sides and roof of this vault or cave; the walls reflected a hundred thousand lights to me from my two candles. What it was in the rock, whether diamonds, or any other precious stones, or gold, which I rather supposed it to be, I knew not.

The place I was in was a most delightful cavity or grotto of its kind, as could be expected, though perfectly dark. The floor was dry and level, and had a sort of small loose gravel upon it, so that there was no nauseous or venomous creature to be seen; neither was there any damp or wet on the sides or roof. The only difficulty in it was the entrance, which, however, as it was a place of security, and such a retreat as I

wanted, I thought that was a convenience; so that I was really rejoiced at the discovery, and resolved, without any delay, to bring some of those things which I was most anxious about to this place; particularly, I resolved to bring hither my magazine of powder, and all my spare arms, viz. two fowling-pieces, for I had three in all, and three muskets, for of them I had eight in all. So I kept at my castle only five, which stood ready-mounted, like pieces of cannon, on my outmost fence; and were ready also to take out upon any expedition.

Upon this occasion of removing my ammunition, I took occasion to open the barrel of powder, which I took out of the sea, and which had been wet; and I found that the water had penetrated about three or four inches into the powder on every side, which caking, and growing hard, had preserved the inside like a kernel in a shell; so that I had near sixty pounds of very good powder in the centre of the cask. And this was an agreeable discovery to me at that time; so I carried all away thither, never keeping above two or three pounds of powder with me in my castle, for fear of a surprise of any kind. I also carried thither all the lead I had left for bullets.

I fancied myself now like one of the ancient giants, which were said to live in caves and holes in the rocks, where none could come at them; for I persuaded myself, while I was here, if five hundred savages were to hunt me, they could never find me out; or, if they did, they would not venture to attack me here.

The old goat, whom I found expiring, died in the mouth of the cave the next day after I made this discovery; and I found it much easier to dig a great hole there, and throw him in and cover him with earth, than to drag him out. So I interred him there, to prevent offence to my nose.

CHAPTER THIRTEEN

I was now in my twenty-third year of residence in this island; and was so naturalised to the place, and to the manner of living, that could I have but enjoyed the certainty that no savages would come to the place to disturb me, I could have been content to have capitulated for spending the rest of my time there, even to the last moment, till I had laid me down and died, like the old goat in the cave. I had also arrived to some little diversions and amusements, which made the time pass more pleasantly with me a great deal than it did before. As, first, I had taught my Poll, as I noted before, to speak; and he did it so familiarly, and talked so articulately and plain, that it was very pleasant to me; and he lived with me no less than six and

twenty years. How long he might live afterwards I know not, though I know they have a notion in the Brazils that they live a hundred years. Perhaps poor Poll may be alive there still, calling after "poor Robin Crusoe" to this day. I wish no Englishman the ill luck to come there and hear him; but if he did, he would certainly believe it was the devil. My dog was a very pleasant and loving companion to me for no less than sixteen years of my time, and then died of mere old age. As for my cats, they multiplied, as I have observed, to that degree, that I was obliged to shoot several of them at first to keep them from devouring me and all I had; but at length, when the two old ones I brought with me were gone, and after some time continually driving them from me, and letting them have no provision with me, they all ran wild into the woods, except two or three favourites, which I kept tame, and whose young, when they had any, I always drowned; and these were part of my family. Besides these, I always kept two or three household kids about me, whom I taught to feed out of my hand. And I had two more parrots, which talked pretty well, and would all call "Robin Crusoe," but none like my first; nor, indeed, did I take the pains with any of them that I had done with him. I had also several tame sea-fowls, whose names I know not, whom I caught upon the shore, and cut their wings; and the little stakes which I had planted before my castle-wall being now grown up to a good thick grove, these fowls all lived among these low trees, and bred there, which was very agreeable to me; so that, as I said above, I began to be very well contented with the life I led, if it might but have been secure from the dread of the savages.

But it was otherwise directed; and it may not be amiss for all people who shall meet with my story, to make this just observation from it, viz. how frequently, in the course of our lives, the evil which in itself we seek most to shun, and which, when we are fallen into it, is the most dreadful to us, is oftentimes the very means or door of our deliverance, by which alone we can be raised again from the affliction we are fallen into. I could give many examples of this in the course of my unaccountable life; but in nothing was it more particularly remarkable, than in the circumstances of my last years of solitary residence in this island.

It was now the month of December, as I said above, in my twenty-third year; and this, being the southern solstice (for winter I cannot call it), was the particular time of my harvest, and required my being pretty much abroad in the fields; when, going out pretty early in the morning, even before it was thorough daylight, I was surprised with seeing a light of some fire upon the shore, at a distance from me of about two mile, towards the end of the island, where I had observed some savages had been, as before. But not on the other side; but, to my great affliction, it was on my side of the island.

I was indeed terribly surprised at the sight, and stopped short within my grove, not daring to go out, lest I might be surprised; and yet I had no more peace within, from the apprehensions I had that if these savages, in rambling over the island, should find my corn standing or cut, or any of my works and improvements, they would immediately conclude that there were people in the place, and would then never give over till they had found me out. In this extremity I went back directly to

my castle, pulled up the ladder after me, and made all things without look as wild and natural as I could.

Then I prepared myself within, putting myself in a posture of defence. I loaded all my cannon, as I called them, that is to say, my muskets, which were mounted upon my new fortification, and all my pistols, and resolved to defend myself to the last gasp; not forgetting seriously to commend myself to the Divine protection, and earnestly to pray to God to deliver me out of the hands of the barbarians. And in this posture I continued about two hours; but began to be mighty impatient for intelligence abroad, for I had no spies to send out.

After sitting a while longer, and musing what I should do in this case, I was not able to bear sitting in ignorance any longer; so setting up my ladder to the side of the hill where there was a flat place, as I observed before, and then pulling the ladder up after me, I set it up again, and mounted to the top of the hill; and pulling out my perspective-glass, which I had taken on purpose, I laid me down flat on my belly on the ground, and began to look for the place. I presently found there was no less than nine naked savages sitting round a small fire they had made, not to warm them, for they had no need of that, the weather being extreme hot, but, as I supposed, to dress some of their barbarous diet of human flesh which they had brought with them, whether alive or dead, I could not know.

They had two canoes with them, which they had hauled up upon the shore; and as it was then tide of ebb, they seemed to me to wait for the return of the flood to go away again. It is not easy to imagine what confusion this sight put me into, especially seeing them come on my side the island, and so near me too. But when I observed their coming must be always with the current of the ebb, I began afterwards to be more sedate in my mind, being satisfied that I might go abroad with safety all the time of the tide of flood, if they were not on shore before; and having made this observation, I went abroad about my harvest-work with the more composure.

As I expected, so it proved; for as soon as the tide made to the westward, I saw them all take boat, and row (or paddle, as we call it) all away. I should have observed, that for an hour and more before they went off, they went to dancing; and I could easily discern their postures and gestures by my glasses. I could not perceive, by my nicest observation, but that they were stark naked, and had not the least covering upon them; but whether they were men or women, I could not distinguish.

As soon as I saw them shipped and gone, I took two guns upon my shoulders, and two pistols at my girdle, and my great sword by my side, without a scabbard, and with all the speed I was able to make I went away to the hill where I had discovered the first appearance of all. And as soon as I got thither, which was not less than two hours (for I could not go apace, being so loaden with arms as I was), I perceived there had been three canoes more of savages on that place; and looking out farther, I saw they were all at sea together, making over for the main.

This was a dreadful sight to me, especially when, going down to the shore, I could see the marks of horror which the dismal work they had been about had left behind it, viz. the blood, the bones, and part of the flesh of human bodies, eaten and devoured by those wretches, with merriment and sport. I was so filled with indignation at the sight, that I began now to premeditate the destruction of the next that I saw there, let them be who or how many soever.

It seemed evident to me that the visits which they thus make to this island are not very frequent, for it was above fifteen months before any more of them came on shore there again; that is to say, I neither saw them, or any footsteps or signals of them, in all that time; for, as to the rainy seasons, then they are sure not to come abroad, at least not so far. Yet all this while I lived uncomfortably, by reason of the constant apprehensions I was in of their coming upon me by surprise: from whence I observe, that the expectation of evil is more bitter than the suffering, especially if there is no room to shake off that expectation, or those apprehensions.

During all this time I was in the murdering humour, and took up most of my hours, which should have been better employed, in contriving how to circumvent and fall upon them, the very next time I should see them; especially if they should be divided, as they were the last time, into two parties: nor did I consider at all, that if I killed one party, suppose ten or a dozen, I was still the next day, or week, or month, to kill another, and so another, even ad infinitum, till I should be at length no less a murderer than they were in being maneaters, and perhaps much more so.

I spent my days now in great perplexity and anxiety of mind, expecting that I should, one day or other, fall into the hands of these merciless creatures; and if I did at any time venture abroad, it was not without looking round me with the greatest care and caution imaginable. And now I found, to my great comfort, how happy it was that I provided for a tame flock or herd of goats: for I durst not, upon any account, fire my gun, especially near that side of the island, where they usually came, lest I should alarm the savages; and if they had fled from me now, I was sure to have them come back again, with perhaps two or three hundred canoes with them, in a few days, and then I knew what to expect.

However, I wore out a year and three months more before I ever saw any more of the savages, and then I found them again, as I shall soon observe. It is true they might have been there once or twice, but either they made no stay, or at least I did not hear them; but in the month of May, as near as I could calculate, and in my four and twentieth year, I had a very strange encounter with them; of which in its place.

Chapter Thirteen

The perturbation of my mind, during this fifteen or sixteen months' interval, was very great. I slept unquiet, dreamed always frightful dreams, and often started out of my sleep in the night. In the day great troubles overwhelmed my mind, and in the night I dreamed often of killing the savages, and of the reasons why I might justify the doing of it. But, to waive all this for a while, it was in the middle of May, on the sixteenth day, I think, as well as my poor wooden calendar would reckon, for I marked all upon the post still; I say, it was the sixteenth of May that it blew a very great storm of wind all day, with a great deal of lightning and thunder, and a very foul night it was after it. I know not what was the particular occasion of it, but as I was reading in the Bible, and taken up with very serious thoughts about my present condition, I was surprised with a noise of a gun, as I thought, fired at sea.

This was, to be sure, a surprise of a quite different nature from any I had met with before; for the notions this put into my thoughts were quite of another kind. I started up in the greatest haste imaginable, and, in a trice, clapped my ladder to the middle place of the rock, and pulled it after me; and mounting it the second time, got to the top of the hill the very moment that a flash of fire bid me listen for a second gun, which accordingly, in about half a minute, I heard; and, by the sound, knew that it was from that part of the sea where I was driven down the current in my boat.

I immediately considered that this must be some ship in distress, and that they had some comrade, or some other ship in company, and fired these guns for signals of distress, and to obtain help. I had this presence of mind, at that minute, as to think that though I could not help them, it may be they might help me; so I brought together all the dry wood I could get at hand, and, making a good handsome pile, I set it on fire upon the hill. The wood was dry, and blazed freely; and though the wind blew very hard, yet it burnt fairly out; so that I was certain, if there was any such thing as a ship, they must needs see it, and no doubt they did; for as soon as ever my fire blazed up I heard another gun, and after that several others, all from the same quarter. I plied my fire all night long till day broke; and when it was broad day, and the air cleared up, I saw something at a great distance at sea, full east of the island, whether a sail or a hull I could not distinguish, no, not with my glasses, the distance was so great, and the weather still something hazy also; at least it was so out at sea.

I looked frequently at it all that day, and soon perceived that it did not move; so I presently concluded that it was a ship at an anchor. And being eager, you may be sure, to be satisfied, I took my gun in my hand and run toward the south side of the island, to the rocks where I had formerly been carried away with the current; and getting up there, the weather by this time being perfectly clear, I could plainly see, to my great sorrow, the wreck of a ship, cast away in the night upon those concealed rocks which I found when I was out in my boat; and which rocks, as they checked the violence of the stream, and made a kind of counter-stream or eddy, were the occasion of my recovering from the most desperate, hopeless condition that ever I had been in in all my life.

Thus, what is one man's safety is another man's destruction; for it seems these men, whoever they were, being out of their knowledge, and the rocks being wholly under water, had been driven upon them in the night, the wind blowing hard at E. and E.N.E. Had they seen the island, as I must necessarily suppose they did not, they must, as I thought, have endeavoured to have saved themselves on shore by the help of their boat; but their firing of guns for help, especially when they saw, as I imagined, my fire, filled me with many thoughts. First, I imagined that upon seeing my light, they might have put themselves into their boat, and have endeavoured to make the shore; but that the sea going very high, they might have been cast away. Other times I imagined that they might have lost their boat before, as might be the case many ways; as, particularly, by the breaking of the sea upon their ship, which many times obliges men to stave, or take in pieces their boat, and sometimes to throw it overboard with their own hands. Other times I imagined they had some other ship or ships in company, who, upon the signals of distress they had made, had taken them up and carried them off. Other whiles I fancied they were all gone off to sea in their boat, and being hurried away by the current that I had been formerly in, were carried out into the great ocean, where there was nothing but misery and perishing; and that, perhaps, they might by this time think of starving, and of being in a condition to eat one another.

As all these were but conjectures at best, so, in the condition I was in, I could do no more than look on upon the misery of the poor men, and pity them; which had still this good effect on my side, that it gave me more and more cause to give thanks to God, who had so happily and comfortably provided for me in my desolate condition; and that of two ships' companies who were now cast away upon this part of the world, not one life should be spared but mine. I learned here again to observe, that it is very rare that the providence of God casts us into any condition of life so low, or any misery so great, but we may see something or other to be thankful for, and may see others in worse circumstances than our own.

Such certainly was the case of these men, of whom I could not so much as see room to suppose any of them were saved; nothing could make it rational so much as to wish or expect that they did not all perish there, except the possibility only of their being taken up by another ship in company; and this was but mere possibility indeed, for I saw not the least sign or appearance of any such thing.

I cannot explain, by any possible energy of words, what a strange longing or hankering of desires I felt in my soul upon this sight, breaking out sometimes thus: "O that there had been but one or two, nay, or but one soul, saved out of this ship, to have escaped to me, that I might but have had one companion, one fellow-creature, to have spoken to me, and to have conversed with!" In all the time of my

"...THE PRINT OF A MANS' NAKED FOOT ON THE SHORE..."
(J. FINNEMORE)

"...NO LESS THAN NINE NAKED SAVAGES SITTING ROUND A SMALL FIRE THEY HAD MADE..."
(A. E. JACKSON)

"AFTER REFRESHING MYSELF, I GOT ALL MY CARGO ON SHORE, AND BEGAN TO EXAMINE THE PARTICULARS."
(N. POCOCK)

"At length he came close to me, and then he kneeled down again..."
(J. Williamson)

solitary life, I never felt so earnest, so strong a desire after the society of my fellow-creatures, or so deep a regret at the want of it.

There are some secret moving springs in the affections, which, when they are set a going by some object in view, or be it some object, though not in view, yet rendered present to the mind by the power of imagination, that motion carries out the soul, by its impetuosity, to such violent, eager embracings of the object, that the absence of it is insupportable. Such were these earnest wishings that but one man had been saved! "O that it had been but one!" I believe I repeated the words, "O that it had been but one!" a thousand times; and the desires were so moved by it, that when I spoke the words my hands would clinch together, and my fingers press the palms of my hands, that if I had had any soft thing in my hand it would have crushed it involuntarily; and the teeth in my head would strike together, and set against one another so strong, that for some time I could not part them again.

Let the naturalists explain these things, and the reason and manner of them: all I can say to them is, to describe the fact, which was even surprising to me, when I found it, though I knew not from whence it proceeded: it was doubtless the effect of ardent wishes, and of strong ideas formed in my mind, realising the comfort which the conversation of one of my fellow-Christians would have been to me.

But it was not to be. Either their fate or mine, or both, forbid it; for, till the last year of my being on this island, I never knew whether any were saved out of that ship or no; and had only the affliction, some days after, to see the corpse of a drowned boy come on shore at the end of the island which was next the shipwreck. He had on no clothes but a seaman's waistcoat, a pair of open-kneed linen drawers, and a blue linen shirt; but nothing to direct me so much as to guess what nation he was of. He had nothing in his pocket but two pieces of eight and a tobacco-pipe. The last was to me of ten times more value than the first.

It was now calm, and I had a great mind to venture out in my boat to this wreck, not doubting but I might find something on board that might be useful to me. But that did not altogether press me so much as the possibility that there might be yet some living creature on board, whose life I might not only save, but might, by saving that life, comfort my own to the last degree. And this thought clung so to my heart, that I could not be quiet night nor day, but I must venture out in my boat on board this wreck; and committing the rest to God's providence, I thought, the impression was so strong upon my mind that it could not be resisted, that it must come from some invisible direction, and that I should be wanting to myself if I did not go.

Under the power of this impression, I hastened back to my castle, prepared everything for my voyage, took a quantity of bread, a great pot for fresh water, a compass to steer by, a bottle of rum (for I had still a great deal of that left), a basket full of raisins. And thus, loading myself with everything necessary, I went down to my boat, got the water out of her, and got her afloat, loaded all my cargo in her and then went home again for more. My second cargo was a great bag full of rice, the umbrella to set up over my head for shade, another large pot full of fresh water, and about two dozen of my small loaves, or barley-cakes, more than before, with a bottle of goat's milk and a cheese; all which, with great labour and sweat, I brought to my boat; and praying to God to direct my voyage, I put out; and rowing, or paddling, the canoe along the shore, I came at last to the utmost point of the island on that side, viz. N.E. And now I was to launch out into the ocean, and either to venture or not to venture. I looked on the rapid currents which ran constantly on both sides of the island at a distance, and which were very terrible to me, from the remembrance of the hazard I had been in before, and my heart began to fail me; for I foresaw that if I was driven into either of those currents, I should be carried a vast way out to sea, and perhaps out of my reach, or sight of the island again; and that then, as my boat was but small, if any little gale of wind should rise, I should be inevitably lost.

These thoughts so oppressed my mind, that I began to give over my enterprise; and having hauled my boat into a little creek on the shore, I stept out, and sate me down upon a little rising bit of ground, very pensive and anxious, between fear and desire, about my voyage; when, as I was musing, I could perceive that the tide was turned, and the flood come on; upon which my going was for so many hours impracticable. Upon this, presently it occurred to me that I should go up to the highest piece of ground I could find and observe, if I could, how the sets of the tide, or currents, lay when the flood came in, that I might judge whether, if I was driven one way out, I might not expect to be driven another way home, with the same rapidness of the currents. This thought was no sooner in my head but I cast my eye upon a little hill, which sufficiently overlooked the sea both ways, and from whence I had a clear view of the currents, or sets of the tide, and which way I was to guide myself in my return. Here I found, that as the current of the ebb set out close by the south point of the island, so the current of the flood set in close by the shore of the north side; and that I had nothing to do but to keep to the north of the island in my return, and I should do well enough.

Encouraged with this observation, I resolved the next morning to set out with the first of the tide, and reposing myself for the night in the canoe, under the great watch-coat I mentioned, I launched out. I made first a little out to sea full north, till I began to feel the benefit of the current which set eastward, and which carried me at a great rate; and yet did not so hurry me as the southern side current had done before, and so as to take from me all government of the boat; but having a strong steerage with

my paddle, I went at a great rate directly for the wreck, and in less than two hours I came up to it.

It was a dismal sight to look at. The ship, which, by it's building was Spanish, stuck fast, jammed in between two rocks. All the stern and quarter of her was beaten to pieces with the sea; and as her forecastle, which stuck in the rocks, had run on with great violence, her mainmast and foremast were brought by the board; that is to say, broken short off; but her boltsprit was sound, and the head and bow appeared firm. When I came close to her a dog appeared upon her, who, seeing me coming, yelped and cried; and as soon as I called to him, jumped into the sea to come to me, and I took him into the boat, but found him almost dead for hunger and thirst. I gave him a cake of my bread, and he eat it like a ravenous wolf that had been starving a fortnight in the snow. I then gave the poor creature some fresh water, with which if I would have let him, he would have burst himself.

After this I went on board; but the first sight I met with was two men drowned in the cook-room, or forecastle of the ship, with their arms fast about one another. I concluded, as is indeed probable, that when the ship struck, it being in a storm, the sea broke so high, and so continually over her, that the men were not able to bear it, and were strangled with the constant rushing in of the water, as much as if they had been under water. Besides the dog, there was nothing left in the ship that had life; nor any goods that I could see, but what were spoiled by the water. There were some casks of liquor, whether wine or brandy I knew not, which lay lower in the hold, and which, the water being ebbed out, I could see; but they were too big to meddle with. I saw several chests, which I believed belonged to some of the seamen; and I got two of them into the boat, without examining what was in them.

Had the stern of the ship been fixed, and the forepart broken off, I am persuaded I might have made a good voyage; for by what I found in these two chests, I had room to suppose the ship had a great deal of wealth on board; and if I may guess by the course she steered, she must have been bound from the Buenos Ayres, or the Rio de la Plata, in the south part of America, beyond the Brazils, to the Havana, in the Gulf of Mexico, and so perhaps to Spain. She had, no doubt, a great treasure in her, but of no use, at that time, to anybody; and what became of the rest of her people, I then knew not.

I found, besides these chests, a little cask full of liquor, of about twenty gallons, which I got into my boat with much difficulty. There were several muskets in a cabin, and a great powder-horn, with about four pounds of powder in it. As for the muskets, I had no occasion for them, so I left them, but took the powder-horn. I took a fire-shovel and tongs, which I wanted extremely; as also two little brass kettles, a copper pot to make chocolate, and a gridiron. And with this cargo, and the dog, I came away, the tide beginning to make home again; and the same evening, about an hour within night, I reached the island again, weary and fatigued to the last degree.

I reposed that night in the boat; and in the morning I resolved to harbour what I had gotten in my new cave, not to carry it home to my castle. After refreshing myself, I got all my cargo on shore, and began to examine the particulars. The cask of liquor I found to be a kind of rum, but not such as we had at the Brazils, and, in a word, not at all good. But when I came to open the chests, I found several things of great use to me. For example, I found in one a fine case of bottles, of an extraordinary kind, and filled with cordial waters, fine, and very good; the bottles held about three pints each, and were tipped with silver. I found two pots of very good succades, or sweetmeats, so fastened also on top, that the salt water had not hurt them; and two more of the same, which the water had spoiled. I found some very good shirts, which were very welcome to me; and about a dozen and a half of linen white handkerchiefs and coloured neckcloths. The former were also very welcome, being exceeding refreshing to wipe my face in a hot day. Besides this, when I came to the till in the chest, I found there three great bags of pieces of eight, which held out about eleven hundred pieces in all; and in one of them, wrapped up in a paper, six doubloons of gold, and some small bars or wedges of gold. I suppose they might all weigh near a pound.

The other chest I found had some clothes in it, but of little value; but by the circumstances, it must have belonged to the gunner's mate; though there was no powder in it, but about two pounds of fine glazed powder, in three small flasks, kept, I suppose, for charging their fowling-pieces on occasion. Upon the whole, I got very little by this voyage that was of any use to me; for as to the money, I had no manner of occasion for it; 'twas to me as the dirt under my feet; and I would have given it all for three or four pair of English shoes and stockings, which were things I greatly wanted, but had not had on my feet now for many years. I had indeed gotten two pair of shoes now, which I took off the feet of the two

drowned men whom I saw in the wreck, and I found two pair more in one of the chests, which were very welcome to me; but they were not like our English shoes, either for ease or service, being rather what we call pumps than shoes. I found in this seaman's chest about fifty pieces of eight in royals, but no gold. I suppose this belonged to a poorer man than the other, which seemed to belong to some officer.

Well, however, I lugged this money home to my cave, and laid it up, as I had done that before which I brought from our own ship; but it was great pity, as I said, that the other part of this ship had not come to my share, for I am satisfied I might have loaded my canoe several times over with money, which, if I had ever escaped to England, would have lain here safe enough till I might have come again and fetched it.

Having now brought all my things on shore, and secured them, I went back to my boat, and rowed or paddled her along the shore to her old harbour, where I laid her up, and made the best of my way to my old habitation, where I found everything safe and quiet. So I began to repose myself, live after my old fashion, and take care of my family affairs; and, for a while, I lived easy enough, only that I was more vigilant than I used to be, looked out oftener, and did not go abroad so much; and if at any time I did stir with any freedom, it was always to the east part of the island, where I was pretty well satisfied the savages never came, and where I could go without so many precautions, and such a load of arms and ammunition as I always carried with me if I went the other way.

CHAPTER FOURTEEN

I lived in this condition near two years more; but my unlucky head, that was always to let me know it was born to make my body miserable, was all this two years filled with projects and designs, how, if it were possible, I might get away from this island; for sometimes I was for making another voyage to the wreck, though my reasons told me that there was nothing left there worth the hazard of my voyage; sometimes for a ramble one way, sometimes another; and I believe verily, if I had had the boat that I went from Sallee in, I should have ventured to sea, bound anywhere, I knew not whither.

I have been, in all my circumstances, a memento to those who are touched with the general plague of mankind, whence, for aught I know, one-half of their miseries flow; I mean, that of not being satisfied with the station wherein God and Nature has placed them: for, not to look back upon my primitive condition, and the excellent advice of my father, the opposition to which was, as I may call it, my original sin, my subsequent mistakes of the same kind had been the means of my coming into this miserable condition; for had that Providence, which so happily seated me at the Brazils as a planter, blessed me with confined desires, and I could have been contented to have gone on gradually, I might have been, by this time, I mean in the time of my being in this island, one of the most considerable planters in the Brazils; nay, I am persuaded, that by the improvements I had made in that little time I lived there, and the increase I should probably have made if I had remained, I might have been worth a hundred thousand moidores. And what business had I to leave a settled fortune, a well-stocked plantation, improving and increasing, to turn supercargo to Guinea to fetch negroes, when patience and time would have so increased our stock at home, that we could have bought them at our own door from those whose business it was to fetch them; and though it had cost us something more, yet the difference of that price was by no means worth saving at so great a hazard.

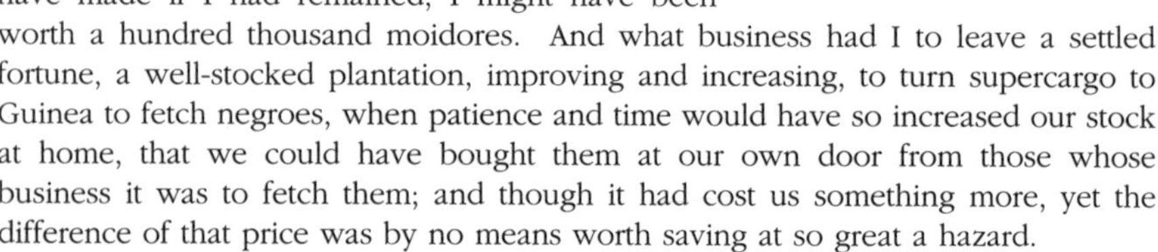

But as this is usually the fate of young heads, so reflection upon the folly of it is as ordinarily the exercise of more years, or of the dear-bought experience of time: and so it was with me now. And yet so deep had the mistake taken root in my temper, that I could not satisfy myself in my station, but was continually poring upon the means and possibility of my escape from this place. And that I may, with the greater pleasure to the reader, bring on the remaining part of my story, it may not be improper to give some account of my first conceptions on the subject of this foolish scheme for my escape, and how, and upon what foundation, I acted.

I am now to be supposed retired into my castle, after my late voyage to the wreck, my frigate laid up and secured under water, as usual, and my condition restored to what it was before; I had more wealth, indeed, than I had before, but was not at all the richer: for I had no more use for it than the Indians of Peru had before the Spaniards came there.

It was one of the nights in the rainy season in March, the four and twentieth year of my first setting foot in this island of solitariness. I was lying in my bed, or hammock, awake, very well in health, had no pain, no distemper, no uneasiness of body, no, nor any uneasiness of mind, more than ordinary, but could by no means close my eyes, that is, so as to sleep; no, not a wink all night long, otherwise than as follows.

It is as impossible, as needless, to set down the innumerable crowd of thoughts that whirled through that great thoroughfare of the brain, the memory, in this night's time. I ran over the whole history of my life in miniature, or by abridgment, as I may call it, to my coming to this island, and also of the part of my life since I came to this

island. In my reflections upon the state of my case since I came on shore on this island, I was comparing the happy posture of my affairs in the first years of my habitation here, compared to the life of anxiety, fear, and care which I had lived in, ever since I had seen the print of a foot in the sand: not that I did not believe the savages had frequented the island even all the while, and might have been several hundreds of them at times on shore there; but I had never known it, and was incapable of any apprehensions about it; my satisfaction was perfect, though my danger was the same, and I was as happy in not knowing my danger, as if I had never really been exposed to it. This furnished my thoughts with many very profitable reflections, and particularly this one: How infinitely good that Providence is, which has provided, in its government of mankind, such narrow bounds to his sight and knowledge of things; and though he walks in the midst of so many thousand dangers, the sight of which, if discovered to him, would distract his mind and sink his spirits, he is kept serene and calm, by having the events of things hid from his eyes, and knowing nothing of the dangers which surround him.

After these thoughts had for some time entertained me, I came to reflect seriously upon the real danger I had been in for so many years in this very island, and how I had walked about in the greatest security, and with all possible tranquillity, even when perhaps nothing but the brow of a hill, a great tree, or the casual approach of night, had been between me and the worst kind of destruction, viz. that of falling into the hands of cannibals and savages, who would have seized on me with the same view as I would of a goat or a turtle, and have thought it no more a crime to kill and devour me, than I did of a pigeon or a curlew. I would unjustly slander myself, if I should say I was not sincerely thankful to my great Preserver, to whose singular protection I acknowledged, with great humility, all these unknown deliverances were due, and without which I must inevitably have fallen into their merciless hands.

When these thoughts were over, my head was for some time taken up in considering the nature of these wretched creatures, I mean the savages, and how it came to pass in the world that the wise Governor of all things should give up any of His creatures to such inhumanity; nay, to something so much below even brutality itself, as to devour its own kind. But as this ended in some (at that time fruitless) speculations, it occurred to me to inquire what part of the world these wretches lived in? how far off the coast was from whence they came? what they ventured over so far from home for? what kind of boats they had? and why I might not order myself and my business so, that I might be as able to go over thither, as they were to come to me.

I never so much as troubled myself to consider what I should do with myself when I came thither; what would become of me, if I fell into the hands of the savages; or how I should escape from them, if they attempted me; no, nor so much as how it was possible for me to reach the coast, and not be attempted by some or other of them, without any possibility of delivering myself; and if I should not fall into their hands, what I should do for provision, or whither I should bend my course. None of these thoughts, I say, so much as came in my way; but my mind was wholly bent upon the notion of my passing over in my boat to the mainland. I looked back upon my present condition as the most miserable that could possibly be; that I was not able to throw myself into anything, but death, that could be called worse; that if I reached the shore of the main, I might perhaps meet with relief, or I might coast along, as I did on the shore of Africa, till I came to some inhabited country, and where I might find some relief; and after all, perhaps I might fall in with some Christian ship that might take me in; and if the worse came to the worst, I could but die, which would put an end to all these miseries at once. Pray note, all this was the fruit of a disturbed mind, an impatient temper, made, as it were, desperate by the long continuance of my troubles, and the disappointments I had met in the wreck I had been on board of, and where I had been so near obtaining what I so earnestly longed for, viz. somebody to speak to, and to learn some knowledge from of the place where I was, and of the probable means of my deliverance. I say, I was agitated wholly by these thoughts; all my calm of mind, in my resignation to Providence, and waiting the issue of the dispositions of Heaven, seemed to be suspended; and I had, as it were, no power to turn my thoughts to any thing but to the project of a voyage to the main, which came upon me with such force, and such an impetuosity of desire, that it was not to be resisted.

When this had agitated my thoughts for two hours, or more, with such violence that it set my very blood into a ferment, and my pulse beat as high as if I had been in a fever, merely with the extraordinary fervour of my mind about it, Nature, as if I had been fatigued and exhausted with the very thought of it, threw me into a sound sleep. One would have thought I should have dreamed of it, but I did not, nor of anything relating to it; but I dreamed that as I was going out in the morning, as usual, from my castle, I saw upon the shore two canoes and eleven savages coming to land, and that they brought with them another savage, who they were going to kill in order to eat him; when, on a sudden, the savage that they were going to kill jumped away and ran for his life. And I thought, in my sleep, that he came running into my little thick grove before my fortification to hide himself; and that I, seeing him alone, and not perceiving that the other sought him that way, showed myself to him, and smiling upon him, encouraged him; that he kneeled down to me, seeming to pray me to assist him; upon which I showed my ladder, made him go up, and carried him into my cave, and he became my servant; and that as soon as I had gotten this man, I said to myself, "Now I may certainly venture to the mainland; for this fellow will serve me as a pilot, and will tell me what to do, and whither to go for provisions, and whither not to go for fear of being devoured; what places to venture into, and what to escape." I waked with this thought, and was under such inexpressible impressions of joy at the prospect of my escape in my dream, that the disappointments which I felt upon coming to myself and finding it was no more than a dream were equally extravagant the other way, and threw me into a very great dejection of spirit.

Upon this, however, I made this conclusion; that my only way to go about an attempt for an escape was, if possible, to get a savage into my possession; and, if possible, it should be one of their prisoners who they had condemned to be eaten, and should bring thither to kill. But these thoughts still were attended with this

difficulty, that it was impossible to effect this without attacking a whole caravan of them, and killing them all; and this was not only a very desperate attempt, and might miscarry, but, on the other hand, I had greatly scrupled the lawfulness of it to me; and my heart trembled at the thoughts of shedding so much blood, though it was for my deliverance. I need not repeat the arguments which occurred to me against this, they being the same mentioned before. But though I had other reasons to offer now, viz. that those men were enemies to my life, and would devour me if they could; that it was self-preservation, in the highest degree, to deliver myself from this death of a life, and was acting in my own defence as much as if they were actually assaulting me, and the like; I say, though these things argued for it, yet the thoughts of shedding human blood for my deliverance were very terrible to me, and such as I could by no means reconcile myself to a great while.

However, at last, after many secret disputes with myself, and after great perplexities about it, for all these arguments, one way and another, struggled in my head a long time, the eager prevailing desire of deliverance at length mastered all the rest, and I resolved, if possible, to get one of those savages into my hands, cost what it would. My next thing then was to contrive how to do it, and this indeed was very difficult to resolve on. But as I could pitch upon no probable means for it, so I resolved to put myself upon the watch, to see them when they came on shore, and leave the rest to the event, taking such measures as the opportunity should present, let be what would be.

With these resolutions in my thoughts, I set myself upon the scout as often as possible, and indeed so often, till I was heartily tired of it; for it was above a year and half that I waited; and for great part of that time went out to the west end, and to the south-west corner of the island, almost every day, to see for canoes, but none appeared. This was very discouraging, and began to trouble me much; though I cannot say that it did in this case, as it had done some time before that, viz. wear off the edge of my desire to the thing. But the longer it seemed to be delayed, the more eager I was for it. In a word, I was not at first so careful to shun the sight of these savages, and avoid being seen by them, as I was now eager to be upon them.

Besides, I fancied myself able to manage one, nay, two or three savages, if I had them, so as to make them entirely slaves to me, to do whatever I should direct them, and to prevent their being able at any time to do me any hurt. It was a great while that I pleased myself with this affair; but nothing still presented. All my fancies and schemes came to nothing, for no savages came near me for a great while.

About a year and half after I had entertained these notions, and by long musing had, as it were, resolved them all into nothing, for want of an occasion to put them in execution, I was surprised, one morning early, with seeing no less than five canoes all on shore together on my side the island, and the people who belonged to them all landed, and out of my sight. The number of them broke all my measures; for seeing so many, and knowing that they always came four, or six, or sometimes more, in a boat, I could not tell what to think of it, or how to take my measures to attack twenty or thirty men single-handed; so I lay still in my castle, perplexed and discomforted. However, I put myself into all the same postures for an attack that I had formerly provided, and was just ready for action if anything had presented. Having waited a good while, listening to hear if they made any noise, at length, being very impatient, I set my guns at the foot of my ladder, and clambered up to the top of the hill, by my two stages, as usual; standing so, however, that my head did not appear above the hill, so that they could not perceive me by any means. Here I observed, by the help of my perspective glass, that they were no less than thirty in number, that they had a fire kindled, that they had had meat dressed. How they had cooked it, that I knew not, or what it was; but they were all dancing, in I know not how many barbarous gestures and figures, their own way, round the fire.

While I was thus looking on them, I perceived by my perspective two miserable wretches dragged from the boats, where, it seems, they were laid by, and were now brought out for the slaughter. I perceived one of them immediately fell, being knocked down, I suppose, with a club or wooden sword, for that was their way, and two or three others were at work immediately, cutting him open for their cookery, while the other victim was left standing by himself, till they should be ready for him. In that very moment this poor wretch seeing himself a little at liberty, Nature inspired him with hopes of life, and he started away from them, and ran with incredible swiftness along the sands directly towards me, I mean towards that part of the coast where my habitation was.

I was dreadfully frighted (that I must acknowledge) when I perceived him to run my way, and especially when, as I thought, I saw him pursued by the whole body; and now I expected that part of my dream was coming to pass, and that he would certainly take shelter in my grove; but I could not depend, by any means, upon my dream for the rest of it, viz. that the other savages would not pursue him thither, and find him there. However, I kept my station, and my spirits began to recover when I found that there was not above three men that followed him; and still more was I encouraged when I found that he outstripped them exceedingly in running, and gained ground of them; so that if he could but hold it for half-an-hour, I saw easily he would fairly get away from them all.

There was between them and my castle the creek, which I mentioned often at the first part of my story, when I landed my cargoes out of the ship; and this I saw plainly he must necessarily swim over, or the poor wretch would be taken there. But when the savage escaping came thither he made nothing of it, though the tide was then up; but plunging in, swam through in about thirty strokes or thereabouts, landed, and ran on with exceeding strength and swiftness. When the three persons came to the creek, I found that two of them could swim, but the third could not, and that, standing on the other side, he looked at the other, but went no further, and soon after went softly back, which, as it happened, was very well for him in the main.

I observed, that the two who swam were yet more than twice as long swimming over the creek as the fellow was that fled from them. It came now very warmly upon my thoughts, and indeed irresistibly, that now was my time to get me a servant, and perhaps a companion or assistant, and that I was called plainly by Providence to save this poor creature's life. I immediately ran down the ladders with all possible expedition, fetched my two guns, for they were both but at the foot of the ladders, as I observed above, and getting up again, with the same haste, to the top of the hill, I crossed toward the sea, and having a very short cut, and all down hill, clapped myself in the way between the pursuers and the pursued, hallooing aloud to him that fled, who, looking back, was at first perhaps as much frighted at me as at them; but I beckoned with my hand to him to come back; and, in the meantime, I slowly advanced towards the two that followed; then rushing at once upon the foremost, I knocked him down with the stock of my piece. I was loth to fire, because I would not have the rest hear; though, at that distance, it would not have been easily heard, and being out of sight of the smoke too, they would not have easily known what to make of it. Having knocked this fellow down, the other who pursued with him stopped, as if he had been frighted, and I advanced apace towards him; but as I came nearer, I perceived presently he had a bow and arrow, and was fitting it to shoot at me; so I was then necessitated to shoot at him first, which I did, and killed him at the first shoot.

The poor savage who fled, but had stopped, though he saw both his enemies fallen and killed, as he thought, yet was so frighted with the fire and noise of my piece, that he stood stock-still, and neither came forward or went backward, though he seemed rather inclined to fly still, than to come on. I hollowed again to him, and made signs to come forward, which he easily understood, and came a little away, then stopped again, and then a little further, and stopped again; and I could then perceive that he stood trembling, as if he had been taken prisoner, and had just been to be killed, as his two enemies were. I beckoned him again to come to me, and gave him all the signs of encouragement that I could think of; and he came nearer and nearer, kneeling down every ten or twelve steps, in token of acknowledgment for my saving his life. I smiled at him, and looked pleasantly, and beckoned to him to come still nearer. At length he came close to me, and then he kneeled down again, kissed the ground, and laid his head upon the ground, and taking me by the foot, set my foot upon his head. This, it seems, was in token of swearing to be my slave for ever. I

took him up, and made much of him, and encouraged him all I could. But there was more work to do yet; for I perceived the savage whom I knocked down was not killed, but stunned with the blow, and began to come to himself; so I pointed to him, and showing him the savage, that he was not dead, upon this he spoke some words to me; and though I could not understand them, yet I thought they were pleasant to hear; for they were the first sound of a man's voice that I had heard, my own excepted, for above twenty-five years. But there was no time for such reflections now. The savage who was knocked down recovered himself so far as to sit up upon the ground, and I perceived that my savage began to be afraid; but when I saw that, I presented my other piece at the man, as if I would shoot him. Upon this my savage, for so I call him now, made a motion to me to lend him my sword, which hung naked in a belt by my side; so I did. He no sooner had it but he runs to his enemy, and, at one blow, cut off his head as cleverly, no executioner in Germany could have done it sooner or better; which I thought very strange for one who, I had reason to believe, never saw a sword in his life before, except their own wooden swords. However, it seems, as I learned afterwards, they make their wooden swords so sharp, so heavy, and the wood is so hard, that they will cut off heads even with them, ay, and arms, and that at one blow too. When he had done this, he comes laughing to me in sign of triumph, and brought me the sword again, and with abundance of gestures, which I did not understand, laid it down, with the head of the savage that he had killed, just before me.

But that which astonished him most, was to know how I had killed the other Indian so far off; so pointing to him, he made signs to me to let him go to him; so I bade him go, as well as I could. When he came to him, he stood like one amazed, looking at him, turned him first on one side, then on t'other, looked at the wound the bullet had made, which, it seems, was just in his breast, where it had made a hole, and no great quantity of blood had followed; but he had bled inwardly, for he was quite dead. He took up his bow and arrows, and came back; so I turned to go away, and beckoned to him to follow me, making signs to him that more might come after them.

Upon this he signed to me that he should bury them with sand, that they might not be seen by the rest if they followed; and so I made signs again to him to do so. He fell to work, and in an instant he had scraped a hole in the sand with his hands big enough to bury the first in, and then dragged him into it, and covered him, and

'I was then necessitated to shoot at him first . . .' (p. 145)

did so also by the other. I believe he had buried them both in a quarter of an hour. Then calling him away, I carried him, not to my castle, but quite away to my cave, on the farther part of the island; so I did not let my dream come to pass in that part, viz. that he came into my grove for shelter.

Here I gave him bread and a bunch of raisins to eat, and a draught of water, which I found he was indeed in great distress for, by his running; and having refreshed him, I made signs for him to go lie down and sleep, pointing to a place where I had laid a great parcel of rice-straw, and a blanket upon it, which I used to sleep upon myself sometimes; so the poor creature laid down, and went to sleep.

He was a comely, handsome fellow, perfectly well made, with straight strong limbs, not too large, tall, and well shaped, and, as I reckon, about twenty-six years of age. He had a very good countenance, not a fierce and surly aspect, but seemed to have something very manly in his face; and yet he had all the sweetness and softness of an European in his countenance too, especially when he smiled. His hair was long and black, not curled like wool; his forehead very high and large; and a great vivacity and sparkling sharpness in his eyes. The colour of his skin was not quite black, but very tawny; and yet not of an ugly, yellow, nauseous tawny as the Brazilians and Virginians and other natives of America are, but of a bright kind of a dun olive colour, that had in it something very agreeable, though not very easy to describe. His face was round and plump; his nose small, not flat like the negroes; a very good mouth, thin lips, and his fine teeth well set, and white as ivory.

After he had slumbered, rather than slept, about half-an-hour, he waked again, and comes out of the cave to me, for I had been milking my goats, which I had in the enclosure just by. When he espied me, he came running to me, laying himself down again upon the ground, with all the possible signs of an humble, thankful disposition, making a many antic gestures to show it. At last he lays his head flat upon the ground, close to my foot, and sets my other foot upon his head, as he had done before, and after this made all the signs to me of subjection, servitude, and submission imaginable, to let me know how he would serve me as long as he lived. I understood him in many things, and let him know I was very well pleased with him. In a little time I began to speak to him, and teach him to speak to me; and, first, I made him know his name should be Friday, which was the day I saved his life. I called him so for the memory of the time. I likewise taught him to say Master, and then let him know that was to be my name. I likewise taught him to say Yes and No, and to know the meaning of them. I gave him some milk in an earthen pot, and let him see me drink it before him, and sop my bread in it; and I gave him a cake of bread to do the like, which he quickly complied with, and made signs that it was very good for him.

I kept there with him all that night; but as soon as it was day, I beckoned to him to come with me, and let him know I would give him some clothes; at which he seemed very glad, for he was stark naked. As we went by the place where he had buried the two men, he pointed exactly to the place, and showed me the marks that he had made to find them again, making signs to me that we should dig them up

again, and eat them. At this I appeared very angry, expressed my abhorrence of it, made as if I would vomit at the thoughts of it, and beckoned with my hand to him to come away; which he did immediately, with great submission. I then led him up to the top of the hill, to see if his enemies were gone; and pulling out my glass, I looked, and saw plainly the place where they had been, but no appearance of them or of their canoes; so that it was plain that they were gone, and had left their two comrades behind them, without any search after them.

But I was not content with this discovery; but having now more courage, and consequently more curiosity, I takes my man Friday with me, giving him the sword in his hand, with the bow and arrows at his back, which I found he could use very dexterously, making him carry one gun for me, and I two for myself, and away we marched to the place where these creatures had been; for I had a mind now to get some fuller intelligence of them. When I came to the place, my very blood ran chill in my veins, and my heart sunk within me, at the horror of the spectacle. Indeed, it was a dreadful sight, at least it was so to me, though Friday made nothing of it. The place was covered with human bones, the ground dyed with their blood, great pieces of flesh left here and there, half-eaten, mangled, and scorched; and, in short, all the tokens of the triumphant feast they had been making there, after a victory over their enemies. I saw three skulls, five hands, and the bones of three or four legs and feet, and abundance of other parts of the bodies; and Friday, by his signs, made me understand that they brought over four prisoners to feast upon; that three of them were eaten up, and that he, pointing to himself, was the fourth; that there had been a great battle between them and their next king, whose subjects it seems he had been one of, and that they had taken a great number of prisoners; all which were carried to several places by those that had taken them in the fight, in order to feast upon them, as was done here by these wretches upon those they brought hither.

I caused Friday to gather all the skulls, bones, flesh, and whatever remained, and lay them together on a heap, and make a great fire upon it, and burn them all to ashes. I found Friday had still a hankering stomach after some of the flesh, and was still a cannibal in his nature; but I discovered so much abhorrence at the very thoughts of it, and at the least appearance of it, that he durst not discover it; for I had, by some means, let him know that I would kill him if he offered it.

When we had done this we came back to our castle, and there I fell to work for my man Friday; and, first of all, I gave him a pair of linen drawers, which I had out of the poor gunner's chest I mentioned, and which I found in the wreck; and which, with a little alteration, fitted him very well. Then I made him a jerkin of goat's-skin, as well as my skill would allow, and I was now grown a tolerable good tailor; and I gave him a cap, which I made of a hare-skin, very convenient and fashionable enough; and thus he was clothed for the present tolerably well, and was mighty well pleased to see himself almost as well clothed as his master. It is true he went awkwardly in these things at first; wearing the drawers was very awkward to him, and the sleeves of the waistcoat galled his shoulders, and the inside of his arms; but a little easing them where he complained they hurt him, and using himself to them, at length he took to them very well.

The next day after I came home to my hutch with him, I began to consider where I should lodge him. And that I might do well for him, and yet be perfectly easy myself, I made a little tent for him in the vacant place between my two fortifications, in the inside of the last and in the outside of the first; and as there was a door or entrance there into my cave, I made a formal framed door-case, and a door to it of boards, and set it up in the passage, a little within the entrance; and causing the door to open on the inside, I barred it up in the night, taking in my ladders too; so that Friday could no way come at me in the inside of my innermost wall without making so much noise in getting over, that it must needs waken me; for my first wall had now a complete roof over it of long poles, covering all my tent, and leaning up to the side of the hill, which was again laid cross with smaller sticks instead of laths, and then thatched over a great thickness with the ricestraw, which was strong, like reeds; and at the hole or place which was left to go in or out by the ladder, I had placed a kind of trap-door, which, if it had been attempted on the outside, would not have opened at all, but would have fallen down, and made a great noise; and as to weapons, I took them all into my side every night.

But I needed none of all this precaution; for never man had a more faithful, loving, sincere servant than Friday was to me; without passions, sullenness, or designs, perfectly obliged and engaged; his very affections were tied to me, like those of a child to a father; and I dare say he would have sacrificed his life for the saving mine, upon any occasion whatsoever. The many testimonies he gave me of this put it out of doubt, and soon convinced me that I needed to use no precautions as to my safety on his account.

This frequently gave me occasion to observe, and that with wonder, that however it had pleased God, in His providence, and in the government of the works of His hands, to take from so great a part of the world of His creatures the best uses to which their faculties and the powers of their souls are adapted, yet that He has bestowed upon them the same powers, the same reason, the same affections, the same sentiments of kindness and obligation, the same passions and resentments of wrongs, the same sense of gratitude, sincerity, fidelity, and all the capacities of doing good, and receiving good, that He has given to us; and that when He pleases to offer to them occasions of exerting these, they are as ready, nay, more ready, to apply them to the right uses for which they were bestowed than we are. And this made me very melancholy sometimes, in reflecting, as the several occasions presented, how mean a use we make of all these, even though we have these powers enlightened by the great lamp of instruction, the Spirit of God, and by the knowledge of His word added to our understanding; and why it has pleased God to hide the like saving knowledge from so many millions of souls, who, if I might judge by this poor savage, would make a much better use of it than we did.

From hence, I sometimes was led too far, to invade the sovereignty of Providence, and, as it were, arraign the justice of so arbitrary a disposition of things, that should hide that light from some, and reveal it to others, and yet expect a like duty from both. But I shut it up, and checked my thoughts with this conclusion: first, That we did not know by what light and law these should be condemned: but that as God was necessarily, and, by the nature of His being, infinitely holy and just, so it could not be, but if these creatures were all sentenced to absence from Himself, it was on account of sinning against that light, which, as the Scripture says, was a law to themselves, and by such rules as their consciences would acknowledge to be just, though the foundation was not discovered to us; and, second, That still, as we all are the clay in the hand of the potter, no vessel could say to Him, "Why hast Thou formed me thus?"

But to return to my new companion. I was greatly delighted with him, and made it my business to teach him everything that was proper to make him useful, handy, and helpful; but especially to make him speak, and understand me when I spake. And he was the aptest scholar that ever was; and particularly was so merry, so constantly diligent, and so pleased when he could but understand me, or make me understand him, that it was very pleasant to me to talk to him. And now my life began to be so easy, that I began to say to myself, that could I but have been safe from more savages, I cared not if I was never to remove from the place while I lived.

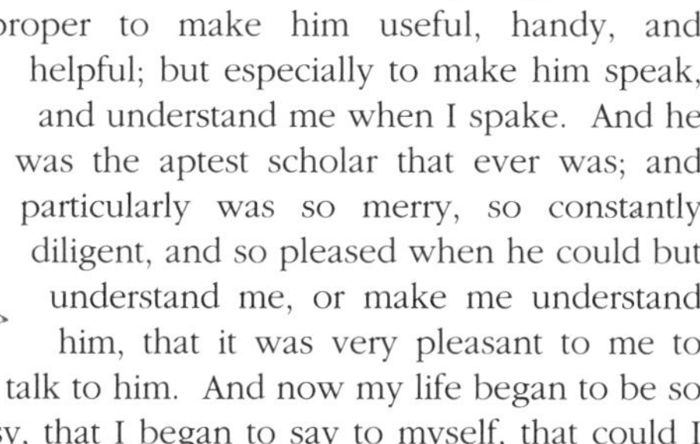

CHAPTER FIFTEEN

After I had been two or three days returned to my castle, I thought that, in order to bring Friday off from his horrid way of feeding, and from the relish of a cannibal's stomach, I ought to let him taste other flesh; so I took him out with me one morning to the woods. I went, indeed, intending to kill a kid out of my own flock, and bring him home and dress it; but as I was going, I saw a she-goat lying down in the shade, and two young kids sitting by her. I catched hold of Friday. "Hold," says I, "stand still," and made signs to him not to stir. Immediately I presented my piece, shot and killed one of the kids. The poor creature, who had, at a distance indeed, seen me kill the savage, his enemy, but did not know, or could imagine, how it was done, was sensibly surprised, trembled and shook, and looked so amazed, that I thought he would have sunk down. He did not see the kid I had shot at, or perceive I had killed it, but ripped up his waistcoat to feel if he was not wounded; and, as I found presently, thought I was resolved to kill him; for he came and kneeled down to me, and embracing my knees, said a great many things I did not understand; but I could easily see that the meaning was to pray me not to kill him.

I soon found a way to convince him that I would do him no harm; and taking him up by the hand, laughed at him, and pointing to the kid which I had killed, beckoned to him to run and fetch it, which he did; and while he was wondering, and looking to see how the creature was killed, I loaded my gun again; and by-and-by I saw a great fowl, like a hawk, sit upon a tree, within shot; so, to let Friday understand a little what I would do, I called him to me again, pointing at the fowl, which was indeed a parrot, though I thought it had been a hawk; I say, pointing to the parrot, and to my gun, and to the ground under the parrot, to let him see I would make it fall, I made him understand that I would shoot and kill that bird. Accordingly I fired, and bade him look, and immediately he saw the parrot fall. He stood like one frighted again, notwithstanding all I had said to him; and I found he was the more amazed, because he did not see me put anything into the gun, but thought that there must be some wonderful fund of death and destruction in that thing, able to kill man, beast, bird, or anything near or far off; and the astonishment this created in him was such as could not wear off for a long time; and I believe, if I would have let him, he would have worshipped me and my gun. As for the gun itself, he would not so much as touch it for several days after; but would speak to it, and talk to it, as if it had answered him, when he was by himself; which, as I afterwards learned of him, was to desire it not to kill him.

Well, after his astonishment was a little over at this, I pointed to him to run and fetch the bird I had shot, which he did, but stayed some time; for the parrot, not being quite dead, was fluttered a good way off from the place where she fell. However, he found her, took her up, and brought her to me; and as I had perceived his ignorance about the gun before, I took this advantage to charge the gun again, and not let him see me do it, that I might be ready for any other mark that might present. But nothing more offered at that time; so I brought home the kid, and the same evening I took the skin off, and cut it out as well as I could; and having a pot for that purpose, I boiled or stewed some of the flesh, and made some very good broth; and after I had begun to eat some, I gave some to my man, who seemed very glad of it, and liked it very well; but that which was strangest to him, was to see me eat salt with it. He made a sign to me that the salt was not good to eat, and putting a little into his own mouth, he seemed to nauseate it, and would spit and sputter at it, washing his mouth with fresh water after it. On the other hand, I took some meat in my mouth without salt, and I pretended to spit and sputter for want of salt, as fast as he had done at the salt. But it would not do; he would never care for salt with

his meat or in his broth; at least, not a great while, and then but a very little.

Having thus fed him with boiled meat and broth, I was resolved to feast him the next day with roasting a piece of the kid. This I did by hanging it before the fire in a string, as I had seen many people do in England, setting two poles up, one on each side of the fire, and one cross on the top, and tying the string to the cross stick, letting the meat turn continually. This Friday admired very much. But when he came to taste the flesh, he took so many ways to tell me how well he liked it, that I could not but understand him; and at last he told me he would never eat man's flesh any more, which I was very glad to hear.

The next day I set him to work to beating some corn out, and sifting it in the manner I used to do, as I observed before; and he soon understood how to do it as well as I, especially after he had seen what the meaning of it was, and that it was to make bread of; for after that I let him see me make my bread, and bake it too; and in a little time Friday was able to do all the work for me, as well as I could do it myself.

I began now to consider that, having two mouths to feed instead of one, I must provide more ground for my harvest, and plant a larger quantity of corn than I used to do; so I marked out a larger piece of land, and began the fence in the same manner as before, in which Friday not only worked very willingly and very hard, but did it very cheerfully; and I told him what it was for; that it was for corn to make more bread, because he was now with me, and that I might have enough for him and myself too. He appeared very sensible of that part, and let me know that he thought I had much more labour upon me on his account, than I had for myself; and that he would work the harder for me, if I would tell him what to do.

This was the pleasantest year of all the life I led in this place. Friday began to talk pretty well, and understand the names of almost everything I had occasion to call for, and of every place I had to send him to, and talk a great deal to me; so that, in short, I began now to have some use for my tongue again, which, indeed, I had very little occasion for before, that is to say, about speech. Besides the pleasure of talking to him, I had a singular satisfaction in the fellow himself. His simple, unfeigned honesty appeared to me more and more every day, and I began really to love the creature; and, on his side, I believe he loved me more than it was possible for him ever to love anything before.

I had a mind once to try if he had any hankering inclination to his own country again; and having learned him English so well that he could answer me almost any questions, I asked him whether the nation that he belonged to never conquered in battle? At which he smiled, and said, "Yes, yes, we always fight the better;" that is, he meant, always get the better in fight; and so we began the following discourse: "You always fight the better," said I. "How came you to be taken prisoner then, Friday?"

Friday. My nation beat much for all that.

Master. How beat? If your nation beat them, how came you to be taken?

Friday. They more many than my nation in the place where me was; they take one, two, three, and me. My nation overbeat them in the yonder place, where me no was; there my nation take one, two, great thousand.

Master. But why did not your side recover you from the hands of your enemies then?

Friday. They run one, two, three, and me, and make go in the canoe; my nation have no canoe that time.

Master. Well, Friday, and what does your nation do with the men they take? Do they carry them away and eat them, as these did?

Friday. Yes, my nation eats mans too; eat all up.

Master. Where do they carry them?

Friday. Go to other place, where they think.

Master. Do they come hither?

Friday. Yes, yes, they come hither; come other else place.

Master. Have you been here with them?

Friday. Yes, I been here. (Ponts to the N.W. side of the Island which, it seems, was their side.)

By this I understood that my man Friday had formerly been among the savages who used to come on shore on the farther part of the island, on the same man-eating occasions that he was now brought for; and, some time after, when I took the courage to carry him to that side, being the same I formerly mentioned, he presently knew the place, and told me he was there once when they eat up twenty men, two women, and one child. He could not tell twenty in English, but he numbered them by laying so many stones on a row, and pointing to me to tell them over.

I have told this passage, because it introduces what follows; that after I had had this discourse with him, I asked him how far it was from our island to the shore, and whether the canoes were not often lost. He told me there was no danger, no canoes ever lost; but that, after a little way out to the sea, there was a current and a wind, always one way in the morning, the other in the afternoon.

This I understood to be no more than the sets of the tide, as going out or coming in; but I afterwards understood it was occasioned by the great draught and reflux of the mighty river Orinoco, in the mouth of the gulf of which river, as I found

afterwards, our island lay; and this land which I perceived to the W. and N.W. was the great island Trinidad, on the north point of the mouth of the river. I asked Friday a thousand questions about the country, the inhabitants, the sea, the coast, and what nations were near. He told me all he knew, with the greatest openness imaginable. I asked him the names of the several nations of his sort of people, but could get no other name than Caribs; from whence I easily understood that these were the Caribbees, which our maps place on the part of America which reaches from the mouth of the river Orinoco to Guiana, and onwards to St. Martha. He told me that up a great way beyond the moon, that was, beyond the setting of the moon, which must be W. from their country, there dwelt white-bearded men, like me, and pointed to my great whiskers, which I mentioned before; and that they had killed much mans, that was his word; by all which I understood he meant the Spaniards, whose cruelties in America had been spread over the whole countries, and was remembered by all the nations from father to son.

I inquired if he could tell me how I might come from this island and get among those white men. He told me, "Yes, yes, I might go in two canoe." I could not understand what he meant, or make him describe to me what he meant by two canoe; till at last, with great difficulty, I found he meant it must be in a large great boat, as big as two canoes.

This part of Friday's discourse began to relish with me very well; and from this time I entertained some hopes that, one time or other, I might find an opportunity to make my escape from this place, and that this poor savage might be a means to help me to do it.

During the long time that Friday had now been with me, and that he began to speak to me, and understand me, I was not wanting to lay a foundation of religious knowledge in his mind; particularly I asked him one time, Who made him? The poor creature did not understand me at all, but thought I had asked who was his father. But I took it by another handle, and asked him who made the sea, the ground we walked on, and the hills and woods? He told me it was one old Benamuckee, that lived beyond all. He could describe nothing of this great person, but that he was very old, much older, he said, than the sea or the land, than the moon or the stars. I asked him then, if this old person had made all things, why did not all things worship him? He looked very grave, and with a perfect look of innocence said, "All things do say O to him." I asked him if the people who die in his country went away anywhere? He said, "Yes, they all went to Benamuckee." Then I asked him whether these they eat up went thither too? He said "Yes."

From these things I began to instruct him in the knowledge of the true God. I told him that the great Maker of all things lived up there, pointing up towards heaven; that He governs the world by the same power and providence by which He had made it; that He was omnipotent, could do everything for us, give everything to us, take everything from us; and thus, by degrees, I opened his eyes. He listened with great attention, and received with pleasure the notion of Jesus Christ being sent to redeem us, and of the manner of making our prayers to God, and His being able to hear us, even into heaven. He told me one day that if our God could hear us up beyond the sun, He must needs be a greater God than their Benamuckee, who lived but a little way off, and yet could not hear till they went up to the great mountains where he dwelt to speak to him. I asked him if he ever went thither to speak to him? He said, No; they never went that were young men; none went thither but the old men, who he called their Oowokakee, that is, as I made him explain it to me, their religious, or clergy; and that they went to say O! (so he called saying prayers), and then came back, and told them what Benamuckee said. By this I observed that there is priestcraft even amongst the most blinded, ignorant pagans in the world; and the policy of making a secret religion in order to preserve the veneration of the people to the clergy is not only to be found in the Roman, but perhaps among all religions in the world, even among the most brutish and barbarous savages.

I endeavoured to clear up this fraud to my man Friday, and told him that the pretence of their old men going up to the mountains to say O to their god Benamuckee was a cheat, and their bringing word from thence what he said was much more so; that if they met with any answer, or spoke with any one there, it must be with an evil spirit; and then I entered into a long discourse with him about the devil, the original of him, his rebellion against God, his enmity to man, the reason of it, his setting himself up in the dark parts of the world to be worshipped instead of God, and as God, and the many stratagems he made use of to delude mankind to their ruin; how he had a secret access to our passions and to our affections, to adapt his snares so to our inclinations, as to cause us even to be our own tempters, and to run upon our destruction by our own choice.

I found it was not so easy to imprint right notions in his mind about the devil, as it was about the being of a God. Nature assisted all my arguments to evidence to him even the necessity of a great First Cause, and overruling, governing Power, a secret, directing Providence, and of the equity and justice of paying homage to Him that made us, and the like. But there appeared nothing of all this in the notion of an evil spirit; of his original, his being, his nature, and, above all, of his inclination to do evil, and to draw us in to do so too: and the poor creature puzzled me once in such a manner, by a question merely natural and innocent, that I scarce knew what to say to him. I had been talking a great deal to him of the power of God, His omnipotence, His aversion to sin, His being a consuming fire to the workers of iniquity; how, as He had made us all, He could destroy us and all the world in a moment; and he listened with great seriousness to me all the while.

After this I had been telling him how the devil was God's enemy in the hearts of

men, and used all his malice and skill to defeat the good designs of Providence, and to ruin the kingdom of Christ in the world, and the like. "Well," says Friday, "but you say God is so strong, so great; is He not much strong, much might as the devil?" "Yes, yes," says I, "Friday, God is stronger than the devil; God is above the devil, and therefore we pray to God to tread him down under our feet, and enable us to resist his temptations, and quench his fiery darts." "But," says he again, "if God much strong, much might as the devil, why God no kill the devil, so make him no more do wicked?"

I was strangely surprised at his question; and after all, though I was now an old man, yet I was but a young doctor, and ill enough qualified for a casuist, or a solver of difficulties; and at first I could not tell what to say; so I pretended not to hear him, and asked him what he said? But he was too earnest for an answer to forget his question, so that he repeated it in the very same broken words as above. By this time I had recovered myself a little, and I said, "God will at last punish him severely; he is reserved for the judgment, and is to be cast into the bottomless pit, to dwell with everlasting fire." This did not satisfy Friday; but he returns upon me, repeating my words, "Reserve, at last, me no understand; but why not kill the devil now? not kill great ago?" "You may as well ask me," said I, "why God does not kill you and I, when we do wicked things here that offend Him; we are preserved to repent and be pardoned." He muses awhile at this. "Well, well," says he, mighty affectionately, "that well; so you, I, devil, all wicked, all preserve, repent, God pardon all." Here I was run down again by him to the last degree; and it was a testimony to me, how the mere notions of nature, though they will guide reasonable creatures to the knowledge of a God, and of a worship or homage due to the supreme being of God, as the consequence of our nature, yet nothing but divine revelation can form the knowledge of Jesus Christ, and of redemption purchased for us, of a Mediator of the new covenant, and of an Intercessor at the footstool of God's throne: I say, nothing but a revelation from Heaven can form these in the soul; and that, therefore, the Gospel of our Lord and Saviour Jesus Christ, I mean the Word of God, and the Spirit of God, promised for the guide and sanctifier of His people, are the absolutely necessary instructors of the souls of men in the saving knowledge of God, and the means of salvation.

I therefore diverted the present discourse between me and my man, rising up hastily, as upon some sudden occasion of going out; then sending him for something a good way off, I seriously prayed to God that He would enable me to instruct savingly this poor savage, assisting by His Spirit the heart of the poor ignorant creature to receive the light of the knowledge of God in Christ, reconciling him to himself, and would guide me to speak so to him from the Word of God as his conscience might be convinced, his eyes opened, and his soul saved. When he came again to me, I entered into a long discourse with him upon the subject of the redemption of man by the Saviour of the world, and of the doctrine of the Gospel preached from Heaven, viz. of repentance towards God, and faith in our blessed Lord Jesus. I then explained to him as well as I could why our blessed redeemer took not on Him the nature of angels, but the seed of Abraham; and how, for that reason, the fallen angels had no share in the redemption; that He came only to the lost sheep of the house of Israel, and the like.

I had, God knows, more sincerity than knowledge in all the methods I took for this poor creature's instruction, and must acknowledge, what I believe all that act upon the same principle will find, that in laying things open to him, I really informed and instructed myself in many things that either I did not know, or had not fully considered before, but which occurred naturally to my mind upon searching into them, for the information of this poor savage; and I had more affection in my inquiry after things upon this occasion than ever I felt before: so that, whether this poor wild wretch was the better for me or no, I had great reason to be thankful that ever he came to me; my grief sat lighter upon me; my habitation grew comfortable to me beyond measure; and when I reflected, that in this solitary life which I had been confined to, I had not only been moved myself to look up to Heaven, and to seek to the hand that had brought me here, but was now to be made an instrument, under Providence, to save the life, and, for aught I know, the soul of a poor savage, and bring him to the true knowledge of religion, and of the Christian doctrine, that he might know Christ Jesus, to know whom is life eternal; I say, when I reflected upon all these things, a secret joy ran through every part of my soul, and I frequently rejoiced that ever I was brought to this place, which I had so often thought the most dreadful of all afflictions that could possibly have befallen me.

In this thankful frame I continued all the remainder of my time, and the conversation which employed the hours between Friday and I was such as made the three years which we lived there together perfectly and completely happy, if any such thing as complete happiness can be formed in a sublunary state. The savage was now a good Christian, a much better than I; though I have reason to hope, and bless God for it, that we were equally penitent, and comforted, restored penitents. We had here the Word of God to read, and no farther off from His Spirit to instruct than if we had been in England.

I always applied myself to reading the Scripture, to let him know, as well as I could, the meaning of what I read; and he again, by his serious inquiries and questionings, made me, as I said before, a much better scholar in the Scripture-

knowledge than I should ever have been by my own private mere reading. Another thing I cannot refrain from observing here also, from experience in this retired part of my life, viz. how infinite and inexpressible a blessing it is that the knowledge of God, and of the doctrine of salvation by Christ Jesus, is so plainly laid down in the Word of God, so easy to be received and understood, that, as the bare reading the Scripture made me capable of understanding enough of my duty to carry me directly on to the great work of sincere repentance for my sins, and laying hold of a Saviour for life and salvation, to a stated reformation in practice, and obedience to all God's commands, and this without any teacher or instructor, I mean human; so, the same plain instruction sufficiently served to the enlightening this savage creature, and bringing him to be such a Christian, as I have known few equal to him in my life.

As to all the disputes, wranglings, strife, and contention which has happened in the world about religion, whether niceties in doctrines, or schemes of Church government, they were all perfectly useless to us; as, for aught I can yet see, they have been to all the rest in the world. We had the sure guide to heaven, viz. the Word of God; and we had, blessed be God, comfortable views of the Spirit of God teaching and instructing us by His Word, leading us into all truth, and making us both willing and obedient to the instruction of His Word; and I cannot see the least use that the greatest knowledge of the disputed points in religion, which have made such confusions in the world, would have been to us if we could have obtained it. But I must go on with the historical part of things, and take every part in its order.

After Friday and I became more intimately acquainted, and that he could understand almost all I said to him, and speak fluently, though in broken English, to me, I acquainted him with my own story, or at least so much of it as related to my coming into the place; how I had lived there, and how long. I let him into the mystery, for such it was to him, of gunpowder and bullet, and taught him how to shoot; I gave him a knife, which he was wonderfully delighted with, and I made him a belt, with a frog hanging to it, such as in England we wear hangers in; and in the frog, instead of a hanger, I gave him a hatchet, which was not only as good a weapon, in some cases, but much more useful upon other occasions.

I described to him the country of Europe, and particularly England, which I came from; how we lived, how we worshipped God, how we behaved to one another, and how we traded in ships to all parts of the world. I gave him an account of the wreck which I had been on board of, and showed him, as near as I could, the place where she lay; but she was all beaten in pieces before, and gone.

I showed him the ruins of our boat, which we lost when we escaped, and which I could not stir with my whole strength then, but was now fallen almost all to pieces. Upon seeing this boat, Friday stood musing a great while, and said nothing. I asked him what it was he studied upon. At last says he, "Me see such boat like come to place at my nation."

I did not understand him a good while; but at last, when I had examined further into it, I understood by him that a boat, such as that had been, came on shore upon the country where he lived; that is, as he explained it, was driven thither by stress of weather. I presently imagined that some European ship must have been cast away upon their coast, and the boat might get loose and drive ashore; but was so dull, that I never once thought of men making escape from a wreck thither, much less whence they might come; so I only inquired after a description of the boat.

Friday described the boat to me well enough; but brought me better to understand him when he added with some warmth, "We save the white mans from drown." Then I presently asked him if there was any white mans, as he called them, in the boat. "Yes," he said, "the boat full of white mans." I asked him how many. He told upon his fingers seventeen. I asked him then what became of them. He told me, "They live, they dwell at my nation."

This put new thoughts into my head; for I presently imagined that these might be the men belonging to the ship that was cast away in sight of my island, as I now call it; and who, after the ship was struck on the rock, and they saw her inevitably lost, had saved themselves in their boat, and were landed upon that wild shore among the savages.

Upon this I inquired of him more critically what was become of them. He assured me they lived still there; that they had been there about four years; that the savages let them alone, and gave them victuals to live. I asked him how it came to pass they did not kill them, and eat them. He said, "No, they make brother with them"; that is, as I understood him, a truce; and then he added, "They no eat mans but when make the war fight"; that is to say, they never eat any men but such as come to fight with them and are taken in battle.

It was after this some considerable time, that being on the top of the hill, at the east side of the island, (from whence as I have said, I had in a clear day discovered the main or continent of America), Friday, the weather being very serene, looks very earnestly towards the mainland, and, in a kind of surprise, falls a-jumping and dancing, and calls out to me, for I was at some distance from him. I asked him what was the matter? "O joy!" says he, "O glad! there see my country, there my nation!"

I observed an extraordinary sense of pleasure appeared in his face, and his eyes sparkled, and his countenance discovered a strange eagerness, as if he had a mind to be in his own country again; and this observation of mine put a great many thoughts into me, which made me at first not so easy about my new man Friday as I was before; and I made no doubt but that if Friday could get back to his own nation again, he would not only forget all his religion, but all his obligation to me; and would be forward enough to give his countrymen an account of me, and come back perhaps with a hundred or two of them, and make a feast upon me, at which he might be as merry as he used to be with those of his enemies, when they were taken in war.

But I wronged the poor honest creature very much, for which I was very sorry afterwards. However, as my jealousy increased, and held me some weeks, I was a little more circumspect, and not so familiar and kind to him as before; in which I was certainly in the wrong too, the honest, grateful creature having no thought about it but what consisted with the best principles, both as a religious Christian and as a grateful friend, as appeared afterwards to my full satisfaction.

While my jealousy of him lasted, you may be sure I was every day pumping him, to see if he would discover any of the new thoughts which I suspected were in him; but I found everything he said was so honest and so innocent, that I could find nothing to nourish my suspicion; and, in spite of all my uneasiness, he made me at last entirely his own again, nor did he in the least perceive that I was uneasy, and therefore I could not suspect him of deceit.

One day, walking up the same hill, but the weather being hazy at sea, so that we could not see the continent, I called to him, and said, "Friday, do not you wish yourself in your own country, your own nation?" "Yes," he said, "I be much O glad to be at my own nation." "What would you do there?" said I. "Would you turn wild again, eat men's flesh again, and be a savage as you were before?" He looked full of concern, and shaking his head said, "No, no; Friday tell them to live good; tell them to pray God; tell them to eat corn-bread, cattle-flesh, milk, no eat man again." "Why then," said I to him, "they will kill you." He looked grave at that, and then said, "No, they no kill me, they willing love learn." He meant by this they would be willing to learn. He added, they learned much of the bearded mans that come in the boat. Then I asked him if he would go back to them? He smiled at that, and told me he could not swim so far. I told him I would make a canoe for him. He told me he would go, if I would go with him. "I go!" says I; "why, they will eat me if I come there." "No, no," says he, "me make they no eat you; me make they much love you." He meant, he would tell them how I had killed his enemies, and saved his life, and so he would make them love me. Then he told me, as well as he could, how kind they were to seventeen white men, or bearded men, as he called them, who came on shore there in distress.

From this time I confess I had a mind to venture over, and see if I could possibly join with these bearded men, who, I made no doubt, were Spaniards or Portuguese; not doubting but, if I could, we might find some method to escape from thence, being upon the continent, and a good company together, better than I could from an island forty miles off the shore, and alone, without help. So, after some days, I took Friday to work again, by way of discourse, and told him I would give him a boat to go back to his own nation; and accordingly I carried him to my frigate, which lay on the other side of the island, and having cleared it of water, for I always kept it sunk in the water, I brought it out, showed it him, and we both went into it.

I found he was a most dexterous fellow at managing it, would make it go almost as swift and fast again as I could. So when he was in I said to him, "Well now, Friday, shall we go to your nation?" He looked very dull at my saying so, which, it seems, was because he thought the boat too small to go so far. I told him then I had a bigger: so the next day I went to the place where the first boat lay which I had made, but which I could not get into water. He said that was big enough; but then, as I had taken no care of it, and it had lain two or three and twenty years there, the sun had split and dried it, that it was in a manner rotten. Friday told me such a boat would do very well, and would carry "much enough victual, drink, bread"; that was his way of talking.

CHAPTER SIXTEEN

Upon the whole, I was by this time so fixed upon my design of going over with him to the continent, that I told him we would go and make one as big as that, and he should go home in it. He answered not one word, but looked very grave and sad. I asked him what was the matter with him? He asked me again thus, "Why you angry mad with Friday? what me done?" I asked him what he meant. I told him I was not angry with him at all. "No angry! no angry!" says he, repeating the words several times. "Why send Friday home away to my nation?" "Why," says I, "Friday, did you not say you wished you were there?" "Yes, yes," says he, "wish be both there, no wish Friday there, no master there." In a word, he would not think of going there without me. "I go there, Friday?" says I; "what shall I do there?" He turned very quick upon me at this: "You do great deal much good," says he; "you teach wild mans to be good, sober, tame mans; you tell them know God, pray God, and live new life." "Alas! Friday," says I, "thou knowest not what you sayest. I am but an ignorant man myself." "Yes, yes," says he, "you teachee me good, you teachee them good." "No, no, Friday," says I, "you shall go without me; leave me here to live by myself, as I did before." He looked confused again at that word, and running to one of the hatchets which he used to wear, he takes it up hastily, comes and gives it me. "What must I do with this?" says I to him. "You take kill Friday," said he. "What must I kill you for?" said I again. He returns very quick, "What you send Friday away for? Take kill Friday, no send Friday away." This he spoke so earnestly, that I saw tears stand in his eyes. In a word, I so plainly discovered the utmost affection in him to me, and a firm resolution in him, that I told him then, and often after, that I would never send him away from me if he was willing to stay with me.

Upon the whole, as I found by all his discourse a settled affection to me, and that nothing should part him from me, so I found all the foundation of his desire to go to his own country was laid in his ardent affection to the people, and his hopes of my doing them good; a thing which, as I had no notion of myself, so I had not the least thought or intention or desire of undertaking it. But still I found a strong inclination to my attempting an escape, as above, founded on the supposition gathered from the

discourse, viz. that there were seventeen bearded men there; and, therefore, without any more delay I went to work with Friday to find out a great tree proper to fell, and make a large periagua, or canoe, to undertake the voyage. There were trees enough in the island to have built a little fleet, not of periaguas and canoes, but even of good large vessels. But the main thing I looked at was, to get one so near the water that we might launch it when it was made, to avoid the mistake I committed at first.

At last Friday pitched upon a tree, for I found he knew much better than I what kind of wood was fittest for it; nor can I tell, to this day, what wood to call the tree we cut down, except that it was very like the tree we call fustic, or between that and the Nicaragua wood, for it was much of the same colour and smell. Friday was for burning the hollow or cavity of this tree out, to make it for a boat, but I showed him how rather to cut it out with tools; which, after I had showed him how to use, he did very handily; and in about a month's hard labour we finished it, and made it very handsome; especially when, with our axes, which I showed him how to handle, we cut and hewed the outside into the true shape of a boat. After this, however, it cost us near a fortnight's time to get her along, as it were inch by inch, upon great rollers into the water; but when she was in, she would have carried twenty men with great ease.

When she was in the water, and though she was so big, it amazed me to see with what dexterity, and how swift my man Friday would manage her, turn her, and paddle her along. So I asked him if he would, and if we might venture over in her. "Yes," he said, "he venture over her very well, though great blow wind." However, I had a farther design that he knew nothing of, and that was to make a mast and sail, and to fit her with an anchor and cable. As to a mast, that was easy enough to get; so I pitched upon a straight young cedar tree, which I found near the place, and which there was great plenty of in the island; and I set Friday to work to cut it down, and gave him directions how to shape and order it. But as to the sail, that was my particular care. I knew I had old sails, or rather pieces of old sails enough; but as I had had them now twenty-six years by me, and had not been very careful to preserve them, not imagining that I should ever have this kind of use for them, I did not doubt but they were all rotten, and, indeed, most of them were so. However, I found two pieces which appeared pretty good, and with these I went to work, and with a great deal of pains, and awkward tedious stitching (you may be sure) for want of needles, I, at length, made a three-corner ugly thing, like what we call in England a shoulder-of-mutton sail, to go with a boom at bottom, and a little short sprit at the top, such as usually our ships' longboats sail with, and such as I best knew how to manage; because it was such a one as I had to the boat in which I made my escape from Barbary, as related in the first part of my story.

I was near two months performing this last work, viz. rigging and fitting my mast and sails; for I finished them very complete, making a small stay, and a sail, or foresail, to it, to assist, if we should turn to windward; and, which was more than all, I fixed a rudder to the stern of her to steer with; and though I was but a bungling shipwright, yet as I knew the usefulness, and even necessity, of such a thing, I applied myself with so much pains to do it, that at last I brought it to pass; though, considering the many dull contrivances I had for it that failed, I think it cost me almost as much labour as making the boat.

After all this was done too, I had my man Friday to teach as to what belonged to the navigation of my boat; for though he knew very well how to paddle a canoe, he knew nothing what belonged to a sail and a rudder; and was the most amazed when he saw me work the boat to and again in the sea by the rudder, and how the sail jibbed, and filled this way, or that way, as the course we sailed changed; I say, when he saw this, he stood like one astonished and amazed. However, with a little use I made all these things familiar to him, and he became an expert sailor, except that as to the compass I could make him understand very little of that. On the other hand, as there was very little cloudy weather, and seldom or never any fogs in those parts, there was the less occasion for a compass, seeing the stars were always to be seen by night, and the shore by day, except in the rainy seasons, and then nobody cared to stir abroad, either by land or sea.

I was now entered on the seven and twentieth year of my captivity in this place; though the three last years that I had this creature with me ought rather to be left out of the account, my habitation being quite of another kind than in all the rest of the time. I kept the anniversary of my landing here with the same thankfulness to God for His mercies as at first; and if I had such cause of acknowledgment at first, I had much more so now, having such additional testimonies of the care of Providence over me, and the great hopes I had of being effectually and speedily delivered; for I had an invincible impression upon my thoughts that my deliverance was at hand, and that I should not be another year in this place. However, I went on with my husbandry, digging, planting, fencing, as usual. I gathered and cured my grapes, and did every necessary thing as before.

The rainy season was, in the meantime, upon me, when I kept more within doors than at other times; so I had stowed our new vessel as secure as we could, bringing her up into the creek, where, as I said, in the beginning I landed my rafts from the ship; and hauling her up to the shore at high-water mark, I made my man Friday dig a little dock, just big enough to hold her, and just deep enough to give her water enough to float in; and then, when the tide was out, we made a strong dam across the end of it, to keep the water out; and so she lay dry, as to the tide from the sea; and to keep the rain off, we laid a great many boughs of trees, so thick, that she was as well thatched as a house; and thus we waited for the month of November and December, in which I designed to make my adventure.

When the settled season began to come in, as the thought of my design returned with the fair weather, I was preparing daily for the voyage; and the first thing I did was to lay by a certain quantity of provisions, being the stores for our voyage; and intended, in a week or a fortnight's time, to open the dock, and launch out our boat. I was busy one morning upon something of this kind, when I called to Friday, and bid him go to the sea-shore and see if he could find a turtle, or tortoise, a thing which we generally got once a week, for the sake of the eggs as well as the flesh. Friday had not been long gone when he came running back, and flew over my outer wall,

or fence, like one that felt not the ground, or the steps he set his feet on; and before I had time to speak to him, he cries out to me, "O master! O master! O sorrow! O bad!" "What's the matter, Friday?" says I. "O yonder, there," says he, "one, two, three canoe! one, two, three!" By his way of speaking, I concluded there were six; but, on inquiry, I found it was but three. "Well, Friday," says I, "do not be frighted." So I heartened him up as well as I could. However, I saw the poor fellow was most terribly scared; for nothing ran in his head but that they were come to look for him, and would cut him in pieces, and eat him; and the poor fellow trembled so, that I scarce knew what to do with him. I comforted him as well as I could, and told him I was in as much danger as he, and that they would eat me as well as him. "But," says I, "Friday, we must resolve to fight them. Can you fight, Friday?" "Me shoot," says he; "but there come many great number." "No matter for that," said I again; "our guns will fright them that we do not kill." So I asked him whether, if I resolved to defend him, he would defend me, and stand by me, and do just as I bid him. He said, "Me die when you bid die, master." So I went and fetched a good dram of rum, and gave him; for I had been so good a husband of my rum, that I had a great deal left. When he had drank it, I made him take the two fowling-pieces, which we always carried, and load them with large swan-shot, as big as small pistol-bullets. Then I took four muskets, and loaded them with two slugs and five small bullets each; and my two pistols I loaded with a brace of bullets each. I hung my great sword, as usual, naked by my side, and gave Friday his hatchet.

When I had thus prepared myself, I took my perspective glass, and went up to the side of the hill to see what I could discover; and I found quickly, by my glass, that there were one and twenty savages, three prisoners, and three canoes, and that their whole business seemed to be the triumphant banquet upon these three human bodies; a barbarous feast indeed, but nothing more than, as I had observed, was usual with them.

I observed also that they were landed, not where they had done when Friday made his escape, but nearer to my creek, where the shore was low, and where a thick wood came close almost down to the sea. This, with the abhorrence of the inhuman errand these wretches came about, filled me with such indignation, that I came down again to Friday, and told him I was resolved to go down to them, and kill them all, and asked him if he would stand by me. He was now gotten over his fright, and his spirits being a little raised with the dram I had given him, he was very cheerful, and told me, as before, he would die when I bid die.

In this fit of fury, I took first and divided the arms which I had charged, as before, between us. I gave Friday one pistol to stick in his girdle, and three guns upon his shoulder; and I took one pistol, and the other three myself, and in this posture we marched out. I took a small bottle of rum in my pocket, and gave Friday a large bag with more powder and bullet; and as to orders, I charged him to keep close behind me, and not to stir, or shoot, or do anything, till I bid him, and in the meantime not to speak a word. In this posture I fetched a compass to my right hand of near a mile, as well to get over the creek as to get into the wood, so that I might come within shot of them before I should be discovered, which I had seen, by my glass, it was easy to do.

While I was making this march, my former thoughts returning, I began to abate my resolution. I do not mean that I entertained any fear of their number; for as they were naked, unarmed wretches, 'tis certain I was superior to them; nay, though I had been alone. But it occurred to my thoughts, what call, what occasion, much less what necessity, I was in to go and dip my hands in blood, to attack people who had neither done or intended me any wrong? Who, as to me, were innocent, and whose barbarous customs were their own disaster; being, in them, a token indeed of God's having left them, with the other nations of that part of the world, to such stupidity, and to such inhuman courses; but did not call me to take upon me to be a judge of their actions, much less an executioner of His justice; that whenever He thought fit, He would take the cause into His own hands, and by national vengeance, punish them, as a people, for national crimes; but that, in the meantime, it was none of my business; that, it was true, Friday might justify it, because he was a declared enemy, and in a state of war with those very particular people, and it was lawful for him to attack them; but I could not say the same with respect to me. These things were so warmly pressed upon my thoughts all the way as I went, that I resolved I would only go and place myself near them, that I might observe their barbarous feast, and that I would act then as God should direct; but that, unless something offered that was more a call to me than yet I knew of, I would not meddle with them.

With this resolution I entered the wood, and with all possible wariness and silence, Friday following close at my heels, I marched till I came to the skirt of the wood, on the side which was next to them; only that one corner of the wood lay between me and them. Here I called softly to Friday, and showing him a great tree, which was just at the corner of the wood, I bade him go to the tree and bring me

word if he could see there plainly what they were doing. He did so, and came immediately back to me, and told me they might be plainly viewed there; that they were all about their fire, eating the flesh of one of their prisoners, and that another lay bound upon the sand, a little from them, which, he said, they would kill next; and, which fired all the very soul within me, he told me it was not one of their nation, but one of the bearded men, whom he had told me of, that came to their country in the boat. I was filled with horror at the very naming the white, bearded man; and going to the tree, I saw plainly, by my glass, a white man, who lay upon the beach of the sea, with his hands and his feet tied with flags, or things like rushes, and that he was an European, and had clothes on.

There was another tree, and a little thicket beyond it, about fifty yards nearer to them than the place where I was, which, by going a little way about, I saw I might come at undiscovered, and that then I should be within half shot of them; so I withheld my passion, though I was indeed enraged to the highest degree; and going back about twenty paces, I got behind some bushes, which held all the way till I came to the other tree; and then I came to a little rising ground, which gave me a full view of them, at the distance of about eighty yards.

I had now not a moment to lose, for nineteen of the dreadful wretches sat upon the ground, all close huddled together, and had just sent the other two to butcher the poor Christian, and bring him, perhaps limb by limb, to their fire; and they were stooped down to untie the bands at his feet. I turned to Friday: "Now, Friday," said I, "do as I bid thee." Friday said he would. "Then, Friday," says I, "do exactly as you see me do; fail in nothing." So I set down one of the muskets and the fowling-piece upon the ground, and Friday did the like by his; and with the other musket I took my aim at the savages, bidding him do the like. Then asking him if he was ready, he said, "Yes," "Then fire at them," said I; and the same moment I fired also.

Friday took his aim so much better than I, that on the side that he shot he killed two of them, and wounded three more; and on my side I killed one, and wounded two. They were, you may be sure, in a dreadful consternation; and all of them who

were not hurt jumped up upon their feet, but did not immediately know which way to run, or which way to look, for they knew not from whence their destruction came. Friday kept his eyes close upon me, that, as I had bid him, he might observe what I did; so as soon as the first shot was made I threw down the piece, and took up the fowling-piece, and Friday did the like. He sees me cock and present; he did the same again. "Are you ready, Friday?" said I. "Yes," says he. "Let fly, then," says I, "in the name of God!" and with that I fired again among the amazed wretches, and so did Friday; and as our pieces were now loaded with what I called swan-shot, or small pistol-bullets, we found only two drop, but so many were wounded, that they ran about yelling and screaming like mad creatures, all bloody, and miserably wounded most of them; whereof three more fell quickly after, though not quite dead.

"Now, Friday," says I, laying down the discharged pieces, and taking up the musket which was yet loaden, "follow me," says I, which he did with a great deal of courage; upon which I rushed out of the wood, and showed myself, and Friday close at my foot. As soon as I perceived they saw me, I shouted as loud as I could, and bade Friday do so too; and running as fast as I could, which, by the way, was not very fast, being loaden with arms as I was, I made directly towards the poor victim, who was, as I said, lying upon the beach, or shore, between the place where they sat and the sea. The two butchers, who were just going to work with him, had left him at the surprise of our first fire, and fled in a terrible fright to the seaside, and had jumped into a canoe, and three more of the rest made the same way. I turned to Friday, and bid him step forwards and fire at them. He understood me immediately, and running about forty yards, to be near them, he shot at them, and I thought he had killed them all, for I saw them all fall of a heap into the boat; though I saw two of them up again quickly. However, he killed two of them, and wounded the third, so that he lay down in the bottom of the boat as if he had been dead.

While my man Friday fired at them, I pulled out my knife and cut the flags that bound the poor victim; and loosing his hands and feet, I lifted him up, and asked him in the Portuguese tongue what he was. He answered in Latin, Christianus; but was so weak and faint, that he could scarce stand or speak. I took my bottle out of my pocket and gave it him, making signs that he should drink, which he did; and I gave him a piece of bread, which he eat. Then I asked him what countryman he was; and he said, Espagniole; and being a little recovered, let me know, by all the signs he could possibly make, how much he was in my debt for his deliverance. "Seignior," said I, with as much Spanish as I could make up, "we will talk afterwards, but we must fight now. If you have any strength left, take this pistol and sword, and lay about you." He took them very thankfully, and no sooner had he the arms in his hands but, as if they had put new vigour into him, he flew upon his murderers like a fury, and had cut two of them in pieces in an instant; for the truth is, as the whole was a surprise to them, so the poor creatures were so much frighted with the noise of our pieces, that they fell down for mere amazement and fear, and had no more power to attempt their own escape, than their flesh had to resist our shot: and that was the case of those five that Friday shot at in the boat; for as three of them

'I made directly towards the poor victim . . .' (p. 168)

fell with the hurt they received, so the other two fell with the fright.

I kept my piece in my hand still without firing, being willing to keep my charge ready, because I had given the Spaniard my pistol and sword. So I called to Friday, and bade him run up to the tree from whence we first fired, and fetch the arms which lay there that had been discharged, which he did with great swiftness; and then giving him my musket, I sat down myself to load all the rest again, and bade them come to me when they wanted. While I was loading these pieces, there happened a fierce engagement between the Spaniard and one of the savages, who made at him with one of their great wooden swords, the same weapon that was to have killed him before if I had not prevented it. The Spaniard, who was as bold and as brave as could be imagined, though weak, had fought this Indian a good while, and had cut him two great wounds on his head; but the savage being a stout, lusty fellow, closing in with him, had thrown him down, being faint, and was wringing my sword out of his hand, when the Spaniard, though undermost, wisely quitting the sword, drew the pistol from his girdle, shot the savage through the body, and killed him upon the spot, before I, who was running to help him, could come near him.

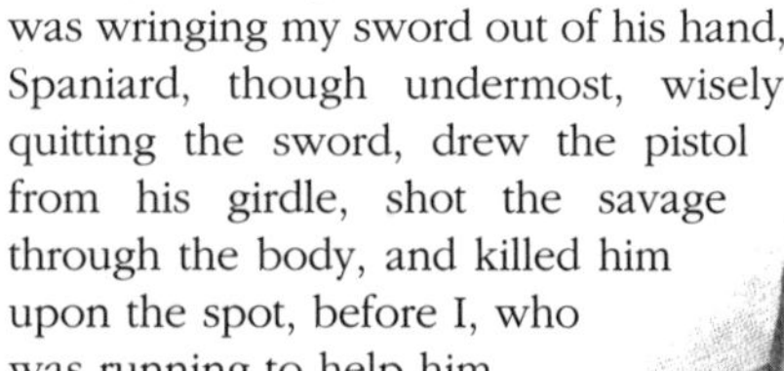

Friday, being now left to his liberty, pursued the flying wretches with no weapon in his hand but his hatchet; and with that he dispatched those three who, as I said before, were wounded at first, and fallen, and all the rest he could come up with; and the Spaniard coming to me for a gun, I gave him one of the fowling-pieces, with which he pursued two of the savages, and wounded them both; but as he was not able to run, they both got from him into the wood, where Friday pursued them, and killed one of them; but the other was too nimble for him, and though he was wounded, yet had plunged himself into the sea and swam with all his might off to those two who were left in the canoe; which three in the canoe, with one wounded, who we know not whether he died or no, were all that escaped our hands of one and twenty. The account of the rest is as follows:

3 killed at our first shot from the tree.
2 killed at the next shot.
2 killed by Friday in the boat.
2 killed by ditto, of those at first wounded.
1 killed by ditto in the wood.
3 killed by the Spaniard.
4 killed, being found dropped here and there of their wounds, or killed by Friday in his chase of them.
4 escaped in the boat, whereof one wounded, if not dead.

---

21 in all.

Those that were in the canoe worked hard to get out of gun-shot; and though Friday made two or three shots at them, I did not find that he hit any of them. Friday would fain have had me take one of their canoes, and pursued them; and, indeed, I was very anxious about their escape, lest carrying the news home to their people they should come back perhaps with two or three hundred of their canoes, and devour us by mere multitude. So I consented to pursue them by sea, and running to one of their canoes I jumped in, and bade Friday follow me. But when I was in the canoe, I was surprised to find another poor creature lie there alive, bound hand and foot, as the Spaniard was, for the slaughter, and almost dead with fear, not knowing what the matter was; for he had not been able to look up over the side of the boat, he was tied so hard, neck and heels, and had been tied so long, that he had really but little life in him.

I immediately cut the twisted flags or rushes, which they had bound him with, and would have helped him up; but he could not stand or speak, but groaned most piteously, believing, it seems, still that he was only unbound in order to be killed.

When Friday came to him, I bade him speak to him, and tell him of his deliverance; and pulling out my bottle, made him give the poor wretch a dram; which, with the news of his being delivered, revived him, and he sat up in the boat. But when Friday came to hear him speak, and look in his face, it would have moved any one to tears to have seen how Friday kissed him, embraced him, hugged him, cried, laughed, hollowed, jumped about, danced, sung; then cried again, wrung his hands, beat his own face and head, and then sung and jumped about again, like a distracted creature. It was a good while before I could make him speak to me, or tell me what was the matter; but when he came a little to himself, he told me that it was his father.

It is not easy for me to express how it moved me to see what ecstasy and filial affection had worked in this poor savage at the sight of his father, and of his being delivered from death; nor, indeed, can I describe half the extravagancies of his affection after this; for he went into the boat, and out of the boat, a great many times. When he went in to him, he would sit down by him, open his breast, and hold his father's head close to his bosom, half-an-hour together, to nourish it; then he took his arms and ankles, which were numbed and stiff with the binding, and chafed and rubbed them with his hands; and I, perceiving what the case was, gave him some rum out of my bottle to rub them with, which did them a great deal of good.

This action put an end to our pursuit of the canoe with the other savages, who were now gotten almost out of sight; and it was happy for us that we did not, for it blew so hard within two hours after, and before they could be gotten a quarter of their way, and continued blowing so hard all night, and that from the north-west, which was against them, that I could not suppose their boat could live, or that they ever reached to their own coast.

But to return to Friday. He was so busy about his father, that I could not find in my heart to take him off for some time; but after I thought he could leave him a little, I called him to me, and he came jumping and laughing, and pleased to the highest extreme. Then I asked him if he had given his father any bread. He shook his head, and said, "None; ugly dog eat all up self." So I gave him a cake of bread out of a little pouch I carried on purpose. I also gave him a dram for himself, but he would not taste it, but carried it to his father. I had in my pocket also two or three bunches of my raisins, so I gave him a handful of them for his father. He had no sooner given his father these raisins, but I saw him come out of the boat and run away, as if he had been bewitched, he ran at such a rate; for he was the swiftest fellow of his foot that ever I saw. I say, he run at such a rate, that he was out of sight, as it were, in an instant; and though I called, and hollowed too, after him, it was all one, away he went; and in a quarter of an hour I saw him come back again, though not so fast as he went; and as he came nearer I found his pace was slacker, because he had something in his hand.

When he came up to me, I found he had been quite home for an earthen jug, or pot, to bring his father some fresh water, and that he had got two more cakes or loaves of bread. The bread he gave me, but the water he carried to his father. However, as I was very thirsty too, I took a little sup of it. This water revived his father more than all the rum or spirits I had given him, for he was just fainting with thirst.

When his father had drank, I called him to know if there was any water left. He said "Yes;" and I bade him give it to the poor Spaniard, who was in as much want of it as his father; and I sent one of the cakes, that Friday brought, to the Spaniard too, who was indeed very weak, and was reposing himself upon a green place under the

shade of a tree; and whose limbs were also very stiff, and very much swelled with the rude bandage he had been tied with. When I saw that upon Friday's coming to him with the water he sat up and drank, and took the bread, and began to eat, I went to him, and gave him a handful of raisins. He looked up in my face with all the tokens of gratitude and thankfulness that could appear in any countenance; but was so weak, notwithstanding he had so exerted himself in the fight, that he could not stand upon his feet. He tried to do it two or three times, but was really not able, his ankles were so swelled and so painful to him; so I bade him sit still, and caused Friday to rub his ankles, and bathe them with rum, as he had done his father's.

I observed the poor affectionate creature, every two minutes, or perhaps less, all the while he was here, turned his head about to see if his father was in the same place and posture as he left him sitting; and at last he found he was not to be seen; at which he started up, and without speaking a word, flew with that swiftness to him, that one could scarce perceive his feet to touch the ground as he went. But when he came, he only found he had laid himself down to ease his limbs; so Friday came back to me presently, and I then spoke to the Spaniard to let Friday help him up, if he could, and lead him to the boat, and then he should carry him to our dwelling, where I would take care of him. But Friday, a lusty strong fellow, took the Spaniard quite up upon his back, and carried him away to the boat, and set him down softly upon the side or gunnel of the canoe with his feet in the inside of it, and then lifted him quite in, and set him close to his father; and presently stepping out again, launched the boat off, and paddled it along the shore faster than I could walk, though the wind blew pretty hard too. So he brought them both safe into our creek, and leaving them in the boat, runs away to fetch the other canoe. As he passed me, I spoke to him, and asked him whither he went. He told me, "Go fetch more boat." So away he went like the wind, for sure never man or horse run like him; and he had the other canoe in the creek almost as soon as I got to it by land; so he wafted me over, and then went to help our new guests out of the boat, which he did; but they were neither of them able to walk, so that poor Friday knew not what to do.

To remedy this I went to work in my thought, and calling to Friday to bid them sit down on the bank while he came to me, I soon made a kind of hand-barrow to lay them on, and Friday and I carried them up both together upon it between us. But when we got them to the outside of our wall, or fortification, we were at a worse loss than before, for it was impossible to get them over, and I was resolved not to break it down. So I set to work again; and Friday and I, in about two hours' time, made a very handsome tent, covered with old sails, and above that with boughs of trees, being in the space without our outward fence, and between that and the grove of young wood which I had planted; and here we made them two beds of such things as I had, viz. of good rice-straw, with blankets laid upon it to lie on, and another to cover them, on each bed.

My island was now peopled, and I thought myself very rich in subjects; and it was a merry reflection, which I frequently made, how like a king I looked. First of all, the whole country was my own mere property, so that I had an undoubted right of

dominion. Secondly, my people were perfectly subjected, I was absolute lord and lawgiver; they all owed their lives to me, and were ready to lay down their lives, if there had been occasion of it, for me. It was remarkable, too, we had but three subjects, and they were of three different religions. My man Friday was a Protestant, his father was a Pagan and a cannibal, and the Spaniard was a Papist. However, I allowed liberty of conscience throughout my dominions. But this is by the way.

As soon as I had secured my two weak rescued prisoners, and given them shelter and a place to rest them upon, I began to think of making some provision for them; and the first thing I did, I ordered Friday to take a yearling goat, betwixt a kid and a goat, out of my particular flock, to be killed; when I cut off the hinder-quarter, and chopping it into small pieces, I set Friday to work to boiling and stewing, and made them a very good dish, I assure you, of flesh and broth, having put some barley and rice also into the broth; and as I cooked it without doors, for I made no fire within my inner wall, so I carried it all into the new tent, and having set a table there for them, I sat down and eat my own dinner also with them, and as well as I could cheered them, and encouraged them; Friday being my interpreter, especially to his father, and, indeed, to the Spaniard too; for the Spaniard spoke the language of the savages pretty well.

After we had dined, or rather supped, I ordered Friday to take one of the canoes and go and fetch our muskets and other firearms, which, for want of time, we had left upon the place of battle; and the next day I ordered him to go and bury the dead bodies of the savages, which lay open to the sun, and would presently be offensive; and I also ordered him to bury the horrid remains of their barbarous feast, which I knew were pretty much, and which I could not think of doing myself; nay, I could not bear to see them, if I went that way. All which he punctually performed, and defaced the very appearance of the savages being there; so that when I went again I could scarce know where it was, otherwise than by the corner of the wood pointing to the place.

I then began to enter into a little conversation with my two new subjects; and first, I set Friday to inquire of his father what he thought of the escape of the savages in that canoe, and whether we might expect a return of them, with a power too great for us to resist. His first opinion was, that the savages in the boat never could live out the storm which blew that night they went off, but must, of necessity, be drowned, or driven south to those other shores, where they were as sure to be devoured as they were to be drowned if they were cast away. But as to what they would do if they came safe on shore, he said he knew not; but it was his opinion that

they were so dreadfully frighted with the manner of their being attacked, the noise, and the fire, that he believed they would tell their people they were all killed by thunder and lightning, not by the hand of man; and that the two which appeared, viz. Friday and me, were two heavenly spirits, or furies, come down to destroy them, and not men with weapons. This, he said, he knew, because he heard them all cry out so in their language to one another; for it was impossible to them to conceive that a man could dart fire, and speak thunder, and kill at a distance without lifting up the hand, as was done now. And this old savage was in the right; for, as I understood since by other hands, the savages never attempted to go over to the island afterwards. They were so terrified with the accounts given by those four men, (for, it seems, they did escape the sea), that they believed whoever went to that enchanted island would be destroyed with fire from the gods.

This, however, I knew not, and therefore was under continual apprehensions for a good while, and kept always upon my guard, me and all my army; for as we were now four of us, I would have ventured upon a hundred of them, fairly in the open field, at any time.

In a little time, however, no more canoes appearing, the fear of their coming wore off, and I began to take my former thoughts of a voyage to the main into consideration; being likewise assured, by Friday's father, that I might depend upon good usage from their nation, on his account, if I would go.

CHAPTER SEVENTEEN

But my thoughts were a little suspended when I had a serious discourse with the Spaniard, and when I understood that there were sixteen more of his countrymen and Portuguese who, having been cast away, and made their escape to that side, lived there at peace, indeed, with the savages, but were very sore put to it for necessaries, and indeed for life. I asked him all the particulars of their voyage, and found they were a Spanish ship bound from the Rio de la Plata to the Havana, being directed to leave their loading there, which was chiefly hides and silver, and to bring back what European goods they could meet with there; that they had five Portuguese seamen on board, whom they took out of another wreck; that five of their own men were drowned when the first ship was lost, and that these escaped, through infinite dangers and hazards, and arrived, almost starved, on the cannibal coast, where they expected to have been devoured every moment.

He told me they had some arms with them, but they were perfectly useless, for that they had neither powder or ball, the washing of the sea having spoiled all their powder but a little, which they used, at their first landing, to provide themselves some food.

I asked him what he thought would become of them there, and if they had formed no design of making any escape? He said they had many consultations about it; but that having neither vessel, or tools to build one, or provisions of any kind, their councils always ended in tears and despair.

I asked him how he thought they would receive a proposal from me, which might tend towards an escape; and whether, if they were all here, it might not be done? I told him with freedom, I feared mostly their treachery and ill usage of me if I put my life in their hands; for that gratitude was no inherent virtue in the nature of man, nor did men always square their dealings by the obligations they had received, so much as they did by the advantages they expected. I told him it would be very hard that I should be the instrument of their deliverance, and that they should afterwards make me their prisoner in New Spain, where an Englishman was certain to be made a sacrifice, what necessity or what accident soever brought him thither; and that I had rather be delivered up to the savages, and be devoured alive, than fall into the merciless claws of the priests, and be carried into the Inquisition. I added, that otherwise I was persuaded, if they were all here, we might, with so many hands, build a bark large enough to carry us all away, either to the Brazils, southward, or to the islands, or Spanish coast, northward; but that if, in requital, they should, when I had put weapons into their hands, carry me by force among their own people, I might be ill used for my kindness to them, and make my case worse than it was before.

He answered, with a great deal of candour and ingenuity, that their condition was so miserable, and they were so sensible of it, that he believed they would abhor the thought of using any man unkindly that should contribute to their deliverance; and that, if I pleased, he would go to them with the old man, and discourse with them about it, and return again, and bring me their answer; that he would make conditions with them upon their solemn oath that they should be absolutely under my leading, as their commander and captain; and that they should swear upon the holy sacraments and the gospel to be true to me, and to go to such Christian country as that I should agree to, and no other, and to be directed wholly and absolutely by my orders till they were landed safely in such country as I intended; and that he would bring a contract from them, under their hands, for that purpose.

Then he told me he would first swear to me himself, that he would never stir from me as long as he lived till I gave him orders; and that he would take my side to the last drop of his blood, if there should happen the least breach of faith among his countrymen.

He told me they were all of them very civil, honest men, and they were under the greatest distress imaginable, having neither weapons or clothes, nor any food, but at the mercy and discretion of the savages; out of all hopes of ever returning to their own country; and that he was sure, if I would undertake their relief, they would live and die by me.

Upon these assurances I resolved to venture to relieve them, if possible, and to send the old savage and this Spaniard over to them to treat. But when we had gotten all things in a readiness to go, the Spaniard himself started an objection, which had so much prudence in it on one hand, and so much sincerity on the other hand, that I could not but be very well satisfied in it, and by his advice put off the deliverance of his comrades for at least half a year. The case was thus.

He had been with us now about a month, during which time I had let him see in what manner I had provided, with the assistance of Providence, for my support; and he saw evidently what stock of corn and rice I had made up; which, as it was more than sufficient for myself, so it was not sufficient, at least without good husbandry, for my family, now it was increased to number four; but much less would it be sufficient if his countrymen, who were, as he said, fourteen still alive, should come over; and least of all would it be sufficient to victual our vessel, if we should build one, for a voyage to any of the Christian colonies of America. So he told me he thought it would be more advisable to let him and the two others dig and cultivate some more land, as much as I could spare seed to sow; and that we should wait another harvest, that we might have a supply of corn for his countrymen when they should come; for want might be a temptation to them to disagree, or not to think themselves delivered, otherwise than out of one difficulty into another. "You know," says he, "the children of Israel, though they rejoiced at first for their being delivered out of Egypt, yet rebelled even against God Himself, that delivered them, when they came to want bread in the wilderness."

His caution was so seasonable, and his advice so good, that I could not but be very well pleased with his proposal, as well as I was satisfied with his fidelity. So we fell to digging all four of us, as well as the wooden tools we were furnished with permitted; and in about a month's time, by the end of which it was seed-time, we had gotten as much land cured and trimmed up as we sowed twenty-two bushels of barley on, and sixteen jars of rice; which was, in short, all the seed we had to spare; nor, indeed, did we leave ourselves barley sufficient for our own food for the six months that we had to expect our crop; that is to say, reckoning from the time we set our seed aside for sowing; for it is not to be supposed it is six months in the ground in that country.

Having now society enough, and our number being sufficient to put us out of fear of the savages, if they had come, unless their number had been very great, we went freely all over the island, wherever we found occasion; and as here we had our escape or deliverance upon our thoughts, it was impossible, at least for me, to have the means of it out of mine. To this purpose I marked out several trees which I thought fit for our work, and I set Friday and his father to cutting them down; and then I caused the Spaniard, to whom I imparted my thought on that affair, to oversee and direct their work. I showed them with what indefatigable pains I had hewed a large tree into single planks, and I caused them to do the like, till they had made about a dozen large planks of good oak, near two foot broad, thirty-five foot long, and from two inches to four inches thick. What prodigious labour it took up, any one may imagine.

At the same time, I contrived to increase my little flock of tame goats as much as I could; and to this purpose I made Friday and the Spaniard go out one day, and myself with Friday the next day, for we took our turns, and by this means we got above twenty young kids to breed up with the rest; for whenever we shot the dam, we saved the kids, and added them to our flock. But above all, the season for curing the grapes coming on, I caused such a prodigious quantity to be hung up in the sun, that I believe, had we been at Alicant, where the raisins of the sun are cured, we could have filled sixty or eighty barrels; and these, with our bread, was a great part of our food, and very good living too, I assure you; for it is an exceeding nourishing food.

It was now harvest, and our crop in good order. It was not the most plentiful increase I had seen in the island, but, however, it was enough to answer our end; for from our twenty-two bushels of barley we brought in and thrashed out above two hundred and twenty bushels, and the like in proportion of the rice; which was store enough for our food to the next harvest, though all the sixteen Spaniards had been on shore with me; or if we had been ready for a voyage, it would very plentifully have victualled our ship to have carried us to any part of the world, that is to say, of America.

When we had thus housed and secured our magazine of corn, we fell to work to make more wicker-work, viz. great baskets, in which we kept it; and the Spaniard was very handy and dexterous at this part, and often blamed me that I did not make some things for defence of this kind of work; but I saw no need of it.

And now having a full supply of food for all the guests I expected, I gave the Spaniard leave to go over to the main, to see what he could do with those he had left behind him there. I gave him a strict charge in writing not to bring any man with him who would not first swear, in the presence of himself and of the old savage, that he would no way injure, fight with, or attack the person he should find in the island, who was so kind to send for them in order to their deliverance; but that they would stand by and defend him against all such attempts, and wherever they went would be entirely under and subjected to his commands; and that this should be put in writing, and signed with their hands. How we were to have this done, when I knew they had neither pen or ink, that indeed was a question which we never asked.

Under these instructions, the Spaniard and the old savage, the father of Friday,

went away in one of the canoes which they might be said to come in, or rather were brought in, when they came as prisoners to be devoured by the savages.

I gave each of them a musket, with a firelock on it, and about eight charges of powder and ball, charging them to be very good husbands of both, and not to use either of them but upon urgent occasion.

This was a cheerful work, being the first measures used by me, in view of my deliverance, for now twenty-seven years and some days. I gave them provisions of bread and of dried grapes sufficient for themselves for many days, and sufficient for all their countrymen for about eight days' time; and wishing them a good voyage, I see them go, agreeing with them about a signal they should hang out at their return, by which I should know them again, when they came back, at a distance, before they came on shore.

They went away with a fair gale on the day that the moon was at full, by my account in the month of October; but as for an exact reckoning of days, after I had once lost it, I could never recover it again; nor had I kept even the number of years so punctually as to be sure that I was right, though as it proved, when I afterwards examined my account, I found I had kept a true reckoning of years.

It was no less than eight days I had waited for them, when a strange and unforeseen accident intervened, of which the like has not perhaps been heard of in history. I was fast asleep in my hutch one morning, when my man Friday came running in to me, and called aloud, "Master, master, they are come, they are come!"

I jumped up, and, regardless of danger, I went out as soon as I could get my clothes on, through my little grove, which, by the way, was by this time grown to be a very thick wood; I say, regardless of danger, I went without my arms, which was not my custom to do; but I was surprised when, turning my eyes to the sea, I presently saw a boat at about a league and half's distance standing in for the shore, with a shoulder-of-mutton sail, as they call it, and the wind blowing pretty fair to bring them in; also I observed presently that they did not come from that side which the shore lay on, but from the southernmost end of the island. Upon this I called Friday in, and bid him lie close, for these were not the people we looked for, and that we might not know yet whether they were friends or enemies.

In the next place, I went in to fetch my perspective glass, to see what I could make of them; and having taken the ladder out, I climbed up to the top of the hill, as I used to do when I was apprehensive of anything, and to take my view the plainer, without being discovered.

I had scarce set my foot on the hill, when my eye plainly discovered a ship lying at an anchor at about two leagues and an half's distance from me, south-south-east, but not above a league and an half from the shore. By my observation, it appeared plainly to be an English ship, and the boat appeared to be an English longboat.

I cannot express the confusion I was in; though the joy of seeing a ship, and one who I had reason to believe was manned by own countrymen, and consequently friends, was such as I cannot describe. But yet I had some secret doubts hung about me, I cannot tell from whence they came, bidding me keep upon my guard. In the

first place, it occurred to me to consider what business an English ship could have in that part of the world, since it was not the way to or from any part of the world where the English had any traffic; and I knew there had been no storms to drive them in there as in distress; and that if they were English really, it was most probable that they were here upon no good design; and that I had better continue as I was, than fall into the hands of thieves and murderers.

Let no man despise the secret hints and notices of danger, which sometimes are given him when he may think there is no possibility of its being real. That such hints and notices are given us, I believe few that have made any observations of things can deny; that they are certain discoveries of an invisible world, and a converse of spirits, we cannot doubt; and if the tendency of them seems to be to warn us of danger, why should we not suppose they are from some friendly agent, (whether supreme, or inferior and subordinate, is not the question), and that they are given for our good?

The present question abundantly confirms me in the justice of this reasoning; for had I not been made cautious by this secret admonition, come it from whence it will, I had been undone inevitably, and in a far worse condition than before, as you will see presently.

I had not kept myself long in this posture, but I saw the boat draw near the shore, as if they looked for a creek to thrust in at, for the convenience of landing. However, as they did not come quite far enough, they did not see the little inlet where I formerly landed my rafts; but run their boat on shore upon the beach, at about half a mile from me, which was very happy for me; for otherwise they would have landed just, as I may say, at my door, and would soon have beaten me out of my castle, and perhaps have plundered me of all I had.

When they were on shore, I was fully satisfied that they were Englishmen, at least most of them; one or two I thought were Dutch, but it did not prove so. There were in all eleven men, whereof three of them I found were unarmed and, as I thought, bound; and when the first four or five of them were jumped on shore, they took those three out of the boat, as prisoners. One of the three I could perceive using the most passionate gestures of entreaty, affliction, and despair, even to a kind of extravagance; and the other two, I could perceive, lifted up their hands sometimes, and appeared concerned indeed, but not to such a degree as the first.

I was perfectly confounded at the sight, and knew not what the meaning of it

should be. Friday called out to me in English as well as he could, "O master! you see English mans eat prisoner as well as savage mans." "Why," says I, "Friday, do you think they are a-going to eat them then?" "Yes," says Friday, "they will eat them." "No, no," says I, "Friday, I am afraid they will murder them indeed, but you may be sure they will not eat them."

All this while I had no thought of what the matter really was, but stood trembling with the horror of the sight, expecting every moment when the three prisoners should be killed; nay, once I saw one of the villains lift up his arm with a great cutlass, as the seamen call it, or sword, to strike one of the poor men; and I expected to see him fall every moment, at which all the blood in my body seemed to run chill in my veins.

I wished heartily now for my Spaniard, and the savage that was gone with him; or that I had any way to have come undiscovered within shot of them, that I might have rescued the three men, for I saw no firearms they had among them; but it fell out to my mind another way.

After I had observed the outrageous usage of the three men by the insolent seamen, I observed the fellows run scattering about the land, as if they wanted to see the country. I observed that the three other men had liberty to go also where they pleased; but they sat down all three upon the ground, very pensive, and looked like men in despair.

This put me in mind of the first time when I came on shore, and began to look about me; how I gave myself over for lost; how wildly I looked round me; what dreadful apprehensions I had; and how I lodged in the tree all night, for fear of being devoured by wild beasts.

As I knew nothing that night of the supply I was to receive by the providential driving of the ship nearer the land by the storms and tide, by which I have since been so long nourished and supported; so these three poor desolate men knew nothing how certain of deliverance and supply they were, how near it was to them, and how effectually and really they were in a condition of safety, at the same time that they thought themselves lost, and their case desperate.

So little do we see before us in the world, and so much reason have we to depend cheerfully upon the great Maker of the world, that He does not leave His creatures so absolutely destitute, but that, in the worst circumstances, they have always something to be thankful for, and sometimes are nearer their deliverance than they imagine; nay, are even brought to their deliverance by the means by which they seem to be brought to their destruction.

It was just at the top of high-water when these people came on shore; and while partly they stood parleying with the prisoners they brought, and partly while they rambled about to see what kind of a place they were in, they had carelessly staid till the tide was spent, and the water was ebbed considerably away, leaving their boat aground.

They had left two men in the boat, who, as I found afterwards, having drank a little too much brandy, fell asleep. However, one of them waking sooner than the other, and finding the boat too fast aground for him to stir it, hollowed for the rest, who were straggling about, upon which they all soon came to the boat; but it was past all their strength to launch her, the boat being very heavy, and the shore on that side being a soft oozy sand, almost like a quicksand.

In this condition, like true seamen, who are perhaps the least of all mankind given to forethought, they gave it over, and away they strolled about the country again; and I heard one of them say aloud to another, calling them off from the boat, "Why, let her alone, Jack, can't ye? she will float next tide;" by which I was fully confirmed in the main inquiry of what countrymen they were.

All this while I kept myself very close, not once daring to stir out of my castle, any farther than to my place of observation near the top of the hill; and very glad I was to think how well it was fortified. I knew it was no less than ten hours before the boat could be on float again, and by that time it would be dark, and I might be at more liberty to see their motions, and to hear their discourse, if they had any.

In the meantime, I fitted myself up for a battle, as before, though with more caution, knowing I had to do with another kind of enemy than I had at first. I ordered Friday also, whom I had made an excellent marksman with his gun, to load himself with arms. I took myself two fowling-pieces, and I gave him three muskets. My figure, indeed, was very fierce. I had my formidable goat-skin coat on, with the great cap I have mentioned, a naked sword by my side, two pistols in my belt, and a gun upon each shoulder.

It was my design, as I said above, not to have made any attempt till it was dark; but about two o'clock, being the heat of the day, I found that, in short, they were all gone straggling into the woods, and, as I thought, were laid down to sleep. The three poor distressed men, too anxious for their condition to get any sleep, were, however, set down under the shelter of a great tree, at about a quarter of a mile from me, and, as I thought, out of sight of any of the rest.

Upon this I resolved to discover myself to them, and learn something of their condition. Immediately I marched in the figure as above, my man Friday at a good distance behind me, as formidable for his arms as I, but not making quite so staring a spectre-like figure as I did.

I came as near them undiscovered as I could, and then, before any of them saw me, I called aloud to them in Spanish, "What are ye, gentlemen?"

They started up at the noise, but were ten times more confounded when they saw me, and the uncouth figure that I made. They made no

"A FIERCE ENGAGEMENT BETWEEN THE SPANIARD AND ONE OF THE SAVAGES..."
(J. FINNEMORE)

"...THEY SET UP TWO OR THREE GREAT SHOUTS, HOLLOWING WITH ALL THEIR MIGHT, TO TRY IF THEY COULD MAKE THEIR COMPANIONS HEAR..." (J. WILLIAMSON)

THE CAPTAIN AND THE MATE, ENTERING FIRST, IMMEDIATELY KNOCKED DOWN THE SECOND MATE & CARPENTER WITH THE BUTT-END OF THEIR MUSKETS…" (J. MATTHEW)

"So he began jumping and shaking the bough, at which the bear began to totter."
(J. Finnemore)

answer at all, but I thought I perceived them just going to fly from me, when I spoke to them in English. "Gentlemen," said I, "do not be surprised at me; perhaps you may have a friend near you, when you did not expect it." "He must be sent directly from Heaven then," said one of them very gravely to me, and pulling off his hat at the same time to me, "for our condition is past the help of man." "All help is from Heaven, sir," said I. "But can you put a stranger in the way how to help you, for you seem to me to be in some great distress? I saw you when you landed; and when you seemed to make applications to the brutes that came with you, I saw one of them lift up his sword to kill you."

The poor man, with tears running down his face, and trembling, looking like one astonished, returned, "Am I talking to God, or man? Is it a real man, or an angel?" "Be in no fear about that, sir," said I. "If God had sent an angel to relieve you, he would have come better clothed, and armed after another manner than you see me in. Pray lay aside your fears; I am a man, an Englishman, and disposed to assist you, you see. I have one servant only; we have arms and ammunition; tell us freely, can we serve you? What is your case?"

"Our case," said he, "sir, is too long to tell you while our murderers are so near; but in short, sir, I was commander of that ship; my men have mutinied against me, they have been hardly prevailed on not to murder me; and at last have set me on shore in this desolate place, with these two men with me, one my mate, the other a passenger, where we expected to perish, believing the place to be uninhabited, and know not yet what to think of it."

"Where are those brutes, your enemies?" said I. "Do you know where they are gone?" "There they lie, sir," said he, pointing to a thicket of trees. "My heart trembles for fear they have seen us, and heard you speak. If they have, they will certainly murder us all."

"Have they any firearms?" said I. He answered, they had only two pieces, and one which they left in the boat. "Well then," said I, "leave the rest to me, I see they are all asleep; it is an easy thing to kill them all; but shall we rather take them prisoners?" He told me there were two desperate villains among them that it was scarce safe to show any mercy to; but if they were secured, he believed all the rest would return to their duty. I asked him which they were. He told me he could not at that distance describe them, but he would obey my orders in anything I would direct. "Well," says I, "let us retreat out of their view or hearing, lest they awake, and we will resolve further." So they willingly went back with me, till the woods covered us from them.

"Look you, sir," said I, "if I venture upon your deliverance, are you willing to make two conditions with me?" He anticipated my proposals, by telling me that both he and the ship, if recovered, should be wholly directed and commanded by me in everything; and if the ship was not recovered, he would live and die with me in what part of the world soever I would send him; and the two other men said the same.

"Well," says I, "my conditions are but two. 1. That while you stay on this island with me, you will not pretend to any authority here; and if I put arms into your hands, you will, upon all occasions, give them up to me, and do no prejudice to me or mine upon this island; and in the meantime, be governed by my orders. 2. That if the ship is, or may be, recovered, you will carry me and my man to England, passage free."

He gave me all the assurances that the invention and faith of man could devise that he would comply with these most reasonable demands; and, besides, would owe his life to me, and acknowledge it upon all occasions, as long as he lived.

"Well then," said I, "here are three muskets for you, with powder and ball; tell me next what you think is proper to be done." He showed all the testimony of his gratitude that he was able, but offered to be wholly guided by me. I told him I thought it was hard venturing anything; but the best method I could think of was to fire upon them at once as they lay; and if any was not killed at the first volley, and offered to submit, we might save them, and so put it wholly upon God's providence to direct the shot.

He said very modestly that he was loth to kill them, if he could help it; but that those two were incorrigible villains, and had been the authors of all the mutiny in the ship, and if they escaped, we should be undone still; for they would go on board and bring the whole ship's company, and destroy us all. "Well then," says I, "necessity legitimates my advice, for it is the only way to save our lives." However, seeing him still cautious of shedding blood, I told him they should go themselves, and manage as they found convenient.

In the middle of this discourse we heard some of them awake, and soon after we saw two of them on their feet. I asked him if either of them were of the men who he had said were the heads of the mutiny. He said, "No." "Well then," said I, "you may let them escape; and Providence seems to have wakened them on purpose to save themselves. "Now," says I, "if the rest escape you, it is your fault."

Animated with this, he took the musket I had given him in his hand, and a pistol in his belt, and his two comrades with him, with each man a piece in his hand. The two men who were with him going first made some noise, at which one of the seamen who was awake turned about, and seeing them coming cried out to the rest; but it was too late then, for the moment he cried out they fired; I mean the two men, the captain wisely reserving his own piece. They had so well aimed their shot at the men they knew, that one of them was killed on the spot, and the other very much wounded; but not being dead, he started up upon his feet, and called eagerly for help to the other. But the captain stepping

to him, told him 'twas too late to cry for help, he should call upon God to forgive his villainy; and with that word knocked him down with the stock of his musket, so that he never spoke more. There were three more in the company, and one of them was also slightly wounded. By this time I was come; and when they saw their danger, and that it was in vain to resist, they begged for mercy. The captain told them he would spare their lives if they would give him any assurance of their abhorrence of the treachery they had been guilty of, and would swear to be faithful to him in recovering the ship, and afterwards in carrying her back to Jamaica, from whence they came. They gave him all the protestations of their sincerity that could be desired, and he was willing to believe them, and spare their lives, which I was not against, only I obliged him to keep them bound hand and foot while they were upon the island.

While this was doing, I sent Friday with the captain's mate to the boat, with orders to secure her, and bring away the oars and sail, which they did; and by-and-by three straggling men, that were (happily for them) parted from the rest, came back upon hearing the guns fired; and seeing their captain, who before was their prisoner, now their conqueror, they submitted to be bound also, and so our victory was complete.

It now remained that the captain and I should inquire into one another's circumstances. I began first, and told him my whole history, which he heard with an attention even to amazement; and particularly at the wonderful manner of my being furnished with provisions and ammunition; and, indeed, as my story is a whole collection of wonders, it affected him deeply. But when he reflected from thence upon himself, and how I seemed to have been preserved there on purpose to save his life, the tears ran down his face, and he could not speak a word more.

After this communication was at an end, I carried him and his two men into my apartment, leading them in just where I came out, viz. at the top of the house, where I refreshed them with such provisions as I had, and showed them all the contrivances I had made during my long, long inhabiting that place.

All I showed them, all I said to them, was perfectly amazing; but above all, the captain admired my fortification, and how perfectly I had concealed my retreat with a grove of trees, which, having been now planted near twenty years, and the trees growing much faster than in England, was become a little wood, and so thick, that it was unpassable in any part of it but at that one side where I had reserved my little winding passage into it. I told him this was my castle and my residence, but that I had a seat in the country, as most princes have, whither I could retreat upon occasion, and I would show him that too another time; but at present, our business was to consider how to recover the ship. He agreed with me as to that, but told me he was perfectly at a loss what measures to take, for that there were still six and twenty hands on board, who having entered into a cursed conspiracy, by which they had all forfeited their lives to the law, would be hardened in it now by desperation, and would carry it on, knowing that if they were reduced, they should be brought to the gallows as soon as they came to England, or to any of the English colonies; and that therefore there would be no attacking them with so small a number as we were.

I mused for some time upon what he said, and found it was a very rational conclusion, and that therefore something was to be resolved on very speedily, as well to draw the men on board into some snare for their surprise, as to prevent their landing upon us, and destroying us. Upon this it presently occurred to me that in a little while the ship's crew, wondering what was become of their comrades, and of the boat, would certainly come on shore in their other boat to see for them; and that then, perhaps, they might come armed, and be too strong for us. This he allowed was rational.

Upon this, I told him the first thing we had to do was to stave the boat, which lay upon the beach, so that they might not carry her off; and taking everything out of her, leave her so far useless as not to be fit to swim. Accordingly we went on board, took the arms which were left on board out of her, and whatever else we found there, which was a bottle of brandy, and another of rum, a few biscuit-cakes, a horn of powder, and a great lump of sugar in a piece of canvas – the sugar was five or six pounds; all which was very welcome to me, especially the brandy and sugar, of which I had had none left for many years.

When we had carried all these things on shore, (the oars, mast, sail, and rudder of the boat were carried away before, as above), we knocked a great hole in her bottom, that if they had come strong enough to master us, yet they could not carry off the boat.

Indeed, it was not much in my thoughts that we could be able to recover the ship; but my view was, that if they went away without the boat, I did not much question to make her fit again to carry us away to the Leeward Islands, and call upon our friends the Spaniards in my way; for I had them still in my thoughts.

CHAPTER EIGHTEEN

While we were thus preparing our designs, and had first, by main strength, heaved the boat up upon the beach so high that the tide would not fleet her off at high-water mark; and besides, had broke a hole in her bottom too big to be quickly stopped, and were sat down musing what we should do, we heard the ship fire a gun, and saw her make a waft with her ancient as a signal for the boat to come on board. But no boat stirred; and they fired several times, making other signals for the boat.

At last, when all their signals and firings proved fruitless, and they found the boat did not stir, we saw them, by the help of my glasses, hoist another boat out, and row

towards the shore; and we found, as they approached, that there was no less than ten men in her, and that they had firearms with them.

As the ship lay almost two leagues from the shore, we had a full view of them as they came, and a plain sight of the men, even of their faces; because the tide having set them a little to the east of the other boat, they rowed up under shore, to come to the same place where the other had landed, and where the boat lay.

By this means, I say, we had a full view of them, and the captain knew the persons and characters of all the men in the boat, of whom he said that there were three very honest fellows, who, he was sure, were led into this conspiracy by the rest, being overpowered and frighted; but that as for the boatswain, who, it seems, was the chief officer among them, and all the rest, they were as outrageous as any of the ship's crew, and were no doubt made desperate in their new enterprise; and terribly apprehensive he was that they would be too powerful for us.

I smiled at him, and told him that men in our circumstances were past the operation of fear; that seeing almost every condition that could be was better than that which we were supposed to be in, we ought to expect that the consequence, whether death or life, would be sure to be a deliverance. I asked him what he thought of the circumstances of my life, and whether a deliverance were not worth venturing for? "And where, sir," said I, "is your belief of my being preserved here on purpose to save your life, which elevated you a little while ago? For my part," said I, "there seems to be but one thing amiss in all the prospect of it." "What's that?" says he. "Why," said I, "'tis that, as you say, there are three or four honest fellows among them, which should be spared; had they been all of the wicked part of the crew I should have thought God's providence had singled them out to deliver them into your hands; for depend upon it, every man of them that comes ashore are our own, and shall die or live as they behave to us."

As I spoke this with a raised voice and cheerful countenance, I found it greatly encouraged him; so we set vigorously to our business. We had, upon the first appearance of the boat's coming from the ship, considered of separating our prisoners, and had, indeed, secured them effectually.

Two of them, of whom the captain was less assured than ordinary, I sent with Friday and one of the three delivered men to my cave, where they were remote enough, and out of danger of being heard or discovered, or of finding their way out of the woods if they could have delivered themselves. Here they left them bound, but gave them provisions, and promised them, if they continued there quietly, to give them their liberty in a day or two; but that if they attempted their escape, they should be put to death without mercy. They promised faithfully to bear their confinement with patience, and were very thankful that they had such good usage as to have provisions and a light left them; for Friday gave them candles (such as we made ourselves) for their comfort; and they did not know but that he stood sentinel over them at the entrance.

The other prisoners had better usage. Two of them were kept pinioned, indeed, because the captain was not free to trust them; but the other two were taken into my service, upon their captain's recommendation, and upon their solemnly engaging to live and die with us; so with them and the three honest men we were seven men well armed; and I made no doubt we should be able to deal well enough with the ten that were a-coming, considering that the captain had said there were three or four honest men among them also.

As soon as they got to the place where their other boat lay, they ran their boat into the beach, and came all on shore, hauling the boat up after them, which I was glad to see; for I was afraid they would rather have left the boat at an anchor some distance from the shore, with some hands in her to guard her, and so we should not be able to seize the boat.

Being on shore, the first thing they did they ran all to their other boat; and it was easy to see that they were under a great surprise to find her stripped, as above, of all that was in her, and a great hole in her bottom.

After they had mused a while upon this, they set up two or three great shouts, hollowing with all their might, to try if they could make their companions hear; but all was to no purpose. Then they came all close in a ring, and fired a volley of their small arms, which, indeed, we heard, and the echoes made the woods ring. But it was all one; those in the cave we were sure could not hear, and those in our keeping, though they heard it well enough, yet durst give no answer to them.

They were so astonished at the surprise of this, that, as they told us afterwards, they resolved to go all on board again, to their ship, and let them know there that the men were all murdered, and the longboat staved. Accordingly, they immediately launched their boat again, and gat all of them on board.

The captain was terribly amazed, and even confounded at this, believing they would go on board the ship again, and set sail, giving their comrades for lost, and so he should still lose the ship, which he was in hopes we should have recovered; but he was quickly as much frighted the other way.

They had not been long put off with the boat but we perceived them all coming on shore again; but with this new measure in their conduct, which it seems they consulted together upon, viz. to leave three men in the boat, and the rest to go on shore, and go up into the country to look for their fellows.

This was a great disappointment to us, for now we were at a loss what to do; for our seizing those seven men on shore would be no advantage to us if we let the boat escape, because they would then row away to the ship, and then the rest of them would be sure to weigh and set sail, and so our recovering the ship would be lost. However, we had no remedy but to wait and see what the issue of things might present. The seven men came on shore, and the three who remained in the boat put her off to a good distance from the shore, and came to an anchor to wait for them; so that it was impossible for us to come at them in the boat.

Those that came on shore kept close together, marching towards the top of the little hill under which my habitation lay; and we could see them plainly, though they could not perceive us. We could have been very glad they would have come nearer to us, so that we might have fired at them, or that they would have gone farther off, that we might have come abroad.

But when they were come to the brow of the hill, where they could see a great way into the valleys and woods which lay towards the north-east part, and where the island lay lowest, they shouted and hollowed till they were weary; and not caring, it seems, to venture far from the shore, nor far from one another, they sat down together under a tree, to consider of it. Had they thought fit to have gone to sleep there, as the other party of them had done, they had done the job for us; but they were too full of apprehensions of danger to venture to go to sleep, though they could not tell what the danger was they had to fear neither.

The captain made a very just proposal to me upon this consultation of theirs, viz. that perhaps they would all fire a volley again, to endeavour to make their fellows hear, and that we should all sally upon them, just at the juncture when their pieces were all discharged, and they would certainly yield, and we should have them without bloodshed. I liked the proposal, provided it was done while we were near enough to come up to them before they could load their pieces again.

But this event did not happen, and we lay still a long time, very irresolute what course to take. At length I told them there would be nothing to be done, in my opinion, till night; and then, if they did not return to the boat, perhaps we might find a way to get between them and the shore, and so might use some stratagem with them in the boat to get them on shore.

We waited a great while, though very impatient for their removing; and were very uneasy when, after long consultations, we saw them start all up, and march down toward the sea. It seems they had such dreadful apprehensions upon them of the danger of the place, that they resolved to go on board the ship again, give their companions over for lost, and so go on with their intended voyage with the ship.

As soon as I perceived them go towards the shore, I imagined it to be, as it really was, that they had given over their search, and were for going back again; and the captain, as soon as I told him my thoughts, was ready to sink at the apprehensions of it; but I presently thought of a stratagem to fetch them back again, and which answered my end to a tittle.

I ordered Friday and the captain's mate to go over the little creek westward, towards the place where the savages came on shore when Friday was rescued, and as soon as they came to a little rising ground, at about half a mile distance, I bade them hollow as loud as they could, and wait till they found the seamen heard them; that as soon as ever they heard the seamen answer them, they should return it again; and then keeping out of sight, take a round, always answering when the other hollowed, to draw them as far into the island, and among the woods, as possible, and then wheel about again to me by such ways as I directed them.

They were just going into the boat when Friday and the mate hollowed; and they presently heard them, and answering, run along the shore westward, towards the voice they heard, when they were presently stopped by the creek, where the water being up, they could not get over, and called for the boat to come up and set them over, as, indeed, I expected.

When they had set themselves over, I observed that the boat being gone up a good way into the creek, and, as it were, in a harbour within the land, they took one of the three men out of her to go along with them, and left only two in the boat, having fastened her to the stump of a little tree on the shore.

That was what I wished for; and immediately leaving Friday and the captain's mate to their business, I took the rest with me, and crossing the creek out of their sight, we surprised the two men before they were aware; one of them lying on shore, and the other being in the boat. The fellow on shore was between sleeping and waking, and going to start up, the captain, who was foremost, ran in upon him, and knocked him down, and then called out to him in the boat to yield, or he was a dead man.

There needed very few arguments to persuade a single man to yield when he saw five men upon him, and his comrade knocked down; besides, this was, it seems, one of the three who were not so hearty in the mutiny as the rest of the crew, and therefore was easily persuaded not only to yield, but afterwards to join very sincerely with us.

In the meantime, Friday and the captain's mate so well managed their business with the rest, that they drew them, by hollowing and answering, from one hill to another, and from one wood to another, till they not only heartily tired them, but left them where they were very sure they could not reach back to the boat before it was dark; and, indeed, they were heartily tired themselves also by the time they came back to us.

We had nothing now to do but to watch for them in the dark, and to fall upon them, so as to make sure work with them.

It was several hours after Friday came back to me before they came back to their boat; and we could hear the foremost of them, long before they came quite up, calling to those behind to come along, and could also hear them answer and complain how lame and tired they were, and not able to come any faster; which was very welcome news to us.

At length they came up to the boat; but 'tis impossible to express their confusion when they found the boat fast aground in the creek, the tide ebbed out, and their two men gone. We could hear them call to one another in a most lamentable manner,

telling one another they were gotten into an enchanted island; that either there were inhabitants in it, and they should all be murdered, or else there were devils and spirits in it, and they should all be carried away and devoured.

They hollowed again, and called their two comrades by their names a great many times; but no answer. After some time we could see them, by the little light there was, run about, wringing their hands like men in despair, and that sometimes they would go and sit down in the boat to rest themselves, then come ashore again, and walk about again, and so the same thing over again.

My men would fain have me give them leave to fall upon them at once in the dark; but I was willing to take them at some advantage, so to spare them, and kill as few of them as I could; and especially I was unwilling to hazard the killing any of our own men, knowing the other were very well armed. I resolved to wait, to see if they did not separate; and, therefore, to make sure of them, I drew my ambuscade nearer, and ordered Friday and the captain to creep upon their hands and feet, as close to the ground as they could, that they might not be discovered, and get as near them as they could possibly, before they offered to fire.

They had not been long in that posture but that the boatswain, who was the principal ringleader of the mutiny, and had now shown himself the most dejected and dispirited of all the rest, came walking towards them, with two more of their crew. The captain was so eager, as having this principal rogue so much in his power, that he could hardly have patience to let him come so near as to be sure of him, for they only heard his tongue before; but when they came nearer, the captain and Friday, starting up on their feet, let fly at them.

The boatswain was killed upon the spot; the next man was shot into the body, and fell just by him, though he did not die till an hour or two after; and the third run for it.

At the noise of the fire I immediately advanced with my whole army, which was now eight men, viz. myself, generalissimo; Friday, my lieutenant-general; the captain and his two men, and the three prisoners of war, whom we had trusted with arms.

We came upon them, indeed, in the dark, so that they could not see our number; and I made the man we had left in the boat, who was now one of us, call to them by name, to try if I could bring them to a parley, and so might perhaps reduce them to terms, which fell out just as we desired; for indeed it was easy to think, as their condition then was, they would be very willing to capitulate. So he calls out as loud as he could to one of them, "Tom Smith! Tom Smith!" Tom Smith answered immediately, "Who's that? Robinson?" For it seems he knew his voice. 'Tother answered, "Ay, ay; for God's sake, Tom Smith, throw down your arms and yield, or you are all dead men this moment."

"Who must we yield to? Where are they?" says Smith again. "Here they are," says he; "here's our captain, and fifty men with him, have been hunting you this two hours; the boatswain is killed, Will Frye is wounded, and I am a prisoner, and if you do not yield, you are all lost."

"Will they give us quarter then," says Tom Smith, "and we will yield?" "I'll go and ask, if you promise to yield," says Robinson. So he asked the captain, and the captain then calls himself out, "You, Smith, you know my voice, if you lay down your arms immediately, and submit, you shall have your lives, all but Will Atkins."

Upon this Will Atkins cried out, "For God's sake, captain, give me quarter; what have I done? They have been all as bad as I": which, by the way, was not true neither; for, it seems, this Will Atkins was the first man that laid hold of the captain when they first mutinied, and used him barbarously, in tying his hands, and giving him injurious language. However, the captain told him he must lay down his arms at discretion, and trust to the governor's mercy; by which he meant me, for they all called me governor.

In a word, they all laid down their arms, and begged their lives; and I sent the man that had parleyed with them and two more, who bound them all; and then my great army of fifty men, which, particularly with those three, were all but eight, came up and seized upon them all, and upon their boat; only that I kept myself and one more out of sight for reasons of state.

Our next work was to repair the boat, and think of seizing the ship; and as for the captain, now he had leisure to parley with them, he expostulated with them upon the villainy of their practices with him, and at length upon the farther wickedness of their design, and how certainly it must bring them to misery and distress in the end, and perhaps to the gallows.

They all appeared very penitent, and begged hard for their lives. As for that, he told them they were none of his prisoners, but the commander of the island; that they thought they had set him on shore in a barren, uninhabited island; but it had pleased God so to direct them that the island was inhabited, and that the governor was an Englishman; that he might hang them all there, if he pleased; but as he had given them all quarter, he supposed he would send them to England, to be dealt with there as justice required, except Atkins, who he was commanded by the governor to advise to prepare for death, for that he would be hanged in the morning.

Though this was all a fiction of his own, yet it had its desired effect. Atkins fell upon his knees, to beg the captain to intercede with the governor for his life; and all the rest begged of him, for God's sake, that they might not be sent to England.

It now occurred to me that the time of our deliverance was come, and that it would be a most easy thing to bring these fellows in to be hearty in getting possession of the ship; so I retired in the dark from them, that they might not see what kind of a governor they had, and called the captain to me. When I called, as at a good distance, one of the men was ordered to speak again, and say to the captain, "Captain, the commander calls for you." And presently the captain replied, "Tell his excellency I am just a-coming." This more perfectly amused them, and they all believed that the commander was just by with his fifty men.

Upon the captain's coming to me, I told him my project for seizing the ship, which he liked of wonderfully well, and resolved to put it in execution the next morning. But in order to execute it with more art, and secure of success, I told him we must divide the prisoners, and that he should go and take Atkins and two more of the worst of them, and send them pinioned to the cave where the others lay. This was committed to Friday and the two men who came on shore with the captain.

They conveyed them to the cave, as to a prison. And it was, indeed, a dismal place, especially to men in their condition. The others I ordered to my bower, as I called it, of which I have given a full description; and as it was fenced in, and they pinioned, the place was secure enough, considering they were upon their behaviour.

To these in the morning I sent the captain, who was to enter into a parley with them; in a word, to try them, and tell me whether he thought they might be trusted or no to go on board and surprise the ship. He talked to them of the injury done him, of the condition they were brought to; and that though the governor had given them quarter for their lives as to the present action, yet that if they were sent to England they would all be hanged in chains, to be sure; but that if they would join in so just an attempt as to recover the ship, he would have the governor's engagement for their pardon.

Any one may guess how readily such a proposal would be accepted by men in their condition. They fell down on their knees to the captain, and promised, with the deepest imprecations, that they would be faithful to him to the last drop, and that they should owe their lives to him, and would go with him all over the world; that they would own him for a father to them as long as they lived.

"Well," says the captain, "I must go and tell the governor what you say, and see what I can do to bring him to consent to it." So he brought me an account of the temper he found them in, and that he verily believed they would be faithful.

However, that we might be very secure, I told him he should go back again and choose out five of them, and tell them they might see that he did not want men, that he would take out those five to be his assistants, and that the governor would keep the other two and the three that were sent prisoners to the castle, my cave, as hostages for the fidelity of those five; and that if they proved unfaithful in the execution, the five hostages should be hanged in chains alive upon the shore.

This looked severe, and convinced them that the governor was in earnest. However, they had no way left them but to accept it; and it was now the business of the prisoners, as much as of the captain, to persuade the other five to do their duty.

Our strength was now thus ordered for the expedition. *1.* The captain, his mate, and passenger. *2.* Then the two prisoners of the first gang, to whom, having their characters from the captain, I had given their liberty, and trusted them with arms. *3.* The other two whom I had kept till now in my bower, pinioned, but upon the captain's motion had now released. *4.* The single man taken in the boat. *5.* These five released at last; so that they were thirteen in all, besides five we kept prisoners in the cave for hostages.

I asked the captain if he was willing to venture with these hands on board the ship; for as for me and my man Friday, I did not think it was proper for us to stir, having seven men left behind, and it was employment enough for us to keep them asunder and supply them with victuals. As to the five in the cave, I resolved to keep them fast; but Friday went in twice a day to them, to supply them with necessaries; and I made the other two carry provisions to a certain distance, where Friday was to take it.

When I showed myself to the two hostages, it was with the captain, who told them I was the person the governor had ordered to look after them, and that it was the governor's pleasure they should not stir anywhere but by my direction; that if they did, they should be fetched into the castle, and be laid in irons; so that as we never suffered them to see me as governor, so I now appeared as another person, and spoke of the governor, the garrison, the castle, and the like, upon all occasions.

The captain now had no difficulty before him but to furnish his two boats, stop the breach of one, and man them. He made his passenger captain of one, with four other men; and himself, and his mate, and five more went in the other; and they contrived their business very well, for they came up to the ship about midnight. As soon as they came within call of the ship, he made

Robinson hail them, and tell them they had brought off the men and the boat, but that it was a long time before they had found them, and the like, holding them in a chat till they came to the ship's side; when the captain and the mate entering first, with their arms, immediately knocked down the second mate and carpenter with the butt-end of their muskets, being very faithfully seconded by their men. They secured all the rest that were upon the main and quarter decks, and began to fasten the hatches to keep them down who were below; when the other boat and their men entering at the fore-chains, secured the fore-castle of the ship, and the scuttle which went down into the cook-room, making three men they found there prisoners.

When this was done, and all safe upon deck, the captain ordered the mate, with three men, to break into the roundhouse, where the new rebel captain lay, and having taken the alarm was gotten up, and with two men and a boy had gotten firearms in their hands; and when the mate with a crow split open the door, the new captain and his men fired boldly among them, and wounded the mate with a musket-ball, which broke his arm, and wounded two more of the men, but killed nobody.

The mate calling for help, rushed however into the roundhouse wounded as he was, and with his pistol shot the new captain through the head, the bullet entering at his mouth and came out again behind one of his ears, so that he never spoke a word; upon which the rest yielded, and the ship was taken effectually, without any more lives lost.

As soon as the ship was thus secured, the captain ordered seven guns to be fired, which was the signal agreed upon with me to give me notice of his success, which you may be sure I was very glad to hear, having sat watching upon the shore for it till near two of the clock in the morning.

Having thus heard the signal plainly, I laid me down; and it having been a day of great fatigue to me, I slept very sound, till I was something surprised with the noise of a gun; and presently starting up, I heard a man call me by the name of "Governor, Governor," and presently I knew the captain's voice; when climbing up to the top of the hill, there he stood, and pointing to the ship, he embraced me in his arms. "My dear friend and deliverer," says he, "there's your ship, for she is all yours, and so are we, and all that belong to her." I cast my eyes to the ship, and there she rode within little more than half a mile of the shore; for they had weighed her anchor as soon as they were masters of her, and the weather being fair, had brought her to an anchor just against the mouth of the little creek, and the tide being up, the captain had brought the pinnace in near the place where I at first landed my rafts, and so landed just at my door.

I was at first ready to sink down with the surprise; for I saw my deliverance, indeed, visibly put into my hands, all things easy, and a large ship just ready to carry me away whither I pleased to go. At first, for some time, I was not able to answer him one word; but as he had taken me in his arms, I held fast by him, or I should have fallen to the ground.

He perceived the surprise, and immediately pulls a bottle out of his pocket, and gave me a dram of cordial, which he had brought on purpose for me. After I had

'The mate . . . shot the new captain through the head . . .' (p. 195)

drank it, I sat down upon the ground; and though it brought me to myself, yet it was a good while before I could speak a word to him.

All this while the poor man was in as great an ecstasy as I, only not under any surprise, as I was; and he said a thousand kind tender things to me, to compose me and bring me to myself. But such was the flood of joy in my breast, that it put all my spirits into confusion. At last it broke out into tears, and in a little while after I recovered my speech.

Then I took my turn, and embraced him as my deliverer, and we rejoiced together. I told him I looked upon him as a man sent from heaven to deliver me, and that the whole transaction seemed to be a chain of wonders; that such things as these were the testimonies we had of a secret hand of Providence governing the world, and an evidence that the eyes of an infinite Power could search into the remotest corner of the world, and send help to the miserable whenever He pleased.

I forgot not to lift up my heart in thankfulness to Heaven; and what heart could forbear to bless Him, who had not only in a miraculous manner provided for one in such a wilderness, and in such a desolate condition, but from whom every deliverance must always be acknowledged to proceed?

When we had talked a while, the captain told me he had brought me some little refreshment, such as the ship afforded, and such as the wretches that had been so long his masters had not plundered him of. Upon this he called aloud to the boat, and bid his men bring the things ashore that were for the governor; and, indeed, it was a present as if I had been one, not that was to be carried away along with them, but as if I had been to dwell upon the island still, and they were to go without me.

First, he had brought me a case of bottles full of excellent cordial waters, six large bottles of Madeira wine, (the bottles held two quarts apiece), two pound of excellent good tobacco, twelve good pieces of the ship's beef, and six pieces of pork, with a bag of pease, and about a hundredweight of biscuit.

He brought me also a box of sugar, a box of flour, a bag full of lemons, and two bottles of lime-juice, and abundance of other things; but besides these, and what was a thousand times more useful to me, he brought me six clean new shirts, six very good neck-cloths, two pair of gloves, one pair of shoes, a hat, and one pair of stockings, and a very good suit of clothes of his own, which had been worn but very little; in a word, he clothed me from head to foot.

It was a very kind and agreeable present, as any one may imagine, to one in my circumstances; but never was anything in the world of that kind so unpleasant, awkward, and uneasy, as it was to me to wear such clothes at their first putting on.

After these ceremonies past, and after all his good things were brought into my little apartment, we began to consult what was to be done with the prisoners we had; for it was worth considering whether we might venture to take them away with us or no, especially two of them, whom we knew to be incorrigible and refractory to the last degree; and the captain said he knew they were such rogues, that there was no obliging them; and if he did carry them away, it must be in irons, as malefactors, to be delivered over to justice at the first English colony he could come at; and I found that the captain himself was very anxious about it.

Upon this I told him that, if he desired it, I durst undertake to bring the two men he spoke of to make it their own request that he should leave them upon the island. "I should be very glad of that," says the captain, "with all my heart."

"Well," says I, "I will send for them up, and talk with them for you." So I caused Friday and the two hostages, for they were now discharged, their comrades having performed their promise; I say, I caused them to go to the cave and bring up the five men, pinioned as they were, to the bower, and keep them there till I came.

After some time I came thither, dressed in my new habit; and now I was called governor again. Being all met, and the captain with me, I caused the men to be brought before me, and I told them I had had a full account of their villainous behaviour to the captain, and how they had run away with the ship, and were preparing to commit farther robberies, but that Providence had ensnared them in their own ways, and that they were fallen into the pit which they had digged for others.

I let them know that by my direction the ship had been seized, that she lay now in the road, and they might see, by and by, that their new captain had received the reward of his villainy, for that they might see him hanging at the yard-arm; that as to them, I wanted to know what they had to say why I should not execute them as pirates, taken in the fact, as by my commission they could not doubt I had authority to do.

One of them answered in the name of the rest that they had nothing to say but this, that when they were taken the captain promised them their lives, and they humbly implored my mercy. But I told them I knew not what mercy to show them; for as for myself, I had resolved to quit the island with all my men, and had taken passage with the captain to go for England. And as for the captain, he could not carry them to England other than as prisoners in irons, to be tried for mutiny, and running away with the ship; the consequence of which, they must needs know, would be the gallows; so that I could not tell which was best for them, unless they had a mind to take their fate in the island. If they desired that, I did not care, as I had liberty to leave it. I had some inclination to give them their lives, if they thought they could shift on shore.

They seemed very thankful for it, said they would much rather venture to stay there than to be carried to England to be hanged; so I left it on that issue.

However, the captain seemed to make some difficulty of it, as if he durst not leave them there. Upon this I seemed a little angry with the captain, and told him that they were my prisoners, not his; and that seeing I had offered them so much favour, I would be as good as my word; and that if he did not think fit to consent to it, I would set them at liberty, as I found them; and if he did not like it, he might take them again if he could catch them.

Upon this they appeared very thankful, and I accordingly set them at liberty, and bade them retire into the woods to the place whence they came, and I would leave

them some firearms, some ammunition, and some directions how they should live very well, if they thought fit.

Upon this I prepared to go on board the ship, but told the captain that I would stay that night to prepare my things, and desired him to go on board in the meantime, and keep all right in the ship, and send the boat on shore the next day for me; ordering him, in the meantime, to cause the new captain, who was killed, to be hanged at the yard-arm, that these men might see him.

When the captain was gone, I sent for the men up to me to my apartment, and entered seriously into discourse with them of their circumstances. I told them I thought they had made a right choice; that if the captain carried them away, they would certainly be hanged. I showed them the new captain hanging at the yard-arm of the ship, and told them they had nothing less to expect.

When they all declared their willingness to stay, I then told them I would let them into the story of my living there, and put them into the way of making it easy to them. Accordingly, I gave them the whole history of the place, and of my coming to it, showing them my fortifications, the way I made my bread, planted my corn, cured my grapes; and in a word, all that was necessary to make them easy. I told them the story also of the sixteen Spaniards that were to be expected, for whom I left a letter, and made them promise to treat them in common with themselves.

I left them my firearms, viz. five muskets, three fowling pieces, and three swords. I had above a barrel and half of powder left; for after the first year or two I used but little, and wasted none. I gave them a description of the way I managed the goats, and directions to milk and fatten them, and to make both butter and cheese.

In a word, I gave them every part of my own story, and I told them I would prevail with the captain to leave them two barrels of gunpowder more, and some garden seeds, which I told them I would have been very glad of. Also I gave them the bag of pease which the captain had brought me to eat, and bade them be sure to sow and increase them.

Having done all this, I left them the next day, and went on board the ship. We prepared immediately to sail, but did not weigh that night. The next morning early two of the five men came swimming to the ship's side, and making a most lamentable complaint of the other three, begged to be taken into the ship for God's sake, for they should be murdered, and begged the captain to take them on board, though he hanged them immediately.

Upon this the captain pretended to have no power without me; but after some difficulty, and after their solemn promises of amendment, they were taken on board, and were some time after soundly whipped and pickled, after which they proved very honest and quiet fellows.

Some time after this the boat was ordered on shore, the tide being up, with the things promised to the men, to which the captain, at my intercession, caused their chests and clothes to be added, which they took, and were very thankful for. I also encouraged them by telling them that if it lay in my way to send any vessel to take them in, I would not forget them.

CHAPTER NINETEEN

When I took leave of this island, I carried on board, for relics, the great goat skin cap I had made, my umbrella, and my parrot; also I forgot not to take the money I formerly mentioned, which had lain by me so long useless that it was grown rusty or tarnished, and could hardly pass for silver till it had been a little rubbed and handled; as also the money I found in the wreck of the Spanish ship.

And thus I left the island, the 19th of December, as I found by the ship's account, in the year 1686, after I had been upon it eight and twenty years, two months, and nineteen days, being delivered from this second captivity the same day of the month that I first made my escape in the barco-longo, from among the Moors of Sallee.

In this vessel, after a long voyage, I arrived in England, the 11th of June, in the year 1687, having been thirty and five years absent.

When I came to England, I was as perfect a stranger to all the world as if I had never been known there. My benefactor and faithful steward, whom I had left in trust with my money, was alive, but had had great misfortunes in the world, was become a widow the second time, and very low in the world. I made her easy as to what she owed me, assuring her I would give her no trouble; but on the contrary, in gratitude to her former care and faithfulness to me, I relieved her as my little stock would afford; which, at that time, would indeed allow me to do but little for her; but I assured her I would never forget her former kindness to me, nor did I forget her when I had sufficient to help her, as shall be observed in its place.

I went down afterwards into Yorkshire; but my father was dead, and my mother and all the family extinct, except that I found two sisters, and two of the children of one of my brothers; and as I had been long ago given over for dead, there had been no provision made for me; so that, in a word, I found nothing to relieve or assist me; and that little money I had would not do much for me as to settling in the world.

I met with one piece of gratitude, indeed, which I did not expect; and this was, that the master of the ship whom I had so happily delivered, and by the same means saved the ship and cargo, having given a very handsome account to the owners of

the manner how I had saved the lives of the men, and the ship, they invited me to meet them, and some other merchants concerned, and all together made me a very handsome compliment upon the subject, and a present of almost £200 sterling.

But after making several reflections upon the circumstances of my life, and how little way this would go towards settling me in the world, I resolved to go to Lisbon, and see if I might not come by some information of the state of my plantation in the Brazils, and of what was become of my partner, who I had reason to suppose had some years now given me over for dead.

With this view I took shipping for Lisbon, where I arrived in April following; my man Friday accompanying me very honestly in all these ramblings, and proving a most faithful servant upon all occasions.

When I came to Lisbon, I found out, by inquiry, and to my particular satisfaction, my old friend the captain of the ship who first took me up at sea, off of the shore of Africa. He was now grown old, and had left off the sea, having put his son, who was far from a young man, into his ship, and who still used the Brazil trade. The old man did not know me; and, indeed, I hardly knew him; but I soon brought him to my remembrance, and as soon brought myself to his remembrance, when I told him who I was.

After some passionate expressions of the old acquaintance, I inquired, you may be sure, after my plantation and my partner. The old man told me he had not been in the Brazils for about nine years; but that he could assure me that, when he came away, my partner was living; but the trustees, whom I had joined with him to take cognisance of my part, were both dead. That, however, he believed that I would have a very good account of the improvement of the plantation; for that upon the general belief of my being cast away and drowned, my trustees had given in the account of the produce of my part of the plantation to the procurator-fiscal, who had appropriated it, in case I never came to claim it, one-third to the king, and two-thirds to the monastery of St. Augustine, to be expended for the benefit of the poor, and for the conversion of the Indians to the Catholic faith; but that if I appeared, or anyone for me to claim the inheritance, it should be restored; only that the improvement, or annual production, being distributed to charitable uses, could not be restored. But he assured me that the steward of the king's revenue from lands, and the provedidore, or steward of the monastery, had taken great care all along that the incumbent, that is to say, my partner, gave every year a faithful account of the produce, of which they received duly my moiety.

I asked him if he knew to what height of improvement he had brought the plantation, and whether he thought it might be worth looking after; or whether, on my going thither, I should meet with no obstruction to my possessing my just right in the moiety.

He told me he could not tell exactly to what degree the plantation was improved; but this he knew, that my partner was growing exceeding rich upon the enjoying but one-half of it; and that, to the best of his remembrance, he had heard that the king's third of my part, which was, it seems, granted away to some other monastery or religious house, amounted to above two hundred moidores a year. That as to my being restored to a quiet possession of it, there was no question to be made of that, my partner being alive to witness my title, and my name being also enrolled in the register of the country. Also he told me that the survivors of my two trustees were very fair, honest people, and very wealthy; and he believed I would not only have their assistance for putting me in possession, but would find a very considerable sum of money in their hands for my account, being the produce of the farm while their fathers held the trust, and before it was given up, as above; which, as he remembered, was for about twelve years.

I showed myself a little concerned and uneasy at this account, and inquired of the old captain how it came to pass that the trustees should thus dispose my effects, when he knew that I had made my will, and had made him, the Portuguese captain, my universal heir, etc.

He told me, that was true; but that as there was no proof of my being dead, he could not act as executor until some certain account should come of my death; and that besides, he was not willing to intermeddle with a thing so remote; that it was true he had registered my will, and put in his claim; and could he have given any account of my being dead or alive, he would have acted by procuration, and taken possession of the ingenio, so they called the sugar-house, and had given his son, who was now at the Brazils, order to do it.

"But," says the old man, "I have one piece of news to tell you, which perhaps may not be so acceptable to you as the rest; and that is, that believing you were lost, and all the world believing so also, your partner and trustees did offer to account to me, in your name, for six or eight of the first years of profits, which I received; but there being at that time," says he, "great disbursements for increasing the works, building an ingenio, and buying slaves, it did not amount to near so much as afterwards it produced. However," says the old man, "I shall give you a true account of what I have received in all, and how I have disposed of it."

After a few days' farther conference with this ancient friend, he brought me an account of the six first years' income of my plantation, signed by my partner and the merchant-trustees, being always delivered in goods, viz. tobacco in roll, and sugar in chests, besides rum, molasses, etc., which is the consequence of a sugar-work; and I found, by this account, that every year the income considerably increased; but, as above, the disbursement being large, the sum at first was small. However, the old man let me see that he was debtor to me 470 moidores of gold, besides 60 chests of

sugar, and 15 double rolls of tobacco, which were lost in his ship, he having been shipwrecked coming home to Lisbon, about eleven years after my leaving the place.

The good man then began to complain of his misfortunes, and how he had been obliged to make use of my money to recover his losses, and buy him a share in a new ship. "However, my old friend," says he, "you shall not want a supply in your necessity; and as soon as my son returns, you shall be fully satisfied."

Upon this he pulls out an old pouch, and gives me 160 Portugal moidores in gold; and giving me the writing of his title to the ship, which his son was gone to the Brazils in, of which he was a quarter-part owner, and his son another, he puts them both into my hands for security of the rest.

I was too much moved with the honesty and kindness of the poor man to be able to bear this; and remembering what he had done for me, how he had taken me up at sea, and how generously he had used me on all occasions, and particularly how sincere a friend he was now to me, I could hardly refrain weeping at what he said to me; therefore first I asked him if his circumstances admitted him to spare so much money at that time, and if it would not straiten him? He told me he could not say but it might straiten him a little; but, however, it was my money, and I might want it more than he.

Everything the good man said was full of affection, and I could hardly refrain from tears while he spoke; in short, I took 100 of the moidores, and called for a pen and ink to give him a receipt for them. Then I returned him the rest, and told him if ever I had possession of the plantation, I would return the other to him also, as, indeed, I afterwards did; and that as to the bill of sale of his part in his son's ship, I would not take it by any means; but that if I wanted the money, I found he was honest enough to pay me; and if I did not, but came to receive what he gave me reason to expect, I would never have a penny more from him.

When this was passed, the old man began to ask me if he should put me into a method to make my claim to my plantation? I told him I thought to go over to it myself. He said I might do so if I pleased; but that if I did not, there were ways enough to secure my right, and immediately to appropriate the profits to my use; and as there were ships in the river of Lisbon just ready to go away to Brazil, he made me enter my name in a public register, with his affidavit, affirming, upon oath, that I was alive, and that I was the same person who took up the land for the planting the said plantation at first.

This being regularly attested by a notary, and a procuration affixed, he directed me to send it, with a letter of his writing, to a merchant of his acquaintance at the place, and then proposed my staying with him till an account came of the return.

Never anything was more honourable than the proceedings upon this procuration; for in less than seven months I received a large packet from the survivors of my trustees, the merchants, for whose account I went to sea, in which were the following particular letters and papers enclosed.

First, there was the account-current of the produce of my farm or plantation from the year when their fathers had balanced with my old Portugal captain, being for six years; the balance appeared to be 1174 moidores in my favour.

Secondly, there was the account of four years more, while they kept the effects in their hands, before the government claimed the administration, as being the effects of a person not to be found, which they called civil death; and the balance of this, the value of the plantation increasing, amounted to 38892 crusadoes, which made 3241 moidores.

Thirdly, there was the prior of the Augustines' account, who had received the profits for above fourteen years; but not being to account for what was disposed to the hospital, very honestly declared he had 872 moidores not distributed, which he acknowledged to my account; as to the king's part, that refunded nothing.

There was a letter of my partner's, congratulating me very affectionately upon my being alive, giving me an account how the estate was improved, and what it produced a year, with a particular of the number of squares or acres that it contained; how planted, how many slaves there were upon it, and making two and twenty crosses for blessings, told me he had said so many Ave Marias to thank the Blessed Virgin that I was alive; inviting me very passionately to come over and take possession of my own; and in the meantime, to give him orders to whom he should deliver my effects, if I did not come myself; concluding with a hearty tender of his friendship, and that of his family; and sent me as a present seven fine leopards' skins, which he had, it seems, received from Africa by some other ship which he had sent thither, and who,

it seems, had made a better voyage than I. He sent me also five chests of excellent sweetmeats, and a hundred pieces of gold uncoined, not quite so large as moidores. By the same fleet, my two merchant trustees shipped me 1200 chests of sugar, 800 rolls of tobacco, and the rest of the whole account in gold.

I might well say now, indeed, that the latter end of Job was better than the beginning. It is impossible to express the flutterings of my very heart when I looked over these letters, and especially when I found all my wealth about me; for as the Brazil ships come all in fleets, the same ships which brought my letters brought my goods, and the effects were safe in the river before the letters came to my hand. In a word, I turned pale, and grew sick; and had not the old man run and fetched me a cordial, I believe the sudden surprise of joy had overset Nature, and I had died upon the spot.

Nay, after that I continued very ill, and was so some hours, till a physician being sent for, and something of the real cause of my illness being known, he ordered me to be let blood, after which I had relief, and grew well; but I verily believe, if it had not been eased by a vent given in that manner to the spirits, I should have died.

I was now master, all on a sudden, of above £5000 sterling in money, and had an estate, as I might well call it, in the Brazils of above a thousand pounds a year, as sure as an estate of lands in England; and in a word, I was in a condition which I scarce knew how to understand, or how to compose myself for the enjoyment of it.

The first thing I did was to recompense my original benefactor, my good old captain, who had been first charitable to me in my distress, kind to me in my beginning, and honest to me at the end. I showed him all that was sent me. I told him that, next to the providence of Heaven, which disposes all things, it was owing to him; and that it now lay on me to reward him, which I would do a hundredfold. So I first returned to him the hundred moidores I had received of him; then I sent for a notary, and caused him to draw up a general release or discharge for the 470 moidores which he had acknowledged he owed me in the fullest and firmest manner possible; after which I caused a procuration to be drawn, empowering him to be my receiver of the annual profits of my plantation, and appointing my partner to account to him, and make the returns by the usual fleets to him in my name; and a clause in the end, being a grant of 100 moidores a year to him, during his life, out of the effects, and 50 moidores a year to his son after him, for his life; and thus I requited my old man.

I was now to consider which way to steer my course next, and what to do with the estate that Providence had thus put into my hands; and, indeed, I had more care upon my head now than I had in my silent state of life in the island, where I wanted nothing but what I had, and had nothing but what I wanted; whereas I had now a great charge upon me, and my business was how to secure it. I had ne'er a cave now to hide my money in, or a place where it might lie without lock or key till it grew mouldy and tarnished before anybody would meddle with it. On the contrary, I knew not where to put it, or whom to trust with it. My old patron, the captain, indeed, was honest, and that was the only refuge I had.

In the next place, my interest in the Brazils seemed to summon me thither; but now I could not tell how to think of going thither till I had settled my affairs, and left my effects in some safe hands behind me. At first I thought of my old friend the widow, who I knew was honest, and would be just to me; but then she was in years, and but poor, and for aught I knew might be in debt; so that, in a word, I had no way but to go back to England myself, and take my effects with me.

It was some months, however, before I resolved upon this; and therefore, as I had rewarded the old captain fully, and to his satisfaction, who had been my former benefactor, so I began to think of my poor widow, whose husband had been my first benefactor, and she, while it was in her power, my faithful steward and instructor. So the first thing I did, I got a merchant in Lisbon to write to his correspondent in London, not only to pay a bill, but to go find her out, and carry her in money an hundred pounds from me, and to talk with her, and comfort her in her poverty, by telling her she should, if I lived, have a further supply. At the same time I sent my two sisters in the country each of them an hundred pounds, they being, though not in want, yet not in very good circumstances; one having been married, and left a widow; and the other having a husband not so kind to her as he should be.

But among all my relations or acquaintances, I could not yet pitch upon one to whom I durst commit the gross of my stock, that I might go away to the Brazils, and leave things safe behind me; and this greatly perplexed me.

I had once a mind to have gone to the Brazils and have settled myself there, for I was, as it were, naturalised to the place. But I had some little scruple in my mind about religion, which insensibly drew me back, of which I shall say more presently. However, it was not religion that kept me from going there for the present; and as I had made no scruple of being openly of the religion of the country all the while I was among them, so neither did I yet; only that, now and then, having of late thought more of it than formerly, when I began to think of living and dying among them I began to regret my having professed myself a papist, and thought it might not be the best religion to die with.

But, as I have said, this was not the main thing that kept me from going to the Brazils, but that really I did not know with whom to leave my effects behind me; so I resolved, at last, to go to England with it, where, if I arrived, I concluded I should make some acquaintance, or find some relations, that would be faithful to me; and accordingly I prepared to go for England with all my wealth.

In order to prepare things for my going home, I first, the Brazil fleet being just going away, resolved to give answers suitable to the just and faithful account of things I had from thence. And first, to the prior of St. Augustine I wrote a letter full of thanks for their just dealings, and the offer of the 872 moidores which was undisposed of, which I desired might be given, 500 to the monastery, and 372 to the poor, as the prior should direct, desiring the good padre's prayers for me, and the like.

I wrote next a letter of thanks to my two trustees, with all the acknowledgment that so much justice and honesty called for. As for sending them any present, they were far above having any occasion of it.

Lastly, I wrote to my partner, acknowledging his industry in the improving the plantation, and his integrity in increasing the stock of the works, giving him instructions for his future government of my part, according to the powers I had left with my old patron, to whom I desired him to send whatever became due to me till he should hear from me more particularly; assuring him that it was my intention not only to come to him, but to settle myself there for the remainder of my life. To this I added a very handsome present of some Italian silks for his wife and two daughters, for such the captain's son informed me he had; with two pieces of fine English broad cloth, the best I could get in Lisbon, five pieces of black baize, and some Flanders lace of a good value.

Having thus settled my affairs, sold my cargo, and turned all my effects into good bills of exchange, my next difficulty was which way to go to England. I had been accustomed enough to the sea, and yet I had a strange aversion to going to England by sea at that time; and though I could give no reason for it, yet the difficulty increased upon me so much, that though I had once shipped my baggage in order to go, yet I altered my mind, and that not once, but two or three times.

It is true I had been very unfortunate by sea, and this might be some of the reason; but let no man slight the strong impulses of his own thoughts in cases of such moment. Two of the ships which I had singled out to go in, I mean more particularly singled out than any other, that is to say, so as in one of them to put my things on board, and in the other to have agreed with the captain; I say, two of these ships miscarried, viz. one was taken by the Algerines, and the other was cast away on the Start, near Torbay, and all the people drowned except three; so that in either of those vessels I had been made miserable; and in which most, it was hard to say.

Having been thus harassed in my thoughts, my old pilot, to whom I communicated everything, pressed me earnestly not to go by sea, but either to go by land to the Groyne, and cross over the Bay of Biscay to Rochelle, from whence it was but an easy and safe journey by land to Paris, and so to Calais and Dover; or to go up to Madrid, and so all the way by land through France.

In a word, I was so prepossessed against my going by sea at all, except from Calais to Dover, that I resolved to travel all the way by land; which, as I was not in haste, and did not value the charge, was by much the pleasanter way. And to make it more so, my old captain brought an English gentleman, the son of a merchant in Lisbon, who was willing to travel with me; after which we picked up two more English merchants also, and two young Portuguese gentlemen, the last going to Paris only; so that we were in all six of us, and five servants; the two merchants and the two Portuguese contenting themselves with one servant between two, to save the charge; and as for me, I got an English sailor to travel with me as a servant, besides my man Friday, who was too much a stranger to be capable of supplying the place of a servant on the road.

In this manner I set out from Lisbon; and our company, being all very well mounted and armed, we made a little troop, whereof they did me the honour to call me captain, as well because I was the oldest man as because I had two servants, and indeed was the original of the whole journey.

As I have troubled you with none of my sea journals, so I shall trouble you now with none of my land journal; but some adventures that happened to us in this tedious and difficult journey I must not omit.

When we came to Madrid, we being all of us strangers to Spain, were willing to stay some time to see the court of Spain, and to see what was worth observing; but it being the latter part of the summer we hastened away, and set out from Madrid about the middle of October; but when we came to the edge of Navarre, we were alarmed at several towns on the way with an account that so much snow was fallen on the French side of the mountains, that several travellers were obliged to come back to Pampeluna, after having attempted, at an extreme hazard, to pass on.

When we came to Pampeluna itself, we found it so indeed; and to me, that had been always used to a hot climate, and indeed to countries where we could scarce bear any clothes on, the cold was insufferable; nor indeed was it more painful than it was surprising to come but ten days before out of the Old Castile, where the weather was not only warm, but very hot, and immediately to feel a wind from the Pyrenean mountains so very keen, so severely cold, as to be intolerable, and to endanger benumbing and perishing of our fingers and toes.

Poor Friday was really frighted when he saw the mountains all covered with snow, and felt cold weather, which he had never seen or felt before in his life.

To mend the matter, when we came to Pampeluna it continued snowing with so much violence, and so long, that the people said winter was become before it's time; and the roads, which were difficult before, were now quite impassable; for, in a word, the snow lay in some places too thick for us to travel, and being not hard frozen, as is the case in northern countries, there was no going without being in danger of being buried alive every step. We staid no less than twenty days at Pampeluna; when seeing the winter coming on, and no likelihood of its being better, for it was the severest winter all over Europe that had been known in the memory of man, I proposed that we should all go away to Fontarabia, and there take shipping for Bordeaux, which was a very little voyage.

But while we were considering this, there came in four French gentlemen, who having been stopped on the French side of the passes, as we were on the Spanish, had found out a guide, who, traversing the country near the head of Languedoc, had brought them over the mountains by such ways, that they were not much incommoded with the snow; and where they met with snow in any quantity, they said it was frozen hard enough to bear them and their horses.

We sent for this guide, who told us he would undertake to carry us the same way with no hazard from the snow, provided we were armed sufficiently to protect us from wild beasts; for he said, upon these great snows it was frequent for some wolves to show themselves at the foot of the mountains, being made ravenous for want of food, the ground being covered with snow. We told him we were well enough prepared for such creatures as they were, if he would ensure us from a kind of two-legged wolves, which, we were told, we were in most danger from, especially on the French side of the mountains.

He satisfied us there was no danger of that kind in the way that we were to go; so we readily agreed to follow him, as did also twelve other gentlemen, with their servants, some French, some Spanish, who, as I said, had attempted to go, and were obliged to come back again.

Accordingly we all set out from Pampeluna, with our guide, on the 15th of November; and, indeed, I was surprised when, instead of going forward, he came directly back with us on the same road that we came from Madrid, above twenty miles; when being passed two rivers, and come into the plain country, we found ourselves in a warm climate again, where the country was pleasant, and no snow to be seen; but on a sudden, turning to his left, he approached the mountains another way; and though it is true the hills and precipices looked dreadful, yet he made so many tours, such meanders, and led us by such winding ways, that we were insensibly passed the height of the mountains without being much encumbered with the snow; and all on a sudden he showed us the pleasant fruitful provinces of Languedoc and Gascoign, all green and flourishing, though, indeed, it was at a great distance, and we had some rough way to pass yet.

We were a little uneasy, however, when we found it snowed one whole day and a night so fast, that we could not travel; but he bid us be easy, we should soon be past it all. We found indeed, that we began to descend every day, and to come more north than before; and so, depending upon our guide, we went on.

It was about two hours before night when, our guide being something before us, and not just in sight, out rushed three monstrous wolves, and after them a bear, out of a hollow way adjoining to a thick wood. Two of the wolves flew upon the guide, and had he been half a mile before us he had been devoured indeed before we could have helped him. One of them fastened upon his horse, and the other attacked the man with that violence, that he had not time, or not presence of mind enough, to draw his pistol, but hollowed and cried out to us most lustily. My man Friday being next to me, I bid him ride up, and see what was the matter. As soon as Friday came in sight of the man, he hollowed as loud as t'other, "O master! O master!" but, like a bold fellow, rode directly up to the poor man, and with his pistol shot the wolf that attacked him into the head.

It was happy for the poor man that it was my man Friday, for he having been used to that kind of creature in his country, had no fear upon him, but went close up to him and shot him, as above; whereas any of us would have fired at a farther distance, and have perhaps either missed the wolf, or endangered shooting the man.

But it was enough to have terrified a bolder man than I; and, indeed, it alarmed all our company, when, with the noise of Friday's pistol, we heard on both sides the dismallest howling of wolves; and the noise, redoubled by the echo of the mountains, that it was to us as if there had been a prodigious multitude of them; and perhaps indeed there was not such a few as that we had no cause of apprehensions.

However, as Friday had killed this wolf, the other that had fastened upon the horse left him immediately and fled, having happily fastened upon his head, where the bosses of the bridle had stuck in his teeth, so that he had not done him much hurt. The man indeed was most hurt; for the raging creature had bit him twice, once on the arm, and the other time a little above his knee; and he was just as it were tumbling down by the disorder of his horse, when Friday came up and shot the wolf.

It is easy to suppose that at the noise of Friday's pistol we all mended our pace, and rid up as fast as the way, which was very difficult, would give us leave, to see what was the matter. As soon as we came clear of the trees, which blinded us before, we saw clearly what had been the case, and how Friday had disengaged the poor guide, though we did not presently discern what kind of creature it was he had killed.

CHAPTER TWENTY

But never was a fight managed so hardily, and in such a surprising manner, as that which followed between Friday and the bear, which gave us all (though at first we were surprised and afraid for him) the greatest diversion imaginable. As the bear is a heavy, clumsy creature, and does not gallop as the wolf does, who is swift and light, so he has two particular qualities, which generally are the rule of his actions: first, as to men, who are not his proper prey; I say, not his proper prey, because, though I cannot say what excessive hunger might do, which was now their case, the ground being all covered with snow; but as to men, he does

not usually attempt them, unless they first attack him. On the contrary, if you meet him in the woods, if you don't meddle with him, he won't meddle with you; but then you must take care to be very civil to him, and give him the road, for he is a very nice gentleman. He won't go a step out of his way for a prince; nay, if you are really afraid, your best way is to look another way, and keep going on; for sometimes if you stop, and stand still, and look steadily at him, he takes it for an affront; but if you throw or toss anything at him, and it hits him, though it were but a bit of a stick as big as your finger, he takes it for an affront, and sets all his other business aside to pursue his revenge; for he will have satisfaction in point of honour. That is his first quality; the next is, that if he be once affronted, he will never leave you, night or day, till he has his revenge, but follows, at a good round rate, till he overtakes you.

My man Friday had delivered our guide, and when we came up to him he was helping him off from his horse; for the man was both hurt and frighted, and indeed the last more than the first; when, on the sudden, we spied the bear come out of the wood, and a vast monstrous one it was, the biggest by far that ever I saw. We were all a little surprised when we saw him; but when Friday saw him, it was easy to see joy and courage in the fellow's countenance. "O! O! O!" says Friday, three times pointing to him. "O master! you give me te leave; me shakee te hand with him; me make you good laugh."

I was surprised to see the fellow so pleased. "You fool you," says I, "he will eat you up." "Eatee me up! eatee me up!" says Friday, twice over again; "me eatee him up; me make you good laugh; you all stay here, me show you good laugh." So down he sits, and gets his boots off in a moment, and put on a pair of pumps, as we call the flat shoes they wear, and which he had in his pocket, gives my other servant his horse, and with his gun away he flew, swift like the wind.

The bear was walking softly on, and offered to meddle with nobody till Friday, coming pretty near, calls to him, as if the bear could understand him, "Hark ye, hark ye," says Friday, "me speakee wit you." We followed at a distance; for now being come down on the Gascoign side of the mountains, we were entered a vast great forest, where the country was plain and pretty open, though many trees in it scattered here and there.

Friday, who had, as we say, the heels of the bear, came up with him quickly, and takes up a great stone and throws at him, and hit him just on the head, but did him no more harm than if he had thrown it against a wall. But it answered Friday's end, for the rogue was so void of fear, that he did it purely to make the bear follow him, and show us some laugh, as he called it.

As soon as the bear felt the stone, and saw him, he turns about, and comes after him, taking devilish long strides, and shuffling along at a strange rate, so as would have put a horse to a middling gallop. Away runs Friday, and takes his course as if he run towards us for help; so we all resolved to fire at once upon the bear, and deliver my man; though I was angry at him heartily for bringing the bear back upon us, when he was going about his own business another way; and especially I was angry that he had turned the bear upon us, and then run away; and I called out, "You dog," said I, "is this your making us laugh? Come away, and take your horse, that we may shoot the creature." He hears me, and cries out, "No shoot, no shoot; stand still, you get much laugh." And as the nimble creature run two feet for the beast's one, he turned on a sudden, on one side of us, and seeing a great oak tree fit for his purpose, he beckoned to us to follow; and doubling his pace, he gets nimbly up the tree, laying his gun down upon the ground, at about five or six yards from the bottom of the tree.

The bear soon came to the tree, and we followed at a distance. The first thing he did, he stopped at the gun, smelt to it, but let it lie, and up he scrambles into the tree, climbing like a cat, though so monstrously heavy. I was amazed at the folly, as I thought it, of my man, and could not for my life see anything to laugh at yet, till seeing the bear get up the tree, we all rode nearer to him.

When we came to the tree, there was Friday got out to the small end of a large limb of the tree, and the bear got about half way to him. As soon as the bear got out to that part where the limb of the tree was weaker, "Ha!" says he to us, "now you see me teachee the bear dance." So he falls a-jumping and shaking the bough, at which the bear began to totter, but stood still, and began to look behind him, to see how he should get back. Then, indeed, we did laugh heartily. But Friday had not done with him by a great deal. When he sees him stand still, he calls out to him again, as if he had supposed the bear could speak English, "What, you no come farther? pray you come farther"; so he left jumping and shaking the tree; and the bear, just as if he had understood what he said, did come a little farther; then he fell a-jumping again, and the bear stopped again.

We thought now was a good time to knock him on the head, and I called to Friday to stand still, and we would shoot the bear; but he cried out earnestly, "O pray! O pray! no shoot, me shoot by and then"; he would have said by-and-by. However, to shorten the story, Friday danced so much, and the bear stood so ticklish, that we had laughing enough indeed, but still could not imagine what the fellow would do: for first we thought he depended upon shaking the bear off; and we found the bear was too cunning for that too; for he would not go out far enough to be thrown down, but clings fast with his great broad claws and feet, so that we could not imagine what would be the end of it, and where the jest would be at last.

But Friday put us out of doubt quickly; for seeing the bear cling fast to the bough, and that he would not be persuaded to come any farther, "Well, well," says Friday, "you no come farther, me go, me go; you no come to me, me go come to you"; and upon this he goes out to the smallest end of the bough, where it would bend with his weight, and gently lets himself down by it, sliding down the bough till he came near enough to jump down on his feet, and away he ran to his gun, takes it up, and stands still.

"Well," said I to him, "Friday, what will you do now? Why don't you shoot him?" "No shoot," says Friday, "no yet; me shoot now, me no kill; me stay, give you one more laugh." And, indeed, so he did, as you will see presently; for when the bear sees his enemy gone, he comes back from the bough where he stood, but did it mighty leisurely, looking behind him every step, and coming backward till he got into the body of the tree; then with the same hinder end foremost he comes down the tree, grasping it with his claws, and moving one foot at a time, very leisurely. At this juncture, and just before he could set his hind feet upon the ground, Friday stepped up close to him, clapped the muzzle of his piece into his ear, and shot him dead as a stone.

Then the rogue turned about to see if we did not laugh; and when he saw we were pleased by our looks, he falls a-laughing himself very loud. "So we kill bear in my country," says Friday. "So you kill them?" says I; "why, you have no guns." "No," says he, "no gun, but shoot great much long arrow."

This was indeed a good diversion to us; but we were still in a wild place, and our guide very much hurt, and what to do we hardly knew. The howling of wolves ran much in my head; and indeed, except the noise I once heard on the shore of Africa, of which I have said something already, I never heard anything that filled me with so much horror.

These things, and the approach of night, called us off, or else, as Friday would have had us, we should certainly have taken the skin of this monstrous creature off, which was worth saving; but we had three leagues to go, and our guide hastened us; so we left him, and went forward on our journey.

The ground was still covered with snow, though not so deep and dangerous as on the mountains; and the ravenous creatures, as we heard afterwards, were come down into the forest and plain country, pressed by hunger, to seek for food, and had done a great deal of mischief in the villages, where they surprised the country people, killed a great many of their sheep and horses, and some people too.

We had one dangerous place to pass, which our guide told us if there were any more wolves in the country we should find them there; and this was in a small plain, surrounded with woods on every side, and a long narrow defile, or lane, which we were to pass to get through the wood, and then we should come to the village where we were to lodge.

It was within half an hour of sunset when we entered the first wood, and a little after sunset when we came into the plain. We met with nothing in the first wood, except that, in a little plain within the wood, which was not above two furlongs over, we saw five great wolves cross the road, full speed one after another, as if they had been in chase of some prey, and had it in view; they took no notice of us, and were gone out of sight in a few moments.

Upon this our guide, who, by the way, was but a fainthearted fellow, bid us keep in a ready posture, for he believed there were more wolves a-coming. We kept our arms ready, and our eyes about us; but we saw no more wolves till we came through that wood, which was near half a league, and entered the plain. As soon as we came into the plain, we had occasion enough to look about us: the first object we met with was a dead horse, that is to say, a poor horse which the wolves had killed, and at least a dozen of them at work, we could not say eating of him, but picking of his bones rather: for they had eaten up all the flesh before.

We did not think fit to disturb them at their feast; neither did they take much notice of us. Friday would have let fly at them, but I would not suffer him by any means; for I found we were like to have more business upon our hands than we were aware of. We were not gone half over the plain, when we began to hear the wolves howl in the wood on our left in a frightful manner, and presently after we saw about a hundred coming on directly towards us, all in a body, and most of them in a line, as regularly as an army drawn up by an experienced officer. I scarce knew in what manner to receive them, but found to draw ourselves in a close line was the only way: so we formed in a moment: but that we might not have too much interval, I ordered that only every other man should fire, and that the others who had not fired should stand ready to give them a second volley immediately, if they continued to advance upon us; and then that those who had fired at first should not pretend to load their fusees again, but stand ready every one with a pistol, for we were all armed with a fusee and a pair of pistols each man; so we were, by this method, able to fire six volleys, half of us at a time. However, at present we had no necessity; for upon firing the first volley, the enemy made a full stop, being terrified as well with the noise as with the fire; four of them, being shot in the head, dropped; several others were wounded, and went bleeding off, as we could see by the snow. I found they stopped, but did not immediately retreat; whereupon, remembering that I had been told that the fiercest creatures were terrified at the voice of a man, I caused all the company to hollow as loud as we could; and I found the notion not altogether mistaken; for upon our shout, they began to retire, and turn about. Then I ordered a second volley to be fired in their rear, which put them to the gallop, and away they went to the woods. This gave us leisure to charge our pieces again; and that we might lose no

time, we kept going; but we had but little more than loaded our fusees, and put ourselves into a readiness, when we heard a terrible noise in the same wood, on our left, only that it was farther onward, the same way we were to go.

The night was coming on, and the light began to be dusky, which made it worse on our side; but the noise increasing, we could easily perceive that it was the howling and yelling of those hellish creatures; and on a sudden, we perceived two or three troops of wolves, one on our left, one behind us, and one on our front, so that we seemed to be surrounded with them. However, as they did not fall upon us, we kept our way forward as fast as we could make our horses go, which, the way being very rough, was only a good large trot, and in this manner we came in view of the entrance of a wood, through which we were to pass, at the farther side of the plain; but we were greatly surprised when, coming nearer the lane, or pass, we saw a confused number of wolves standing just at the entrance.

On a sudden, at another opening of the wood, we heard the noise of a gun, and looking that way, out rushed a horse, with a saddle and a bridle on him, flying like the wind, and sixteen or seventeen wolves after him, full speed; indeed, the horse had the heels of them; but as we supposed that he could not hold it at that rate, we doubted not but they would get up with him at last, and no question but they did.

But here we had a most horrible sight; for riding up to the entrance where the horse came out, we found the carcass of another horse and of two men, devoured by the ravenous creatures; and one of the men was no doubt the same whom we heard fire the gun, for there lay a gun just by him fired off; but as to the man, his head and the upper part of his body was eaten up.

This filled us with horror, and we knew not what course to take; but the creatures resolved us soon, for they gathered about us presently in hopes of prey, and I verily believe there were three hundred of them. It happened very much to our advantage that, at the entrance into the wood, but a little way from it, there lay some large timber-trees, which had been cut down the summer before, and I suppose lay there for carriage. I drew my little troop in among those trees, and placing ourselves in a line behind one long tree, I advised them all to light, and keeping that tree before us for a breastwork, to stand in a triangle, or three fronts, enclosing our horses in the centre.

We did so, and it was well we did; for never was a more furious charge than the creatures made upon us in the place. They came on us with a growling kind of a noise, and mounted the piece of timber, which, as I said, was our breastwork, as if they were only rushing upon their prey; and this fury of theirs, it seems, was principally occasioned by their seeing our horses behind us, which was the prey they aimed at. I ordered our men to fire as before, every other man; and they took their aim so sure, that indeed they killed several of the wolves at the first volley; but there was a necessity to keep a continual firing, for they came on like devils, those behind pushing on those before.

When we had fired our second volley of our fusees, we thought they stopped a little, and I hoped they would have gone off; but it was but a moment, for others came forward again; so we fired two volleys of our pistols; and I believe in these four firings we had killed seventeen or eighteen of them, and lamed twice as many, yet they came on again.

I was loth to spend our last shot too hastily; so I called my servant, not my man Friday, for he was better employed, for with the greatest dexterity imaginable he had charged my fusee, and his own while we were engaged; but as I said, I called my other man, and giving him a horn of powder, I bade him lay a train all along the piece of timber, and let it be a large train. He did so, and had but just time to get away when the wolves came up to it, and some were got up upon it, when I, snapping an uncharged pistol close to the powder, set it on fire. Those that were upon the timber were scorched with it, and six or seven of them fell, or rather jumped, in among us with the force and fright of the fire. We despatched these in an instant, and the rest were so frighted with the light, which the night, for it was now very near dark, made more terrible, that they drew back a little; upon which I ordered our last pistol to be fired off in one volley, and after that we gave a shout. Upon this the wolves turned tail, and we sallied immediately upon near twenty lame ones, whom we found struggling on the ground, and fell a-cutting them with our swords, which answered our expectation; for the crying and howling they made was better understood by their fellows, so that they all fled and left us.

We had, first and last, killed about threescore of them, and had it been daylight, we had killed many more. The field of battle being thus cleared, we made forward again, for we had still near a league to go. We heard the ravenous creatures howl and yell in the woods as we went several times, and sometimes we fancied we saw some of them, but the snow dazzling our eyes, we were not certain. So in about an hour more we came to the town where we were to lodge, which we found in a

terrible fright, and all in arms; for it seems that the night before the wolves and some bears had broke into the village in the night, and put them in a terrible fright; and they were obliged to keep guard night and day, but especially in the night, to preserve their cattle, and, indeed, their people.

The next morning our guide was so ill, and his limbs swelled with the rankling of his two wounds, that he could go no farther; so we were obliged to take a new guide there, and go to Toulouse, where we found a warm climate, a fruitful, pleasant country, and no snow, no wolves, or anything like them. But when we told our story at Toulouse, they told us it was nothing but what was ordinary in the great forest at the foot of the mountains, especially when the snow lay on the ground; but they inquired much what kind of a guide we had gotten that would venture to bring us that way in such a severe season, and told us it was very much we were not all devoured. When we told them how we placed ourselves, and the horses in the middle they blamed us exceedingly, and told us it was fifty to one but we had been all destroyed; for it was the sight of the horses which made the wolves so furious, seeing their prey; and that, at other times, they are really afraid of a gun; but the being excessive hungry, and raging on that account, the eagerness to come at the horses had made them senseless of danger; and that if we had not, by the continued fire, and at last by the stratagem of the train of powder, mastered them, it had been great odds but that we had been torn to pieces; whereas had we been content to have sat still on horseback, and fired as horsemen, they would not have taken the horses for so much their own, when men were on their backs, as otherwise; and withal they told us, that at last, if we had stood all together, and left our horses, they would have been so eager to have devoured them, that we might have come off safe, especially having our firearms in our hands, and being so many in number.

For my part, I was never so sensible of danger in my life; for seeing above three hundred devils come roaring and open-mouthed to devour us, and having nothing to shelter us or retreat to, I gave myself over for lost, and as it was, I believe I shall never care to cross those mountains again. I think I would much rather go a thousand leagues by sea, though I were sure to meet with a storm once a week.

I have nothing uncommon to take notice of in my passage through France; nothing but what other travellers have given an account of with much more advantage than I can. I travelled from Toulouse to Paris, and without any considerable stay came to Calais, and landed safe at Dover, the 14th of January, after having had a severe cold season to travel in.

I was now come to the centre of my travels, and had in a little time all my new-discovered estate safe about me, the bills of exchange which I brought with me having been very currently paid.

My principal guide and privy councillor was my good ancient widow; who, in gratitude for the money I had sent her, thought no pains too much, or care too great, to employ for me; and I trusted her so entirely with everything, that I was perfectly easy as to the security of my effects; and indeed I was very happy from my beginning, and now to the end, in the unspotted integrity of this good gentlewoman.

And now I began to think of leaving my effects with this woman and setting out for Lisbon, and so to the Brazils. But now another scruple came in my way, and that was religion; for as I had entertained some doubts about the Roman religion even while I was abroad, especially in my state of solitude, so I knew there was no going to the Brazils for me, much less going to settle there, unless I resolved to embrace the Roman Catholic religion without any reserve; unless on the other hand I resolved to be a sacrifice to my principles, be a martyr for religion, and die in the Inquisition. So I resolved to stay at home, and if I could find means for it, to dispose of my plantation.

To this purpose I wrote to my old friend at Lisbon, who in return gave me notice that he could easily dispose of it there; but that if I thought fit to give him leave to offer it in my name to the two merchants, the survivors of my trustees, who lived in the Brazils, who must fully understand the value of it, who lived just upon the spot, and whom I knew were very rich, so that he believed they would be fond of buying it, he did not doubt but I should make 4000 or 5000 pieces of eight the more of it.

Accordingly I agreed, gave him order to offer it to them and he did so; and in about eight months more, the ship being then returned, he sent me an account that they had accepted the offer, and had remitted 33000 pieces of eight to a correspondent of theirs at Lisbon to pay for it.

In return, I signed the instrument of sale in the form which they sent from Lisbon, and sent it to my old man, who sent me bills of exchange for 32800 pieces of eight to me, for the estate; reserving the payment of 100 moidores a year to him, the old man, during his life, and 50 moidores afterwards to his son for his life, which I had promised them, which the plantation was to make good as a rent-charge. And thus I have given the first part of a life of fortune and adventure, a life of Providence's chequer-work, and of a variety which the world will seldom be able to show the like of; beginning foolishly, but closing much more happily than any part of it ever gave me leave so much as to hope for.

Any one would think that in this state of complicated good fortune I was past running any more hazards; and so indeed I had been, if other circumstances had concurred. But I was inured to a wandering life, had no family, not many relations, nor, however rich, had I contracted much acquaintance; and though I had sold my estate in the Brazils, yet I could not keep the country out of my head, and had a great mind to be upon the wing again; especially I could not resist the strong inclination I had to see my island, and to know if the poor Spaniards were in being there, and how the rogues I left there had used them.

My true friend, the widow, earnestly dissuaded me from it, and so far prevailed with me, that for almost seven years she prevented my running abroad, during which time I took my two nephews, the children of one of my brothers, into my care. The eldest having something of his own, I bred up as a gentleman, and gave him a settlement of some addition to his estate after my decease. The other I put out to a captain of a ship, and after five years, finding him a sensible, bold, enterprising young fellow, I put him into a good ship, and sent him to sea; and this young fellow afterwards drew me in, as old as I was, to farther adventures myself.

In the meantime, I in part settled myself here; for, first of all, I married, and that not either to my disadvantage or dissatisfaction, and had three children, two sons and one daughter; but my wife dying, and my nephew coming home with good success from a voyage to Spain, my inclination to go abroad, and his importunity, prevailed, and engaged me to go in his ship as a private trader to the East Indies. This was in the year 1694.

In this voyage I visited my new colony in the island, saw my successors the Spaniards, had the whole story of their lives, and of the villains I left there; how at first they insulted the poor Spaniards, how they afterwards agreed, disagreed, united, separated, and how at last the Spaniards were obliged to use violence with them; how they were subjected to the Spaniards; how honestly the Spaniards used them; a history, if it were entered into, as full of variety and wonderful accidents as my own part; particularly also as to their battles with the Caribbeans, who landed several times upon the island, and as to the improvement they made upon the island itself; and how five of them made an attempt upon the mainland, and brought away eleven men and five women prisoners, by which, at my coming, I found about twenty young children on the island.

Here I stayed about twenty days, left them supplies of all necessary things, and particularly of arms, powder, shot, clothes, tools, and two workmen, which I brought from England with me, viz. a carpenter and a smith.

Besides this, I shared the island into parts with them, reserved to myself the property of the whole, but gave them such parts respectively as they agreed on; and having settled all things with them, and engaged them not to leave the place, I left them there.

From thence I touched at the Brazils, from whence I sent a bark, which I bought there, with more people, to the island; and in it, besides other supplies, I sent seven women, being such as I found proper for service, or for wives to such as would take them. As to the Englishmen, I promised them to send them some women from England, with a good cargo of necessaries, if they would apply themselves to planting; which I afterwards performed; and the fellows proved very honest and diligent after they were mastered, and had their properties set apart for them. I sent them also from the Brazils five cows, three of them being big with calf, some sheep, and some hogs, which, when I came again, were considerably increased.

But all these things, with an account how three hundred Caribbees came and invaded them, and ruined their plantations, and how they fought with that whole number twice and were at first defeated and three of them killed; but at last a storm destroying their enemies' canoes, they famished or destroyed almost all the rest, and renewed and recovered the possession of their plantation, and still lived upon the island: – all these things, with some very surprising incidents in some new adventures of my own, for ten years more, I may perhaps give a farther account of hereafter.